W9-CDN-751

THE OLD ADAM

ARNOLD BENNETT

BY ARNOLD BENNETT

NOVELS

The Old Wives' Tale
Helen with the High Hand
The Matador of the Five Towns
The Book of Carlotta
Buried Alive
A Great Man
Leonora
Whom God Hath Joined
A Man from the North
Anna of the Five Towns
The Glimpse

POCKET PHILOSOPHIES

How to Live on 24 Hours A Day
The Human Machine
Literary Taste
Mental Efficiency

PLAYS

Cupid and Commonsense
What the Public Wants
Polite Farces
Milestones
The Honeymoon

MISCELLANEOUS

The Truth About an Author
The Feast of St. Friend

GEORGE H. DORAN COMPANY
NEW YORK

THE OLD ADAM

An Adventure

BY

ARNOLD BENNETT

AUTHOR OF "THE OLD WIVES' TALE," "HOW TO LIVE
ON TWENTY-FOUR HOURS A DAY," ETC.

Fitz Memorial Library

Endicott College
Beverly, Massachusetts 01915

NEW YORK
GEORGE H. DORAN COMPANY

Copyright, 1913
BY GEORGE H. DORAN COMPANY

Fic
Ben

CONTENTS

PART I

CHAPTER   PAGE

   I DOG-BITE 3

  II THE BANK-NOTE 37

 III WILKINS'S 72

 IV ENTRY INTO THE THEATRICAL WORLD . . 107

  V MR. SACHS TALKS 137

 VI LORD WOLDO AND LADY WOLDO 172

PART II

 VII CORNER-STONE 215

VIII DEALING WITH ELSIE 257

 IX THE FIRST NIGHT 300

  X ISABEL 339

794 Gift of Deborah Locke 20.00

THE OLD ADAM

PART I

THE OLD ADAM

CHAPTER I

DOG-BITE

I.

"A ND yet," Edward Henry Machin reflected
as at six minutes to six he approached his
own dwelling at the top of Bleakridge,
" and yet — I don't feel so jolly after all ! "

The first two words of this disturbing meditation
had reference to the fact that, by telephoning twice
to his stockbrokers at Manchester, he had just made
the sum of three hundred and forty-one pounds in a
purely speculative transaction concerning Rubber
shares. (It was in the autumn of the great gambling
year, 1910). He had simply opened his lucky and
wise mouth at the proper moment, and the money,
like ripe golden fruit, had fallen into it, a gift from
benign Heaven, surely a cause for happiness ! And
yet — he did not feel so jolly ! He was surprised,
he was even a little hurt, to discover by introspec-
tion that monetary gain was not necessarily accompanied by felicity. Nevertheless, this very successful man of the world of the Five Towns, having been

3

born on the 27th of May, 1867, had reached the age
of forty-three and a half years.

" I must be getting older," he reflected.

He was right. He was still young, as every man
of forty-three will agree, but he was getting older.
A few years ago a windfall of Three hundred and
forty-one pounds would not have been followed by
morbid self-analysis; it would have been followed by
unreasoning instinctive elation, which elation would
have endured at least twelve hours.

As he disappeared within the reddish garden wall
which sheltered his abode from the publicity of
Trafalgar Road, he half hoped to see Nellie waiting for him on the famous marble step of the porch,
for the woman had long, long since invented a way
of scouting for his advent from the small window
in the bathroom. But there was nobody on the
marble step. His melancholy increased. At the
midday meal he had complained of neuralgia, and
hence this was an evening upon which he might fairly
have expected to see sympathy charmingly attired
on the porch. It is true that the neuralgia had completely gone. " Still," he said to himself with justifiable sardonic gloom, " how does she know my
neuralgia's gone? She doesn't know."

Having opened the front door with the thinnest,
neatest latchkey in the Five Towns, he entered his
home and stumbled slightly over a brush that was
lying against the sunk door-mat. He gazed at that
brush with resentment. It was a dilapidated hand-
brush. The offensive object would have been out of

place, at nightfall, in the lobby of any house. But in the lobby of his house — the house which he had planned a dozen years earlier to the special end of minimising domestic labour, and which he had always kept up to date with the latest devices — in his lobby the spectacle of a vile outworn hand-brush at tea-time amounted to a scandal. Less than a fortnight previously he had purchased and presented to his wife a marvellous electric vacuum-cleaner, surpassing all former vacuum-cleaners. You simply attached this machine by a cord to the wall, like a dog, and waved it in mysterious passes over the floor, like a fan, and the house was clean! He was as proud of this machine as though he had invented it, instead of having merely bought it; every day he enquired about its feats, expecting enthusiastic replies as a sort of reward for his own keenness; and be it said that he had had enthusiastic replies.

And now this obscene hand-brush!

As he carefully removed his hat and his beautiful new Melton overcoat (which had the colour and the soft smoothness of a damson), he animadverted upon the astounding negligence of women. There were Nellie, his wife; his mother, the nurse, the cook, the maid — five of them; and in his mind they had all plotted together — a conspiracy of carelessness — to leave the inexcusable tool in his lobby for him to stumble over. What was the use of accidentally procuring three hundred and forty-one pounds?

Still no sign of Nellie, though he purposely made

a noisy rattle with his ebon walking-stick. Then the maid burst out of the kitchen with a tray and the principal utensils for high tea thereon. She had a guilty air. The household was evidently late. Two steps at a time he rushed up-stairs to the bathroom, so as to be waiting in the dining-room at six precisely, in order, if possible, to shame the household and fill it with remorse and unpleasantness. Yet, ordinarily, he was not a very prompt man, nor did he delight in giving pain. On the contrary, he was apt to be casual, blithe, and agreeable.

The bathroom was his pecular domain, which he was always modernising, and where his talent for the ingenious organisation of comfort and his utter indifference to esthetic beauty had the fullest scope. By universal consent admitted to be the finest bathroom in the Five Towns, it typified the whole house. He was disappointed on this occasion to see no untidy trace in it of the children's ablution; some transgression of the supreme domestic law that the bathroom must always be free and immaculate when Father wanted it would have suited his gathering humour. As he washed his hands and cleansed his well-trimmed nails with a nail-brush that had cost five shillings and sixpence, he glanced at himself in the mirror which he was splashing. A stoutish, broad-shouldered, fair, chubby man with a short bright beard and plenteous bright hair! His necktie pleased him; the elegance of his turned-back wristbands pleased him; and he liked the rich down on his forearms.

He could not believe that he looked forty-three
and a half. And yet he had recently had an idea
of shaving off his beard, partly to defy time, but
partly, also (I must admit), because a friend had
suggested to him, wildly perhaps, that if he dispensed with a beard his hair might grow more sturd-
ily. Yes, there was one weak spot in the middle
of the top of his head where the crop had of late
disconcertingly thinned. The hair-dresser had informed him that the symptom would vanish under
electric massage, and that, if he doubted the bona-
fides of hair-dressers, any doctor would testify to
the value of electric massage. But now Edward
Henry Machin, strangely discouraged, inexplicably
robbed of the zest of existence, decided that it was
not worth while to shave off his beard. Nothing
was worth while. If he was forty-three and a half,
he was forty-three and a half. To become bald
was the common lot. Moreover, beardless, he
would need the service of a barber every day. And
he was absolutely persuaded that not a barber worth
the name could be found in the Five Towns. He
actually went to Manchester, thirty-six miles, to get
his hair cut. The operation never cost him less
than a sovereign and half a day's time. And he
honestly deemed himself to be a fellow of simple
tastes! Such is the effect of the canker of luxury.
Happily he could afford these simple tastes; for,
although not rich in the modern significance of
the term, he paid income tax on some five thousand pounds a year, without quite convincing the

Surveyor of Taxes that he was an honest man.

He brushed the thick hair over the weak spot, he turned down his wristbands, he brushed the collar of his jacket, and lastly his beard; and he put on his jacket — with a certain care, for he was very neat. And then, reflectively twisting his moustache to military points, he spied through the smaller window to see whether the new high hoarding of the football-ground really did prevent a serious observer from descrying wayfarers as they breasted the hill from Hanbridge. It did not. Then he spied through the larger window upon the yard, to see whether the wall of the new rooms which he had lately added to his house showed any further trace of damp, and whether the new chauffeur was washing the new motor-car with all his heart. The wall showed no further trace of damp, and the new chauffeur's bent back seemed to symbolise an extreme conscientiousness.

Then the clock on the landing struck six, and he hurried off to put the household to open shame.

II.

Nellie came into the dining-room two minutes after her husband. As Edward Henry had laboriously counted these two minutes almost second by second on the dining-room clock, he was very tired of waiting. His secret annoyance was increased by the fact that Nellie took off her white apron in the doorway and flung it hurriedly on to the table-tray which, during the progress of meals, was established outside the dining-room door. He did not actually witness this operation of undressing, because Nellie was screened by the half-closed door; but he was entirely aware of it. He disliked it, and he had always disliked it. When Nellie was at work, either as a mother or as the owner of certain fine silver ornaments, he rather enjoyed the wonderful white apron, for it suited her temperament; but as the head of a household with six thousand pounds a year at its disposal, he objected to any hint of the thing at meals. And to-night he objected to it altogether. Who could guess from the homeliness of their family life that he was in a position to spend a hundred pounds a week and still have enough income left over to pay the salary of a town clerk or so? Nobody could guess; and he felt that people ought to be able to guess. When he was young he would have esteemed an income of six thousand pounds a year as necessarily implicating feudal state, valets, castles, yachts, family solicitors, racing-stables, county society, dinner-calls, and a drawling London accent. Why should his wife wear an apron at all? But the sad truth was that neither his wife nor his mother ever *looked* rich, nor even endeavoured to look rich. His mother would carry an eighty-pound sealskin as though she had picked it up at a jumble sale, and his wife put such simplicity into the wearing of a hundred-and-eighty pound diamond ring that its expensiveness was generally quite wasted.

And yet, while the logical male in him scathingly

condemned this feminine defect of character, his private soul was glad of it, for he well knew that he would have been considerably irked by the complexities and grandeurs of high life. But never would he have admitted this.

Nellie's face as she sat down was not limpid. He understood naught of it. More than twenty years had passed since they had first met — he and a wistful little creature — at a historic town-hall dance. He could still see the wistful little creature in those placid and pure features, in that buxom body; but now there was a formidable, capable, and experienced woman there too. Impossible to credit that the wistful little creature was thirty-seven! But she was. Indeed, it was very doubtful if she would ever see thirty-eight again. Once he had had the most romantic feelings about her. He could recall the slim flexibility of her waist, the timorous, melting invitation of her eyes. And now — such was human existence!

She sat up erect on her chair. She did not apologise for being late. She made no inquiry as to his neuralgia. On the other hand, she was not cross. She was just neutral, polite, cheerful, and apparently conscious of perfection. He strongly desired to inform her of the exact time of day, but his lips would not articulate the words.

"Maud," she said with divine calm to the maid who bore in the baked York ham under its silver canopy, "you haven't taken away that brush that's in the passage." Another illustration of Nellie's inability to live up to six thousand pounds a year; she would always refer to the hall as the "passage."

"Please'm, I did, m'm," replied Maud, now as conscious of perfection as her mistress. "He must have took it back again."

"Who's 'he'?" demanded the master.

"Carlo, sir." Upon which triumph Maud retired.

Edward Henry was dashed. Nevertheless, he quickly recovered his presence of mind, and sought about for a justification of his previous verdict upon the negligence of five women.

"It would have been easy enough to put the brush where the dog couldn't get at it," he said. But he said this strictly to himself. He could not say it aloud. Nor could he say aloud the words "neuralgia," "three hundred and forty-one pounds," any more than he could say "late."

That he was in a peculiar mental condition is proved by the fact that he did not remark the absence of his mother until he was putting her share of baked ham on to a plate.

He thought, "This is a bit thick, this is!" meaning the extreme lateness of his mother for the meal. But his only audible remark was a somewhat impatient banging down of the hot plate in front of his mother's empty chair.

In answer to this banging, Nellie quietly began:

" Your mother —"

(He knew instantly, then, that Nellie was disturbed about something or other. Mother-in-law and daughter-in-law lived together under one roof in perfect amity. Nay more, they often formed powerful and unscrupulous leagues against him. But whenever Nellie was disturbed, by no matter what, she would say " your mother " instead of merely " Mother." It was an extraordinary subtle, silly, and effective way of putting him in the wrong.)

" Your mother is staying up-stairs with Robert."

Robert was the eldest child, aged eight.

" Oh ! " breathed Edward Henry. He might have enquired what the nurse was for ; he might have enquired how his mother meant to get her tea ; but he refrained, adding simply, " What's up now? "

And in retort to his wife's " your," he laid a faint emphasis on the word " now," to imply that those women were always inventing some fresh imaginary woe for the children.

" Carlo's bitten him — in the calf," said Nellie, tightening her lips.

This, at any rate, was not imaginary.

" The kid was teasing him as usual, I suppose? " he suggested.

" That I don't know," said Nellie. " But I know we must get rid of that dog."

" Serious? "

" Of course we must," Nellie insisted, with an inadvertent heat which she immediately cooled.

" I mean the bite."

" Well — it's a bite right enough."

" And you're thinking of hydrophobia, death amid horrible agony, and so on."

" No, I'm not," she said stoutly, trying to smile.

But he knew she was. And he knew also that the bite was a trifle. If it had been a good bite, she would have made it enormous; she would have hinted that the dog had left a chasm in the boy's flesh.

" Yes, you are," he continued to twit her, encouraged by her attempt at a smile.

However, the smile expired.

" I suppose you won't deny that Carlo's teeth may have been dirty? He's always nosing in some filth or other," she said challengingly, in a measured tone of sagacity. " And there may be blood-poisoning."

" Blood-fiddlesticks ! " exclaimed Edward Henry.

Such a nonsensical and infantile rejoinder deserved no answer, and it received none. Shortly afterwards Maud entered and whispered that Nellie was wanted up-stairs. As soon as his wife had gone, Edward Henry rang the bell.

" Maud," he said, " bring me the *Signal* out of my left-hand overcoat-pocket."

And he defiantly finished his meal at leisure, with the news of the day propped up against the flower-pot, which he had set before him instead of the dish of ham.

III.

Later, catching through the open door fragments of a conversation on the stairs which indicated that his mother was at last coming down
for tea, he sped like a threatened delinquent
into the drawing-room. He had no wish to encounter his mother, though that woman usually said
little.

The drawing-room, after the bathroom, was Edward Henry's favourite district in the home. Since
he could not spend the whole of his time in the bathroom,— and he could not! — he wisely gave a
special care to the drawing-room, and he loved it
as one always loves that upon which one has bestowed
benefits. He was proud of the drawing-room, and
he had the right to be. The principal object in it,
at night, was the electric chandelier, which would
have been adequate for a lighthouse. Edward
Henry's eyes were not what they used to be; and the
minor advertisements in the *Signal*, which constitu-
ted his sole evening perusals, often lacked legibility.
Edward Henry sincerely believed in light and heat;
he was almost the only person in the Five Towns
who did. In the Five Towns people have fires in
their grates — not to warm the room, but to make
the room bright. Seemingly they use their pride to
keep themselves warm. At any rate, whenever Edward Henry talked to them of radiators, they would
sternly reply that a radiator did not and could not
brighten a room. Edward Henry had made the

great discovery that an efficient chandelier will
brighten a room better even than a fire; and he had
gilded his radiator. The notion of gilding the radiator was not his own; he had seen a gilded radiator
in the newest hotel at Birmingham, and had rejoiced as some peculiar souls rejoice when they
meet a fine line in a new poem. (In concession to
popular prejudice, Edward Henry had fire-grates in
his house, and fires therein during exceptionally
frosty weather; but this did not save him from being regarded in the Five Towns as in some ways a
peculiar soul.) The effulgent source of dark heat
was scientifically situated in front of the window, and
on ordinarily cold evenings Edward Henry and his
wife and mother, and an acquaintance if one happened to come in, would gather round the radiator
and play bridge or dummy whist.

The other phenomena of the drawing-room which
particularly interested Edward Henry were the
Turkey carpet, the four vast easy chairs, the sofa,
the imposing cigar-cabinet, and the mechanical piano-
player. At one brief period he had hovered a good
deal about the revolving bookcase containing the
encyclopedia, to which his collection of books was
limited; but the frail passion for literature had not
survived a struggle with the seductions of the mechanical piano-player.

The walls of the room never drew his notice.
He had chosen, some years before, a patent wash-
able kind of wall-paper (which could be wiped over
with a damp cloth), and he had also chosen the

pattern of the paper, but it is a fact that he could spend hours in any room without even seeing the pattern of its paper. In the same way, his wife's cushions and little draperies and bows were invisible to him, though he had searched for and duly obtained the perfect quality of swansdown which filled the cushions.

The one ornament of the walls which attracted him was a large and splendidly framed oil-painting of a ruined castle in the midst of a sombre forest through which cows were strolling. In the tower of the castle was a clock, and this clock was a realistic timepiece whose fingers moved and told the hour. Two of the oriel windows of the castle were realistic holes in its masonry; through one of them you could put a key to wind up the clock, and through the other you could put a key to wind up a secret musical box which played sixteen different tunes. He had bought this handsome relic of the Victorian era (not less artistic, despite your scorn, than many devices for satisfying the higher instincts of the present day) at an auction sale in the Strand, London. But it, too, had been supplanted in his esteem by the mechanical piano-player.

He now selected an example of the most expensive cigar in the cigar-cabinet, and lighted it as only a connoisseur can light a cigar — lovingly; he blew out the match lingeringly, with regret, and dropped it and the cigar's red collar with care into a large copper bowl on the centre table, instead of flinging it against the Japanese umbrella in the fireplace.

(A grave disadvantage of radiators is that you cannot throw odds and ends into them.) He chose the most expensive cigar because he wanted comfort and peace. The ham was not digesting very well.

Then he sat down and applied himself to the property advertisements in the *Signal,* a form of sensational serial which usually enthralled him — but not to-night. He allowed the paper to lapse on to the floor, and then rose impatiently, rearranged the thick dark blue curtains behind the radiator, and finally yielded to the silent call of the mechanical piano-player. He quite knew that to dally with the piano-player while smoking a high-class cigar was to insult the cigar; but he did not care. He tilted the cigar upwards from an extreme corner of his mouth, and through the celestial smoke gazed at the titles of the new music-rolls which had been delivered that day, and which were ranged on the top of the piano itself.

And while he did so he was thinking:

" Why in thunder didn't the little thing come and tell me at once about that kid and his dog-bite? I wonder why she didn't! She seemed only to mention it by accident. I wonder why she didn't bounce into the bathroom and tell me at once? "

But it was untrue that he sought vainly for an answer to this riddle. He was aware of the answer. He even kept saying over the answer to himself:

" She's made up her mind I've been teasing her a bit too much lately about those kids and their precious illnesses. And she's doing the dignified. That's what she's doing! She's doing the dignified!"

Of course, instantly after his tea he ought to have gone up-stairs to inspect the wounded victim of dogs. The victim was his own child, and its mother was his wife. He knew that he ought to have gone up-stairs long since. He knew he ought now to go, and the sooner the better. But somehow he could not go; he could not bring himself to go. In the minor and major crises of married life there are not two partners but four; each partner has a dual personality; each partner is indeed two different persons, and one of these fights against the other, with the common result of a fatal inaction.

The wickeder of the opposing persons in Edward Henry, getting the upper hand of the more virtuous, sniggered. " Dirty teeth, indeed! Blood-poisoning, indeed! Why not rabies, while she's about it? I guarantee she's dreaming of coffins and mourning coaches already! "

Scanning nonchalantly the titles of the music-rolls, he suddenly saw: " Funeral March. Chopin."

" She shall have it," he said, affixing the roll to the mechanism. And added, " Whatever it is! "

For he was not acquainted with the Funeral March from Chopin's Pianoforte Sonata. His musical education had in truth begun only a year earlier, with the advertisement of the " Pianisto " mechanical player. He was a judge of advertisements, and the " Pianisto " literature pleased him in a high degree. He justifiably reckoned that he could distinguish between honest and dishonest advertising. He made a deep study of the question of mechanical players, and deliberately came to the conclusion that the " Pianisto " was the best. It was also the most costly; but one of the conveniences of having six thousand pounds a year is that you need not deny yourself the best mechanical player because it happens to be the most costly. He bought a " Pianisto," and incidentally he bought a superb grand piano, and exiled the old cottage piano to the nursery.

The " Pianisto " was the best, partly because, like the vacuum-cleaner, it could be operated by electricity, and partly because, by means of certain curved lines on the unrolling paper, and of certain gun-metal levers and clutches, it enabled the operator to put his secret ardent soul into the music. Assuredly it had given Edward Henry a taste for music. The whole world of musical compositions was his to conquer, and he conquered it at the rate of about two great masters a month. From Handel to Richard Strauss, even from Palestrina to Debussy, the achievements of genius lay at his mercy. He criticised them with a freedom that was entirely unprejudiced by tradition. Beethoven was no more to him than Arthur Sullivan; indeed, was rather less. The works of his choice were the "Tannhäuser" overture, a potpourri of Verdi's " Aïda," Chopin's Study in Thirds — which ravished him — and a selection from " The Merry Widow,"

which also ravished him. So that on the whole it
may be said that he had a very good natural taste.

He at once liked Chopin's Funeral March. He
entered profoundly into the spirit of it. With the
gun-metal levers he produced in a marvellous fashion
the long tragic roll of the drums, and by the manipu-
lation of a clutch he distilled into the chant at the
graveside a melancholy sweetness that rent the
heart. The later crescendi were overwhelming.
And as he played there, with the bright blaze of
the chandelier on his fair hair and beard, and the
blue cigar-smoke in his nostrils, and the effluence
of the gilded radiator behind him, and the intimacy
of the drawn window curtains and the closed and cur-
tained door folding him in from the world, and the
agony of the music grieving his artistic soul to the
core — as he played there, he grew gradually happier and happier, and the zest of existence seemed
to return. It was not only that he felt the ele-
mental, unfathomable satisfaction of a male who is
sheltered in solitude from a pack of women that
have got on his nerves; there was also the more
piquant assurance that he was behaving in a very
sprightly manner. How long was it since he had
accomplished anything worthy of his ancient reputation as a " card," as " the " card of the Five
Towns? He could not say; but now he knew that
he was being a card again. The whole town would
smile and forgive and admire if it learnt that —

Nellie invaded the room. She had resumed the
affray.

"Denry!" she reproached him, in an uncontrolled voice. "I'm ashamed of you! I really am!" She was no longer doing the dignified. The mask was off, and the unmistakable lineaments of the outraged mother appeared. That she should address him as "Denry" proved the intensity of her agitation. Years ago, when he had been made an alderman, his wife and his mother had decided that "Denry" was no longer a suitable name for him, and had abandoned it in favour of "Edward Henry."

He ceased playing.

"Why?" he protested, with a ridiculous air of innocence. "I'm only playing Chopin. Can't I play Chopin?"

He was rather surprised and impressed that she had recognised the piece for what it was. But of course she did, as a fact, know something about music, he remembered, though she never touched the "Pianisto."

"I think it's a pity you can't choose some other evening for your funeral marches!" she exclaimed.

"If that's it," said Edward Henry like lightning, "why did you stick me out you weren't afraid of hydrophobia?"

"I'll thank you to come up-stairs," she replied with warmth.

"Oh, all right, my dear! All right!" he cooed.

And they went up-stairs in a rather solemn procession.

IV.

Nellie led the way to the chamber known as " Maisie's room," where the youngest of the Machins was wont to sleep in charge of the nurse, who, under the supervision of the mother of all three, had dominion over Robert, Ralph, and their little sister. The first thing that Edward Henry noticed was the screen which shut off one of the beds. The unfurling of the four-fold screen was always a sure sign that Nellie was taking an infantile illness seriously. It was an indication to Edward Henry of the importance of the dog-bite in Nellie's esteem. When all the chicks of the brood happened to be simultaneously sound, the screen reposed, inconspicuous, at an angle against a wall behind the door; but when pestilence was abroad, the screen travelled from one room to another in the wake of it, and, spreading wide, took part in the battle of life and death.

In an angle of the screen, on the side of it away from the bed and near the fire (in times of stress Nellie would not rely on radiators), sat old Mrs. Machin, knitting. She was a thin, bony woman of sixty-nine years, and as hard and imperishable as teak. So far as her son knew, she had only had two illnesses in her life. The first was an attack of influenza, and the second was an attack of acute rheumatism, which had incapacitated her for several weeks. Edward Henry and Nellie had taken advantage of her helplessness, then, to force her to give up her barbaric cottage in Brougham Street and share permanently the splendid comfort of their home. She existed in their home like a philosophic prisoner of war at the court of conquerors, behaving faultlessly, behaving magnanimously in the melancholy grandeur of her fall, but never renouncing her soul's secret independence, nor permitting herself to forget that she was on foreign ground. When Edward Henry looked at those yellow and seasoned fingers which, by hard manual labour, had kept herself and him in the young days of his humble obscurity, and which, during sixty years had not been idle for more than six weeks in all, he grew almost apologetic for his wealth. They reminded him of the day when his total resources were five pounds, won in a wager, and of the day when he drove proudly about behind a mule collecting other people's rents, and of the glittering day when he burst in on her from Llandudno with over a thousand gold sovereigns in a hat-box,— product of his first great picturesque coup,— imagining himself to be an English Jay Gould. She had not blenched even then. She had not blenched since. And she never would blench. In spite of his gorgeous position and his unique reputation, in spite of her well-concealed but notorious pride in him, he still went in fear of that ageless woman, whose undaunted eye always told him that he was still the lad Denry, and her inferior in moral force. The curve of her thin lips seemed ever to be warning him that with her pretensions were quite useless, and that she saw through him, and through him to the innermost grottoes of his poor human depravity.

He caught her eye guiltily.

"Behold the alderman!" she murmured with grimness.

That was all. But the three words took thirty years off his back, snatched the half-crown cigar out of his hand, and reduced him again to the raw, hungry boy of Brougham Street. And he knew that he had sinned gravely in not coming up-stairs very much earlier.

"Is that you, Father?" called the high voice of Robert from the back of the screen.

He had to admit to his son that it was he.

The infant lay on his back in Maisie's bed, while his mother sat lightly on the edge of nurse's bed near-by.

"Well, you're a nice chap!" said Edward Henry, avoiding Nellie's glance, but trying to face his son as one innocent man may face another, and not perfectly succeeding. He never could feel like a real father somehow.

"My temperature's above normal," announced Robert proudly, and then added with regret, "but not much!"

There was the clinical thermometer — instrument which Edward Henry despised and detested as being an inciter of illnesses — in a glass of water on the table between the two beds.

"Father!" Robert began again.

"Well, Robert?" said Edward Henry cheerfully.

He was glad that the child was in one of his rare loquacious moods, because the chatter not only proved that the dog had done no serious damage, —it also eased the silent strain between himself and Nellie.

"Why did you play the Funeral March, Father?" asked Robert; and the question fell into the tranquillity of the room rather like a bomb that had not quite decided whether or not to burst.

For the second time that evening Edward Henry was dashed.

"Have you been meddling with my music-rolls?"

"No, Father. I only read the labels."

This child simply read everything.

"How did you know I was playing a funeral march?" Edward Henry demanded.

"Oh, *I* didn't tell him!" Nellie put in, excusing herself before she was accused. She smiled benignly, as an angel woman, capable of forgiving all. But there were moments when Edward Henry hated moral superiority and Christian meekness in a wife. Moreover, Nellie somewhat spoiled her own effect by adding with an artificial continuation of the smile, "You needn't look at *me!*"

Edward Henry considered the remark otiose. Though he had indeed ventured to look at her, he had not looked at her in the manner which she implied.

"It made a noise like funerals and things," Robert explained.

"Well, it seems to me, *you* have been playing a funeral march," said Edward Henry to the child.

He thought this rather funny, rather worthy of himself, but the child answered with ruthless gravity and a touch of disdain, for he was a disdainful child, without bowels:

" I don't know what you mean, Father." The curve of his lips (he had his grandmother's lips) appeared to say, " I wish you wouldn't try to be silly, Father." However, youth forgets very quickly, and the next instant Robert was beginning once more, " Father! "

" Well, Robert? "

By mutual agreement of the parents, the child was never addressed as " Bob " or " Bobby," or by any other diminutive. In their practical opinion a child's name was his name, and ought not to be mauled or dismembered on the pretext of fondness. Similarly, the child had not been baptised after his father, or after any male member of either the Machin or the Cotterill family. Why should family names be perpetuated merely because they were family names? A natural human reaction, this, against the excessive sentimentalism of the Victorian era!

" What does ' stamped out ' mean? " Robert enquired.

Now Robert, among other activities, busied himself in the collection of postage-stamps, and in consequence his father's mind, under the impulse of the question, ran immediately to postage-stamps.

"Stamped out?" said Edward Henry, with the air of omniscience that a father is bound to assume. "Postage-stamps are stamped-out — by a machine — you see."

Robert's scorn of this explanation was manifest.

"Well," Edward Henry, piqued, made another attempt, "you stamp a fire out with your feet." And he stamped illustratively on the floor. After all, the child was only eight.

"I knew all that before," said Robert coldly. "You don't understand."

"What makes you ask, dear? Let us show Father your leg." Nellie's voice was soothing.

"Yes," Robert murmured, staring reflectively at the ceiling. "That's it. It says in the encyclopedia that hydrophobia is stamped out in this country — by Mr. Long's muzzling order. Who is Mr. Long?"

A second bomb had fallen on exactly the same spot as the first, and the two exploded simultaneously. And the explosion was none the less terrible because it was silent and invisible. The tidy domestic chamber was strewn in a moment with an awful mass of wounded susceptibilities. Beyond the screen the *nick-nick* of grandmother's steel needles stopped and started again. It was characteristic of her temperament that she should recover before the younger generations could recover. Edward Henry, as befitted his sex, regained his nerve a little earlier than Nellie.

"I told you never to touch my encyclopedia," said

he sternly. Robert had twice been caught on his stomach on the floor with a vast volume open under his chin, and his studies had been traced by vile thumb-marks.

" I know," said Robert.

Whenever anybody gave that child a piece of un-solicited information, he almost invariably replied, " I know."

" But hydrophobia ! " cried Nellie. " How did you know about hydrophobia ? "

" We had it in spellings last week," Robert ex-plained.

" The deuce you did ! " muttered Edward Henry.

The one bright fact of the many-sided and gloomy crisis was the very obvious truth that Robert was the most extraordinary child that ever lived.

" But when on earth did you get at the encyclo-pedia, Robert ? " his mother exclaimed, completely at a loss.

" It was before you came in from Hillport," the wondrous infant answered. " After my leg had stopped hurting me a bit."

" But when I came in Nurse said it had only just happened ! "

" Shows how much *she* knew ! " said Robert, with contempt.

" Does your leg hurt you now ? " Edward Henry enquired.

" A bit. That's why I can't go to sleep, of course."

" Well, let's have a look at it." Edward Henry
attempted jollity.

" Mother's wrapped it all up in boracic wool."

The bed-clothes were drawn down and the leg
gradually revealed. And the sight of the little soft
leg, so fragile and defenceless, really did touch Edward Henry. It made him feel more like an authentic father than he had felt for a long time.
And the sight of the red wound hurt him. Still,
it was a beautifully clean wound, and it was not
a large wound.

" It's a clean wound," he observed judiciously.
In spite of himself, he could not keep a certain flip-
pant harsh quality out of his tone.

" Well, I've naturally washed it with carbolic,"
Nellie returned sharply.

He illogically resented this sharpness.

" Of course he was bitten through his stocking? "

" Of course," said Nellie, re-enveloping the wound
hastily, as though Edward Henry was not worthy to
regard it.

" Well, then, by the time they got through the
stocking, the animal's teeth couldn't be dirty.
Every one knows that."

Nellie shut her lips.

" Were you teasing Carlo? " Edward Henry demanded curtly of his son.

" I don't know."

Whenever anybody asked that child for a piece
of information, he almost invariably replied, " I
don't know."

"How, you don't know? You must know whether you were teasing the dog or not!" Edward Henry was nettled.

The renewed spectacle of his own wound had predisposed Robert to feel a great and tearful sympathy for himself. His mouth now began to take strange shapes and to increase magically in area, and beads appeared in the corners of his large eyes.

"I — I was only measuring his tail by his hind leg," he blubbered, and then sobbed.

Edward Henry did his best to save his dignity.

"Come, come!" he reasoned, less menacingly. "Boys who can read enyclopedias mustn't be crybabies. You'd no business measuring Carlo's tail by his hind leg. You ought to remember that that dog's older than you." And this remark, too, he thought rather funny, but apparently he was alone in his opinion.

Then he felt something against his calf. And it was Carlo's nose. Carlo was a large, very shaggy and unkempt Northern terrier, but owing to vagueness of his principal points, due doubtless to a vagueness in his immediate ancestry, it was impossible to decide whether he had come from the north or the south side of the Tweed. This aging friend of Edward Henry's, surmising that something unusual was afoot in his house, and having entirely forgotten the trifling episode of the bite, had unobtrusively come to make enquiries.

"Poor old boy!" said Edward Henry, stooping

to pat the dog. " Did they try to measure his tail
with his hind leg? "

The gesture was partly instinctive, for he loved
Carlo; but it also had its origin in sheer nervousness,
in sheer ignorance of what was the best thing to do.
However, he was at once aware that he had done the
worst thing. Had not Nellie announced that the
dog must be got rid of? And here he was fondly
caressing the bloodthirsty dog! With a hysterical
movement of the lower part of her leg, Nellie pushed
violently against the dog,— she did not kick, but she
nearly kicked,— and Carlo, faintly howling a protest, fled.

Edward Henry was hurt. He escaped from between the beds, and from that close, enervating domestic atmosphere where he was misunderstood by
women and disdained by infants. He wanted fresh
air; he wanted bars, whiskies, billiard-rooms, and
the society of masculine men about town. The
whole of his own world was against him.

As he passed by his knitting mother, she ignored
him and moved not. She had a great gift of holding aloof from conjugal complications.

On the landing he decided that he would go out
at once into the major world. Half-way down the
stairs he saw his overcoat on the hall-stand, beckoning to him and offering release.

Then he heard the bedroom door and his wife's
footsteps.

" Edward Henry! "

" Well? "

He stopped and looked up inimically at her face, which overhung the banisters. It was the face of a woman outraged in her most profound feelings, but amazingly determined to be sweet.

" What do you think of it? "

" What do I think of what? The wound? "

" Yes."

" Why, it's simply nothing. Nothing at all. You know how that kid always heals up quickly. You won't be able to find the wound in a day or two."

" Don't you think it ought to be cauterised at once? "

He moved downwards.

" No, I don't. I've been bitten three times in my life by dogs, and I was never cauterised."

" Well, I *do* think it ought to be cauterised." She raised her voice slightly as he retreated from her. " And I shall be glad if you'll call in at Dr. Stirling's and ask him to come round."

He made no reply, but put on his overcoat and his hat, and took his stick. Glancing up the stairs, he saw Nellie was now standing at the head of them, under the electric light there, and watching him. He knew that she thought he was cravenly obeying her command. She could have no idea that before she spoke to him he had already decided to put on his overcoat and hat and take his stick and go forth into the major world. However, that was no affair of his.

He hesitated a second. Then the nurse appeared

out of the kitchen with a squalling Maisie in her
arms, and ran up-stairs. Why Maisie was squalling, and why she should have been in the kitchen
at such an hour instead of in bed, he could not
guess; but he could guess that if he remained one
second longer in that exasperating minor world he
would begin to smash furniture, and so he quitted it.

v.

It was raining slightly, but he dared not return
to the house for his umbrella. In the haze
and wet of the shivering October night, the clock
of Bleakridge Church glowed like a fiery disk
suspended in the sky; and, mysteriously hanging
there, without visible means of support, it seemed
to him somehow to symbolise the enigma of the universe and intensify his inward gloom. Never before
had he had such feelings to such a degree. It is
scarcely an exaggeration to say that never before
had the enigma of the universe occurred to him.
The side gates clicked as he stood hesitant under
the shelter of the wall, and a figure emerged from
his domain. It was Bellfield, the new chauffeur, going across to his home in the little square in front
of the church. Bellfield touched his cap with an
eager and willing hand, as new chauffeurs will.

" Want the car, sir? Setting in for a wet night! "
" No, thanks."

It was a lie. He did want the car. He wanted
the car so that he might ride right away into a new
and more interesting world, or at any rate into

Hanbridge, centre of the pleasures, the wickedness, and the commerce of the Five Towns. But he dared not have the car. He dared not have his own car. He must slip off, noiseless and unassuming. Even to go to Dr. Stirling's he dared not have the car. Besides, he could have walked down the hill to Dr. Stirling's in three minutes. Not that he had the least intention of going to Dr. Stirling's. No! His wife imagined that he was going; but she was mistaken. Within an hour, when Dr. Stirling had failed to arrive, she would doubtless telephone, and get her Dr. Stirling. Not, however, with Edward Henry's assistance!

He reviewed his conduct throughout the evening. In what particular had it been sinful? In no particular. True, the accident to the boy was a misfortune, but had he not borne that misfortune lightly, minimised it, and endeavoured to teach others to bear it lightly? His blithe humour ought surely to have been an example to Nellie! And as for the episode of the funeral march on the "Pianisto," really, really, the tiresome little thing ought to have better appreciated his whimsical drollery!

But Nellie was altered; he was altered; everything was altered. He remembered the ecstasy of their excursion to Switzerland. He remembered the rapture with which, on their honeymoon, he had clasped a new opal bracelet on her exciting arm. He could not possibly have such sensations now. What was the meaning of life? Was life worth

living? The fact was, he was growing old. Useless to pretend to himself that it was not so. Both
he and she were growing old. Only, she seemed
to be placidly content, and he was not content.
And more and more the domestic atmosphere and
the atmosphere of the district fretted and even annoyed him. To-night's affair was not unique, but
it was a culmination. He gazed pessimistically
north and south along the slimy expanse of Trafalgar Road, which sank northwards in the direction
of Dr. Stirling's, and southwards in the direction
of joyous Hanbridge. He loathed and despised
Trafalgar Road. What was the use of making
three hundred and forty-one pounds by a shrewd
speculation? None. He could not employ three
hundred and forty-one pounds to increase his happiness. Money had become futile for him. Astounding thought! He desired no more of it. He
had a considerable income from investments, and
also at least four thousand a year from the Five
Towns Universal Thrift Club, that wonderful but
unpretentious organisation which now embraced
every corner of the Five Towns; that gorgeous in-
vention for profitably taking care of the pennies of
the working classes; that excellent device, his own,
for selling the working classes every kind of goods
at credit prices after having received part of the
money in advance!

"I want a change!" he said to himself, and
threw away his cigar.

After all, the bitterest thought in his heart was

perhaps that on that evening he had tried to be a
" card," and, for the first time in his brilliant career
as a " card," had failed. He, Henry Machin, who
had been the youngest mayor of Bursley years and
years ago; he, the recognised amuser of the Five
Towns; he, one of the greatest " characters " that
the Five Towns had ever produced — he had failed
of an effect!

He slipped out on to the pavement, and saw, under the gas-lamp, on the new hoarding of the football-ground, a poster intimating that during that particular week there was a gigantic attraction at the
Empire Music Hall at Hanbridge. According to
the posters, there was a gigantic attraction every
week at the Empire, but Edward Henry happened
to know that this week the attraction was indeed
somewhat out of the common. And to-night was
Friday, the fashionable night for the bloods and
the modishness of the Five Towns. He looked at
the church clock, and then at his watch. He would
be in time for the " second house," which started
at nine o'clock. At the same moment an electric
tram-car came thundering up out of Bursley. He
boarded it, and was saluted by the conductor. Remaining on the platform, he lit a cigarette, and
tried to feel cheerful; but he could not conquer his
depression.

"Yes," he thought, "what I want is change —
and a lot of it too!"

CHAPTER II

THE BANK-NOTE

I.

ALDERMAN MACHIN had to stand at the back, and somewhat towards the side, of that part of the auditorium known as the Grand Circle at the Empire Music Hall, Hanbridge. The attendants at the entrance and in the lounge, where the salutation "Welcome" shone in electricity over a large Cupid-surrounded mirror, had compassionately and yet exultingly told him that there was not a seat left in the house. He had shared their exultation. He had said to himself, full of honest pride in the Five Towns: "This music-hall, admitted by the press to be one of the finest in the provinces, holds over two thousand five hundred people. And yet we can fill it to overflowing twice every night! And only a few years ago there wasn't a decent music-hall in the entire district!"

The word "progress" flitted through his head.

It was not strictly true that the Empire was or could be filled to overflowing twice every night, but it was true that at that particular moment not a seat was unsold; and the aspect of a crowded auditorium is apt to give an optimistic quality to broad

37

generalisations. Alderman Machin began instinctively to calculate the amount of money in the house, and to wonder whether there would be a chance for a second music-hall in the dissipated town of Hanbridge. He also wondered why the idea of a second music-hall in Hanbridge had never occurred to him before.

The Grand Circle was so-called because it was grand. Its plush fauteuils cost a shilling, no mean price for a community where seven pounds of potatoes can be bought for sixpence, and the view of the stage therefrom was perfect. But the alderman's view was far from perfect, since he had to peer as best he could between and above the shoulders of several men, each apparently, but not really, taller than himself. By constant slight movements to comply with the movements of the rampart of shoulders, he could discern fragments of various advertisements of soap, motor-cars, whisky, shirts, perfume, pills, bricks, and tea, for the drop-curtain was down. And, curiously, he felt obliged to keep his eyes on the drop-curtain, and across the long intervening vista of hats and heads and smoke, to explore its most difficult corners again and again, lest, when it went up, he might not be in proper practice for seeing what was behind it.

Nevertheless, despite the marked inconveniences of his situation, he felt brighter, he felt almost happy in this dense atmosphere of success. He even found a certain peculiar and perverse satisfaction in the fact that he had as yet been recognised by nobody. Once or twice the owners of shoulders had turned and deliberately glared at the worrying fellow who had the impudence to be all the time peeping over them and between them; they had not distinguished the fellow from any ordinary fellow. Could they have known that he was the famous Alderman Edward Henry Machin, founder and sole proprietor of the Thrift Club, into which their wives were probably paying so much a week, they would most assuredly have glared to another tune, and they would have said with pride afterwards, " That chap Machin o' Bursley was standing behind me at the Empire to-night." And though Machin is amongst the commonest names in the Five Towns, all would have known that the great and admired Denry was meant. It was astonishing that a personage so notorious should not have been instantly " spotted " in such a resort as the Empire. More proof that the Five Towns was a vast and seething concentration of cities, and no longer a mere district where everybody knew everybody.

The curtain rose, and, as it did so, a thunderous, crashing applause of greeting broke forth — applause that thrilled and impressed and inspired; applause that made every individual in the place feel right glad that he was there. For the curtain had risen on the gigantic attraction which many members of the audience were about to see for the fifth time that week; in fact, it was rumoured that certain men of fashion, whose habit was to refuse themselves nothing, had attended every performance

of the gigantic attraction since the second house on
Monday.

The scene represented a restaurant of quiet aspect, into which entered a waiter bearing a pile of
plates some two feet high. The waiter being intoxicated, the tower of plates leaned this way and
that as he staggered about, and the whole house
really did hold its breath in the simultaneous hope
and fear of an enormous and resounding smash.
Then entered a second intoxicated waiter, also bearing a pile of plates some two feet high; and the
risk of destruction was thus more than doubled —
it was quadrupled, for each waiter, in addition to
the risks of his own inebriety, was now subject to
the dreadful peril of colliding with the other.
However, there was no catastrophe.

Then arrived two customers, one in a dress suit
and an eye-glass, and the other in a large violet
hat, a diamond necklace, and a yellow satin skirt.
The which customers, seemingly well used to the
sight of drunken waiters tottering to and fro with
towers of plates, sat down at a table and waited
calmly for attention. The popular audience, with
that quick mental grasp for which popular audi-
ences are so renowned, soon perceived that the
table was in close proximity to a lofty sideboard,
and that on either hand of the sideboard were two
chairs, upon which the two waiters were trying to
climb in order to deposit their plates on the topmost shelf of the sideboard. The waiters successfully mounted the chairs, and successfully lifted

their towers of plates to within half an inch of the desired shelf, and then the chairs began to show signs of insecurity. By this time the audience was stimulated to an ecstasy of expectation, whose painfulness was only equalled by its extreme delectability. The sole unmoved persons in the building were the customers awaiting attention at the restaurant table.

One tower was safely lodged on the shelf. But was it? It was not! Yes? No! It curved; it straightened; it curved again. The excitement was as keen as that of watching a drowning man attempt to reach the shore. It was simply excruciating. It could not be borne any longer, and when it could not be borne any longer, the tower sprawled irrevocably, and seven dozen plates fell in a cascade on the violet hat, and so, with an inconceivable clatter, to the floor. Almost at the same moment the being in the dress suit and the eye-glass — becoming aware of the phenomena — slightly unusual even in a restaurant, dropped his eye-glass, turned round to the sideboard, and received the other waiter's seven dozen plates in the face and on the crown of his head.

No such effect had ever been seen in the Five Towns, and the felicity of the audience exceeded all previous felicities. The audience yelled, roared, shrieked, gasped, trembled, and punched itself in a furious passion of pleasure. They make plates in the Five Towns. They live by making plates. They understand plates. In the Five Towns a man will carry not seven but twenty-seven dozen plates on a swaying plank for eight hours a day, up steps and down steps, and in doorways and out of doorways, and not break one plate in seven years! Judge, therefore, the simple but terrific satisfaction of a Five Towns' audience in the hugeness of the calamity. Moreover, every plate smashed means a demand for a new plate and increased prosperity for the Five Towns. The grateful crowd in the auditorium of the Empire would have covered the stage with wreaths if it had known that wreaths were used for other occasions than funerals; which it did not know.

Fresh complications instantly ensued which cruelly cut short the agreeable exercise of uncontrolled laughter. It was obvious that one of the waiters was about to fall. And in the enforced tranquillity of a new dread, every dyspeptic person in the house was deliciously conscious of a sudden freedom from indigestion, due to the agreeable exercise of uncontrolled laughter, and wished fervently that he could laugh like that after every meal. The waiter fell; he fell through the large violet hat and disappeared beneath the surface of a sea of crockery. The other waiter fell too, but the sea was not deep enough to drown a couple of them. Then the customers, recovering themselves, decided that they must not be outclassed in this competition of havoc, and they overthrew the table and everything on it, and all the other tables, and everything on all the other tables. The audience was now a field of artillery which nothing could silence. The waiters arose, and, opening the sideboard, disclosed many hundreds of unsuspected plates of all kinds, ripe for smashing. Niagaras of plates surged on to the stage. All four performers revelled and wallowed in smashed plates. New supplies of plates were constantly being produced from strange concealments, and finally the tables and chairs were broken to pieces, and each object on the walls was torn down and flung in bits on to the gorgeous general débris, to the top of which clambered the violet hat, necklace, and yellow petticoat, brandishing one single little plate, whose life had been miraculously spared. Shrieks of joy in that little plate played over the din like lightning in a thunder-storm. And the curtain fell.

It was rung up fifteen times, and fifteen times the quartette of artists, breathless, bowed in acknowledgment of the frenzied and boisterous testimony to their unique talents. No singer, no tragedian, no comedian, no wit, could have had such a triumph, could have given such intense pleasure. And yet none of the four had spoken a word. Such is genius!

At the end of the fifteenth call the stage-manager came before the curtain and guaranteed that two thousand four hundred plates had been broken.

The lights went up. Strong men were seen to be wiping tears from their eyes. Complete strangers were seen addressing each other in the manner of old friends. Such is art!

"Well, that was worth a bob, that was!" muttered Edward Henry to himself. And it was. Edward Henry had not escaped the general fate. Nobody, being present, could have escaped it. He was enchanted. He had utterly forgotten every care.

"Good evening, Mr. Machin," said a voice at his side. Not only he turned, but nearly every one in the vicinity turned. The voice was the voice of the stout and splendid managing director of the Empire, and it sounded with the ring of authority above the rising tinkle of the bar behind the Grand Circle.

"Oh! How d'ye do, Mr. Dakins?" Edward Henry held out a cordial hand, for even the greatest men are pleased to be greeted in a place of entertainment by the managing director thereof. Further, his identity was now recognised.

"Haven't you seen those gentlemen in that box beckoning to you?" said Mr. Dakins, proudly deprecating complimentary remarks on the show.

"Which box?"

Mr. Dakins' hand indicated the stage-box. And Henry, looking, saw three men, one unknown to him; the second, Robert Brindley, the architect, of Bursley; and the third, Dr. Stirling.

Instantly his conscience leapt up within him. He thought of rabies. Yes, sobered in the fraction of a second, he thought of rabies. Supposing that, after all, in spite of Mr. Long's muzzling order, as cited by his infant son, an odd case of rabies should have lingered in the British Isles, and supposing that

Carlo had been infected! Not impossible! Was it providential that Dr. Stirling was in the auditorium?

" You know two of them? " said Mr. Dakins.

" Yes."

" Well, the third's a Mr. Bryany. He's manager to Mr. Seven Sachs." Mr. Dakins' tone was respectful.

" And who's Mr. Seven Sachs? " asked Edward Henry absently. It was a stupid question.

He was impressively informed that Mr. Seven Sachs was the arch-famous American actor-playwright, now nearing the end of a provincial tour which had surpassed all records of provincial tours, and that he would be at the Theatre Royal, Hanbridge, next week. Edward Henry then remembered that the hoardings had been full of Mr. Seven Sachs for some time past.

" They keep on making signs to you," said Mr. Dakins, referring to the occupants of the stage-box.

Edward Henry waved a reply to the box.

" Here! I'll take you there the shortest way," said Mr. Dakins.

II.

" Welcome to Stirling's box, Machin! " Robert Brindley greeted the alderman with an almost imperceptible wink. Edward Henry had encountered this wink once or twice before; he could not decide precisely what it meant; it was apt to make him reflective. He did not dislike Robert Brindley, his habit was not to dislike people; he admitted Brindley to be a clever architect, though he objected to the "modern" style of the fronts of his houses and schools. But he did take exception to the man's attitude towards the Five Towns, of which, by the way, Brindley was just as much a native as himself. Brindley seemed to live in the Five Towns like a highly cultured stranger in a savage land, and to derive rather too much sardonic amusement from the spectacle of existence therein. Brindley was a very special crony of Stirling's, and had influenced Stirling. But Stirling was too clever to submit unduly to the influence. Besides, Stirling was not a native; he was only a Scotchman, and Edward Henry considered that what Stirling thought of the district did not matter. Other details about Brindley which Edward Henry deprecated were his necktie, which, for Edward Henry's taste, was too flowing, his scorn of the "Pianisto" (despite the man's tremendous interest in music), and his incipient madness on the subject of books — a madness shared by Stirling. Brindley and the doctor were forever chattering about books, and buying them.

So that, on the whole, Dr. Stirling's box was not a place where Edward Henry felt entirely at home. Nevertheless, the two men, having presented Mr. Bryany, did their best, each in his own way, to make him feel at home.

"Take this chair, Machin," said Stirling, indicating a chair at the front.

"Oh, I can't take the front chair!" Edward Henry protested.

"Of course you can, my dear Machin," said Brindley sharply. "The front chair in a stage-box is the one proper seat in the house for you. Do as your doctor prescribes."

And Edward Henry accordingly sat down at the front, with Mr. Bryany by his side; and the other two sat behind. But Edward Henry was not quite comfortable. He faintly resented that speech of Brindley's. And yet he did feel that what Brindley had said was true, and he was indeed glad to be in the front chair of a brilliant stage-box on the grand tier, instead of being packed away in the nethermost twilight of the Grand Circle. He wondered how Brindley and Stirling had managed to distinguish his face among the confusion of faces in that distant obscurity; he, Edward Henry, had failed to notice them, even in the prominence of their box. But that they had distinguished him showed how familiar and striking a figure he was. He wondered, too, why they should have invited him to hobnob with them. He was not of their set. Indeed, like many very eminent men, he was not to any degree in anybody's set. Of one thing he was sure,— because he had read it on the self-conscious faces of all three of them,— namely, that they had been discussing him. Possibly he had been brought up for Mr. Bryany's inspection as a major lion and character of the district. Well, he did not mind that; nay, he enjoyed that. He could feel Mr. Bryany

covertly looking him over. And he thought:
" Look, my boy! I make no charge." He smiled
and nodded to one or two people who with pride
saluted him from the stalls. It was meet that he
should be visible there on that Friday night!

" A full house! " he observed, to break the rather
awkward silence of the box, as he glanced round at
the magnificent smoke-veiled pageant of the aristocracy and the democracy of the Five Towns
crowded together, tier above gilded tier, up to the
dim roof where ragged lads and maids giggled and
flirted while waiting for the broken plates to be
cleared away and the moving pictures to begin.

" You may say it! " agreed Mr. Bryany, who
spoke with a very slight American accent. " Dakins positively hadn't a seat to offer me. I happened to have the evening free. It isn't often I do
have a free evening. And so I thought I'd pop in
here. But if Dakins hadn't introduced me to these
gentlemen, my seat would have had to be a standing
one."

" So that's how they got to know him, is it? "
thought Edward Henry.

And then there was another short silence.

" Hear you've been doing something striking in
rubber shares, Machin? " said Brindley at length.

Astonishing how these things got abroad!

" Oh, very little, very little! " Edward Henry
laughed modestly. " Too late to do much! In another fortnight the bottom will be all out of the
rubber market! "

" Of course I'm an Englishman —" Mr. Bryany
began.

" Why ' of course '? " Edward Henry interrupted
him.

" Hear! Hear! Alderman. Why ' of course '? "
said Brindley approvingly, and Stirling's rich laugh
was heard. " Only it does just happen," Brindley
added, " that Mr. Bryany did us the honour to be
born in the district."

" Yes. Longshaw," Mr. Bryany admitted, half
proud and half apologetic, " which I left at the age
of two."

" Oh, Longshaw! " murmured Edward Henry
with a peculiar inflection, which had a distinct meaning for at least two of his auditors.

Longshaw is at the opposite end of the Five
Towns from Bursley, and the majority of the inhabitants of Bursley have never been to Longshaw
in their lives, have only heard of it, as they hear
of Chicago or Bangkok. Edward Henry had often
been to Longshaw, but, like every visitor from
Bursley, he instinctively regarded it as a foolish and
unnecessary place.

" As I was saying," resumed Mr. Bryany, quite
unintimidated, " I'm an Englishman. But I've lived
eighteen years in America, and it seems to me the
bottom will soon be knocked out of pretty nearly
all the markets in England. Look at the Five
Towns! "

" No, don't, Mr. Bryany! " said Brindley.
" Don't go to extremes."

" Personally, I don't mind looking at the Five
Towns," said Edward Henry. " What of it? "

" Well, did you ever see such people for looking
twice at a five-pound note? "

Edward Henry most certainly did not like this
aspersion on his native district. He gazed in silence
at Mr. Bryany's brassy and yet simple face, and did
not like the face either.

And Mr. Bryany, beautifully unaware that he had
failed in tact, continued: " The Five Towns is the
most English place I've ever seen, believe me! Of
course it has its good points, and England has her
good points; but there's no money stirring. There's
no field for speculation on the spot, and as for outside investment, no Englishman will touch anything
that really is good." He emphasised the last three
words.

" What d'ye do yeself, Mr. Bryany? " inquired
Dr. Stirling.

" What do I do with my little bit? " cried Mr.
Bryany. " Oh, I know what to do with my little
bit. I can get ten per cent. in Seattle, and twelve
to fifteen in Calgary, on my little bit; and security
just as good as English railway stock — *and* better."

The theatre was darkened, and the cinematograph began its reckless twinkling.

Mr. Bryany went on offering to Edward Henry,
in a suitably lowered voice, his views on the great
questions of investment and speculation; and Edward Henry made cautious replies.

" And even when there *is* a good thing going at

home," Mr. Bryany said, in a wounded tone, " what Englishman'd look at it?"

" I would," said Edward Henry with a blandness that was only skin-deep, for all the time he was cogitating the question whether the presence of Dr. Stirling in the audience ought or ought not to be regarded as providential.

"Now, I've got the option on a little affair in London," said Mr. Bryany, while Edward Henry glanced quickly at him in the darkness, " and can I get anybody to go into it? I can't."

"What sort of a little affair?"

" Building a theatre in the West End."

Even a less impassive man than Edward Henry would have started at the coincidence of this remark. And Edward Henry started. Twenty minutes ago he had been idly dreaming of theatrical speculation, and now he could almost see theatrical speculation shimmering before him in the pale shifting rays of the cinematograph that cut through the gloom of the mysterious auditorium.

"Oh!" And in this new interest he forgot the enigma of the ways of Providence.

"Of course, you know, I'm in the business," said Mr. Bryany. "I'm Seven Sachs's manager." It was as if he owned and operated Mr. Seven Sachs.

"So I heard," said Edward Henry, and then remarked with mischievous cordiality: "And I suppose these chaps told you I was the sort of man you were after. And you got them to ask me in, eh, Mr. Bryany?"

Mr. Bryany gave an uneasy laugh, but seemed to find naught to say.

" Well, what *is* your little affair? " Edward Henry encouraged him.

" Oh, I can't tell you now," said Mr. Bryany. " It would take too long. The thing has to be explained."

" Well, what about to-morrow? "

" I have to leave for London by the first train in the morning."

" Well, some other time? "

" After to-morrow will be too late."

" Well, what about to-night? "

" The fact is, I've half promised to go with Dr. Stirling to some club or other after the show. Otherwise we might have had a quiet confidential chat in my rooms over the Turk's Head. I never dreamt—" Mr. Bryany was now as melancholy as a greedy lad who regards rich fruit at arm's length through a plate-glass window, and he had ceased to be patronising.

" I'll soon get rid of Stirling for you," said Edward Henry, turning instantly towards the doctor. The ways of Providence had been made plain to Edward Henry. " I say, Doc! " But the Doctor and Brindley were in conversation with another man at the open door of the box.

" What is it? " said Stirling.

" I've come to fetch you. You're wanted at my place."

" Well, you're a caution! " said Stirling.

"Why am I a caution?" Edward Henry smoothly protested. "I didn't tell you before because I didn't want to spoil your fun."

Stirling's mien was not happy.

"Did they tell you I was here?" he asked.

"You'd almost think so, wouldn't you?" said Edward Henry in a playful, enigmatic tone. After all, he decided privately, his wife was right: it was better that Stirling should see the infant. And there was also this natural human thought in his mind: he objected to the doctor giving an entire evening to diversions away from home; he considered that a doctor, when not on a round of visits, ought to be forever in his consulting-room, ready for a sudden call of emergency. It was monstrous that Stirling should have proposed, after an escapade at the music-hall, to spend further hours with chance acquaintances in vague clubs! Half the town might fall sick and die while the doctor was vainly amusing himself. Thus the righteous layman in Edward Henry!

"What's the matter?" asked Stirling.

"My eldest's been rather badly bitten by a dog, and the missis wants it cauterized."

"Really?"

"Well, you bet she does!"

"Where's the bite?"

"In the calf."

The other man at the door having departed, Robert Brindley abruptly joined the conversation at this point.

" I suppose you've heard of that case of hydrophobia at Bleakridge? " said Brindley.

Edward Henry's heart jumped.

" No, I haven't," he said anxiously. " What is
it? "

He gazed at the white blur of Brindley's face in
the darkened box, and he could hear the rapid
clicking of the cinematograph behind him.

" Didn't you see it in the *Signal?* "

" No."

" Neither did I," said Brindley.

At the same moment the moving pictures came
to an end, the theatre was filled with light, and the
band began to play, " God Save the King."
Brindley and Stirling were laughing. And indeed,
Brindley had scored, this time, over the unparalleled
card of the Five Towns.

" I make you a present of that," said Edward
Henry. " But my wife's most precious infant has
to be cauterized, Doctor," he added firmly.

" Got your car here? " Stirling questioned.

" No. Have you? "

" No."

" Well, there's the tram. I'll follow you later.
I've some business round this way. Persuade my
wife not to worry, will you? "

And when a discontented Dr. Stirling had made
his excuses and adieux to Mr. Bryany, and Robert
Brindley had decided that he could not leave his
crony to travel by tram-car alone, and the two men

had gone, then Edward Henry turned to Mr. Bryany:

"That's how I get rid of the doctor, you see."

"But *has* your child been bitten by a dog?" asked Mr. Bryany, acutely perplexed.

"You'd almost think so, wouldn't you?" Edward Henry replied, carefully non-committal. "What price going to the Turk's Head now?"

He remembered with satisfaction, and yet with misgiving, a remark made to him, a judgment passed on him, by a very old woman very many years before. This discerning hag, the Widow Hullins by name, had said to him briefly, "Well, you're a queer 'un!"

III.

Within five minutes he was following Mr. Bryany into a small parlour on the first floor of the Turk's Head, a room with which he had no previous acquaintance, though, like most industrious men of affairs in metropolitan Hanbridge, he reckoned to know something about the Turk's Head. Mr. Bryany turned up the gas (the Turk's Head took pride in being a "hostelry," and, while it had accustomed itself to incandescent mantles on the ground floor, it had not yet conquered a natural distaste for electricity) and Edward Henry saw a smart despatch-box, a dress suit, a trouser-stretcher, and other necessaries of theatrical business life at large in the apartment.

"I've never seen this room before," said Edward Henry.

"Take your overcoat off and sit down, will you?" said Mr. Bryany as he turned to replenish the fire from a bucket. "It's my private sitting-room. Whenever I am on my travels, I always take a private sitting-room. It pays, you know. Of course I mean if I'm alone. When I'm looking after Mr. Sachs, of course we share a sitting-room."

Edward Henry agreed lightly:

"I suppose so."

But the fact was that he was much impressed. He himself had never taken a private sitting-room in any hotel. He had sometimes felt the desire, but he had not had the "face," as they say down there, to do it. To take a private sitting-room in a hotel was generally regarded in the Five Towns as the very summit of dashing expensiveness and futile luxury.

"I didn't know they had private sitting-rooms in this shanty," said Edward Henry.

Mr. Bryany, having finished with the fire, fronted him, shovel in hand, with a remarkable air of consummate wisdom, and replied:

"You can generally get what you want if you insist on having it, even in this 'shanty.'"

Edward Henry regretted his use of the word "shanty." Inhabitants of the Five Towns may allow themselves to twit the historic and excellent Turk's Head, but they do not extend the privilege to strangers. And in justice to the Turk's Head, it is to be clearly stated that it did no more to cow and discourage travellers than any other provincial hotel in England. It was a sound and serious English provincial hotel; and it linked century to century.

Said Mr. Bryany:

" 'Merica's the place for hotels."

"Yes, I expect it is."

"Been to Chicago?"

"No, I haven't."

Mr. Bryany, as he removed his overcoat, could be seen politely forbearing to raise his eyebrows.

"Of course you've been to New York?"

Edward Henry would have given all he had in his pockets to be able to say that he had been to New York, but, by some inexplicable negligence, he had hitherto omitted to go to New York, and, being a truthful person, except in the gravest crises, he was obliged to answer miserably:

"No, I haven't."

Mr. Bryany gazed at him with amazement and compassion, apparently staggered by the discovery that there existed in England a man of the world who had contrived to struggle on for forty years without perfecting his education by a visit to New York.

Edward Henry could not tolerate Mr. Bryany's look. It was a look which he had never been able to tolerate on the features of anybody whatsoever. He reminded himself that his secret object in accompanying Mr. Bryany to the Turk's Head was to

repay Mr. Bryany — in what coin he knew not yet
— for the aspersions which at the music-hall he had
cast upon England in general and upon the Five
Towns in particular, and also to get revenge for
having been tricked into believing, even for a moment, that there was really a case of hydrophobia
at Bleakridge.   It is true that Mr. Bryany was innocent of this deception, which had been accomplished by Robert Brindley, but that was a detail
which did not trouble Edward Henry, who lumped
his grievances together — for convenience.

He had been reflecting that some sentimental people, unused to the ways of paternal affection in the
Five Towns, might consider him a rather callous
father; he had been reflecting, again, that Nellie's
suggestion of blood-poisoning might not be as
entirely foolish as feminine suggestions in such
circumstances too often are.   But now he put these
thoughts away, reassuring himself against hydrophobia anyhow, by the recollection of the definite
statement of the Encyclopedia.   Moreover, had he
not inspected the wound — as healthy a wound as
you could wish for?

And he said in a new tone, very curtly:

"Now, Mr. Bryany, what about this little affair
of yours?"

He saw that Mr. Bryany accepted the implied re-
buke with the deference properly shown by a man
who needs something towards the man in possession of what he needs.   And studying the fellow's
countenance, he decided that, despite its brassiness

and simple cunning, it was scarcely the countenance of a rascal.

"Well, it's like this," said Mr. Bryany, sitting down opposite Edward Henry at the centre table, and reaching with obsequious liveliness for the despatch-box.

He drew from the despatch-box, which was lettered "W. C. B.," first a cut-glass flask of whisky, with a patent stopper, and then a spacious box of cigarettes.

"I always travel with the right sort," he remarked, holding the golden liquid up to the light. "It's safer, and it saves any trouble with orders after closing-time. These English hotels, you know —!"

So saying, he dispensed whisky and cigarettes, there being a siphon and glasses, and three matches in a match-stand, on the table.

"Here's looking!" he said, with raised glass.

And Edward Henry responded, in conformity with the changeless ritual of the Five Towns:

"I looks!"

And they sipped.

Whereupon Mr. Bryany next drew from the despatch-box a piece of transparent paper.

"I want you to look at this plan of Piccadilly Circus and environs," said he.

Now there is a Piccadilly in Hanbridge; also a Pall Mall, and a Chancery Lane. The adjective "metropolitan," applied to Hanbridge is just.

"London?" questioned Edward Henry. "I

understood London when we were chatting over there." With his elbow he indicated the music-hall, somewhere vaguely outside the room.

"London," said Mr. Bryany.

And Edward Henry thought:

"What on earth am I meddling with London for? What use should I be in London?"

"You see the plot marked in red?" Mr. Bryany proceeded. "Well, that's the site. There's an old chapel on it now."

"What do all these straight lines mean?" Edward Henry inquired, examining the plan. Lines radiated from the red plot in various directions.

"Those are the lines of vision," said Mr. Bryany. "They show just where an electric sign at the corner of the front of the proposed theatre could be seen from. You notice the site is not in the Circus itself — a shade to the north." Mr. Bryany's finger approached Edward Henry's on the plan and the clouds from their cigarettes fraternally mingled. "Now you see by those lines that the electric sign of the proposed theatre would be visible from nearly the whole of Piccadilly Circus, parts of Lower Regent Street, Coventry Street, and even Shaftesbury Avenue. You see what a site it is — absolutely unique."

Edward Henry asked coldly:

"Have you bought it?"

"No," Mr. Bryany seemed to apologise, "I haven't exactly bought it; but I've got an option on it."

The magic word " option " wakened the drowsy speculator in Edward Henry. And the mere act of looking at the plan endowed the plot of land with reality. There it was. It existed.

" An option to buy it? "

" You can't buy land in the West End of London," said Mr. Bryany sagely. " You can only lease it."

" Well, of course," Edward Henry concurred.

" The freehold belongs to Lord Woldo, now aged six months."

" Really! " murmured Edward Henry.

" I've got an option to take up the remainder of the lease, with sixty-four years to run, on the condition I put up a theatre. And the option expires in exactly a fortnight's time."

Edward Henry frowned, and then asked:

" What are the figures? "

" That is to say," Mr. Bryany corrected himself, smiling courteously, " I've got half the option."

" And who's got the other half? "

" Rose Euclid's got the other half."

At the mention of the name of one of the most renowned star actresses in England, Edward Henry excusably started.

" Not *the* —? " he exclaimed.

Mr. Bryany nodded proudly, blowing out much smoke.

" Tell me," asked Edward Henry, confidentially, leaning forward, " where do those ladies get their names from? "

"It happens in this case to be her real name," said Mr. Bryany. "Her father kept a tobacconists' shop in Cheapside. The sign was kept up for many years, until Rose paid to have it changed."

"Well, well!" breathed Edward Henry, secretly thrilled by these extraordinary revelations. "And so you and she have got it between you?"

Mr. Bryany said:

"I bought half of it from her some time ago. She was badly hard up for a hundred pounds, and I let her have the money." He threw away his cigarette half-smoked, with a free gesture that seemed to imply that he was capable of parting with a hundred pounds just as easily.

"How did she *get* the option?" Edward Henry inquired, putting into the query all the innuendo of a man accustomed to look at great worldly affairs from the inside.

"How did she get it? She got it from the late Lord Woldo. She was always very friendly with the late Lord Woldo, you know." Edward Henry nodded. "Why, she and the Countess of Chell are as thick as thieves! You know something about the countess down here, I reckon?"

The Countess of Chell was the wife of the supreme local magnate.

Edward Henry answered calmly, "We do."

He was tempted to relate a unique adventure of his youth, when he had driven the countess to a public meeting in his mule-carriage; but sheer pride kept him silent.

"I asked you. for the figures," he added in a manner which requested Mr. Bryany to remember that he was the founder, chairman, and proprietor of the Five Towns Universal Thrift Club, one of the most successful business organisations in the Midlands.

"Here they are," said Mr. Bryany, passing across the table a sheet of paper.

And as Edward Henry studied them he could hear Mr. Bryany faintly cooing into his ear: "Of course Rose got the ground-rent reduced. And when I tell you that the demand for theatres in the West End far exceeds the supply, and that theatre rents are always going up; when I tell you that a theatre costing £25,000 to build can be let for £11,000 a year, and often £300 a week on a short term —" And he could hear the gas singing over his head; and also, unhappily, he could hear Dr. Stirling talking to his wife and saying to her that the bite was far more serious than it looked, and Nellie hoping very audibly that nothing had "happened" to him, her still absent husband. And then he could hear Mr. Bryany again:

"When I tell you —"

"When you tell me all this, Mr. Bryany," he interrupted with the ferocity which in the Five Towns is regarded as mere directness, "I wonder why the devil you want to sell your half of the option if you *do* want to sell it. Do you want to sell it?"

"To tell you the truth," said Mr. Bryany as if

up to that moment he had told naught but lies, " I
do."

" Why? "

" Oh, I'm always travelling about, you see.   England one day, America the next."   Apparently he
had quickly abandoned the strictness of veracity.
" All depends on the governor's movements.   I
couldn't keep a proper eye on an affair of that kind."

Edward Henry laughed :

" And could I? "

" Chance for you to go a bit oftener to London,"
said Mr. Bryany, laughing too.   Then, with extreme and convincing seriousness, " You're the very
man for a thing of that kind.   And you know it."

Edward Henry was not displeased by this flattery.

" How much? "

" How much?   Well, I told you frankly what I
paid.   I made no concealment of that, did I now?
Well, I want what I paid.   It's worth it! "

" Got a copy of the option, I hope! "

Mr. Bryany produced a copy of the option.

" I am nothing but an infernal ass to mix myself up in a mad scheme like this," said Edward
Henry to his soul, perusing the documents.   " It's
right off my line, right bang off it.   But what a lark! "
But even to his soul he did not utter the remainder
of the truth about himself, namely, " I should like
to cut a dash before this insufferable patroniser of
England and the Five Towns."

Suddenly something snapped within him, a.,d he
said to Mr. Bryany :

" I'm on! "

Those words and no more!

" You are? " Mr. Bryany exclaimed, mistrusting his ears.

Edward Henry nodded.

" Well, that's business anyway," said Mr. Bryany, taking a fresh cigarette and lighting it.

" It's how we do business down here," said Edward Henry, quite inaccurately; for it was not in the least how they did business down there.

Mr. Bryany asked, with a rather obvious anxiety:

" But when can you pay?

" Oh, I'll send you a cheque in a day or two." And Edward Henry in his turn took a fresh cigarette.

" That won't do! That won't do! " cried Mr. Bryany. " I absolutely must have the money to-morrow morning in London. I can sell the option in London for eighty pounds, I know that."

" You must have it? "

" Must! "

They exchanged glances. And Edward Henry, rapidly acquiring new knowledge of human nature on the threshold of a world strange to him, understood that Mr. Bryany, with his private sitting-room and his investments in Seattle and Calgary, was at his wits' end for a bag of English sovereigns, and had trusted to some chance encounter to save him from a calamity. And his contempt for Mr. Bryany was that of a man to whom his bankers are positively servile.

Fitz Memorial Library

Endicott College
Beverly, Massachusetts 01915

" Here," Mr. Bryany almost shouted, " don't light your cigarette with my option ! "

" I beg pardon," Edward Henry apologised, dropping the document which he had creased into a spill. There were no matches left on the table.

" I'll find you a match."

" It's of no consequence," said Edward Henry, feeling in his pockets. Having discovered therein a piece of paper, he twisted it and rose to put it to the gas.

" Could you slip round to your bank and meet me at the station in the morning with the cash ? " suggested Mr. Bryany.

" No, I couldn't," said Edward Henry.

" Well, then, what — ? "

" Here, you'd better take this," the Card, reborn, soothed his host, and, blowing out the spill which he had just ignited at the gas, he offered it to Mr. Bryany.

" What ? "

" This, man ! "

Mr. Bryany, observing the peculiarity of the spill, seized it and unrolled it, not without a certain agitation.

He stammered:

" Do you mean to say it's genuine ? "

" You'd almost think so, wouldn't you ? " said Edward Henry. He was growing fond of this reply, and of the enigmatic playful tone that he had invented for it.

" But —"

" We may, as you say, look twice at a fiver," continued Edward Henry, " but we're apt to be careless about hundred-pound notes in this district. I daresay that's why I always carry one."

" But it's burnt! "

" Only just the edge, not enough to harm it. If any bank in England refuses it, return it to me, and I'll give you a couple more in exchange. Is that talking? "

" Well, I'm dashed! " Mr. Bryany attempted to rise, and then subsided back into his chair. " I am simply and totally dashed! " He smiled weakly, hysterically.

And in that instant Edward Henry felt all the sweetness of a complete and luscious revenge.

He said commandingly:

" You must sign me a transfer. I'll dictate it."

Then he jumped up.

" You're in a hurry? "

" I am. My wife is expecting me. You promised to find me a match." Edward Henry waved the unlit cigarette as a reproach to Mr. Bryany's imperfect hospitality.

IV.

The clock of Bleakridge Church, still imperturbably shining in the night, showed a quarter to one when he saw it again on his hurried and guilty way home. The pavements were drying in the fresh night wind, and he had his overcoat buttoned up to the neck. He was absolutely solitary in the long,

muddy perspective of Trafalgar Road.　He walked
because the last tram-car was already housed in its
shed at the other end of the world, and he walked
quickly because his conscience drove him onwards.
And yet he dreaded to arrive, lest a wound in the
child's leg should have maliciously decided to fester
in order to put him in the wrong.　He was now as
apprehensive concerning that wound as Nellie herself had been at tea-time.

But in his mind, above the dark gulf of anxiety,
there floated brighter thoughts.　Despite his fears
and his remorse as a father, he laughed aloud in
the deserted street when he remembered Mr. Bryany's visage of astonishment upon uncreasing the
note.　Indubitably, he made a terrific and everlasting impression upon Mr. Bryany.　He was sending
Mr. Bryany out of the Five Towns a different man.
He had taught Mr. Bryany a thing or two.　To
what brilliant use had he turned the purely acci-
dental possession of a hundred-pound note!　One
of his finest inspirations — an inspiration worthy of
the great days of his youth!　Yes, he had had his
hour that evening, and it had been a glorious one.
Also, it had cost him a hundred pounds, and he did
not care; he would retire to bed with a net gain of
two hundred and forty-one pounds instead of three
hundred and forty-one pounds, that was all.

For he did not mean to take up the option.　The
ecstasy was cooled now, and he saw clearly that
London and theatrical enterprises therein would not
be suited to his genius.　In the Five Towns he was

on his own ground; he was a figure; he was sure of himself. In London he would be a provincial, with the diffidence and the uncertainty of a provincial. Nevertheless, London seemed to be summoning him from afar off, and he dreamt agreeably of London as one dreams of the impossible East.

As soon as he opened the gate in the wall of his property, he saw that the drawing-room was illuminated and all the other front rooms in darkness. Either his wife or his mother, then, was sitting up in the drawing-room. He inserted a cautious latch-key into the door, and entered the silent home like a sinner. The dim light in the hall gravely reproached him. All his movements were modest and restrained; no noisy rattling of his stick now.

The drawing-room door was slightly ajar. He hesitated, and then, nerving himself, pushed against it.

Nellie, with lowered head, was seated at a table, mending, the image of tranquillity and soft resignation. A pile of children's garments lay by her side, but the article in her busy hands appeared to be an undershirt of his own. None but she ever reinforced the buttons on his linen. Such was her wifely rule, and he considered that there was no sense in it. She was working by the light of a single lamp on the table, the splendid chandelier being out of action. Her economy in the use of electricity was incurable, and he considered that there was no sense in that either.

She glanced up with a guarded expression that might have meant anything.

He said:

" Aren't you trying your eyes? "

And she replied:

" Oh, no! "

Then, plunging, he came to the point:

" Well, doctor been here? "

She nodded.

" What does he say? "

" It's quite all right.   He did nothing but cover up the place with a bit of cyanide gauze."

Instantly, in his own esteem, he regained perfection as a father.   Of course the bite was nothing!   Had he not said so from the first?   Had he not been quite sure throughout that the bite was nothing?

" Then why did you sit up? " he asked, and there was a faint righteous challenge in his tone.

" I was anxious about you.   I was afraid —"

" Didn't Stirling tell you I had some business? "

" I forget —"

" I told him to, anyhow — important business."

" It must have been," said Nellie in an inscrutable voice.

She rose and gathered together her paraphernalia, and he saw that she was wearing the damnable white apron.   The close atmosphere of the home enveloped and stifled him once more.   How different was this exasperating interior from the large jolly freedom of the Empire Music Hall, and from the whisky, cigarettes, and masculinity of that private room at the Turk's Head!

"It was!" he repeated grimly and resentfully. "Very important! And I'll tell you another thing, I shall probably have to go to London."

He said this just to startle her.

"It will do you all the good in the world," she replied angelically, but unstartled. "It's just what you need." And she gazed at him as though his welfare and felicity were her sole preoccupation.

"I meant I might have to stop there quite a while," he insisted.

"If you ask me," she said, "I think it would do us all good."

So saying she retired, having expressed no curiosity whatever as to the nature of the very important business in London.

For a moment, left alone, he was at a loss. Then, snorting, he went to the table and extinguished the lamp. He was now in darkness. The light in the hall showed him the position of the door.

He snorted again. "Oh, very well then!" he muttered. "If that's it! I'm hanged if I don't go to London! I'm hanged if I don't go to London!"

CHAPTER III

WILKINS'S

I.

THE early adventures of Alderman Machin of Bursley at Wilkins' Hotel, London, were so singular and to him so refreshing that they must be recounted in some detail.

He went to London by the morning express from Knype, on the Monday week after his visit to the music-hall. In the meantime he had had some correspondence with Mr. Bryany, more poetic than precise, about the option, and had informed Mr. Bryany that he would arrive in London several days before the option expired. But he had not given a definite date. The whole affair, indeed, was amusingly vague; and, despite his assurances to his wife that the matter was momentous, he did not regard his trip to London as a business trip at all, but rather as a simple freakish change of air. The one certain item in the whole situation was that he had in his pocket a quite considerable sum of actual money, destined — he hoped but was not sure — to take up the option at the proper hour.

Nellie, impeccable to the last, accompanied him in the motor to Knype, the main-line station. The drive, superficially pleasant, was in reality very disconcerting to him. For nine days the household had talked in apparent cheerfulness of Father's visit to London, as though it were an occasion for joy on Father's behalf, tempered by affectionate sorrow for his absence. The official theory was that all was for the best in the best of all possible homes, and this theory was admirably maintained. And yet everybody knew — even to Maisie — that it was not so; everybody knew that the master and the mistress of the home, calm and sweet as was their demeanour, were contending in a terrific silent and mysterious altercation, which in some way was connected with the visit to London. So far as Edward Henry was concerned, he had been hoping for some decisive event — a tone, gesture, glance, pressure — during the drive to Knype, which offered the last chance of a real concord. No such event occurred. They conversed with the same false cordiality as had marked their relations since the evening of the dog-bite. On that evening Nellie had suddenly transformed herself into a distressingly perfect angel, and not once had she descended from her high estate. At least daily she had kissed him — what kisses! Kisses that were not kisses! Tasteless mockeries, like non-alcoholic ale! He could have killed her, but he could not put a finger on a fault in her marvellous wifely behaviour; she would have died victorious.

So that his freakish excursion was not starting very auspiciously. And, waiting with her for the train on the platform at Knype, he felt this more and more. His old clerk Penkethman was there to receive certain final instructions on Thrift Club matters, and the sweetness of Nellie's attitude towards the ancient man, and the ancient's man's naïve pleasure therein, positively maddened Edward Henry. To such an extent that he began to think: " Is she going to spoil my trip for me? "

Then Brindley came up. Brindley, too, was going to London. And Nellie's saccharine assurances to Brindley that Edward Henry really needed a change just about completed Edward Henry's desperation. Not even the uproarious advent of two jolly wholesale grocers, Messieurs Garvin and Quorrall, also going to London, could effectually lighten his pessimism.

When the train steamed in, Edward Henry, in fear, postponed the ultimate kiss as long as possible. He allowed Brindley to climb before him into the second-class compartment, and purposely tarried in finding change for the porter; and then he turned to Nellie, and stooped. She raised her white veil and raised the angelic face. They kissed,— the same false kiss,— and she was withdrawing her lips. But suddenly she put them again to his for one second, with a hysterical clinging pressure. It was nothing. Nobody could have noticed it. She herself pretended that she had not done it. Edward Henry had to pretend not to notice it. But to him it was everything. She had relented. She had surrendered. The sign had come from her. She wished him to enjoy his visit to London.

He said to himself:

" Dashed if I don't write to her every day!"

He leaned out of the window as the train rolled away, and waved and smiled to her, not concealing his sentiments now; nor did she conceal hers as she replied with exquisite pantomime to his signals. But if the train had not been rapidly and infallibly separating them, the reconciliation could scarcely have been thus open. If for some reason the train had backed into the station and ejected its passengers, those two would have covered up their feelings again in an instant. Such is human nature in the Five Towns.

When Edward Henry withdrew his head into the compartment, Brindley and Mr. Garvin, the latter standing at the corridor door, observed that his spirits had shot up in the most astonishing manner, and in their blindness they attributed the phenomenon to Edward Henry's delight in a temporary freedom from domesticity.

Mr. Garvin had come from the neighbouring compartment, which was first-class, to suggest a game at bridge. Messieurs Garvin and Quorrall journeyed to London once a week and sometimes oftener, and, being traders, they had special season-tickets. They travelled first-class because their special season-tickets were first-class. Brindley said that he didn't mind a game, but that he had not the slightest intention of paying excess fare for the privilege. Mr. Garvin told him to come along and trust in Messieurs Garvin and Quorrall. Edward

Henry, not nowadays an enthusiastic card-player, enthusiastically agreed to join the hand, and announced that he did not care if he paid forty excess fares. Whereupon Robert Brindley grumbled enviously that it was "all very well for millionaires . . ." They followed Mr. Garvin into the first-class compartment; and it soon appeared that Messrs. Garvin and Quorrall did in fact own the train, and that the London and North Western Railway was no more than their wash-pot.

"Bring us a cushion from somewhere, will ye?" said Mr. Quorrall casually to a ticket-collector who entered.

And the resplendent official obeyed. The long cushion, rapt from another compartment, was placed on the knees of the quartette, and the game began. The ticket-collector examined the tickets of Brindley and Edward Henry, and somehow failed to notice that they were of the wrong colour. And at this proof of their influential greatness, Messieurs Garvin and Quorrall were both secretly proud.

The last rubber finished in the neighbourhood of Willesden, and Edward Henry, having won eighteen pence halfpenny, was exuberantly content, for Messrs. Garvin, Quorrall, and Brindley were all renowned card-players. The cushion was thrown away, and a fitful conversation occupied the few remaining minutes of the journey.

"Where do you put up?" Brindley asked Edward Henry.

" Majestic," said Edward Henry. " Where do you? "

" Oh! Kingsway, I suppose."

The Majestic and the Kingsway were two of the half-dozen very large and very mediocre hotels in London which, from causes which nobody, and especially no American, has ever been able to discover, are particularly affected by Midland provincials " on the jaunt." Both had an immense reputation in the Five Towns.

There was nothing new to say about the Majestic and the Kingsway, and the talk flagged until Mr. Quorrall mentioned Seven Sachs. The mighty Seven Sachs, in his world-famous play, " Overheard," had taken precedence of all other topics in the Five Towns during the previous week. He had crammed the theatre and half emptied the Empire Music Hall for six nights; a wonderful feat. Incidentally, his fifteen hundredth appearance in " Overheard " had taken place in the Five Towns, and the Five Towns had found in this fact a peculiar satisfaction, as though some deep merit had thereby been acquired or rewarded. Seven Sachs's tour was now closed, and on the Sunday he had gone to London, en route for America.

" I heard *he* stops at Wilkins's," said Mr. Garvin.

" Wilkins's your grandmother! " Brindley essayed to crush Mr. Garvin.

" I don't say he *does* stop at Wilkins's," said Mr. Garvin, an individual not easy to crush, " I only say I heard as he did."

"They wouldn't have him!" Brindley insisted firmly.

Mr. Quorrall at any rate seemed tacitly to agree with Brindley. The august name of Wilkins's was in its essence so exclusive that vast numbers of fairly canny provincials had never heard of it. Ask ten well-informed provincials which is the first hotel in London, and nine of them would certainly reply, the Grand Babylon. Not that even wealthy provincials from the industrial districts are in the habit of staying at the Grand Babylon! No! Edward Henry, for example, had never stayed at the Grand Babylon, no more than he had ever bought a first-class ticket on a railroad. The idea of doing so had scarcely occurred to him. There are certain ways of extravagant smartness which are not considered to be good form among solid wealthy provincials. Why travel first-class (they argue), when second is just as good and no one can tell the difference once you get out of the train? Why ape the tricks of another stratum of society? They like to read about the dinner-parties and supper-parties at the Grand Babylon; but they are not emulous, and they do not imitate. At their most adventurous they would lunch or dine in the neutral region of the grill-room at the Grand Babylon. As for Wilkins's, in Devonshire Square, which is infinitely better known among princes than in the Five Towns, and whose name is affectionately pronounced with a "V" by half the monarchs of Europe, few industrial provincials had ever seen it. The class which is the back-bone of England left it serenely alone to royalty and the aristocratic parasites of royalty.

"I don't see why they shouldn't have him," said Edward Henry, as he lifted a challenging nose in the air.

"Perhaps you don't, Alderman!" said Brindley.

"*I* wouldn't mind going to Wilkins's," Edward Henry persisted.

"I'd like to see you," said Brindley, with curt scorn.

"Well," said Edward Henry, "I'll bet you a fiver I do." Had he not won eighteen pence half-penny? And was he not securely at peace with his wife?

"I don't bet fivers," said the cautious Brindley. "But I'll bet you half a crown."

"Done!" said Edward Henry.

"When will you go?"

"Either to-day or to-morrow. I must go to the Majestic first, because I've ordered a room and so on."

"Ha!" hurled Brindley, as if to insinuate that Edward Henry was seeking to escape from the consequences of his boast.

And yet he ought to have known Edward Henry. He did know Edward Henry. And he hoped to lose his half-crown. On his face and on the faces of the other two was the cheerful admission that

tales of the doings of Alderman Machin, the great
local card, at Wilkins's — if he succeeded in getting in — would be cheap at half a crown.

Porters cried out " Euston! "

II.

It was rather late in the afternoon when Edward
Henry arrived in front of the façade of Wilkins's.
He came in a taxicab, and though the distance from
the Majestic to Wilkins's is not more than a couple
of miles, and he had had nothing else to preoccupy
him after lunch, he had spent some three hours in
the business of transferring himself from the portals
of the one hotel to the portals of the other. Two
hours and three-quarters of this period of time had
been passed in finding courage merely to start.
Even so, he had left his luggage behind him. He
said to himself that, first of all, he would go and spy
out Wilkins's; in the perilous work of scouting he
rightly wished to be unhampered by impedimenta;
moreover, in case of repulse or accident, he must have
a base of operations upon which he could retreat
in good order.

He now looked on Wilkins's for the first time in
his life; and he was even more afraid of it than he
had been while thinking about it in the vestibule of
the Majestic. It was not larger than the Majestic;
it was perhaps smaller; it could not show more
terra cotta, plate glass, and sculptured cornice than
the Majestic. But it had a demeanour . . . and
it was in a square which had a demeanour. . . .

In every window-sill — not only of the hotel, but of nearly every mighty house in the square — there were boxes of bright-blooming flowers. These he could plainly distinguish in the October dusk, and they were a wonderful phenomenon — say what you will about the mildness of that particular October! A sublime tranquillity reigned over the scene. A liveried keeper was locking the gate of the garden in the middle of the square as if potentates had just quitted it and rendered it forever sacred. And between the sacred shadowed grove and the inscrutable fronts of the stately houses, there flitted automobiles of the silent and expensive kind, driven by chauffeurs in pale grey or dark purple, who reclined as they steered, and who were supported on their left sides by footmen who reclined as they contemplated the grandeur of existence.

Edward Henry's taxicab in that square seemed like a homeless cat that had strayed into a dog-show.

At the exact instant when the taxicab came to rest under the massive portico of Wilkins's, a chamberlain in white gloves bravely soiled the gloves by seizing the vile brass handle of its door. He bowed to Edward Henry, and assisted him to alight on to a crimson carpet. The driver of the taxi glanced with pert and candid scorn at the chamberlain, but Edward Henry looked demurely aside, and then in abstraction mounted the broad carpeted steps.

"What about poor little me?" cried the driver, who was evidently a ribald socialist, or at best a republican.

The chamberlain, pained, glanced at Edward Henry for support and direction in this crisis.

" Didn't I tell you I'd keep you? " said Edward Henry, raised now by the steps above the driver.

" Between you and me, you didn't," said the driver.

The chamberlain, with an ineffable gesture, wafted the taxicab away into some limbo appointed for waiting vehicles.

A page opened a pair of doors, and another page opened another pair of doors, each with eighteen-century ceremonies of deference, and Edward Henry stood at length in the hall of Wilkins's. The sanctuary, then, was successfully defiled, and up to the present nobody had demanded his credentials! He took breath.

In its physical aspects Wilkins's appeared to him to resemble other hotels — such as the Majestic. And so far he was not mistaken. Once Wilkins's had not resembled other hotels. For many years it had deliberately refused to recognise that even the Nineteenth Century had dawned, and its magnificent antique discomfort had been one of its main attractions to the elect. For the elect desired nothing but their own privileged society in order to be happy in a hotel. A hip bath on a blanket in the middle of the bedroom floor richly sufficed them, provided they could be guaranteed against the calamity of meeting the unelect in the corridors or at *table d'hôte*. But the rising waters of democracy — the intermixture of classes — had reacted ad-

versely on Wilkins's. The fall of the Emperor
Maximilian of Mexico had given Wilkins's sad food
for thought long, long ago, and the obvious general
weakening of the monarchical principle had most
considerably shaken it. Came the day when Wilkins's reluctantly decided that even *it* could not fight
against the tendency of the whole world, and then,
at one superb stroke, it had rebuilt and brought itself utterly up-to-date.

Thus it resembled other hotels. (Save possibly
in the reticence of its advertisements! The Majestic would advertise bathrooms as a miracle of
modernity, just as though common dwelling-houses
had not possessed bathrooms for the past thirty
years. Wilkins's had superlative bathrooms, but it
said nothing about them. Wilkins's would as soon
have advertised two hundred bathrooms as two hundred bolsters; and for the new Wilkins's a bathroom
was not more modern than a bolster.) Also, other
hotels resembled Wilkins's. The Majestic, too, had
a chamberlain at its portico, and an assortment of
pages to prove to its clients that they were incapable
of performing the simplest act for themselves.
Nevertheless, the difference between Wilkins's and
the Majestic was enormous; and yet so subtle was
it that Edward Henry could not immediately detect
where it resided. Then he understood. The difference between Wilkins's and the Majestic resided
in the theory which underlay its manner. And the
theory was that every person entering its walls was
of royal blood until he had admitted the contrary.

Within the hotel it was already night.

Edward Henry self-consciously crossed the illuminated hall, which was dotted with fashionable figures. He knew not whither he was going, until by chance he saw a golden grille with the word " Reception " shining over it in letters of gold. Behind this grille, and still further protected by an impregnable mahogany counter, stood three young dandies in attitudes of graceful ease. He approached them. The fearful moment was upon him. He had never in his life been so genuinely frightened. Abject disgrace might be his portion within the next ten seconds.

Addressing himself to the dandy in the middle, he managed to articulate:

" What have you got in the way of rooms ? "

Could the Five Towns have seen him then, as he waited, it would hardly have recognised its " card," its character, its mirror of aplomb and inventive audacity, in this figure of provincial and plebeian diffidence.

The dandy bowed.

" Do you want a suite, sir ? "

" Certainly ! " said Edward Henry. Rather too quickly, rather too defiantly; in fact, rather rudely! A habitué would not have so savagely hurled back in the dandy's teeth the insinuation that he wanted only one paltry room.

However, the dandy smiled, accepting with meekness Edward Henry's sudden arrogance, and consulted a sort of pentateuch that was open in front of him.

No person in the hall saw Edward Henry's hat fly up into the air and fall back on his head. But in the imagination of Edward Henry, that was what his hat did.

He was saved. He would have a proud tale for Brindley. The thing was as simple as the alphabet. You just walked in and they either fell on your neck or kissed your feet.

Wilkins's indeed!

A very handsome footman, not only in white gloves but in white calves, was soon supplicating him to deign to enter a lift. And when he emerged from the lift another dandy —in a frock-coat of Paradisê — was awaiting him with obeisances. Apparently it had not yet occurred to anybody that he was not the younger son of some aged king.

He was prayed to walk into a gorgeous suite consisting of a corridor, a noble drawing-room (with portrait of His Majesty of Spain on the walls), a large bedroom with two satinwood beds, a small bedroom, and a bathroom, all gleaming with patent devices in porcelain and silver that fully equalled those at home.

Asked if this suite would do, he said it would, trying as well as he could to imply that he had seen better. Then the dandy produced a note-book and a pencil, and impassively waited. The horrid fact that he was un-elect could no longer be concealed.

" E. H. Machin, Bursley," he said shortly, and added: " Alderman Machin." After all, why should he be ashamed of being an alderman?

To his astonishment the dandy smiled very cordially, though always with profound respect.

" Ah, yes! " said the dandy. It was as though he had said: " We have long wished for the high patronage of this great reputation." Edward Henry could make naught of it.

His opinion of Wilkins's went down.

He followed the departing dandy up the corridor to the door of the suite in an entirely vain attempt to enquire the price of the suite per day. Not a syllable would pass his lips. The dandy bowed and vanished. Edward Henry stood lost at his own door, and his wandering eye caught sight of a pile of trunks near to another door in the main corridor. These trunks gave him a terrible shock. He shut out the rest of the hotel and retired into his private corridor to reflect. He perceived only too plainly that his luggage, now at the Majestic, never could come into Wilkins's. It was not fashionable enough. It lacked elegance. The lounge suit that he was wearing might serve, but his luggage was totally impossible. Never before had he imagined that the aspect of one's luggage could have the least importance in one's scheme of existence. He was learning, and he frankly admitted that he was in an incomparable mess.

III.

At the end of an extensive stroll through and round his new vast domain, he had come to no decision upon a course of action. Certain details of the strange adventure pleased him — as for instance the dandy's welcoming recognition of his name; that, though puzzling, was a source of comfort to him in his difficulties. He also liked the suite; nay more, he was much impressed by its gorgeousness, and such novel complications as the forked electric switches, all of which he turned on, and the double windows, one within the other, appealed to the domestic expert in him; indeed, he at once had the idea of doubling the window of the best bedroom at home; to do so would be a fierce blow to the Five Towns Electric Traction Company, which, as everybody knew, delighted to keep everybody awake at night and at dawn by means of its late and its early tram-cars. However, he could not wander up and down the glittering solitude of his extensive suite for ever. Something must be done. Then he had the notion of writing to Nellie; he had promised himself to write to her daily; moreover, it would pass the time and perhaps help him to some resolution.

He sat down to a delicate Louis XVI desk on which lay a Bible, a Peerage, a telephone-book, a telephone, a lamp, and much distinguished stationery. Between the tasselled folds of plushy curtains that

pleated themselves with the grandeur of painted curtains in a theatre, he glanced out at the lights of
Devonshire Square, from which not a sound came.
Then he lit the lamp and unscrewed his fountain
pen.

" My dear wife —"

That was how he always began, whether in storm
or sunshine. Nellie always began, " My darling
husband "; but he was not a man to fling darlings
about. Few husbands in the Five Towns are. He
thought " darling," but he never wrote it, and he
never said it, save quizzingly.

After these three words the composition of the
letter came to a pause. What was he going to tell
Nellie? He assuredly was not going to tell her that
he had engaged an unpriced suite at Wilkins's. He
was not going to mention Wilkins's. Then he in-
telligently perceived that the note-paper and also
the envelope mentioned Wilkins's in no ambiguous
manner. He tore up the sheet and searched for
plain paper. Now, on the desk there was the ordinary hotel stationery, mourning stationery, cards,
letter-cards, and envelopes for every mood; but not
a piece that was not embossed with the historic name
in royal blue. The which appeared to Edward
Henry to point to a defect of foresight on the part
of Wilkins's. At the gigantic political club to
which he belonged, and which he had occasionally
visited in order to demonstrate to himself and
others that he was a club-man, plain stationery
was everywhere provided for the use of husbands

with a taste for reticence. Why not at Wilkins's also?

On the other hand, why should he *not* write to his wife on Wilkins's paper? Was he afraid of his wife? He was not. Would not the news ultimately reach Bursley that he had stayed at Wilkins's? It would. Nevertheless, he could not find the courage to write to Nellie on Wilkins's paper.

He looked around. He was fearfully alone. He wanted the companionship, were it only momentary, of something human. He decided to have a look at a flunkey, and he rang a bell.

Immediately, just as though wafted thither on a magic carpet, from the court of Austria, a gentleman in waiting arrived in the doorway of the drawing-room, planted himself gracefully on his black silk calves, and bowed.

" I want some plain note-paper, please."

" Very good, sir." Oh! Perfection of tone and of mien!

Three minutes later the plain note-paper and envelopes were being presented to Edward Henry on a salver. As he took them, he looked enquiringly at the gentleman in waiting, who supported his gaze with an impenetrable, invulnerable servility. Edward Henry, beaten off with great loss, thought: " There's nothing doing here just now in the human companionship line," and assumed the mask of a hereditary prince.

The black calves carried away their immaculate living burden, set above all earthly ties.

He wrote nicely to Nellie about the weather and the journey, and informed her also that London seemed as full as ever, and that he might go to the theatre, but he wasn't sure. He dated the letter from the Majestic.

As he was finishing it, he heard mysterious, disturbing footfalls in his private corridor, and after trying for some time to ignore them, he was forced by a vague alarm to investigate their origin. A short middle-aged, pallid man, with a long nose and long moustaches, wearing a red and black-striped sleeved waistcoat and a white apron, was in the corridor. At the Turk's Head such a person would have been the boots. But Edward Henry remembered a notice under the bell, advising visitors to ring once for the waiter, twice for the chambermaid, and three times for the valet. This, then, was the valet. In certain picturesque details of costume Wilkins's was coquettishly French.

"What is it?" he demanded.

"I came to see if your luggage had arrived, sir. No doubt your servant is bringing it. Can I be of any assistance to you?"

The man thoughtfully twirled one end of his moustache. It was an appalling fault in demeanour; but the man was proud of his moustache.

"The first human being I've met here!" thought Edward Henry, attracted too by a gleam in the eye of this eternal haunter of corridors.

"His servant!" He saw that something must be done, and quickly. Wilkins's provided valets for emergencies, but obviously it expected visitors to bring their own valets in addition. Obviously existence without a private valet was inconceivable to Wilkins's.

"The fact is," said Edward Henry, "I'm in a very awkward situation." He hesitated, seeking to and fro in his mind for particulars of the situation.

"Sorry to hear that, sir."

"Yes, a very awkward position." He hesitated again. "I'd booked passages for myself and my valet on the *Minnetonka,* sailing from Tilbury at noon to-day, and sent him on in front with my stuff, and at the very last moment I've been absolutely prevented from sailing! You see how awkward it is! I haven't a thing here."

"It is indeed, sir! And I suppose *he's* gone on, sir?"

"Of course he has! He wouldn't find out till after she sailed that I wasn't on board. You know the crush and confusion there is on those big liners just before they start." Edward Henry had once assisted, under very dramatic circumstances, at the departure of a transatlantic liner from Liverpool.

"Just so, sir!"

"I've neither servant nor clothes!" He considered that so far he was doing admirably. Indeed, the tale could not have been bettered, he thought. His hope was that the fellow would not have the idea of consulting the shipping intelligence in order to confirm the departure of the *Minnetonka* from Tilbury that day. Possibly the *Minnetonka* never

had sailed and never would sail from Tilbury.
Possibly she had been sold years ago. He had se-
lected the first ship's name that came into his head.
What did it matter?

"My man," he added to clinch — the proper word
"man" had only just occurred to him —"my man
can't be back again under three weeks at the
soonest."

The valet made one half-eager step towards him.

"If you're wanting a temporary valet, sir, my
son's out of a place for the moment — through no
fault of his own. He's a very good valet, sir, and
soon learns a gentleman's ways."

"Yes," said Edward Henry judiciously. "But
could he come at once? That's the point." And
he looked at his watch, as if to imply that another
hour without a valet would be more than human
nature could stand.

"I could have him round here in less than an
hour, sir," said the hotel valet, comprehending the
gesture. "He's at Norwich Mews — Berkeley
Square way, sir."

Edward Henry hesitated.

"Very well, then!" he said commandingly.
"Send for him. Let me see him."

He thought:

"Dash it! I'm at Wilkins's — I'll be *at* Wilkins's!"

"Certainly, sir! Thank you very much, sir."

The hotel valet was retiring when Edward Henry
called him back.

" Stop a moment.   I'm just going out.   Help me
on with my overcoat, will you? "

The man jumped.

" And you might get me a tooth-brush," Edward
Henry airily suggested.   " And I've a letter for the
post."

As he walked down Devonshire Square in the
dark, he hummed a tune: certain sign that he was
self-conscious, uneasy, and yet not unhappy.   At a
small but expensive hosier's in a side street he bought
a shirt and a suit of pajamas, and also permitted himself to be tempted by a special job line of hair-
brushes that the hosier had in his fancy department.
On hearing the powerful word " Wilkins's," the
hosier promised with passionate obsequiousness that
the goods should be delivered instantly.

Edward Henry cooled his excitement by an ex-
tended stroll, and finally re-entered the outer hall of
the hotel at half-past seven, and sat down therein
to see the world.   He knew by instinct that the
boldest lounge suit must not at that hour penetrate
further into the public rooms of Wilkins's.

The world at its haughtiest was driving up to
Wilkins's to eat its dinner in the unrivalled restaurant, and often guests staying at the hotel came
into the outer hall to greet invited friends.   And
Edward Henry was so overfaced by visions of
woman's brilliance and man's utter correctness that
he scarcely knew where to look — so apologetic was
he for his grey lounge suit and the creases in his
boots.   In less than a quarter of an hour he ap-

preciated with painful clearness that his entire conception of existence had been wrong, and that he
must begin again at the beginning. Nothing in his
luggage at the Majestic would do. His socks
would not do, nor his shoes, nor the braid on his
trousers, nor his cuff-links, nor his ready-made white
bow, nor the number of studs in the shirt-front, nor
the collar of his coat. Nothing! Nothing! To-
morrow would be a full day.

He ventured apologetically into the lift. In his
private corridor a young man respectfully waited,
hat in hand, the paternal red-and-black waistcoat by
his side for purposes of introduction. The young
man was wearing a rather shabby blue suit, but a
rich and distinguished overcoat that fitted him ill.
In another five minutes Edward Henry had engaged a skilled valet, aged twenty-four, name Joseph,
with a testimonial of efficiency from Sir Nicholas
Winkworth, Bart., at a salary of a pound a week and
all found.

Joseph seemed to await instructions. And Edward Henry was placed in a new quandary. He
knew not whether the small bedroom in the suite
was for a child, or for his wife's maid, or for his
valet. Quite probably it would be a sacrilegious defiance of precedent to put a valet in the small bedroom. Quite probably Wilkins's had a floor for
private valets in the roof. Again, quite probably,
the small bedroom might be after all specially
destined for valets! He could not decide, and the
most precious thing in the universe to him in that

crisis was his reputation as a man about town in the eyes of Joseph.

But something had to be done.

" You'll sleep in this room," said Edward Henry, indicating the door. " I may want you in the night."

" Yes, sir," said Joseph.

" I presume you'll dine up here, sir," said Joseph, glancing at the lounge suit. His father had informed him of his new master's predicament.

" I shall," said Edward Henry. " You might get the menu."

IV.

He had a very bad night indeed, owing no doubt partly to a general uneasiness in his unusual surroundings, and partly also to a special uneasiness caused by the propinquity of a sleeping valet; but the main origin of it was certainly his dreadful anxiety about the question of a first-class tailor. In the organisation of his new life a first-class tailor was essential, and he was not acquainted with a first-class London tailor. He did not know a great deal concerning clothes, though quite passably well dressed for a provincial, but he knew enough to be sure that it was impossible to judge the merits of a tailor by his sign-board, and therefore that if, wandering in the precincts of Bond Street, he entered the first establishment that " looked likely," he would have a good chance of being " done in the eye." So he phrased it to himself as he lay in bed. He wanted a definite and utterly reliable address.

He rang the bell. Only, as it happened to be the wrong bell, he obtained the presence of Joseph in a round-about way, through the agency of a gentleman in waiting. Such, however, is the human faculty of adaptation to environment that he was merely amused in the morning by an error which, on the previous night, would have put him into a sweat.

"Good morning, sir," said Joseph.

Edward Henry nodded, his hands under his head as he lay on his back. He decided to leave all initiative to Joseph. The man drew up the blinds, and, closing the double windows at the top, opened them very wide at the bottom.

"It is a rainy morning, sir," said Joseph, letting in vast quantities of air from Devonshire Square. Clearly, Sir Nicholas Winkworth had been a breezy master.

"Oh!" murmured Edward Henry.

He felt a careless contempt for Joseph's flunkey-ism. Hitherto he had had a theory that footmen, valets, and all male personal attendants were an inexcusable excrescence on the social fabric. The mere sight of them often angered him, though for some reason he had no objection whatever to servility in a nice-looking maid — indeed, rather enjoyed it. But now, in the person of Joseph, he saw that there were human or half-human beings born to self-abasement, and that, if their destiny was to be fulfilled, valetry was a necessary institution. He had no pity for Joseph, no shame in employing him.

He scorned Joseph; and yet his desire, as a man about town, to keep Joseph's esteem was in no way diminished.

"Shall I prepare your bath, sir?" asked Joseph, stationed in a supple attitude by the side of the bed.

Edward Henry was visited by an idea.

"Have you had yours?" he demanded like a pistol-shot.

Edward Henry saw that Sir Nicholas had never asked that particular question.

"No, sir."

"Not had your bath, man! What on earth do you mean by it? Go and have your bath at once!"

A faint sycophantic smile lightened the amazed features of Joseph. And Edward Henry thought: "It's astonishing, all the same, the way they can read their masters. This chap has seen already that I'm a card. And yet how?"

"Yes, sir," said Joseph.

"Have your bath in the bathroom here. And be sure to leave everything in order for me."

"Yes, sir."

As soon as Joseph had gone, Edward Henry jumped out of bed and listened. He heard the discreet Joseph respectfully push the bolt of the bathroom door. Then he crept with noiseless rapidity to the small bedroom, and was aware therein of a lack of order and of ventilation. The rich and distinguished overcoat was hanging on the brass knob at the foot of the bed. He seized it, and, scrutinizing the loop, read in yellow letters: *Quay-*

ther and Cuthering, 47 Vigo Street, W. He knew
that Quayther and Cuthering must be the tailors of
Sir Nicholas Winkworth, and hence first-class.

Hoping for the best, and putting his trust in the
general decency of human nature, he did not trouble
himself with the problem: was the overcoat a gift
or an appropriation? But he preferred to assume
the generosity of Sir Nicholas rather than the dis-
honesty of Joseph.

Repassing the bathroom door, he knocked loudly
on its glass.

" Don't be all day! " he cried. He was in a
hurry now.

An hour later he said to Joseph:

" I'm going down to Quayther and Cuthering's."

" Yes, sir," said Joseph, obviously much reassured.

" Nincompoop! " Edward Henry exclaimed secretly. " The fool thinks better of me because my
tailors are first-class."

But Edward Henry had failed to notice that he
himself was thinking better of himself because he
had adopted first-class tailors.

Beneath the main door of his suite, as he went
forth, he found a business card of the West End
Electric Brougham Supply Agency. And downstairs, solely to impress his individuality on the hall-
porter, he showed the card to that vizier with the
casual question:

" These people any good? "

" An excellent firm, sir."

" What do they charge? "

" By the week, sir? "

He hesitated.   " Yes, by the week? "

" Twenty guineas, sir."

" Well, you might telephone for one.   Can you get it at once? "

" Certainly, sir."

The vizier turned towards the telephone in his lair.

" I say —" said Edward Henry.

" Sir? "

" I suppose one will be enough? "

" Well, sir, as a rule, yes," said the vizier calmly. " Sometimes I get a couple for one family, sir."

Though he had started jocularly, Edward Henry finished by blenching.   " I think one will do. . . . I may possibly send for my own car."

He drove to Quayther and Cuthering's in his electric brougham, and there dropped casually the name of Winkworth.   He explained humourously his singular misadventure of the *Minnetonka,* and was very successful therewith, so successful indeed, that he actually began to believe in the reality of the adventure himself, and had an irrational impulse to despatch a wireless message to his bewildered valet on board the *Minnetonka.*

Subsequently he paid other fruitful visits in the neighbourhood, and at about half-past eleven the fruit was arriving at Wilkins's in the shape of many parcels and boxes, comprising diverse items in the equipment of a man about town, such as tie-clips and Innovation trunks.

Returning late to Wilkins's for lunch, he marched jauntily into the large brilliant restaurant, and commenced an adequate repast. Of course he was still wearing his mediocre lounge suit (his sole suit for another two days), but somehow the consciousness that Quayther and Cutherings were cutting out wondrous garments for him in Vigo Street stiffened his shoulders and gave a mysterious style to that lounge suit.

At lunch he made one mistake, and enjoyed one very remarkable piece of luck.

The mistake was to order an artichoke. He did not know how to eat an artichoke. He had never tried to eat an artichoke, and his first essay in this difficult and complex craft was a sad fiasco. It would not have mattered if, at the table next to his own, there had not been two obviously experienced women, one ill dressed, with a red hat, the other well dressed, with a blue hat; one middle-aged, the other much younger; but both very observant. And even so, it would scarcely have mattered, had not the younger woman been so slim, pretty, and alluring. While tolerably careless of the opinion of the red-hatted plain woman of middle age, he desired the unqualified approval of the delightful young thing in the blue hat. They certainly interested themselves in his manœuvres with the artichoke, and their amusement was imperfectly concealed. He forgave the blue hat, but considered that the red hat ought to have known better. They could not be princesses, nor even titled aristocrats. He supposed them to belong to some baccarat-playing county family.

The piece of luck consisted in the passage down the restaurant of the Countess of Chell, who had been lunching there with a party, and whom he had known locally in more gusty days. The countess bowed stiffly to the red hat, and the red hat responded with eager fulsomeness. It seemed to be here as it no longer was in the Five Towns: everybody knew everybody! The red hat and the blue might be titled, after all, he thought. Then, by sheer accident, the countess caught sight of him, and stopped dead, bringing her escort to a standstill behind her. Edward Henry blushed and rose.

"Is it *you*, Mr. Machin?" murmured the still lovely creature warmly.

They shook hands. Never had social pleasure so thrilled him. The conversation was short. He did not presume on the past. He knew that here he was not on his own ash-pit, as they say in the Five Towns. The countess and her escort went forward. Edward Henry sat down again.

He gave the red and the blue hats one calm glance, which they failed to withstand. The affair of the artichoke was forever wiped out.

After lunch he went forth again in his electric brougham. The weather had cleared. The opulent streets were full of pride and sunshine. And as he penetrated into one shop after another, re-

ceiving kowtows, obeisances, curtsies, homage, sur-
render, resignation, submission, he gradually comprehended that it takes all sorts to make a world,
and that those who are called to greatness must accept with dignity the ceremonials inseparable from
greatness. And the world had never seemed to him
so fine, nor any adventure so diverting and uplifting
as this adventure.

When he returned to his suite, his private corridor was piled up with a numerous and excessively
attractive assortment of parcels. Joseph took his
overcoat and hat and a new umbrella, and placed
an easy chair conveniently for him in the drawing-
room.

"Get my bill," he said shortly to Joseph as he
sank into the gilded fauteuil.

"Yes, sir."

One advantage of a valet, he discovered, is that
you can order him to do things which to do yourself
would more than exhaust your moral courage.

The black-calved gentleman in waiting brought the
bill. It lay on a salver, and was folded, conceivably so as to break the shock of it to the recipient.

Edward Henry took it.

"Wait a minute," he said.

He read on the bill: "Apartment £8. Dinner
£1-2-0. Breakfast 6s. 6d. Lunch 18s. Half
Chablis 6s. 6d. Valet's board 10s. Tooth-brush
2s. 6d.

"That's a bit thick, half a crown for that tooth-
brush!" he said to himself. "However —"

The next instant he blenched once more.

" Gosh! " he privately exclaimed as he read:
" Paid driver of taxicab £2-3-6."

He had forgotten the taxi. But he admired the
sang-froid of Wilkins's, which paid such trifles as a
matter of course, without deigning to disturb a guest
by an enquiry. Wilkins's rose again in his esteem.

The total of the bill exceeded thirteen pounds.

" All right," he said to the gentleman in waiting.

" Are you leaving to-day, sir? " the being permitted himself to ask.

" Of course I'm not leaving to-day! Haven't I
hired an electric brougham for a week? " Edward
Henry burst out. " But I suppose I'm entitled to
know how much I'm spending! "

The gentleman in waiting humbly bowed, and
departed.

Alone in the splendid chamber, Edward Henry
drew out a swollen pocketbook and examined its
crisp, crinkly contents, which made a beauteous and
a reassuring sight.

" Pooh! " he muttered.

He reckoned he would be living at the rate of
about fifteen pounds a day, or five thousand five
hundred a year. (He did not count the cost of
his purchases, because they were in the nature of a
capital expenditure.)

" Cheap! " he muttered. " For once I'm about
living up to my income! "

The sensation was exquisite in its novelty.

He ordered tea, and afterwards, feeling sleepy, he went fast asleep.

He awoke to the ringing of the telephone-bell.   It was quite dark.   The telephone-bell continued to ring.

"Joseph!" he called.

The valet entered.

"What time is it?"

"After ten o'clock, sir."

"The deuce it is!"

He had slept over four hours!

"Well, answer that confounded telephone."

Joseph obeyed.

"It's a Mr. Bryany, sir, if I catch the name right," said Joseph.

Bryany!   For twenty-four hours he had scarcely thought of Bryany, or the option either.

"Bring the telephone here," said Edward Henry.

The cord would just reach to his chair.

"Hello!   Bryany!   Is that you?" cried Edward Henry gaily.

And then he heard the weakened voice of Mr. Bryany in his ear:

"How d'ye do, Mr. Machin.   I've been after you for the better part of two days, and now I find you're staying in the same hotel as Mr. Sachs and me!"

"Oh!" said Edward Henry.

He understood now why on the previous day the dandy introducing him to his suite had smiled a

welcome at the name of Alderman Machin, and why
Joseph had accepted so naturally the command to
take a bath. Bryany had been talking. Bryany
had been recounting his exploits as a card.

The voice of Bryany in his ear continued:

"Look here! I've got Miss Euclid here and
some friends of hers. Of course she wants to see
you at once. Can you come down?"

"Er—" He hesitated.

He could not come down. He would have no
evening wear till the next day but one.

Said the voice of Bryany:

"What?"

"I can't," said Edward Henry. "I'm not very
well. But listen. All of you come up to my rooms
here and have supper, will you? Suite 48."

"I'll ask the lady," said the voice of Bryany, altered now, and a few seconds later: "We're coming."

"Joseph," Edward Henry gave orders rapidly as
he took off his coat and removed the pocketbook
from it. "I'm ill, you understand. Anyhow, not
well. Take this," handing him the coat, "and bring
me the new dressing-gown out of that green card-
board box from Rollet's — I think it is. And then
get the supper menu. I'm very hungry. I've had
no dinner."

Within sixty seconds he sat in state, wearing a
grandiose yellow dressing-gown. The change was
accomplished just in time. Mr. Bryany entered,

and not only Mr. Bryany, but Mr. Seven Sachs, and not only these, but the lady who had worn a red hat at lunch.

"Miss Rose Euclid," said Mr. Bryany, puffing and bending.

CHAPTER IV

ENTRY INTO THE THEATRICAL WORLD

I.

ONCE, on a short visit to London, Edward Henry had paid half a crown to be let into a certain enclosure with a very low ceiling. This enclosure was already crowded with some three hundred people, sitting and standing. Edward Henry had stood in the only unoccupied spot he could find, behind a pillar. When he had made himself as comfortable as possible by turning up his collar against the sharp winds that continually entered from the street, he had peered forward, and seen in front of this enclosure another and larger enclosure also crowded with people, but more expensive people. After a blank interval of thirty minutes a band had begun to play at an incredible distance in front of him, extinguishing the noises of traffic in the street. After another interval an oblong space, rather further off even than the band, suddenly grew bright, and Edward Henry, by curving his neck, first to one side of the pillar and then to the other, had had tantalising glimpses of the interior of a doll's drawing-room and of male and female dolls therein.

He could only see, even partially, the interior half

of the drawing-room,— a little higher than the heads of the dolls,— because the rest was cut off from his vision by the lowness of his own ceiling.

The dolls were talking, but he could not catch clearly what they said, save at the rare moments when an omnibus or a van did not happen to be thundering down the street behind him. Then one special doll had come exquisitely into the drawing-room, and at the sight of her the five hundred people in front of him, and numbers of other people perched hidden beyond his ceiling, had clapped fervently and even cried aloud in their excitement. And he, too, had clapped fervently, and had muttered "Bravo!" This special doll was a marvel of touching and persuasive grace, with a voice — when Edward Henry could hear it — that melted the spine. This special doll had every elegance, and seemed to be in the highest pride of youth. At the close of the affair, as this special doll sank into the embrace of a male doll from whom she had been unjustly separated, and then straightened herself, deliciously and confidently smiling, to take the tremendous applause of Edward Henry and the rest, Edward Henry thought that he had never assisted at a triumph so genuine and so inspiring. Oblivious of the pain in his neck, and of the choking foul atmosphere of the enclosure, accurately described as the pit, he had gone forth into the street with a subconscious notion in his head that the special doll was more than human, was half divine. And he had

said afterwards, with immense satisfaction, at Bursley: "Yes, I saw Rose Euclid in 'Flower of the
Heart.'"

He had never set eyes on her since.

And now, on this day at Wilkins's, he had seen
in the restaurant, and he saw again before him in
his private parlour, a faded and stoutish woman,
negligently if expensively dressed, with a fatigued,
nervous, watery glance, an unnatural, pale-violet
complexion, a wrinkled skin, and dyed hair; a
woman of whom it might be said that she had escaped grandmotherhood, if indeed she had escaped
it, by mere luck — and he was pointblank commanded to believe that she and Rose Euclid were
the same person.

It was one of the most shattering shocks of all
his career, which, nevertheless, had not been un-
tumultuous. And within his dressing-gown —
which nobody remarked upon — he was busy pick-
ing up and piecing together, as quickly as he could,
the shivered fragments of his ideas.

He literally did not recognise Rose Euclid.
True, fifteen years had passed since the night in the
pit! And he himself was fifteen years older. But
in his mind he had never pictured any change in
Rose Euclid. True, he had been familiar with the
enormous renown of Rose Euclid as far back as he
could remember taking any interest in theatrical advertisements! But he had not permitted her to
reach an age of more than about thirty-one or
two. Whereas he now perceived that even the ex-

quisite doll in paradise that he had gloated over
from his pit must have been quite thirty-five —
then. . . .

Well, he scornfully pitied Rose Euclid. He
blamed her for not having accomplished the miracle
of eternal youth. He actually considered that she
had cheated him. " Is this all? What a swindle! "
he thought, as he was piecing together the shivered
fragments of his ideas into a new pattern. He had
felt much the same as a boy, at Bursley Annual
Wakes once, on entering a booth which promised
horrors and did not supply them. He had been
" done " all these years. . . .

Reluctantly he admitted that Rose Euclid could
not help her age. But, at any rate, she ought to
have grown older beautifully, with charming dignity
and vivacity — in fact, she ought to have contrived
to be old and young simultaneously. Or, in the alternative, she ought to have modestly retired into
the country and lived on her memories and such
money as she had not squandered. She had no
right to be abroad. At worst, she ought to have
looked famous. And, because her name and fame
and photographs, as an emotional actress had been
continually in the newspapers, therefore she ought
to have been refined, delicate, distinguished, and full
of witty and gracious small talk. That she had
played the heroine of " Flower of the Heart " four
hundred times, and the heroine of " The Grena-
dier " four hundred and fifty times, and the heroine
of " The Wife's Ordeal " nearly five hundred times,

made it incumbent upon her, in Edward Henry's subconscious opinion, to possess all the talents of a woman of the world and all the virgin freshness of a girl. Which shows how cruelly stupid Edward Henry was in comparison with the enlightened rest of us.

Why (he protested secretly), she was even tongue-tied!

" Glad to meet you, Mr. Machin," she said awkwardly, in a weak voice, with a peculiar gesture as she shook hands. Then, a mechanical nervous giggle — and then silence.

" Happy to make your acquaintance, sir," said Mr. Seven Sachs, and the arch-famous American actor-author also lapsed into silence. But the silence of Mr. Seven Sachs was different from Rose Euclid's. He was not shy. A dark and handsome, tranquil, youngish man, with a redoubtable square chin, delicately rounded at the corners, he strikingly resembled his own figure on the stage; and, moreover, he seemed to regard silence as a natural and proper condition. He simply stood, in a graceful posture, with his muscles at ease, and waited.

Mr. Bryany, behind, seemed to be reduced in stature, and to have become apologetic for himself in the presence of greatness.

Still, Mr. Bryany did say something.

Said Mr. Bryany:

" Sorry to hear you've been seedy, Mr. Machin! "

" Oh, yes! " Rose Euclid blurted out, as if shot. " It's very good of you to ask us up here."

Mr. Seven Sachs concurred, adding that he hoped the illness was not serious.

Edward Henry said it was not.

" Won't you sit down, all of you? " said Edward Henry.   " Miss — er — Euclid —"

They all sat down except Mr. Bryany.

" Sit down, Bryany," said Edward Henry.   " I'm glad to be able to return your hospitality at the Turk's Head."

This was a blow for Mr. Bryany, who obviously felt it, and grew even more apologetic as he fumbled with assumed sprightliness at a chair.

" Fancy your being here all the time! " said he, " and me looked for you everywhere —"

" Mr. Bryany," Seven Sachs interrupted him calmly, " have you got those letters off? "

" Not yet, sir."

Seven Sachs urbanely smiled.   " I think we ought to get them off to-night."

" Certainly," agreed Mr. Bryany with eagerness, and moved towards the door.

" Here's the key of my sitting-room," Seven Sachs stopped him, producing a key.

Mr. Bryany, by a mischance catching Edward Henry's eye as he took the key, blushed.

In a moment Edward Henry was alone with the two silent celebrities.

" Well," said Edward Henry to himself, " I've let myself in for it this time — no mistake!   What in the name of common sense am I doing here? "

Rose Euclid coughed, and arranged the folds of her dress.

" I suppose, like most Americans, you see all the sights," said Edward Henry to Seven Sachs, " the Five Towns is much visited by Americans. What do you think of my dressing-gown? "

" Bully! " said Seven Sachs, with the faintest twinkle. And Rose Euclid gave the mechanical nervous giggle.

" I can do with this chap," thought Edward Henry.

The gentleman in waiting entered with the supper menu.

" Thank Heaven! " thought Edward Henry.

Rose Euclid, requested to order a supper after her own mind, stared vaguely at the menu for some moments, and then said that she did not know what to order.

" Artichokes? " Edward Henry blandly suggested.

Again the giggle, followed this time by a flush! And suddenly Edward Henry recognised in her the entrancing creature of fifteen years ago! Her head thrown back, she had put her left hand behind her, and was groping with her long fingers for an object to touch. Having found at length the arm of another chair, she drew her fingers feverishly along its surface. He vividly remembered the gesture in " Flower of the Heart." She had used it with terrific effect at every grand emotional crisis of the play. He now recognised even her face!

" Did Mr. Bryany tell you that my two boys are coming up ? " said she.   " I left them behind to do some telephoning for me."

" Delighted ! " said Edward Henry.   " The more the merrier ! "

And he hoped that he spoke true.

But her two boys !

" Mr. Marrier — he's a young manager.   I don't know whether you know him; very, very talented. And Carlo Trent."

" Same name as my dog," Edward Henry indiscreetly murmured; and his fancy flew back to the home he had quitted, and Wilkins's and everybody in it grew transiently unreal to him.

" Delighted ! " he said again.

He was relieved that her two boys were not her offspring.   That at least was something gained.

" *You* know — the dramatist," said Rose Euclid, apparently disappointed by the effect on Edward Henry of the name of Carlo Trent.

" Really ! " said Edward Henry.   " I hope he won't mind me being in a dressing-gown."

The gentleman in waiting, obsequiously restive, managed to choose the supper himself.   Leaving, he reached the door just in time to hold it open for the entrance of Mr. Marrier and Mr. Carlo Trent, who were talking, with noticeable freedom and emphasis, in an accent which in the Five Towns is known as the " haw-haw," the " lah-di-dah," or the " Kensingtonian " accent.

II.

Within ten minutes, within less than ten minutes, Alderman Edward Henry Machin's supper-party at Wilkins's was so wonderfully changed for the better that Edward Henry might have been excused for not recognising it as his own.

The service at Wilkins's, where they profoundly understood human nature, was very intelligent. Somewhere in a central bureau at Wilkins's sat a psychologist who knew, for example, that a supper commanded on the spur of the moment must be produced instantly if it is to be enjoyed. Delay in these capricious cases impairs the ecstasy, and therefore lessens the chance of other similar meals being commanded at the same establishment. Hence, no sooner had the gentleman in waiting disappeared with the order, than certain esquires appeared with the limbs and body of a table which they set up in Edward Henry's drawing-room; and they covered the board with a damask cloth and half covered the damask cloth with flowers, glasses, and plates, and laid a special private wire from the skirting-board near the hearth to a spot on the table beneath Edward Henry's left hand, so that he could summon courtiers on the slightest provocation with the minimum of exertion. Then immediately brown bread and butter and lemons and red-pepper came, followed by oysters, followed by bottles of pale wine, both still and sparkling. Thus, before the principal dishes had even begun to frizzle in the distant kitchens, the revellers were under the illusion that the entire supper was waiting just outside the door.

Yes, they were revellers now! For the advent of her young men had transformed Rose Euclid, and Rose Euclid had transformed the general situation. At the table, Edward Henry occupied one side of it, Mr. Seven Sachs occupied the side opposite, Mr. Marrier, the very, very talented young manager, occupied the side to Edward Henry's left, and Rose Euclid and Carlo Trent together occupied the side to his right.

Trent and Marrier were each about thirty years of age. Trent, with a deep voice, had extremely lustrous eyes, which eyes continually dwelt on Rose Euclid in admiration. Apparently, all she needed in this valley was oysters and admiration, and she now had both in unlimited quantities.

" Oysters are darlings," she said, as she swallowed the first.

Carlo Trent kissed her hand respectfully — for she was old enough to be his mother.

" And you are the greatest tragic actress in the world, Ra-ose! " said he in the Kensingtonian bass.

A few moments earlier Rose Euclid had whispered to Edward Henry that Carlo Trent was the greatest dramatic poet in the world. She flowered now beneath the sun of those dark lustrous eyes and the soft rain of that admiration from the greatest dramatic poet in the world. It really did seem to Edward Henry that she grew younger. Assuredly she grew more girlish, and her voice improved. And then the bottles began to pop, and it was as though the action of uncorking wine automatically uncorked hearts also. Mr. Seven Sachs, sitting square and upright, smiled gaily at Edward Henry across the gleaming table, and raised a glass. Little Marrier, who at nearly all times had a most enthusiastic smile, did the same. In the result, five glasses met over the central bed of chrysanthemums. Edward Henry was happy. Surrounded by enigmas, — for he had no conception whatever why Rose Euclid had brought any of the three men to his table, — he was nevertheless uplifted.

As he looked about him, at the rich table, and at the glittering chandelier overhead (albeit the lamps thereof were inferior to his own), and at the expanses of soft carpet, and at the silken-textured walls, and at the voluptuous curtains, and at the couple of impeccable gentlemen in waiting, and at Joseph who knew his place behind his master's chair, — he came to the justifiable conclusion that money was a marvellous thing, and the workings of commerce mysterious and beautiful. He had invented the Five Towns Thrift Club; working men and their wives in the Five Towns were paying their two-pences, and sixpenses, and shillings weekly into his Club, and finding the transaction a real convenience — and lo! he was entertaining celebrities at Wilkins's.

For, mind you, they were celebrities. He knew Seven Sachs was a celebrity because he had verily seen him act — and act very well — in his own play, and because his name in letters a foot high had dominated all the hoardings of the Five Towns. As for Rose Euclid, could there be a greater celebrity? Such was the strange power of the popular legend concerning her, that even now, despite the first fearful shock of disappointment, Edward Henry could not call her by her name, without self-consciously stumbling over it, without a curious thrill. And further, he was revising his judgment of her, as well as lowering her age slightly. On coming into the room she had doubtless been almost as startled as himself, and her constrained muteness had been probably due to a guilty feeling in the matter of passing too open remarks to a friend about a perfect stranger's manner of eating artichokes. The which supposition flattered him. (By the way, he wished she had brought the young friend who had shared her amusement over his artichoke.) With regard to the other two men, he was quite ready to believe that Carlo Trent was the world's greatest poet, and to admit the exceeding talent of Mr. Marrier as a theatrical manager. . . . In fact, unmistakable celebrities, one and all! He himself was a celebrity. A certain quality in the attitude of each of his guests showed clearly that they considered him a celebrity, and not only a celebrity, but a card,— Bryany must have been talking,— and the conviction of this rendered him happy. His magnificent hunger rendered him still happier. And the reflection that Brindley owed him half a crown put a top on his bliss!

"I like your dressing-gown, Mr. Machin," said Carlo Trent suddenly, after his first spoonful of soup.

"Then I needn't apologise for it!" Edward Henry replied.

"It is the dressing-gown of my dreams," Carlo Trent went on.

"Well," said Edward Henry, "as we're on the subject, I like your shirt-front."

Carlo Trent was wearing a soft shirt. The other three shirts were all rigidly starched. Hitherto Edward Henry had imagined that a fashionable evening shirt should be, before aught else, bullet-proof. He now appreciated the distinction of a frilled and gently flowing breastplate, especially when a broad purple eye-glass ribbon wandered across it. Rose Euclid gazed in modest transport at Carlo's chest.

"The colour," Carlo proceeded, ignoring Edward Henry's compliment, "the colour is inspiring. So is the texture. I have a woman's delight in textures. I could certainly produce better hexameters in such a dressing-gown."

Although Edward Henry, owing to an unfortunate hiatus in his education, did not know what a hexameter might be, he was artist enough to comprehend the effect of attire on creative work, for he had noticed that he himself could make more money in one necktie than in another, and he would instinctively take particular care in the morning choice of a cravat on days when he meditated a great coup.

"Why don't you get one?" Marrier suggested.

"Do you really think I could?" asked Carlo Trent, as if the possibility were shimmering far out of his reach like a rainbow.

"Rather!" smiled Marrier. "I don't mind laying a fiver that Mr. Machin's dressing-gown came from Drook's in Old Bond Street." But instead of saying "old" he said "ehoold."

"It did," Edward Henry admitted.

Mr. Marrier beamed with satisfaction.

"Drook's, you say?" murmured Carlo Trent. "Old Bond Street?" and wrote down the information on his shirt-cuff.

Rose Euclid watched him write.

"Yes, Carlo," said she. "But don't you think we'd better begin to talk about the theatre? You haven't told me yet if you got hold of Longay on the 'phone."

"Of course we got hold of him," said Marrier. "He agrees with me that 'The Intellectual' is a better name for it."

Rose Euclid clapped her hands.

"I'm so glad!" she cried. "Now what do *you* think of it as a name, Mr. Machin,—'The Intellectual Theatre?' You see it's most important we should settle on the name, isn't it?"

It is no exaggeration to say that Edward Henry felt a wave of cold in the small of his back, and also a sinking away of the nevertheless quite solid chair on which he sat. He had more than the typical Englishman's sane distrust of that morbid word "Intellectual." His attitude towards it amounted to ac-

tive dislike.   If ever he used it, he would on no account use it alone; he would say, " Intellectual, and
all that sort of thing! " with an air of pushing violently away from him everything that the phrase
implied.   The notion of baptising a theatre with the
fearsome word horrified him.   Still he had to main-
tain his nerve and his repute.   So he drank some
champagne, and smiled nonchalantly as the imperturbable duellist smiles while the pistols are being
examined.

"Well —" he murmured.

"You see," Marrier broke in, with the smile
ecstatic, almost dancing on his chair.   "There's no
use in compromise.   Compromise is and always has
been the curse of this country.   The unintellectual
drahma is dead — dead.   Naoobody can deny that.
All the box-offices in the West are proclaiming it."

"Should you call your play intellectual, Mr.
Sachs? " Edward Henry inquired across the table.

"I scarcely know," said Mr. Seven Sachs calmly.
"I know I've played it myself fifteen hundred and
two times, and that's saying nothing of my three sub-
sidiary companies on the road."

"What *is* Mr. Sach's play? " asked Carlo Trent
fretfully.

"Don't you know, Carlo? " Rose Euclid patted
him.   " ' Overheard.' "

"Oh!   I've never seen it."

"But it was on all the hoardings! "

"I never read the hoardings," said Carlo.   "Is
it in verse? "

" No, it isn't," Mr. Seven Sachs briefly responded. " But I've made over six hundred thousand dollars out of it."

" Then of course it's intellectual! " asserted Mr. Marrier positively. " That proves it. I'm very sorry I've not seen it either; but it must be intellectual. The day of the unintellectual drama is over. The people won't have it. We must have faith in the people, and we can't show our faith better than by calling our theatre by its proper name —' The Intellectual Theatre! ' "

(*"His* theatre!" thought Edward Henry. " What's he got to do with it? ")

" I don't know that I'm so much in love with your ' Intellectual,' " muttered Carlo Trent.

"*Are*n't you? " protested Rose Euclid, shocked.

" Of course I'm not," said Carlo. " I told you before, and I tell you now, that there's only one name for the theatre —' The Muses' Theatre! ' "

" Perhaps you're right! " Rose agreed, as if a swift revelation had come to her. " Yes, you're right."

(" She'll make a cheerful sort of partner for a fellow," thought Edward Henry, " if she's in the habit of changing her mind like that every thirty seconds." His appetite had gone. He could only drink.)

" Naturally, I'm right! Aren't we going to open with my play, and isn't my play in verse? . . . I'm sure you'll agree with me, Mr. Machin, that there is no real drama except the poetical drama."

Edward Henry was entirely at a loss. Indeed, he was drowning in his dressing-gown, so favourable to the composition of hexameters.

"Poetry . . ." he vaguely breathed.

"Yes, sir," said Carlo Trent. "Poetry."

"I've never read any poetry in my life," said Edward Henry, like a desperate criminal. "Not a line."

Whereupon Carlo Trent rose up from his seat, and his eye-glasses dangled in front of him.

"Mr. Machin," said he with the utmost benevolence. "This is the most interesting thing I've ever come across. Do you know, you're precisely the man I've always been wanting to meet? . . . The virgin mind. The clean slate. . . . Do you know, you're precisely the man that it's my ambition to write for?"

"It's very kind of you," said Edward Henry feebly, beaten, and consciously beaten.

(He thought miserably: "What would Nellie think if she saw me in this gang?")

Carlo Trent went on, turning to Rose Euclid:

"Rose, will you recite those lines of Nashe?"

Rose Euclid began to blush.

"That bit you taught me the day before yesterday?"

"Only the three lines! No more! They are the very essence of poetry — poetry at its purest. We'll see the effect of them on Mr. Machin. We'll just see. It's the ideal opportunity to test my theory. Now, there's a good girl!"

"Oh! I can't. I'm too nervous," stammered Rose.

"You can, and you must," said Carlo, gazing at her in homage. "Nobody in the world can say them as well as you can. Now!"

Rose Euclid stood up.

"One moment," Carlo stopped her. "There's too much light. We can't do with all this light. Mr. Machin — do you mind?"

A wave of the hand, and all the lights were extinguished, save a lamp on the mantelpiece, and in the disconcertingly darkened room Rose Euclid turned her face towards the ray from this solitary silk-shaded globe.

Her hand groped out behind her, found the tablecloth and began to scratch it agitatedly. She lifted her head. She was the actress, impressive and subjugating, and Edward Henry felt her power. Then she intoned:

> *"Brightness falls from the air;*
> *Queens have died young and fair;*
> *Dust hath closed Helen's eye."*

And she ceased and sat down. There was a silence.

"*Bravo!*" murmured Carlo Trent.

"*Bravo!*" murmured Mr. Marrier.

Edward Henry in the gloom caught Mr. Seven Sachs's unalterable observant smile across the table.

"Well, Mr. Machin?" said Carlo Trent.

Edward Henry had felt a tremor at the vibrations of Rose Euclid's voice. But the words she uttered had set up no clear image in his mind, unless it might be of some solid body falling from the air, or of a young woman named Helen walking along Trafalgar Road, Bursley, on a dusty day, and getting the dust in her eyes.   He knew not what to answer.

"Is that all there is of it?" he asked at length. Carlo Trent said:

"It's from Thomas Nashe's 'Song in Time of Pestilence.' The closing lines of the verse are:

> *"I am sick, I must die —*
> *Lord, have mercy on me!"*

"Well," said Edward Henry, recovering, "I rather like the end.   I think the end's very appropriate."

Mr. Seven Sachs choked over his wine, and kept on choking.

III.

Mr. Marrier was the first to recover from this blow to the prestige of poetry.   Or perhaps it would be more honest to say that Mr. Marrier had suffered no inconvenience from the contretemps.   His apparent gleeful zest in life had not been impaired.   He was a born optimist, of an extreme type unknown beyond the circumferences of theatrical circles.

"I *say*," he emphasised, "I've got an ideah.   We ought to be photographed like that.   Do you no end of good."   He glanced encouragingly at Rose Euclid.   "Don't you see it in the illustrated papers? 'A prayvate supper-party at Wilkins's Hotel.   Miss Ra-ose Euclid reciting verse at a discussion of

the plans for her new theatre in Piccadilly Circus.
The figures reading from left to right are: Mr.
Seven Sachs, the famous actor-author; Miss Rose
Euclid; Mr. Carlo Trent, the celebrated dramatic
poet; Mr. Alderman Machin, the well-known Midlands capitalist,' and so on! " Mr. Marrier repeated,
" and so on."

" It's a notion," said Rose Euclid dreamily.

" But how *can* we be photographed? " Carlo
Trent demanded with irritation.

" Perfectly easy."

" Now? "

" In ten minutes. I know a photographer in
Brook Street."

" Would he come at once? " Carlo Trent frowned
at his watch.

" Rather! " Mr. Marrier gaily soothed him, as
he went over to the telephone. And Mr. Marrier's
bright boyish face radiated forth the assurance that
nothing in all his existence had more completely
filled him with sincere joy than this enterprise of
procuring a photograph of the party. Even in giving the photographer's number,— he was one of
those prodigies who remember infallibly all telephone numbers,— his voice seemed to gloat upon his
project.

(And while Mr. Marrier, having obtained communication with the photographer, was saying gloriously into the telephone: " Yes, Wilkins's. No.
Quite private. I've got Miss Rose Euclid here, and
Mr. Seven Sachs —" while Mr. Marrier was thus

proceeding with his list of star attractions, Edward
Henry was thinking: " ' *Her* new theatre,'— now!
It was ' his ' a few minutes back! . . .

" The well-known Midland capitalist, eh?   Oh!
Ah!")

He drank again.   He said to himself: " I've
had all I can digest of this beastly balloony stuff."
(He meant the champagne.)   " If I finish this glass,
I'm bound to have a bad night."   And he finished
the glass, and planked it down firmly on the table.

" Well," he remarked aloud cheerfully, " if we're
to be photographed, I suppose we shall want a bit
more light on the subject."

Joseph sprang to the switches.

" Please! " Carlo Trent raised a protesting hand.

The switches were not turned.   In the beautiful
dimness the greatest tragic actress in the world and
the greatest dramatic poet in the world gazed at
each other, seeking and finding solace in mutual esteem.

" I suppose it wouldn't do to call it the Euclid
Theater? " Rose questioned casually, without moving her eyes.

" Splendid! " cried Mr. Marrier from the telephone.

" It all depends whether there are enough mathe-
matical students in London to fill the theater for a
run," said Edward Henry.

" Oh!   D'you think so? " murmured Rose, surprised and vaguely puzzled.

At that instant Edward Henry might have rushed

from the room and taken the night mail back to the
Five Towns, and never any more have ventured
into the perils of London, if Carlo Trent had not
turned his head and signified by a curt reluctant laugh
that he saw the joke. For Edward Henry could no
longer depend on Mr. Seven Sachs. Mr. Seven
Sachs had to take the greatest pains to keep the
muscles of his face in strict order. The slightest lax-
ity with them — and he would have been involved in
another and more serious suffocation.

" No," said Carlo Trent, " ' The Muses' Theatre '
is the only possible title. There is money in the
poetical drama." He looked hard at Edward Henry,
as though to stare down the memory of the failure
of Nashe's verse. " I don't want money. I hate
the thought of money. But money is the only proof
of democratic appreciation, and that is what I need,
and what every artist needs. . . . Don't you think
there's money in the poetical drama, Mr. Sachs? "

" Not in America," said Mr. Sachs. " London
is a queer place."

" Look at the runs of Stephen Phillips's plays! "

" Yes. . . . I only reckon to know America."

" Look at what Pilgrim's made out of Shakespeare."

" I thought you were talking about poetry," said
Edward Henry too hastily.

" And isn't Shakespeare poetry? " Carlo Trent
challenged.

" Well, I suppose if you put it in that way, he *is!* "
Edward Henry cautiously admitted, humbled. He

was under the disadvantage of never having seen or read " Shakespeare." His sure instinct had always warned him against being drawn into " Shakespeare."

" And has Miss Euclid ever done anything finer than Constance? "

" I don't know," Edward Henry pleaded.

" Why — Miss Euclid in ' King John '—"

" I never saw ' King John,' " said Edward Henry.

" *Do you mean to say,*" expostulated Carlo Trent in italics, " *that you never saw Rose Euclid as Constance?* "

And Edward Henry, shaking his abashed head, perceived that his life had been wasted.

Carlo, for a few moments, grew reflective and softer.

" It's one of my earliest and most precious boyish memories," he murmured, as he examined the ceiling. " It must have been in eighteen —"

Rose Euclid abandoned the ice with which she had just been served, and by a single gesture drew Carlo's attention away from the ceiling and towards the fact that it would be clumsy on his part to indulge further in the chronology of her career. She began to blush again.

Mr. Marrier, now back at the table after a successful expedition, beamed over his ice:

" It was your ' Constance ' that led to your friendship with the Countess of Chell, wasn't it, Ra-ose? You know," he turned to Edward Henry, " Miss Euclid and the countess are virry intimate."

" Yes, I know," said Edward Henry.

Rose Euclid continued to blush. Her agitated hand scratched the back of the chair behind her.

" Even Sir John Pilgrim admits I can act Shakespeare," she said in a thick, mournful voice, looking at the cloth as she pronounced the august name of the head of the dramatic profession. " It may surprise you to know, Mr. Machin, that about a month ago, after he'd quarrelled with Selina Gregory, Sir John asked me if I'd care to star with him on his Shakespearean tour round the world next spring, and I said I would if he'd include Carlo's poetical play, ' The Orient Pearl,' and he wouldn't! No, he wouldn't! And now he's got little Cora Pryde! She isn't twenty-two, and she's going to play Juliet! Can you imagine such a thing? As if a mere girl could play Juliet! "

Carlo observed the mature actress with deep satisfaction, proud of her, and proud also of himself.

" I wouldn't go with Pilgrim now," exclaimed Rose passionately, " not if he went down on his knees to me! "

" And nothing on earth would induce me to let him have ' The Orient Pearl '! " Carlo Trent asseverated with equal passion. " He's lost that forever," he added grimly. " It won't be he who'll collar the profits out of that! It'll just be ourselves! "

" Not if he went down on his knees to me! " Rose was repeating to herself with fervency.

The calm of despair took possession of Edward Henry. He felt that he must act immediately — he

knew his own mood, by long experience. Exploring
the pockets of the dressing-gown which had aroused
the longing of the greatest dramatic poet in the
world, he discovered in one of them precisely the
piece of apparatus he required; namely, a slip of
paper suitable for writing. It was a carbon dupli-
cate of the bill for the dressing-gown, and showed
the word " Drook " in massive printed black, and
the figures £4-4-0 in faint blue. He drew a pencil
from his waistcoat and inscribed on the paper:

" Go out, and then come back in a couple of minutes and tell me someone wants to speak to me urgently in the next room."

With a minimum of ostentation he gave the document to Joseph, who, evidently well trained under Sir
Nicholas, vanished into the next room before at-
tempting to read it.

" I hope," said Edward Henry to Carlo Trent,
" that this money-making play is reserved for the
new theatre."

" Utterly," said Carlo Trent.

" With Miss Euclid in the principal part? "

" Rather! " sang Mr. Marrier.   " Rather! "

" I shall never, never appear at any other theatre,
Mr. Machin! " said Rose with tragic emotion, once
more feeling with her fingers along the back of her
chair.   " So I hope the building will begin at once.
In less than six months we ought to open."

" Easily! " sang the optimist.

Joseph returned to the room, and sought his master's attention in a whisper.

" What is it? " Edward Henry asked irritably.
" Speak up ! "

" A gentleman wishes to know if he can speak to
you in the next room, sir."

" Well, he can't."

" He said it was urgent, sir."

Scowling, Edward Henry rose. " Excuse me,"
he said.   " I won't be a moment.   Help yourselves
to the liqueurs.   You chaps can go, I fancy."   The
last remark was addressed to the gentlemen in waiting.

The next room was the vast bedroom with two beds
in it.   Edward Henry closed the door carefully, and
drew the portière across it.   Then he listened.   No
sound penetrated from the scene of the supper.

" There *is* a telephone in this room, isn't there? "
he said to Joseph.   " Oh, yes; there it is!   Well,
you can go."

" Yes, sir."

Edward Henry sat down on one of the beds by
the hook on which hung the telephone.   And he
cogitated upon the characteristics of certain members of the party which he had just left.   " I'm a
' virgin mind,' am I? " he thought.   " I'm a ' clean
slate '?   Well! . . . Their notion of business is to
begin by discussing the name of the theatre!   And
they haven't even taken up the option!   Ye gods!
' Intellectual! '   ' Muses! '   ' The   Orient   Pearl.'
And she's fifty — that I swear!   Not a word yet of
real business — not one word!   He may be a poet.
I dare say he is.   He's a conceited ass.   Why, even

Bryany was better than that lot. Only Sachs turned Bryany out. I like Sachs. But he won't open his mouth. . . . 'Capitalist!' Well, they spoilt my appetite, and I hate champagne! . . . The poet hates money. . . . No, he 'hates the thought of money.' And she's changing her mind the whole blessed time! A month ago she'd have gone over to Pilgrim, and the poet too, like a house a fire! . . . Photographed indeed! The bally photographer will be here in a minute! . . . They take me for a fool! . . . Or don't they know any better? . . . Anyhow, I am a fool. . . . I must teach 'em summat!"

He seized the telephone.

"Hello!" he said into it. "I want you to put me on to the drawing-room of Suite No. 48, please. Who? Oh, me! I'm in the bedroom of Suite No. 48. Machin, Alderman Machin. Thanks. That's all right."

He waited. Then he heard Marrier's Kensingtonian voice in the telephone, asking who he was.

"Is that Mr. Machin's room?" he continued, imitating with a broad farcical effect the acute Kensingtonianism of Mr. Marrier's tones. "Is Miss Ra-ose Euclid there? Oh! She is? Well, you tell her that Sir John Pilgrim's private secretary wishes to speak to her. Thanks. All right. *I'll* hold the line."

A pause. Then he heard Rose's voice in the telephone, and he resumed:

"Miss Euclid? Yes. Sir John Pilgrim. I beg

pardon! Banks? Oh, *Banks!* No, I'm not
Banks. I suppose you mean my predecessor. He's
left. Left last week. No, I don't know why.
Sir John instructs me to ask if you and Mr. Trent
could lunch with him to-morrow at wun-thirty?
What? Oh! At his house. Yes. I mean flat.
Flat! I said flat. You think you could?"

Pause. He could hear her calling to Carlo
Trent.

"Thanks. No, I don't know exactly," he went
on again. "But I know the arrangement with Miss
Pryde is broken off. And Sir John wants a play at
once. He told me that. At once! Yes. 'The
Orient Pearl.' That was the title. At the Royal
first, and then the world's tour. Fifteen months at
least, in all, so I gathered. Of course I don't speak
officially. Well, many thanks. Saoo good of you.
I'll tell Sir John it's arranged. One-thirty to-morrow. Good-bye!"

He hung up the telephone. The excited, eager,
effusive tones of Rose Euclid remained in his ears.
Aware of a strange phenomenon on his forehead, he
touched it. He was perspiring.

"I'll teach 'em a thing or two," he muttered.

And again:

"Serves her right. . . . 'Never, never appear at
any other theatre, Mr. Machin!' . . . 'Bended
knees!' . . . 'Utterly!' . . . Cheerful partners!
Oh, cheerful partners!"

He returned to his supper-party. Nobody said

a word about the telephoning.   But Rose Euclid and
Carlo Trent looked even more like conspirators than
they did before; and Mr. Marrier's joy in life
seemed to be just the least bit diminished.

"So sorry!" Edward Henry began hurriedly,
and, without consulting the poet's wishes, subtly
turned on all the lights. "Now, don't you think
we'd better discuss the question of taking up the option? You know, it expires on Friday."

"No," said Rose Euclid girlishly. "It expires
to-morrow. That's why it's so *fortunate* we got
hold of you to-night."

"But Mr. Bryany told me Friday. And the date
was clear enough on the copy of the option he gave
me."

"A mistake of copying," beamed Mr. Marrier.
"However, it's all right."

"Well," observed Edward Henry with heartiness,
"I don't mind telling you that for sheer calm cool-
ness you take the cake. However, as Mr. Marrier
so ably says, it's all right. Now, I understand if I
go into this affair I can count on you absolutely, and
also on Mr. Trent's services." He tried to talk as
if he had been diplomatising with actresses and poets
all his life.

"Absolutely!" said Rose.

And Mr. Carlo Trent nodded.

"You Iscariots!" Edward Henry addressed them,
in the silence of the brain, behind his smile. "You
Iscariots!"

The photographer arrived with certain cases, and at once Rose Euclid and Carlo Trent began instinctively to pose.

" To think," Edward Henry pleasantly reflected, " that they are hugging themselves because Sir John Pilgrim's secretary happened to telephone just while I was out of the room! "

CHAPTER V

MR. SACHS TALKS

I.

IT was the sudden flash of the photographer's magnesium light, plainly felt by him through his closed lids, that somehow instantly inspired Edward Henry to a definite and ruthless line of action. He opened his eyes and beheld the triumphant group, and the photographer himself, victorious over even the triumphant, in a superb pose that suggested that all distinguished mankind in his presence was naught but food for the conquering camera. The photographer smiled indulgently, and his smile said: "Having been photographed by me, you have each of you reached the summit of your career. Be content. Retire! Die! Destiny is accomplished!"

"Mr. Machin," said Rose Euclid, "I do believe your eyes were shut!"

"So do I!" Edward Henry curtly agreed.

"But you'll spoil the group!"

"Not a bit of it!" said Edward Henry. "I always shut my eyes when I'm being photographed by flash-light. I open my mouth instead. So long as something's open, what does it matter?"

The truth was that only in the nick of time had he,

137

by a happy miracle of ingenuity, invented a way of ruining the photograph. The absolute necessity for its ruin had presented itself to him rather late in the proceedings, when the photographer had already finished arranging the hands and shoulders of everybody in an artistic pattern. The photograph had to be spoilt for the imperative reason that his mother, though she never read a newspaper, did as a fact look at a picture newspaper, *The Daily Film,* which from pride she insisted on paying for out of her own purse, at the rate of one halfpenny a day. Now *The Daily Film* specialised in theatrical photographs, on which it said it spent large sums of money; and Edward Henry in a vision had seen the historic group in a future issue of the *Film.* He had also, in the same vision, seen his mother conning the said issue, and the sardonic curve of her lips as she recognised her son therein, and he had even heard her dry, cynical, contemptuous exclamation: " Bless us ! " He could never have looked squarely in his mother's face again if that group had appeared in her chosen organ! Her silent and grim scorn would have crushed his self-conceit to a miserable, hopeless pulp. Hence his resolve to render the photograph impossible.

" Perhaps I'd better take another one? " the photographer suggested. " Though I think Mr.— er — Machin was all right." At the supreme crisis the man had been too busy with his fireworks to keep a watch on every separate eye and mouth of the assemblage.

" Of course I was all right! " said Edward Henry, almost with brutality. " Please take that thing away as quickly as you can. We have business to attend to."

" Yes, sir," agreed the photographer, no longer victorious.

Edward Henry rang the bell, and two gentlemen in waiting arrived.

" Clear this table immediately! "

The tone of the command startled everybody except the gentlemen in waiting and Mr. Seven Sachs. Rose Euclid gave vent to her nervous giggle. The poet and Mr. Marrier tried to appear detached and dignified, and succeeded in appearing guiltily confused — for which they contemned themselves. Despite their volition, the glances of all three of them too clearly signified: " This capitalist must be humoured. He has an unlimited supply of actual cash, and therefore he has the right to be peculiar. Moreover, we know that he is a card. . . . And, curiously, Edward Henry himself was deriving great force of character from the simple reflection that he had indeed a lot of money, real available money, his to do utterly as he liked with it, hidden in a secret place in that very room. " I'll show 'em what's what! " he privately mused. " Celebrities or not, I'll show 'em! If they think they can come it over me — ! "

It was, I regret to say, the state of mind of a bully. Such is the noxious influence of excessive coin!

He reproached the greatest actress and the greatest dramatic poet for deceiving him, and quite ignored the nevertheless fairly obvious fact that he had first deceived them.

"Now then," he began, with something of the pomposity of a chairman at a directors' meeting, as soon as the table had been cleared and the room emptied of gentlemen in waiting and photographer and photographic apparatus, "let us see exactly where we stand."

He glanced specially at Rose Euclid, who with an air of deep business acumen returned the glance.

"Yes," she eagerly replied, as one seeking after righteousness, "*do* let's see."

"The option must be taken up to-morrow. Good! That's clear. It came rather casual-like, but it's now clear. £4,500 has to be paid down to buy the existing building on the land and so on. . . . Eh?"

"Yes. Of course Mr. Bryany told you all that, didn't he?" said Rose brightly.

"Mr. Bryany did tell me," Edward Henry admitted sternly. "But if Mr. Bryany can make a mistake in the day of the week he might make a mistake in a few naughts at the end of a sum of money."

Suddenly Mr. Seven Sachs startled them all by emerging from his silence with the words:

"The figure is O. K."

Instinctively Edward Henry waited for more; but no more came. Mr. Seven Sachs was one of those rare and disconcerting persons who do not keep on talking after they have finished. He resumed his tranquillity, he re-entered into his silence, with no symptom of self-consciousness, entirely cheerful and at ease. And Edward Henry was aware of his observant and steady gaze. Edward Henry said to himself: " This man is expecting me to behave in a remarkable way. Bryany has been telling him all about me, and he is waiting to see if I really am as good as my reputation. I have just got to be as good as my reputation!" He looked up at the electric chandelier, almost with regret that it was not gas. One cannot light one's cigarette by twisting a hundred-pound bank-note and sticking it into an electric chandelier. Moreover, there were some thousands of matches on the table. Still further, he had done the cigarette-lighting trick once for all. A first-class card must not repeat himself.

" This money," Edward Henry proceeded, " has to be paid to Slossons, Lord Woldo's solicitors, tomorrow, Wednesday, rain or shine? " He finished the phrase on a note of interrogation, and as nobody offered any reply, he rapped on the table, and repeated, half menacingly: " Rain or shine! "

" Yes," said Rose Euclid, leaning timidly forward, and taking a cigarette from a gold case that lay on the table. All her movements indicated an earnest desire to be thoroughly businesslike.

" So that, Miss Euclid," Edward Henry continued impressively but with a wilful touch of incredulity, " you are in a position to pay your share of this money to-morrow? "

" Certainly! " said Miss Euclid. And it was as

if she had said, aggrieved: " Can you doubt my honour? "

" To-morrow morning? "

" Ye-es."

" That is to say, to-morrow morning you will have £2,250 in actual cash — coin, notes — actually in your possession? "

Miss Euclid's disengaged hand was feeling out behind her again for some surface upon which to express its emotion and hers.

" Well —" she stopped, flushing.

(" These people are astounding," Edward Henry reflected, like a god. " She's not got the money. I knew it! ")

" It's like this, Mr. Machin," Marrier began.

" Excuse me, Mr. Marrier," Edward Henry turned on him, determined if he could to eliminate the optimism from that beaming face. " Any friend of Miss Euclid's is welcome here, but you've already talked about this theatre as ' ours,' and I just want to know where you come in."

" Where I come in? " Marrier smiled, absolutely unperturbed. " Miss Euclid has appointed me general manajah."

" At what salary, if it isn't a rude question? "

" Oh! We haven't settled details yet. You see the theatre isn't built yet."

" True! " said Edward Henry. " I was forgetting! I was thinking for the moment that the theatre was all ready and going to be opened to-morrow night with ' The Orient Pearl.' Have you

had much experience of managing theatres, Mr.
Marrier? I suppose you have."

"Eho, yes!" exclaimed Mr. Marrier. "I began life as a lawyah's clerk, but —"

"So did I," Edward Henry interjected.

"How interesting!" Rose Euclid murmured
with fervency, after puffing forth a long shaft of
smoke.

"However, I threw it up," Marrier went on.

"I didn't," said Edward Henry. "I got thrown
out!"

Strange that in that moment he was positively
proud of having been dismissed from his first situation! Strange that all the company, too, thought
the better of him for having been dismissed!
Strange that Marrier regretted that he also had not
been dismissed! But so it was. The possession
of much ready money emits a peculiar effluence in
both directions — back to the past, forward into the
future.

"I threw it up," said Marrier, "because the
stage had an irresistible attraction for me. I'd
been stage-manajah for an amateur company, you
knaoo. I found a shop as stage-manajah of a company touring ' Uncle Tom's Cabin.' I stuck to that
for six years, and then I threw that up too. Then
I've managed one of Miss Euclid's provincial tours.
And since I met our friend Trent, I've had the
chance to show what my ideas about play-producing
really are. I fancy my production of Trent's one-
act play won't be forgotten in a hurry. . . . You

know —' The Nymph?' You read about it, didn't you?"

"I did not," said Edward Henry. "How long did it run?"

"Oh! it didn't run. It wasn't put on for a run. It was part of one of the Sunday-night shows of the Play-Producing Society, at the Court Theatre. Most intellectual people in London, you know. No such audience anywhere else in the wahld!" His rather chubby face glistened and shimmered with enthusiasm. "You bet!" he added. "But that was only by the way. My real game is management — general management. And I think I may say I know what it is."

"Evidently!" Edward Henry concurred. "But shall you have to give up any other engagement in order to take charge of the Muses' Theatre? Because if so —"

Mr. Marrier replied:

"No."

Edward Henry observed:

"Oh!"

"But," said Marrier reassuringly, "if necessary I would throw up any engagement — you understand me, any — in favour of the Intellectual Theatah as I prefer to call it. You see, as I own part of the option —"

By these last words Edward Henry was confounded, even to muteness.

"I forgot to mention, Mr. Machin," said Rose Euclid very quickly. "I've disposed of a quarter of my half of the option to Mr. Marrier. He fully agreed with me it was better that he should have a proper interest in the theatre."

"Why of course!" cried Mr. Marrier, uplifted.

"Let me see," said Edward Henry, after a long breath, "a quarter — that makes it that you have to find £562 10s, to-morrow, Mr. Marrier."

"Yes."

"To-morrow morning — you'll be all right?"

"Well, I won't swear for the morning, but I shall turn up with the stuff in the afternoon any-how. I've two men in tow, and one of them's a cer-tainty."

"Which?"

"I don't know which," said Mr. Marrier. "Howevah, you may count on yours sincerly, Mr. Machin."

There was a pause.

"Perhaps I ought to tell you," Rose Euclid smiled, "perhaps I ought to tell you that Mr. Trent is also one of our partners. He has taken another quarter of my half."

Edward Henry controlled himself.

"Excellent!" said he with glee. "Mr. Trent's money all ready too?"

"I am providing most of it — temporarily," said Rose Euclid.

"I see. Then I understand you have your three quarters of £2,250 all ready in hand."

She glanced at Mr. Seven Sachs.

"Have I, Mr. Sachs?"

And Mr. Sachs, after an instant's hesitation, bowed in assent.

" Mr. Sachs is not exactly going into the speculation, but he is lending us money on the security of our interests.   That's the way to put it, isn't it, Mr. Sachs ? "

Mr. Sachs once more bowed.

And Edward Henry exclaimed:

" Now I really do see ! "

He gave one glance across the table at Mr. Seven Sachs, as who should say: " And have you too allowed yourself to be dragged into this affair?   I really thought you were cleverer.   Don't you agree with me that we're both fools of the most arrant description? "   And under the brief glance Mr. Seven Sachs's calm deserted him as it had never deserted him on the stage, where for over fifteen hundred nights he had withstood the menace of revolvers, poison, and female treachery through three hours and four acts without a single moment of agitation.

Apparently Miss Rose Euclid could exercise a siren's charm upon nearly all sorts of men.   But Edward Henry knew one sort of men upon whom she could not exercise it; namely, the sort of men who are born and bred in the Five Towns.   His instinctive belief in the Five Towns as the sole cradle of hard practical common sense was never stronger than just now.   You might by wiles get the better of London and America, but not of the Five Towns. If Rose Euclid were to go around and about the

Five Towns trying to do the siren business, she would pretty soon discover that she was up against something rather special in the way of human nature!

Why, the probability was that these three — Rose Euclid (only a few hours since a glorious name and legend to him), Carlo Trent, and Mr. Marrier — could not at that moment produce even ten pounds between them! . . . And Marrier offering to lay fivers! . . . He scornfully pitied them. And he was not altogether without pity for Seven Sachs, who had doubtless succeeded in life by sheer accident and knew no more than an infant what to do with his too easily earned money.

II.

"Well," said Edward Henry, "shall I tell you what I've decided?"

"Please do!" Rose Euclid entreated him.

"I've decided to make you a present of my half of the option."

"But aren't you going in with us?" exclaimed Rose, horror-struck.

"No, madam."

"But Mr. Bryany told us positively you were! He said it was all arranged!"

"Mr. Bryany ought to be more careful," said Edward Henry. "If he doesn't mind, he'll be telling a downright lie some day."

"But you bought half the option!"

"Well," said Edward Henry, reasoning. "What

is an option? What does it mean? It means you are free to take something or leave it. I'm leaving it."

" But why? " demanded Mr. Marrier, gloomier.

Carlo Trent played with his eye-glasses and said not a word.

" Why? " Edward Henry replied. " Simply because I feel I'm not fitted for the job. I don't know enough. I don't understand. I shouldn't go the right way about the affair. For instance, I should never have guessed by myself that it was the proper thing to settle the name of the theatre before you'd got the lease of the land you're going to build it on. Then I'm old-fashioned. I hate leaving things to the last moment; but seemingly there's only one proper moment in these theatrical affairs, and that's the very last. I'm afraid there'd be too much trusting in Providence for my taste. I believe in trusting in Providence, but I can't bear to see Providence overworked. And I've never even tried to be intellectual, and I'm a bit frightened of poetry plays —"

" But you've not read my play! " Carlo Trent mutteringly protested.

" That is so," admitted Edward Henry.

" Will you read it? "

" Mr. Trent," said Edward Henry. " I'm not so young as I was."

" We're ruined! " sighed Rose Euclid with a tragic gesture.

" Ruined? " Edward Henry took her up, smiling.

"Nobody is ruined who knows where he can get a square meal. Do you mean to tell me you don't know where you're going to lunch to-morrow?" And he looked hard at her.

It was a blow. She blenched under it.

"Oh, yes," she said, with her giggle, "I know that."

("Well you just don't!" he answered her in his heart. "You think you're going to lunch with John Pilgrim. And you aren't. And it serves you right!")

"Besides," he continued aloud, "how can you say you're ruined when I'm making you a present of something that I paid £100 for?"

"But where am I to find the other half of the money — £2,250?" she burst out. "We were depending absolutely on you for it. If I don't get it, the option will be lost, and the option's very valuable."

"All the easier to find the money then!"

"What? In less than twenty-four hours? It can't be done. I couldn't get it in all London."

"Mr. Marrier will get it for you . . . one of his certainties!" Edward Henry smiled in the Five Towns' manner.

"I might, you knaoo!" said Marrier, brightening to full hope in the fraction of a second.

But Rose Euclid only shook her head.

"Mr. Seven Sachs, then?" Edward Henry suggested.

"I should have been delighted," said Mr. Sachs

with the most perfect gracious tranquillity. "But
I cannot find another £2,250 to-morrow."

"I shall just speak to that Mr. Bryany!" said
Rose Euclid, in the accents of homicide.

"I think you ought to," Edward Henry concurred. "But that won't help things. I feel a little
responsible, especially to a lady. You have a quarter of the whole option left in your hands, Miss
Euclid. I'll pay you at the same rate as Bryany
sold to me. I gave £100 for half. Your quarter
is therefore worth £50. Well, I'll pay you £50."

"And then what?"

"Then let the whole affair slide."

"But that won't help me to my theatre!" Rose
Euclid said, pouting. She was now decidedly less
unhappy than her face pretended, because Edward
Henry had reminded her of Sir John Pilgrim, and
she had dreams of world triumphs for herself and
for Carlo Trent's play. She was almost glad to
be rid of all the worry of the horrid little prospec-
tive theatre.

"I have bank-notes," cooed Edward Henry
softly.

Her head sank.

Edward Henry rose in the incomparable yellow
dressing-gown and walked to and fro a little, and
then from his secret store he produced a bundle of
notes, and counted out five tens and, coming behind Rose, stretched out his arm and laid the treas-
ure on the table in front of her under the brilliant
chandelier.

" I don't want you to feel you have anything against me," he cooed still more softly.

Silence reigned. Edward Henry resumed his chair and gazed at Rose Euclid. She was quite a dozen years older than his wife, and she looked more than a dozen years older. She had no fixed home, no husband, no children, no regular situation. She accepted the homage of young men, who were cleverer than herself save in one important respect. She was always in and out of restaurants and hotels and express trains. She was always committing hygienic indiscretions. She could not refrain from a certain girlishness which, having regard to her years, her waist, and her complexion, was ridiculous. His wife would have been afraid of her, and would have despised her, simultaneously. She was coarsened by the continual gaze of the gaping public. No two women could possibly be more utterly dissimilar than Rose Euclid and the cloistered Nellie. . . . And yet, as Rose Euclid's hesitant fingers closed on the bank-notes with a gesture of relief, Edward Henry had an agreeable and kindly sensation that all women were alike, after all, in the need of a shield, a protection, a strong and generous male hand. He was touched by the spectacle of Rose Euclid, as naïve as any young lass when confronted by actual bank-notes; and he was touched also by the thought of Nellie and the children afar off, existing in comfort and peace, but utterly, wistfully, dependent on himself.

" And what about me? " growled Carlo Trent.

" You? "

The fellow was only a poet. He negligently dropped him five fivers, his share of the option's value.

Mr. Marrier said nothing, but his eye met Edward Henry's, and in silence five fivers were meted out to Mr. Marrier also. . . . It was so easy to delight these persons who apparently seldom set eyes on real ready money.

" You might sign receipts, all of you, just as a matter of form," said Edward Henry.

A little later, the three associates were off.

" As we're both in the hotel, Mr. Sachs," said Edward Henry, " you might stay for a chat and a drink."

Mr. Seven Sachs politely agreed.

Edward Henry accompanied the trio of worshippers and worshipped to the door of his suite, but no further, because of his dressing-gown. Rose Euclid had assumed a resplendent opera-cloak. They rang imperially for the lift. Lackeys bowed humbly before them. They spoke of taxicabs and other luxuries. They were perfectly at home in the grandeur of the hotel. As the illuminated lift carried them down out of sight, their smiling heads disappearing last, they seemed exactly like persons of extreme wealth. And indeed for the moment they were wealthy. They had parted with certain hopes, but they had had a windfall; and two of them were looking forward with absolute assurance

to a profitable meal and deal with Sir John Pilgrim
on the morrow.

"Funny place, London!" said the provincial to
himself as he re-entered his suite to rejoin Mr.
Seven Sachs.

III.

"Well, sir," said Mr. Seven Sachs, "I have to
thank you for getting me out of a very unsatisfac-
tory situation."

"Did you really want to get out of it?" asked
Edward Henry.

Mr. Sachs replied simply.

"I did, sir. There were too many partners for
my taste."

They were seated more familiarly now in the
drawing-room, being indeed separated only by a
small table upon which were glasses. And whereas
on a night in the previous week Edward Henry
had been entertained by Mr. Bryany in a private
parlour at the Turk's Head, Hanbridge, on this
night he was in a sort repaying the welcome to Mr.
Bryany's master in a private parlour at Wilkins's,
London. The sole difference in favour of Mr.
Bryany was that, while Mr. Bryany provided
cigarettes and whisky, Edward Henry was providing only cigarettes and Vichy water. Mr. Seven
Sachs had said that he never took whisky; and
though Edward Henry's passion for Vichy water
was not quite ungovernable, he thought well to give

rein to it on the present occasion, having read somewhere that Vichy water placated the stomach.

Joseph had been instructed to retire.

" And not only that," resumed Mr. Seven Sachs, " but you've got a very good thing entirely into your own hands! Masterly, sir! Masterly! Why, at the end you positively had the air of doing them a favour! You made them believe you *were* doing them a favour."

" And don't you think I was?"

Mr. Sachs reflected, and then laughed.

" You were," he said. " That's the beauty of it. But at the same time you were getting away with the goods!"

It was by sheer instinct, and not by learning, that Edward Henry fully grasped, as he did, the deep significance of the American idiom employed by Mr. Seven Sachs. He, too, laughed, as Mr. Sachs had laughed. He was immeasurably flattered. He had not been so flattered since the Countess of Chell had permitted him to offer her China tea, meringues, and Berlin pancakes at the Sub Rosa tea-rooms in Hanbridge — and that was a very long time ago.

" You really *do* think it's a good thing?" Edward Henry ventured, for he had not yet been convinced of the entire goodness of theatrical enterprise near Piccadilly Circus.

Mr. Seven Sachs convinced him — not by argument, but by the sincerity of his gestures and tones; for it was impossible to question that Mr. Seven

Sachs knew what he was talking about. The shape of Mr. Seven Sachs' chin was alone enough to prove that Mr. Sachs was incapable of a mere ignorant effervescence. Everything about Mr. Sachs was persuasive and confidence-inspiring. His long silences had the easy vigour of oratory, and they served also to make his speech peculiarly impressive. Moreover, he was a handsome and a dark man, and probably half a dozen years younger than Edward Henry. And the discipline of lime-light had taught him the skill to be forever graceful. And his smile, rare enough, was that of a boy.

"Of course," said he, "if Miss Euclid and the others had had any sense, they might have done very well for themselves. If you ask me, the option alone is worth ten thousand dollars. But then they haven't any sense! And that's all there is to it!"

"So you'd advise me to go ahead with the affair on my own?"

Mr. Seven Sachs, his black eyes twinkling, leaned forward and became rather intimately humorous:

"You look as if you wanted advice, don't you?" said he.

"I suppose I do, now I come to think of it!" agreed Edward Henry with a most admirable quizzicalness; in spite of the fact that he had not really meant to "go ahead with the affair," being in truth a little doubtful of his capacity to handle it.

But Mr. Seven Sachs was, all unconsciously, forcing Edward Henry to believe in his own capacities;

and the two, as it were, suddenly developed a more
cordial friendliness.   Each felt the quick lifting of
the plane of their relations, and was aware of a
pleasurable emotion.

"I'm moving onwards — gently onwards,"
crooned Edward Henry to himself.   "What price
Brindley and his half-crown now?"   Londoners
might call him a provincial, and undoubtedly would
call him a provincial; he admitted, even, that he
felt like a provincial in the streets of London.
And yet here he was, "doing Londoners in the eye
all over the place," and receiving the open homage
of Mr. Seven Sachs, whose name was the basis of
a cosmopolitan legend.

And now he made the cardinal discovery, which
marks an epoch in the life of every man who arrives
at it, that world-celebrated persons are very like
other persons.   And he was happy and rather proud
in this discovery, and began to feel a certain vague
desire to tell Mr. Seven Sachs the history of his
career — or at any rate the picturesque portions of
it.   For he, too, was famous in his own sphere;
and in the drawing-room of Wilkins's one celebrity
was hobnobbing with another!   ("Put that in your
pipe and smoke it, Mr. Brindley!")   Yes, he was
happy, both in what he had already accomplished,
and in the contemplation of romantic adventures to
come.

And yet his happiness was marred — not fatally,
but quite appreciably — by a remorse that no
amount of private argument with himself would con-

jure away. Which was the more singular in that a morbid tendency to remorse had never been among Edward Henry's defects! He was worrying, foolish fellow, about the false telephone-call in which, for the purpose of testing Rose Euclid's loyalty to the new enterprise, he had pretended to be the new private secretary of Sir John Pilgrim. Yet what harm had it done? And had it not done a lot of good? Rose Euclid and her youthful worshipper were no worse off than they had been before being victimised by the deceit of the telephone-call. Prior to the call they had assumed themselves to be deprived forever of the benefits which association with Sir John Pilgrim could offer, and as a fact they were deprived forever of such benefits. Nothing changed there! Before the call they had had no hope of lunching with the enormous Sir John on the morrow, and as a fact they would not lunch with the enormous Sir John on the morrow. Nothing changed there either! Again, in no event would Edward Henry have joined the trio in order to make a quartette in partnership. Even had he been as convinced of Rose's loyalty as he was convinced of her disloyalty, he would never have been rash enough to co-operate with such a crew. Again, nothing changed!

On the other hand, he had acquired an assurance of the artiste's duplicity, which assurance had made it easier for him to disappoint her, while the prospect of a business repast with Sir John had helped her to bear the disappointment as a brave woman should. It was true that on the morrow, about lunch-time, Rose Euclid and Carlo Trent might have to live through a few rather trying moments, and they would certainly be very angry; but these drawbacks would have been more than compensated for in advance by the pleasures of hope. And had they not between them pocketed seventy-five pounds which they had stood to lose?

Such reasoning was unanswerable, and his remorse did not attempt to answer it. His remorse was not open to reason; it was one of those stupid, primitive sentiments which obstinately persist in the refined and rational fabric of modern humanity.

He was just sorry for Rose Euclid.

" Do you know what I did? " he burst out confidentially, and confessed the whole telephone trick to Mr. Seven Sachs.

Mr. Seven Sachs, somewhat to Edward Henry's surprise, expressed high admiration of the device.

" A bit mean, though, don't you think? " Edward Henry protested weakly.

" Not at all! " cried Mr. Sachs. " You got the goods on her. And she deserved it."

(Again this enigmatic and mystical word " goods "! But he understood it.)

Thus encouraged, he was now quite determined to give Mr. Seven Sachs a brief episodic account of his career. A fair conversational opening was all he wanted in order to begin.

" I wonder what will happen to her — ultimately? " he said, meaning to work back from the ends of careers to their beginnings, and so to himself.

" Rose Euclid? "

" Yes."

Mr. Sachs shook his head compassionately.

" How did Mr. Bryany get in with her? " asked Edward Henry.

" Bryany is a highly peculiar person," said Mr. Seven Sachs familiarly. " He's all right so long as you don't unstrap him. He was born to convince newspaper reporters of his own greatness."

" I had a bit of talk with him myself," said Edward Henry.

" Oh, yes! He told me all about you."

" But *I* never told him anything about myself," said Edward Henry quickly.

" No, but he has eyes, you know, and ears too. Seems to me the people of the Five Towns do little else of a night but discuss you, Mr. Machin. *I* heard a good bit when *I* was down there, though I don't go about much when I'm on the road. I reckon I could write a whole biography of you."

Edward Henry smiled self-consciously. He was of course enraptured, but at the same time it was disappointing to find Mr. Sachs already so fully informed as to the details of his career. However, he did not intend to let that prevent him from telling the story afresh, in his own manner.

" I suppose you've had your adventures too," he remarked with nonchalance, partly from politeness, but mainly in order to avoid the appearance of hurry in his egotism.

IV.

" You bet I have ! " Mr. Seven Sachs cordially agreed, abandoning the end of a cigarette, putting his hands behind his head, and crossing his legs.

Whereupon there was a brief pause.

" I remember —" Edward Henry began.

" I dare say you've heard —" began Mr. Seven Sachs simultaneously.

They were like two men who by inadvertence had attempted to pass through a narrow doorway abreast. Edward Henry, as the host, drew back.

" I beg your pardon ! " he apologised.

" Not at all," said Seven Sachs. " I was only going to say you've probably heard that I was always up against Archibald Florance."

" Really ! " murmured Edward Henry, impressed in spite of himself; for the renown of Archibald Florance exceeded that of Seven Sachs as the sun the moon, and was older and more securely established than it as the sun the moon. The renown of Rose Euclid was as naught to it. Doubtful it was whether, in the annals of modern histrionics, the grandeur and the romance of that American name could be surpassed by any renown save that of the incomparable Henry Irving. The retirement of Archibald Florance from the stage a couple of years earlier had caused crimson gleams of sunset splendour to shoot across the Atlantic and irradiate even the Garrick Club, London, so that the members thereof had to shade their offended eyes. Edward Henry had never seen Archibald Florance, but it was not necessary to have seen him in order to appreciate the majesty of his glory. No male in the history of the world was ever more photographed, and few have been the subject of more anecdotes.

"I expect he's a wealthy chap in his old age," said Edward Henry.

"Wealthy!" exclaimed Mr. Sachs. "He's the richest actor in America, and that's saying in the world. He had the greatest reputation. He's still the handsomest man in the United States — that's admitted — with his white hair! They used to say he was the cruellest, but it's not so. Though of course he could be a perfect terror with his companies."

"And so you knew Archibald Florance?"

"You bet I did. He never had any friends — never — but I knew him as well as anybody could. Why, in San Francisco, after the show, I've walked with him back to his hotel, and he's walked with me back to mine, and so on, and so on, till three or four o'clock in the morning. You see, we couldn't stop until it happened that he finished a cigar at the exact moment when we got to his hotel door. If the cigar wasn't finished, then he must needs stroll back a bit, and before I knew where

I was he'd be lighting a fresh one. He smoked the finest cigars in America. I remember him telling me they cost him three dollars apiece."

And Edward Henry then perceived another profound truth, his second cardinal discovery on that notable evening; namely, that no matter how high you rise, you will always find that others have risen higher. Nay, it is not until you have achieved a considerable peak that you are able to appreciate the loftiness of those mightier summits. He himself was high, and so he could judge the greater height of Seven Sachs; and it was only through the greater height of Seven Sachs that he could form an adequate idea of the pinnacle occupied by the unique Archibald Florance. Honestly, he had never dreamt that there existed a man who habitually smoked twelve-shilling cigars — and yet he reckoned to know a thing or two about cigars!

" I am nothing! " he thought modestly. Nevertheless, though the savour of the name of Archibald Florance was agreeable, he decided that he had heard enough for the moment about Archibald Florance, and that he would relate to Mr. Sachs the famous episode of his own career in which the Countess of Chell and a mule had so prominently performed.

" I remember —" he recommenced.

" My first encounter with Archibald Florance was very funny," proceeded Mr. Seven Sachs, blandly deaf. " I was starving in New York,— trying to sell a new razor on commission,— and I was de-

termined to get on to the stage. I had one visiting card left — just one. I wrote ' Important ' on
it, and sent it up to Wunch. I don't know whether
you've ever heard of Wunch. Wunch was Archibald Florance's stage-manager, and nearly as famous
as Archibald himself. Well, Wunch sent for me
up-stairs to his room, but when he found I was only
the usual youngster after the usual job he just had
me thrown out of the theatre. He said I'd no
right to put ' Important ' on a visiting card. ' Well,'
I said to myself, ' I'm going to get back into that
theatre somehow! ' So I went up to Archibald's
private house — Sixtieth Street I think it was, and
asked to see him, and I saw him. When I got
into his room, he was writing. He kept on writing
for some minutes, and then he swung round on his
chair.

"' And what can I do for you, sir? ' he said.

"' Do you want any actors, Mr. Florance? ' I
said.

"' Are you an actor? ' he said.

"' I want to be one,' I said.

"' Well,' he said, ' there's a school round the
corner.'

"' Well,' I said, ' you might give me a card of
introduction, Mr. Florance.'

"He gave me the card. I didn't take it to the
school. I went straight back to the theatre with it,
and had it sent up to Wunch. It just said, ' Introducing Mr. Sachs, a young man anxious to get on.'
Wunch took it for a positive order to find me a

place.   The company was full, so he threw out one
poor devil of a super to make room for me.   Curious thing — old Wunchy got it into his head that
I was a *protégé* of Archibald's, and he always looked
after me.   What d'ye think about that?"

"Brilliant!" said Edward Henry.   And it was!
The simplicity of the thing was what impressed him.
Since winning a scholarship at school by altering the
number of marks opposite his name on a paper lying on the master's desk, Edward Henry had never
achieved advancement by a device so simple.   And
he thought: "I am nothing!   The Five Towns
is nothing!   All that one hears about Americans and
the United States is true.   As far as getting on
goes, they can make rings round us.   Still, I shall
tell him about the countess and the mule —"

"Yes," continued Mr. Seven Sachs, "Wunch was
very kind to me.   But he was pretty well down and
out, and he left, and Archibald got a new stage-
manager, and I was promoted to do a bit of assistant stage-managing.   But I got no increase of
salary.   There were two women stars in the play
Archibald was doing then —'The Forty-Niners.'
Romantic drama, you know!   Melodrama you'd
call it over here.   He never did any other sort of
play.   Well, these two women stars were about
equal, and when the curtain fell on the first act
they'd both make a bee-line for Archibald to see
who'd get to him first and engage him in talk.   They
were jealous enough of each other to kill.   Anybody could see that Archibald was frightfully bored.

but he couldn't escape. They got him on both sides, you see, and he just *had* to talk to 'em, both at once. I used to be fussing around fixing the properties for the next act. Well, one night he comes up to me, Archibald does, and he says:

" ' Mr. — what's your name?'

" ' Sachs, sir,' I says.

" ' You notice when those two ladies come up to me after the first act. Well, when you see them talking to me, I want you to come right along and interrupt,' he says.

" ' What shall I say, sir?'

" ' Tap me on the shoulder, and say I'm wanted about something very urgent. You see?'

" So the next night when those women got hold of him, sure enough, I went up between them and tapped him on the shoulder. 'Mr. Florance,' I said, 'something very urgent.' He turned on me and scowled: 'What is it?' he said, and he looked very angry. It was a bit of the best acting the old man ever did in his life. It was so good that at first I thought it was real. He said again louder, 'What is it?' So I said, 'Well, Mr. Florance, the most urgent thing in this theatre is that I should have an increase in salary!' I guess I licked the stuffing out of him that time."

Edward Henry gave vent to one of those cordial and violent guffaws which are a specialty of the humorous side of the Five Towns. And he said to himself: "I should never have thought of anything as good as that."

" And did you get it? " he asked.

" The old man said not a word," Mr. Seven Sachs went on in the same even tranquil smiling voice. " But next pay-day I found I'd got a rise of ten dollars a week. And not only that, but Mr. Florance offered me a singing part in his new drama, if I could play the mandolin. I naturally told him I'd played the mandolin all my life. I went out and bought a mandolin and hired a teacher. He wanted to teach me the mandolin, but I only wanted him to teach me that one accompaniment. So I fired him, and practised by myself night and day for a week. I got through all the rehearsals without ever singing that song. Cleverest dodging I ever did! On the first night I was so nervous I could scarcely hold the mandolin. I'd never played the infernal thing before anybody at all — only up in my bedroom. I struck the first chord, and found the darned instrument was all out of tune with the orchestra. So I just pretended to play it, and squawked away with my song, and never let my fingers touch the strings at all. Old Florance was waiting for me in the wings. I knew he was going to fire me. But no! ' Sachs,' he said, ' that accompaniment was the most delicate piece of playing I ever heard. I congratulate you.' He was quite serious. Everybody said the same! Luck, eh? "

" I should say so," said Edward Henry, gradually beginning to be interested in the odyssey of Mr. Seven Sachs. " I remember a funny thing that happened to me —"

"However," Mr. Sachs swept smoothly along, "that piece was a failure. And Archibald arranged to take a company to Europe with 'Forty-Niners.' And I was left out! This rattled me, specially after the way he liked my mandolin-playing. So I went to see him about it in his dressing-room one night, and I charged around a bit. He did rattle me! Then I rattled him. I would get an answer out of him. He said:

"'I'm not in the habit of being cross-examined in my own dressing-room.'

"I didn't care what happened then, so I said:

"'And I'm not in the habit of being treated as you're treating me.'

"All of a sudden he became quite quiet, and patted me on the shoulder. 'You're getting on very well, Sachs,' he said. 'You've only been at it one year. It's taken me twenty-five years to get where I am.'

"However, I was too angry to stand for that sort of talk. I said to him:

"'I dare say you're a very great and enviable man, Mr. Florance, but I propose to save fifteen years on your twenty-five. I'll equal or better your position in ten years.'

"He shoved me out — just shoved me out of the room. . . . It was that that made me turn to play-writing. Florance wrote his own plays sometimes, but it was only his acting and his face that saved them. And they were too American. He never did really well outside America except in one play, and that wasn't his own. Now, I was out after money. And I still am. I wanted to please the largest possible public. So I guessed there was nothing for it but the universal appeal. I never write a play that won't appeal to England, Germany, France, just as well as to America. America's big, but it isn't big enough for me. . . . Well, as I was saying, soon after that I got a one-act play produced at Hannibal, Missouri. And the same week there was a company at another theatre there playing the old man's 'Forty-Niners.' And the next morning the theatrical critic's article in the Hannibal *Courier-Post* was headed: 'Rival attractions. Archibald Florance's "Forty-Niners" and new play by Seven Sachs.' I cut that heading out and sent it to the old man in London, and I wrote under it, 'See how far I've got in six months.' When he came back he took me into his company again. . . . What price that, eh?"

Edward Henry could only nod his head. The customarily silent Seven Sachs had little by little subdued him to an admiration as mute as it was profound.

"Nearly five years after that I got a Christmas card from old Florance. It had the usual printed wishes,—'Merriest possible Christmas, and so on,'—but underneath that Archibald had written in pencil, 'You've still five years to go.' That made me roll my sleeves up, as you may say. Well, a long time after that I was standing at the corner of Broadway and Forty-fourth Street, and looking at my own name in electric letters on the Criterion Theatre. First time I'd ever seen it in electric letters on Broadway. It was the first night of 'Overheard.' Florance was playing at the Hudson Theatre, which is a bit higher up Forty-fourth Street, and *his* name was in electric letters too, but further off Broadway than mine. I strolled up, just out of idle curiosity, and there the old man was standing in the porch of the theatre, all alone! 'Hullo, Sachs,' he said, 'I'm glad I've seen you. It's saved me twenty-five cents.' I asked how. He said, 'I was just going to send you a telegram of congratulations.' He liked me, old Archibald did. He still does. But I hadn't done with him. I went to stay with him at his house on Long Island in the spring. 'Excuse me, Mr. Florance,' I says to him. 'How many companies have you got on the road?' He said, 'Oh! I haven't got many now. Five, I think.' 'Well,' I says. 'I've got six here in the United States, two in England, three in Austria, and one in Italy.' He said, 'Have a cigar, Sachs; you've got the goods on me!' He was living in that magnificent house all alone, with a whole regiment of servants."

v.

"Well," said Edward Henry, "you're a great man!"

"No, I'm not," said Mr. Seven Sachs. "But my income is four hundred thousand dollars a year, and rising. I'm out after the stuff, that's all."

"I say you are a great man!" Edward Henry repeated. Mr. Sachs' recital had inspired him. He kept saying to himself: "And I'm a great man too. And I'll show 'em."

Mr. Sachs, having delivered himself of his load, had now lapsed comfortably back into his original silence, and was prepared to listen. But Edward Henry somehow had lost the desire to enlarge on his own variegated past. He was absorbed in the greater future.

At length he said very distinctly:

"You honestly think I could run a theatre?"

"You were born to run a theatre," said Seven Sachs.

Thrilled, Edward Henry responded:

"Then I'll write to those lawyer people, Slossons, and tell 'em I'll be around with the brass about eleven to-morrow."

Mr. Sachs rose. A clock had delicately chimed two.

"If ever you come to New York, and I can do anything for you —" said Mr. Sachs heartily.

"Thanks," said Edward Henry. They were shaking hands. "I say," Edward Henry went on, "there's one thing I want to ask you. Why *did* you promise to back Rose Euclid and her friends? You must surely have known —" He threw up his hands.

Mr. Sachs answered:

"I'll be frank with you. It was her cousin that persuaded me into it — Elsie April."

" Elsie April? Who's she? "

" Oh! You must have seen them about together — her and Rose Euclid. They're nearly always together."

" I saw her in the restaurant here to-day with a rather jolly girl — blue hat."

" That's the one. As soon as you've made her acquaintance you'll understand what I mean," said Mr. Seven Sachs.

" Ah! But I'm not a bachelor like you," Edward Henry smiled archly.

" Well, you'll see when you meet her," said Mr. Sachs. Upon which enigmatic warning he departed, and was lost in the immense glittering nocturnal silence of Wilkins's.

Edward Henry sat down to write to Slossons by the three A. M. post. But as he wrote he kept saying to himself: " So Elsie April's her name, is it? And she actually persuaded Sachs — Sachs — to make a fool of himself! "

CHAPTER VI

LORD WOLDO AND LADY WOLDO

I.

THE next morning Joseph, having opened wide the window, informed his master that the weather was bright and sunny, and Edward Henry arose with just that pleasant degree of fatigue which persuades one that one is, if anything, rather more highly vitalised than usual. He sent for Mr. Bryany, as for a domestic animal, and Mr. Bryany, ceremoniously attired, was received by a sort of jolly king who happened to be trimming his beard in the royal bathroom, but who was too good-natured to keep Mr. Bryany waiting. It is remarkable how the habit of royalty, having once taken root, will flourish in the minds of quite unmonarchical persons. Edward Henry first enquired after the health of Mr. Seven Sachs, and then obtained from Mr. Bryany all remaining papers and trifles of information concerning the affair of the option. Whereupon Mr. Bryany, apparently much elated by the honour of an informal reception, effusively retired. And Edward Henry too was so elated, and his faith in life so renewed and invigorated that he said to himself:

" It might be worth while to shave my beard off
after all! "

As in his electric brougham he drove along muddy
and shining Piccadilly, he admitted that Joseph's account of the weather had been very accurate. The
weather was magnificent; it presented the best features of summer combined with the salutary pun-
gency of autumn. And flags were flying over the
establishments of tobacconists, soothsayers, and in-
surance companies in Piccadilly. And the sense of
empire was in the very air, like an intoxication.
And there was no place like London. When, however, having run through Piccadilly into streets less
superb, he reached the Majestic, it seemed to him
that the Majestic was not a part of London, but a
bit of the provinces surrounded by London. He
was very disappointed with the Majestic, and took
his letters from the clerk with careless condescen-
sion. In a few days the Majestic had sunk from
being one of " London's huge caravanserais " to the
level of a swollen Turk's Head. So fragile are reputations!

From the Majestic, Edward Henry drove back
into the regions of Empire, between Piccadilly and
Regent Street, and deigned to call upon his tailors.
A morning suit which he had commanded being
miraculously finished, he put it on, and was at once
not only spectacularly but morally regenerated.
The old suit, though it had cost five guineas in its
time, looked a paltry and a dowdy thing as it lay,
flung down anyhow, on one of Messrs. Quayther and

Cuthering's cane chairs in the mirrored cubicle where baronets and even peers showed their braces to the benign Mr. Cuthering.

" I want to go to Piccadilly Circus now. Stop at the fountain," said Edward Henry to his chauffeur. He gave the order somewhat defiantly, because he was a little self-conscious in the new and gleaming suit, and because he had an absurd idea that the chauffeur might guess that he, a provincial from the Five Towns, was about to venture into West End theatrical enterprise, and sneer at him accordingly.

But the chauffeur merely touched his cap with an indifferent lofty gesture, as if to say:

" Be at ease. I have driven more persons more moonstruck even than you. Human eccentricity has long since ceased to surprise me."

The fountain in Piccadilly Circus was the gayest thing in London. It mingled the fresh tingling of water with the odour and flame of autumn blossoms and the variegated colours of shawled women who passed their lives on its margin engaged in the commerce of flowers. Edward Henry bought an aster from a fine, bold, red-cheeked, blowsy, dirty wench with a baby in her arms, and left some change for the baby. He was in a very tolerant and charitable mood, and could excuse the sins and the stupidity of all mankind. He reflected forgivingly that Rose Euclid and her friends had perhaps not displayed an abnormal fatuity in discussing the name of the theatre before they had got the lease of the

site for it. Had not he himself bought all the option without having even seen the site? The fact
was that he had had no leisure in his short royal
career for such details as seeing the site. He was
now about to make good the omission.

It is a fact that as he turned northward from
Piccadilly Circus, to the right of the County Fire
Office, in order to spy out the land upon which his
theatre was to be built, he hesitated, under the
delusion that all the passers-by were staring at him!
He felt just as he might have felt had he been engaged upon some scheme nefarious. He even went
back and pretended to examine the windows of the
County Fire Office. Then, glancing self-consciously
about, he discerned — not unnaturally — the words
" Regent Street " on a sign.

" There you are! " he murmured with a thrill.
" There you are! There's obviously only one name
for that theatre —' The Regent.' It's close to
Regent Street. No other theatre is called ' The
Regent.' Nobody before ever had the idea of
' Regent ' as a name for a theatre. ' Muses ' indeed! . . . ' Intellectual! ' . . . ' The Regent Theatre! ' How well it comes off the tongue! It's
a great name! It'll be the finest name of any theatre in London! And it took yours truly to think
of it! "

Then he smiled privately at his own weakness.
. . . He too, like the despised Rose, was baptising
the unborn! Still, he continued to dream of the
theatre, and began to picture to himself the ideal

theatre. He discovered that he had quite a number of startling ideas about theatre-construction,
based on his own experience as a playgoer.

When, with new courage, he directed his feet towards the site, upon which he knew there was an
old chapel known as Queen's Glasshouse Chapel,
whose ownership had slipped from the nerveless
hand of a dying sect of dissenters, he could not
find the site, and he could not see the chapel. For
an instant he was perturbed by a horrid suspicion
that he had been victimised by a gang of swindlers
posing as celebrated persons. Everything was possible in this world and century. None of the people who had appeared in the transaction had resembled his previous conceptions of such people!
And confidence-thieves always operated in the
grandest hotels! He immediately decided that if
the sequel should prove him to be a simpleton and
gull he would at any rate be a silent simpleton and
gull. He would stoically bear the loss of two
hundred pounds, and breathe no word of woe.

But then he remembered with relief that he had
genuinely recognised both Rose Euclid and Seven
Sachs; and also that Mr. Bryany, among other
documents, had furnished him with a photograph
of the chapel and surrounding property. The
chapel therefore existed. He had a plan in his
pocket. He now opened this plan and tried to
consult it in the middle of the street, but his agitation was such that he could not make out on it
which was north and which was south. After he

had been nearly prostrated by a taxicab, a policeman
came up to him and said with all the friendly disdain
of a London policeman addressing a provincial:

" Safer to look at that on the pavement, sir!"

Edward Henry glanced up from the plan.

" I was trying to find the Queen's Glasshouse
Chapel, Officer," said he. " Have you ever heard
of it?" (In Bursley, members of the town council
always flattered members of the force by addressing
them as " Officer "; and Edward Henry knew exactly the effective intonation.)

" It *was there,* sir," said the policeman, less disdainful, pointing to a narrow hoarding behind which
could be seen the back walls of high buildings in
Shaftesbury Avenue. " They've just finished pulling it down."

" Thank you," said Edward Henry quietly, with
a superb and successful effort to keep as much colour
in his face as if the policeman had not dealt him a
dizzying blow.

He then walked towards the hoarding, but could
scarcely feel the ground under his feet. From a
wide aperture in the palisades a cartful of earth
was emerging; it creaked and shook as it was
dragged by a labouring horse over loose planks into
the roadway; a whip-cracking carter hovered on its
flank. Edward Henry approached the aperture and
gazed within. An elegant young man stood solitary
inside the hoarding and stared at a razed expanse
of land in whose furthest corner some navvies were
digging a hole. . . .

The site!

But what did this sinister destructive activity mean? Nobody was entitled to interfere with property on which he, Alderman Machin, held an unexpired option! But was it the site? He perused the plan again with more care. Yes, there could be no doubt that it was the site. His eye roved round, and he admitted the justice of the boast that an electric sign displayed at the southern front corner of the theatre would be visible from Piccadilly Circus, lower Regent Street, Shaftesbury Avenue, etc. He then observed a large notice-board, raised on posts above the hoardings, and read the following:

Site
of the
First New Thought Church
to be opened next Spring.
Subscriptions invited.
Rollo Wrissell, Senior Trustee.
Ralph Alloyd, Architect.
Dicks and Pato, Builders.

The name of Rollo Wrissell seemed familiar to him, and after a few moments' searching he recalled that Rollo Wrissell was one of the trustees and executors of the late Lord Woldo, the other being the widow, and the mother of the new Lord Woldo. In addition to the lettering, the notice-board held a graphic representation of the First New Thought Church as it would be when completed.

"Well," said Edward Henry, not perhaps un-justifiably, "this really is a bit thick! Here I've got an option on a plot of land for building a theatre, and somebody else has taken it to put up a church!"

He ventured inside the hoarding, and, addressing the elegant young man, asked:

"You got anything to do with this, Mister?"

"Well," said the young man, smiling humor-ously, "I'm the architect. It's true that nobody ever pays any attention to an architect in these days."

"Oh! You're Mr. Alloyd?"

"I am."

Mr. Alloyd had black hair, intensely black, changeful eyes, and the expressive mouth of an actor.

"I thought they were going to build a theatre here," said Edward Henry.

"I wish they had been!" said Mr. Alloyd. "I'd just like to design a theatre! But of course I shall never get the chance."

"Why not?"

"I know I sha'n't," Mr. Alloyd insisted with gloomy disgust. "Only obtained this job by sheer accident! . . . You got any ideas about theatres?"

"Well, I have," said Edward Henry.

Mr. Alloyd turned on him with a sardonic and half-benevolent gleam.

"And what are your ideas about theatres?"

"Well," said Edward Henry, "I should like to meet an architect who had thoroughly got it into his head that when people pay for seats to see a play they want to be able to *see* it, and not just get a look at it now and then over other people's heads and round corners of boxes and things.   In most theatres that I've been in, the architects seemed to think that iron pillars and wooden heads are transparent.   Either that, or the architects were rascals. Same with hearing.   The pit costs half a crown, and you don't pay half a crown to hear glasses rattled in a bar, or motor-omnibuses rushing down the street.   I was never yet in a London theatre where the architect had really understood that what the people in the pit wanted to hear was the play, and nothing but the play."

"You're rather hard on us," said Mr. Alloyd.

"Not so hard as you are on *us!*" said Edward Henry.   "And then draughts!   I suppose you think a draught on the back of the neck is good for us! . . . But of course you'll say all this has nothing to do with architecture!"

"Oh, no, I sha'n't!   Oh, no, I sha'n't!" exclaimed Mr. Alloyd.   "I quite agree with you!"

"You *do?*"

"Certainly.   You seem to be interested in theatres?"

"I am a bit."

"You come from the North?"

"No, I don't," said Edward Henry.   Mr. Alloyd had no right to be aware that he was not a Londoner.·

"I beg your pardon."

"I come from the Midlands."

"Oh! . . . Have you seen the Russian ballet?"

Edward Henry had not, nor heard of it. "Why?" he asked.

"Nothing," said Mr. Alloyd. "Only I saw it the night before last in Paris. You never saw such dancing. It's enchanted — enchanted! The most lovely thing I ever saw in my life. I couldn't sleep for it. Not that I ever sleep very well! I merely thought, as you were interested in theatres — and Midland people are so enterprising! . . . Have a cigarette?"

Edward Henry, who had begun to feel sympathetic, was somewhat repelled by these odd last remarks. After all the man, though human enough, was an utter stranger.

"No, thanks," he said. "And so you're going to put up a church here?"

"Yes."

"Well, I wonder whether you are."

He walked abruptly away under Alloyd's riddling stare, and he could almost hear the man saying, "Well, he's a queer lot, if you like."

At the corner of the site, below the spot where his electric sign was to have been, he was stopped by a well-dressed middle aged lady who bore a bundle of papers.

"Will you buy a paper for the cause?" she suggested in a pleasant, persuasive tone. "One penny."

He obeyed, and she handed him a small blue-printed periodical of which the title was, *Azure,*

" the Organ of the New Thought Church." He glanced at it, puzzled, and then at the middle-aged lady.

" Every penny of profit goes to the Church-Building Fund," she said, as if in defence of her action.

Edward Henry burst out laughing; but it was a nervous, half-hysterical laugh that he laughed.

II.

In Carey Street, Lincoln's Inn Fields, he descended from his brougham in front of the offices of Messrs. Slosson, Hodge, Budge, Slosson, Maveringham, Slosson, and Vulto, Solicitors, known in the profession by the compendious abbreviation of Slossons. Edward Henry, having been a lawyer's clerk some twenty-five years earlier, was aware of Slossons. Although on the strength of his youthful clerkship he claimed, and was admitted, to possess a very special knowledge of the law,— enough to silence argument when his opponent did not happen to be an actual solicitor,— he did not in truth possess a very special knowledge of the law,— how should he, seeing that he had only been a practitioner of short-hand? — but the fame of Slosson he positively was acquainted with! He had even written letters to the mighty Slossons.

Every lawyer and lawyer's clerk in the realm knew the greatness of Slossons, and crouched before it, and also, for the most part, impugned its right-eousness with sneers. For Slossons acted for the ruling classes of England, who only get value for their money when they are buying something that they can see, smell, handle, or intimidate — such as a horse, a motor-car, a dog, or a lackey. Slossons, those crack solicitors, like the crack nerve specialists in Harley Street and the crack fortune-tellers in Bond Street, sold their invisible, inodorous, and intangible wares of advice at double, treble, or decuple their worth, according to the psychology of the customer. They were great bullies. And they were, further, great money-lenders — on behalf of their wealthier clients. In obedience to a convenient theory that it is imprudent to leave money too long in one place, they were continually calling in mortgages and re-lending the sums so collected on fresh investments, thus achieving two bills of costs on each transaction, and sometimes three, besides employing an army of valuers, surveyors, and mortgage-insurance brokers. In short, Slossons had nothing to learn about the art of self-enrichment.

Three vast motor-cars waited in front of their ancient door, and Edward Henry's hired electric vehicle was diminished to a trifle.

He began by demanding the senior partner, who was denied to him by an old clerk with a face like a stone wall. Only his brutal Midland insistence, and the mention of the important letter which he had written to the firm in the middle of the night, saved him from the ignominy of seeing no partner at all. At the end of the descending ladder of partners he clung desperately to Mr. Vulto, and he saw Mr. Vulto — a youngish and sarcastic person with blue eyes, lodged in a dark room at the back of the house. It occurred fortunately that his letter had been allotted to precisely Mr. Vulto for the purpose of being answered.

"You got my letter?" said Edward Henry cheerfully as he sat down at Mr. Vulto's flat desk on the side opposite from Mr. Vulto.

"We got it, but frankly we cannot make head or tail of it! . . . *What* option?" Mr. Vulto's manner was crudely sarcastic.

"*This* option!" said Edward Henry, drawing papers from his pocket and putting down the right paper in front of Mr. Vulto with an uncompromising slap.

Mr. Vulto picked up the paper with precautions, as if it were a contagion, and, assuming eye-glasses, perused it with his mouth open.

"We know nothing of this," said Mr. Vulto, and it was as though he had added, "Therefore this does not exist." He glanced with sufferance at the window, which offered a close-range view of a whitewashed wall.

"Then you weren't in the confidence of your client?"

"The late Lord Woldo?"

"Yes."

"Pardon me."

"Obviously you weren't in his confidence as regards this particular matter."

"As you say," said Mr. Vulto with frigid irony.

"Well, what are you going to do about it?"

"Well — nothing." Mr. Vulto removed his eye-glasses and stood up.

"Well, good morning. I'll walk round to *my* solicitors." Edward Henry seized the option.

"That will be simpler," said Mr. Vulto. Slossons much preferred to deal with lawyers than with laymen, because it increased costs and vitalised the profession.

At that moment a stout, red-faced, and hoary man puffed very authoritatively into the room.

"Vulto," he cried sharply, "Mr. Wrissell's here. Didn't they tell you?"

"Yes, Mr. Slosson," answered Vulto, suddenly losing all his sarcastic quality and becoming a very junior partner. "I was just engaged with Mr. — " (he paused to glance at his desk)—"Machin, whose singular letter we received this morning about an alleged option on the lease of the chapel-site at Piccadilly Circus — the Woldo estate, sir. You remember, sir?"

"This the man?" enquired Mr. Slosson, ex-president of the Law Society, with a jerk of the thumb.

Edward Henry said: "This is the man."

"Well," said Mr. Slosson, lifting his chin and still puffing, "it would be extremely interesting to hear his story, at any rate. I was just telling Mr. Wrissell about it. Come this way, sir. I've heard some strange things in my time, but — " He stopped. "Please follow me, sir," he ordained.

"I'm dashed if I'll follow you!" Edward Henry

desired to say, but he had not the courage to say it. And because he was angry with himself he determined to make matters as unpleasant as possible for the innocent Mr. Slosson, who was used to bullying, and so well paid for bullying, that really no blame could be apportioned to him. It would have been as reasonable to censure an ordinary person for breathing as to censure Mr. Slosson for bullying. And so Edward Henry was steeling himself: " I'll do him in the eye for that, even if it costs me every cent I've got." (A statement characterised by poetical licence!)

III.

Mr. Slosson, senior, heard Edward Henry's story, but seemingly did not find it quite as interesting as he had prophesied it would be. When Edward Henry had finished the old man drummed on an enormous table, and said:

" Yes, yes. And then? " His manner was far less bullying than in the room of Mr. Vulto.

" It's your turn now, Mr. Slosson," said Edward Henry.

" My turn? How? "

" To go on with the story." He glanced at the clock. " I've brought it up to date — eleven fifteen o'clock this morning, *anno domini.*" And as Mr. Slosson continued to drum on the table and to look out of the window, Edward Henry also drummed on the table and looked out of the window.

The chamber of the senior partner was a very

different matter from Mr. Vulto's. It was immense.
It was not disfigured by japanned boxes inartistically
lettered in white, as are most lawyers' offices. Indeed, in aspect it resembled one of the cosier rooms
in a small and decaying but still comfortable club.
It had easy chairs and cigar-boxes. Moreover, the
sun got into it, and there was a view of the comic
yet stately Victorian Gothic of the Law Courts.
The sun enheartened Edward Henry. And he felt
secure in an unimpugnable suit of clothes; in the
shape of his collar, the colour of his necktie, the
style of his creaseless boots; and in the protuberance
of his pocketbook in his pocket.

As Mr. Slosson had failed to notice the competition of his drumming, he drummed still louder.
Whereupon Mr. Slosson stopped drumming. Edward Henry gazed amiably around. Right at the
back of the room, before a back window that gave
on the whitewashed wall, a man was rapidly putting
his signature to a number of papers. But Mr. Slosson had ignored the existence of this man, treating
him apparently as a figment of the disordered brain,
or as an optical illusion.

" I've nothing to say," said Mr. Slosson.

" Or to do? "

" Or to do."

" Well, Mr. Slosson," said Edward Henry, " your
junior partner has already outlined your policy of
masterly inactivity. So I may as well go. I did
say I'd go to my solicitors; but it's occurred to me
that as I'm a principal I may as well first of all see

the principals on the other side. I only came here because it mentions in the option that the matter is to be completed here; that's all."

" You a principal! " exclaimed Mr. Slosson. " It seems to me you're a long way removed from a principal. The alleged option is given to a Miss Rose Euclid."

" Excuse me — *the* Miss Rose Euclid."

" Miss Rose Euclid. She divides up her alleged interest into fractions and sells them here and there, and you buy them up one after another." Mr. Slosson laughed, not unamiably. " You're a principal about five times removed."

" Well," said Edward Henry, " whatever I am, I have a sort of idea I'll go and see this Mr. Gristle or Wrissell. Can you —"

The man at the distant desk turned his head. Mr. Slosson coughed. The man rose.

" This is Mr. Wrissell," said Mr. Slosson with a gesture from which confusion was not absent.

" Good morning," said the advancing Mr. Rollo Wrissell, and he said it with an accent more Kensingtonian than any accent that Edward Henry had ever heard. His lounging and yet elegant walk assorted well with the accent. His black clothes were loose and untidy. Such boots as his could not have been worn by Edward Henry even in the Five Towns without blushing shame, and his necktie looked as if a baby or a puppy had been playing with it. Nevertheless, these shortcomings made absolutely no difference whatever to the impressiveness of Mr. Rollo

Wrissell, who was famous for having said once: " I put on whatever comes to hand first, and people don't seem to mind."

Mr. Rollo Wrissell belonged to one of the seven great families which once governed — and, by the way, still do govern — England, Scotland, and Ireland. The members of these families may be divided into two species: those who rule, and those who are too lofty in spirit even to rule — those who exist. Mr. Rollo Wrissell belonged to the latter species. His nose and mouth had the exquisite refinement of the descendant of generations of art-collectors and poet-patronisers. He enjoyed life, but not with rude activity, like the grosser members of the ruling caste, rather with a certain rare languor. He sniffed and savoured the whole spherical surface of the apple of life with those delicate nostrils rather than bit into it. His one conviction was that in a properly managed world nothing ought to occur to disturb or agitate the perfect tranquillity of his existing. And this conviction was so profound, so visible even in his lightest gesture and glance, that it exerted a mystic influence over the entire social organism, with the result that practically nothing ever did occur to disturb or agitate the perfect tranquillity of Mr. Rollo Wrissell's existing. For Mr. Rollo Wrissell the world was indeed almost ideal.

Edward Henry breathed to himself:
" This is the genuine article."
And, being an Englishman, he was far more im-

pressed by Mr. Wrissell than he had been by the much vaster reputations of Rose Euclid, Seven Sachs, Mr. Slosson, senior. At the same time he inwardly fought against Mr. Wrissell's silent and unconscious dominion over him, and all the defiant Midland belief that one body is as good as anybody else surged up in him — but stopped at his lips.

"Please don't rise," Mr. Wrissell entreated, waving both hands. " I'm very sorry to hear of this unhappy complication," he went on to Edward Henry with the most adorable and winning politeness. "It pains me." (His martyred expression said: "And really I ought not to be pained.") " I'm quite convinced that you are here in absolute good faith — the most absolute good faith, Mr.—"

"Machin," suggested Mr. Slosson.

"Ah! Pardon me, Mr. Machin. "And, naturally, in the management of enormous estates such as Lord Woldo's little difficulties are apt to occur. . . . I'm sorry you've been put in a false position. You have all my sympathies. But of course you understand that in this particular case. . . . I myself have taken up the lease from the estate. I happen to be interested in a great movement. The plans of my church have been passed by the county council. Building operations have indeed begun."

"Oh, chuck it!" said Edward Henry inexcusably — but such were his words. A surfeit of Mr. Wrissell's calm egotism and accent and fatigued harmonious gestures drove him to commit this outrage upon the very fabric of civilisation.

Mr. Wrissell, if he had ever met with the phrase, — which is doubtful,— had certainly never heard it addressed to himself; conceivably he might have once come across it in turning over the pages of a slang dictionary. A tragic expression traversed his bewildered features; and then he recovered himself somewhat.

"I —"

"Go and bury yourself!" said Edward Henry, with increased savagery.

Mr. Wrissell, having comprehended, went. He really did go. He could not tolerate scenes, and his glance showed that any forcible derangement of his habit of existing smoothly would nakedly disclose the unyielding adamantine selfishness that was the basis of the Wrissell philosophy. His glance was at least harsh and bitter. He went in silence, and rapidly. Mr. Slosson, senior, followed him at a great pace.

Edward Henry was angry. Strange though it may seem, the chief cause of his anger was the fact that his own manners and breeding were lower, coarser, clumsier, more brutal, than Mr. Wrissell's.

After what appeared to be a considerable absence Mr. Slosson, senior, returned into the room. Edward Henry, steeped in peculiar meditations, was repeating:

"So this is Slosson's!"

"What's that?" demanded Mr. Slosson with a challenge in his ancient but powerful voice.

"Nowt!" said Edward Henry.

" Now, sir," said Mr. Slosson, " we'd better come
to an understanding about this so-called option.   It's
not serious, you know."

" You'll find it is."

" It's not commercial."

" I fancy it is — for me! " said Edward Henry.

" The premium mentioned is absurdly inadequate,
and the ground-rent is quite improperly low."

" That's just why I look on it as commercial —
from my point of view," said Edward Henry.

" It isn't worth the paper it's written on," said
Mr. Slosson.

" Why? "

" Because, seeing the unusual form of it, it ought
to be stamped, and it isn't stamped."

" Listen here, Mr. Slosson," said Edward Henry,
" I want you to remember that you're talking to a
lawyer."

" A lawyer? "

" I was in the law for years," said Edward Henry.
" And you know as well as I do that I can get the
option stamped at any time by paying a penalty,
which at worst will be a trifle compared to the value
of the option."

" Ah! "   Mr. Slosson paused, and resumed his
puffing, which exercise — perhaps owing to undue
excitement — he had pretermitted.   " Then further,
the deed isn't drawn up."

" That's not my fault."

" Further, the option is not transferable."

" We shall see about that."

" And the money ought to be paid down to-day, even on your own showing — every cent of it, in cash."

" Here is the money," said Edward Henry, drawing his pocketbook from his breast. " Every cent of it, in the finest brand of bank-notes! "

He flung down the notes with the impulsive gesture of an artist; then, with the caution of a man of the world, gathered them in again.

" The whole circumstances under which the alleged option is alleged to have been given would have to be examined," said Mr. Slosson.

" *I* sha'n't mind," said Edward Henry; " others might."

" There is such a thing as undue influence."

" Miss Euclid is fifty if she's a day," replied Edward Henry.

" I don't see what Miss Euclid's age has to do with the matter."

" Then your eyesight must be defective, Mr. Slosson."

" The document might be a forgery."

" It might. But I've got an autograph letter written entirely in the last Lord Woldo's hand, enclosing the option."

" Let me see it, please."

" Certainly, but in a court of law," said Edward Henry. " You know you're hungry for a good action, followed by a bill of costs as long as from here to Jericho."

" Mr. Wrissell will assuredly fight," said Mr.

Slosson. "He has already given me the most explicit instructions. Mr. Wrissell's objection to a certain class of theatres is well-known."

"And does Mr. Wrissell settle everything?"

"Mr. Wrissell and Lady Woldo settle everything between them, and Lady Woldo is guided by Mr. Wrissell. There is an impression abroad that because Lady Woldo was originally connected — er — with the stage, she and Mr. Wrissell are not entirely at one in the conduct of her and her son's interests. Nothing could be further from the fact."

Edward Henry's thoughts dwelt for a few moments upon the late Lord Woldo's picturesque and far-resounding marriage.

"Can you give me Lady Woldo's address?"

"I can't," said Mr. Slosson after an instant's hesitation.

"You mean you won't!"

Mr. Slosson pursed his lips.

"Well, you can do the other thing!" said Edward Henry, insolent to the last.

As he left the premises he found Mr. Rollo Wrissell and his own new acquaintance, Mr. Alloyd, the architect, chatting in the portico. Mr. Wrissell was calm, bland, and attentive; Mr. Alloyd was eager, excited, and deferential.

Edward Henry caught the words "Russian ballet." He reflected upon an abstract question oddly disconnected with the violent welter of his sensations: "Can a man be a good practical architect who isn't able to sleep because he's seen a Russian ballet? "

The alert chauffeur of the electric brougham, who had an excellent idea of effect, brought the admirable vehicle to the curb exactly in front of Edward Henry as Edward Henry reached the edge of the pavement. Ejaculating a brief command, Edward Henry disappeared within the vehicle, and was whirled away in a style whose perfection no scion of a governing family could have bettered.

IV.

The next scene in the exciting drama of Edward Henry's existence that day took place in a building as huge as Wilkins's itself. As the brougham halted at its portals an old and medalled man rushed forth, touched his cap, and assisted Edward Henry to alight. Within the groined and echoing hall of the establishment a young boy sprang out and, with every circumstance of deference, took Edward Henry's hat and stick. Edward Henry then walked a few steps to a lift, and said " Smoking-room! " to another menial, who bowed humbly before him, and at the proper moment bowed him out of the lift. Edward Henry, crossing a marble floor, next entered an enormous marble apartment chiefly populated by easy chairs and tables. He sat down to a table, and fiercely rang a bell which reposed thereon. Several other menials simultaneously appeared out of invisibility, and one of them hurried obsequiously towards him.

" Bring me a glass of water and a peerage," said Edward Henry.

" I beg pardon, sir.   A glass of water and ——"

" A peerage.   P double e-r-a-g-e."

" I beg your pardon, sir.   I didn't catch.   Which peerage, sir?   We have several."

" All of them."

In a hundred seconds, the last menial having thanked him for kindly taking the glass and the pile of books, Edward Henry was sipping water and studying peerages.   In two hundred seconds he was off again.   A menial opened the swing-doors of the smoking-room for him, and bowed.   The menial of the lift bowed, wafted him downwards, and bowed.   The infant menial produced his hat and stick and bowed.   The old and medalled menial summoned his brougham with a frown at the chauffeur and a smile at Edward Henry, bowed, opened the door of the brougham, helped Edward Henry in, bowed, and shut the door.

" Where to, sir? "

" 262 Eaton Square," said Edward Henry.

" Thank you, sir," said the aged menial, and repeated in a curt and peremptory voice to the chauffeur, " 262 Eaton Square! "   Lastly he touched his cap.

And Edward Henry swiftly left the precincts of the headquarters of political democracy in London.

V.

As he came within striking distance of 262 Eaton Square he had the advantage of an unusual and brilliant spectacle.

Lord Woldo was one of the richest human beings in England — and incidentally he was very human. If he had been in a position to realise all his assets and go to America with the ready money, his wealth was such that even amid the luxurious society of Pittsburg he could have cut quite a figure for some time. He owned a great deal of the land between Oxford Street and Regent Street, and again a number of the valuable squares north of Oxford Street were his, and as for Edgware Road — just as auctioneers advertise a couple of miles of trout-stream or salmon-river as a pleasing adjunct to a country estate, so, had Lord Woldo's estate come under the hammer, a couple of miles of Edgware Road might have been advertised as among its charms. Lord Woldo owned four theatres, and to each theatre he had his private entrance, and in each theatre his private box, over which the management had no sway. The Woldos in their leases had always insisted on this.

He never built in London; his business was to let land for others to build upon, the condition being that what others built should ultimately belong to him. Thousands of people in London were only too delighted to build on these terms: he could pick and choose his builders. (The astute Edward Henry

himself, for example, wanted furiously to build for
him, and was angry because obstacles stood in the
path of his desire.)   It was constantly happening
that under legal agreements some fine erection put
up by another hand came into the absolute possession of Lord Woldo without one halfpenny of expense to Lord Woldo.   Now and then a whole
street would thus tumble all complete into his hands.
The system, most agreeable for Lord Woldo and
about a dozen other landlords in London, was called
the leasehold system; and when Lord Woldo became the proprietor of some bricks and mortar that
had cost him nothing, it was said that one of Lord
Woldo's leases had " fallen in," and everybody was
quite satisfied by this phrase.

In the provinces, besides castles, forests, and
moors, Lord Woldo owned many acres of land
under which was coal, and he allowed enterprising
persons to dig deep for this coal, and often explode
themselves to death in the adventure, on the understanding that they paid him sixpence for every ton
of coal brought to the surface, whether they made
any profit on it or not.   This arrangement was
called " mining rights "— another phrase that apparently satisfied everybody.

It might be thought that Lord Woldo was, as
they say, on velvet.   But the velvet, if it could be so
described, was not of so rich and comfortable a
pile after all; for Lord Woldo's situation involved
many and heavy responsibilities, and was surrounded
by grave dangers.   He was the representative of an

old order going down in the unforeseeable welter of twentieth-century politics.   Numbers of thoughtful students of English conditions spent much of their time in wondering what would happen one day to the Lord Woldos of England.   And when a really great strike came, and a dozen ex-artisans met in a private room of a West End hotel and decided, without consulting Lord Woldo, or the Prime Minister, or anybody, that the commerce of the country should be brought to a standstill, these thoughtful students perceived that even Lord Woldo's situation was no more secure than other people's; in fact, that it was rather less so.

There could be no doubt that the circumstances of Lord Woldo furnished him with food for thought, and very indigestible food too. . . . Why, at least one hundred sprightly female creatures were being brought up in the hope of marrying him.   And they would all besiege him, and he could only marry one of them — at once!

Now, as Edward Henry stopped as near to No. 262 as the presence of a waiting two-horse carriage permitted, he saw a gray-haired and blue-cloaked woman solemnly descending the steps of the portico of No. 262.   She was followed by another similar woman, and watched by a butler and a footman at the summit of the steps, and by a footman on the pavement, and by the coachman on the box of the carriage.   She carried a thick and lovely white shawl, and in this shawl was Lord Woldo and all his many and heavy responsibilities.   It was his fancy to take the air thus, in the arms of a woman. He allowed himself to be lifted into the open carriage, and the door of the carriage was shut; and off went the two ancient horses, slowly, and the two adult fat men and the two mature spinsters, and the vehicle weighing about a ton; and Lord Woldo's morning promenade had begun.

"Follow that!" said Edward Henry to the chauffeur, and nipped into his brougham again. Nobody had told him that the being in the shawl was Lord Woldo, but he was sure that it must be so.

In twenty minutes he saw Lord Woldo being carried to and fro amid the groves of Hyde Park (one of the few bits of London earth that did not belong to him nor to his more or less distant connections) while the carriage waited. Once Lord Woldo sat on a chair, but the chief nurse's lap was between him and the chair-seat. Both nurses chattered to him in Kensingtonian accents, but he offered no replies.

"Go back to 262," said Edward Henry to his chauffeur.

Arrived again in Eaton Equare, he did not give himself time to be imposed upon by the grandiosity of the square in general nor of No. 262 in particular. He just ran up the steps and rang the visitors' bell.

"After all," he said to himself as he waited, "these houses aren't even semi detached! They're just houses in a row, and I bet every one of 'em can hear the piano next door!"

The butler whom he had previously caught sight of opened the great portal.

" I want to see Lady Woldo."

" Her ladyship —" began the formidable official.

" Now look here my man," said Edward Henry rather in desperation, " I must see Lady Woldo instantly. It's about the baby —"

" About his lordship? "

" Yes. And look lively, please."

He stepped into the sombre and sumptuous hall.

" Well," he reflected, " I *am* going it — no mistake! "

VI.

He was in a large back drawing-room, of which the window, looking north, was in rich stained glass. " No doubt because they're ashamed of the view," he said to himself. The size of the chimneypiece impressed him, and also its rich carving. " But what an old-fashioned grate! " he said to himself. " They need gilt radiators here." The doorway was a marvel of ornate sculpture, and he liked it. He liked too the effect of the oil-paintings — mainly portraits — on the walls, and the immensity of the brass fender, and the rugs, and the leatherwork of the chairs. But there could be no question that the room was too dark for the taste of any householder clever enough to know the difference between a house and a church.

There was a plunging noise at the door behind him.

"What's amiss?" he heard a woman's voice. And as he heard it he thrilled with sympathetic vibrations. It was not a North Staffordshire voice, but it was a South Yorkshire voice, which is almost the same thing. It seemed to him to be the first un-Kensingtonian voice to soothe his ears since he had left the Five Towns. Moreover, nobody born south of the Trent would have said, "What's amiss?" A Southerner would have said, "What's the matter?" Or, more probably, "What's the mattah?"

He turned and saw a breathless and very beautiful woman of about twenty-nine or thirty, clothed in black, and she was in the act of removing from her lovely head what looked like a length of red flannel. He noticed too, simultaneously, that she was suffering from a heavy cold. A majestic footman behind her closed the door and disappeared.

"Are you Lady Woldo?" Edward Henry asked.

"Yes," she said. "What's this about my baby?"

"I've just seen him in Hyde Park," said Edward Henry. "And I observed that a rash had broken out all over his face."

"I know that," she replied. "It began this morning, all of a sudden like. But what of it? I was rather alarmed myself, as it's the first rash he's had, and he's the first baby I've had — and he'll be the last too. But everybody said it was nothing. He's never been out without me before, but I had such a cold. Now, you don't mean to tell me that you've come down specially from Hyde Park to in-

form me about that rash.   I'm not such a simpleton
as all that."   She spoke in one long breath.

" I'm sure you're not," said he.   " But we've had
a good deal of rash in our family, and it just happens that I've got a remedy — a good, sound, north-
country remedy, and it struck me you might like to
know of it.   So, if you like, I'll telegraph to my
missis for the recipe.   Here's my card."

She read his name, title, and address.

" Well," she said, " it's very kind of you, I'm sure,
Mr. Machin.   I knew you must come from up there
the moment ye spoke.   It does one good above a
bit to hear a plain north-country voice after all this
fal-lalling."

She blew her lovely nose.

" Doesn't it! " Edward Henry agreed.   " That
was just what I thought when I heard you say ' Bless
us! '   Do you know, I've been in London only a
two-three days, and I assure you I was beginning to
feel lonely for a bit of the Midland accent! "

" Yes," she said, " London's lonely! " and sighed.

" My eldest was bitten by a dog the other day,"
he went on in the vein of gossip.

" Oh, don't! " she protested.

" Yes.   Gave us a lot of anxiety.   All right now!
You might like to know that cyanide gauze is a good
thing to put on a wound — supposing anything should
happen to yours —"

" Oh, don't! " she protested.   " I do hope and
pray Robert will never be bitten by a dog.   Was it
a big dog? "

"Fair," said Edward Henry. "So his name's Robert! So's my eldest's!"

"Really now! They wanted him to be called Robert Philip Stephen Darrand Patrick. But I wouldn't have it. He's just Robert. I did have my own way *there!* You know he was born six months after his father's death."

"And I suppose he's ten months now?"

"No; only six."

"Great Scott! He's big!" said Edward Henry.

"Well," said she, "he is. I am, you see."

"Now, Lady Woldo," said Edward Henry in a new tone, "as we're both from the same part of the country, I want to be perfectly straight and above board with you. It's quite true — all that about the rash. And I *did* think you'd like to know. But that's not really what I came to see you about. You understand, not knowing you, I fancied there might be some difficulty in getting at you —"

"Oh, no!" she said simply. "Everybody gets at me."

"Well, I didn't know, you see. So I just mentioned the baby to begin with, like!"

"I hope you're not after money," she said almost plaintively.

"I'm not," he said. "You can ask anybody in Bursley or Hanbridge whether I'm the sort of man to go out on the cadge."

"I once was in the chorus in a panto at Hanbridge," she said. "Don't they call Bursley 'Bosley' down there —'owd Bosley'?"

Edward Henry dealt suitably with these remarks,
and then gave her a judicious version of the nature
of his business, referring several time to Mr. Rollo
Wrissell.

" Mr. Wrissell ! " she murmured, smiling.

" In the end I told Mr. Wrissell to go and bury
himself," said Edward Henry. " And that's about
as far as I've got."

" Oh, don't ! " she said, her voice weak from
suppressed laughter, and then the laughter burst forth
uncontrollable.

" Yes," he said, delighted with himself and her,
" I told him to go and bury himself ! "

" I suppose you don't like Mr. Wrissell ? "

" Well —" he temporised.

" I didn't at first," she said. " I hated him. But
I like him now, though I must say I adore teasing
him. Mr. Wrissell is what I call a gentleman.
You know he was Lord Woldo's heir. And when
Lord Woldo married me it was a bit of a blow for
him ! But he took it like a lamb. He never turned
a hair, and he was more polite than any of them.
I dare say you know Lord Woldo saw me in a musical comedy at Scarborough — he has a place near
there, ye know. Mr. Wrissell had made him angry
about some of his New Thought fads, and I do believe he asked me to marry him just to annoy Mr.
Wrissell. He used to say to me, my husband did,
that he'd married me in too much of a hurry, and
that it was too bad on Mr. Wrissell. And then he
laughed, and I laughed too. ' After all,' he used

to say, my husband did, ' to marry an actress is an
accident that might happen to any member of the
House of Lords; and it does happen to a lot of 'em,
but they don't marry anything as beautiful as you,
Blanche?' he used to say. 'And you stick up for
yourself, Blanche,' he used to say. 'I'll stand by
you,' he said. He was a straight 'un, my husband
was.

"They left me alone until he died. And then
they began — I mean *his* folks. And when Bobby
was born it got worse. Only I must say even then
Mr. Wrissell never turned a hair. Everybody
seemed to make out that I ought to be very grateful
to him, and I ought to think myself very lucky. Me
— a peeress of the realm! They wanted me to
change. But how could I change? I was Blanche
Wilmot, on the road for ten years, — never got a
show in London, — and Blanche Wilmot I shall ever
be, peeress or no peeress! It was no joke being
Lord Woldo's wife, I can tell you; and it's still less
of a joke being Lord Woldo's mother. You imagine
it. It's worse than carrying about a china vase all
the time on a slippery floor. Am I any happier now
than I was before I married? Well, I *am!*
There's more worry in one way, but there's less in
another. And of course I've got Bobby! But it
isn't all beer and skittles, and I let 'em know it, too.
I can't do what I like. And I'm just a sort of exile,
you know. I used to enjoy being on the stage, and
showing myself off. A hard life, but one does enjoy
it. And one gets used to it. One gets to need it.

Sometimes I feel I'd give anything to be able to go on the stage again — oh — oh —! "

She sneezed; then took breath.

" Shall I put some more coal on the fire? " Edward Henry suggested.

" Perhaps I'd better ring," she hesitated.

" No, I'll do it."

He put coal on the fire.

" And if you'd feel easier with that flannel round your head, please do put it on again."

" Well," she said, " I will. My mother used to say there was naught like red flannel for a cold."

With an actress' skill she arranged the flannel, and from its encircling folds her face emerged bewitching — and she knew it. Her complexion had suffered in ten years of the road, but its extreme beauty could not yet be denied. And Edward Henry thought: " All the *really* pretty girls come from the Midlands! "

" Here I am rambling on," she said. " I always was a rare rambler. What do you want me to do? "

" Exert your influence," he replied. " Don't you think it's rather hard on Rose Euclid — treating her like this? Of course people say all sorts of things about Rose Euclid —"

" I won't hear a word against Rose Euclid," cried Lady Woldo. " Whenever she was on tour, if she knew any of us were resting in the town where she was, she'd send us seats. And many's the time I've cried and cried at her acting. And then she's the life and soul of the Theatrical Ladies' Guild."

"And isn't that your husband's signature?" he demanded, showing the precious option.

"Of course it is."

He did not show her the covering letter.

"And I've no doubt my husband *wanted* a theatre built there, and he wanted to do Rose Euclid a good turn. And I'm quite positive certain sure that he didn't want any of Mr. Wrissell's rigmaroles on his land. He wasn't that sort, my husband wasn't. . . . You must go to law about it," she finished.

"Yes," said Edward Henry protestingly. "And a pretty penny it would cost me! And supposing I lost, after all? . . . You never know. There's a much easier way than going to law."

"What is it?"

"As I say, you exert your influence, Lady Woldo. Write and tell them I've seen you and you insist —"

"Eh! Bless you! They'd twist me round their little finger. I'm not a fool, but I'm not very clever; I know that. I shouldn't know whether I was standing on my head or my heels by the time they'd done with me. I've tried to face them out before — about things."

"Who, Mr. Wrissell or Slossons?"

"Both! Eh, but I should like to put a spoke in Mr. Wrissell's wheel, gentleman as he is. You see, he's just one of those men you can't help wanting to tease. When you're on the road you meet lots of 'em."

"I tell you what you can do!"

" What? "

" Write and tell Slossons that you don't wish them to act for you any more, and you'll go to another firm of solicitors. That would bring 'em to their senses."

" Can't! They're in the will. *He* settled that. That's why they're so cocky."

Edward Henry persisted, and this time with an exceedingly impressive and conspiratorial air:

" I tell you another thing you could do — you really *could* do — and it depends on nobody but yourself."

" Well," she said with decision, " I'll do it."

" Whatever it is? "

" If it's straight."

" Of course it's straight. And it would be a grand way of teasing Mr. Wrissell and all of 'em! A simply grand way! I should die of laughing."

" Well —"

At this critical point the historic conversation was interrupted by phenomena in the hall which Lady Woldo recognised with feverish excitement. Lord Woldo had safely returned from Hyde Park. Starting up, she invited Edward Henry to wait a little. A few moments later they were bending over the infant together, and Edward Henry was offering his views on the cause and cure of rash.

VII.

Early on the same afternoon Edward Henry managed by a somewhat excessive obstreperousness

to penetrate once more into the private room of Mr.
Slosson, senior, who received him in silence.

He passed a document to Mr. Slosson.

"It's only a copy," he said, "but the originai is
in my pocket, and to-morrow it will be duly stamped.
I'll give you the original in exchange for the
stamped lease of my Piccadilly Circus plot of land.
You know the money is waiting."

Mr. Slosson perused the document; and it was
certainly to his credit that he did so without any
superficial symptoms of dismay.

"What will Mr. Wrissell and the Woldo family
say about that, do you think?" asked Edward
Henry.

"Lady Woldo will never be allowed to carry it
out," said Mr. Slosson.

"Who's going to stop her? She must carry it
out. She wants to carry it out. She's dying to
carry it out. Moreover, I shall communicate it to
the papers to-night — unless you and I come to an
arrangement. And if by any chance she doesn't
carry it out — well, there'll be a fine society action
about it, you can bet your boots, Mr. Slosson."

The document was a contract made between
Blanche Lady Woldo of the one part and Edward
Henry Machin of the other part, whereby Blanche
Lady Woldo undertook to appear in musical comedy
at any West End theatre to be named by Edward
Henry, at a salary of two hundred pounds a week,
for the period of six months.

"You've not got a theatre," said Mr. Slosson.

"I can get half a dozen in an hour — with that contract in my hand," said Edward Henry.

And he knew from Mr. Slosson's face that he had won.

VIII.

That evening, feeling that he had earned a little recreation, he went to the Empire Theatre — not in Hanbridge, but in Leicester Square, London. The lease, with a prodigious speed hitherto unknown at Slossons, had been drawn up, engrossed, and executed. The Piccadilly Circus land was his for sixty-four years.

"And I've got the old chapel pulled down for nothing," he said to himself.

He was rather happy as he wandered about amid the brilliance of the Empire Promenade. But after half an hour of such exercise, and of vain efforts to see or hear what was afoot on the stage, he began to feel rather lonely. Then it was that he caught sight of Mr. Alloyd the architect, also lonely.

"Well," said Mr. Alloyd curtly, with a sardonic smile, "they've telephoned me all about it. I've seen Mr. Wrissell. Just my luck! So you're the man! He pointed you out to me this morning. My design for that church would have knocked the West End! Of course Mr. Wrissell will pay me compensation, but that's not the same thing. I wanted the advertisement of the building. . . . Just my luck! Have a drink, will you?"

Edward Henry ultimately went with the plaintive

Mr. Alloyd to his rooms in Adelphi Terrace. He quitted those rooms at something after two o'clock in the morning. He had practically given Mr. Alloyd a definite commission to design the Regent Theatre. Already he was practically the proprietor of a first-class theatre in the West End of London!

"I wonder whether Master Seven Sachs could have bettered my day's work to-day!" he reflected as he got into a taxicab. He had dismissed his electric brougham earlier in the evening. "I doubt if even Master Seven Sachs himself wouldn't be proud of my little scheme in Eaton Square!" said he. . . . "Wilkins's Hotel, please, driver."

THE OLD ADAM
PART II

CHAPTER VII

CORNER-STONE

I.

ON a morning in spring Edward Henry got out of an express at Euston, which had come, not from the Five Towns, but from Birmingham. Having on the previous day been called to Birmingham on local and profitable business, he had found it convenient to spend the night there and telegraph home that London had summoned him. It was in this unostentatious, this half-furtive fashion, that his visits to London now usually occurred. Not that he was afraid of his wife! Not that he was afraid even of his mother! Oh, no! He was merely rather afraid of himself,— of his own opinion concerning the metropolitan, non-local, speculative, and perhaps unprofitable business to which he was committed. The fact was that he could scarcely look his women in the face when he mentioned London. He spoke vaguely of "real estate" enterprise, and left it at that. The women made no enquiries; they too, left it at that. Nevertheless. . . .

The episode of Wilkins's was buried, but it was imperfectly buried. The Five Towns definitely knew that he had stayed at Wilkins's for a bet, and that Brindley had discharged the bet. And rumours of his valet, his electric brougham, his theatrical supper-parties, had mysteriously hung in the streets of the Five Towns like a strange vapour. Wisps of the strange vapour had conceivably entered the precincts of his home, but nobody ever referred to them; nobody ever sniffed apprehensively, nor asked anybody else whether there was not a smell of fire. The discreetness of the silence was disconcerting. Happily his relations with that angel, his wife, were excellent. She had carried angelicism so far as not to insist on the destruction of Carlo; and she had actually applauded, while sticking to her white apron, the sudden and startling extravagances of his toilette.

On the whole, though little short of thirty-five thousand pounds would ultimately be involved,— not to speak of liability of nearly three thousand a year for sixty-four years for ground-rent,— Edward Henry was not entirely gloomy as to his prospects. He was indubitably thinner in girth; novel problems and anxieties, and the constant annoyance of being in complete technical ignorance of his job, had removed some flesh. (And not a bad thing either!) But, on the other hand, his chin exhibited one proof that life was worth living, and that he had discovered new faith in life and a new conviction of youthfulness.

He had shaved off his beard.

" Well, sir! " a voice greeted him full of hope and cheer, immediately his feet touched the platform.

It was the voice of Mr. Marrier. Edward Henry and Mr. Marrier were now in regular relations. Before Edward Henry had paid his final bill at Wilkins's and relinquished his valet and his electric brougham, and disposed forever of his mythical " man " on board the *Minnetonka,* and got his original luggage away from the Hotel Majestic, Mr. Marrier had visited him and made a certain proposition. And such was the influence of Mr. Marrier's incurable smile, and of his solid optimism, and of his obvious talent for getting things done on the spot (as witness the photography), that the proposition had been accepted. Mr. Marrier was now Edward Henry's " representative " in London. At the Green Room Club Mr. Marrier informed reliable cronies that he was Edward Henry's " confidential adviser." At the Turk's Head, Hanbridge, Edward Henry informed reliable cronies that Mr. Marrier was a sort of clerk, factotum, or maid of all work. A compromise between these two very different conceptions of Mr. Marrier's position had been arrived at in the word " representative." The real truth was that Edward Henry employed Mr. Marrier in order to listen to Mr. Marrier. He turned to Mr. Marrier like a tap, and nourished himself from a gushing stream of useful information concerning the theatrical world. Mr. Marrier, quite unconsciously, was bit by bit remedying Edward Henry's acute ignorance.

The question of wages had caused Edward Henry some apprehension. He had learnt in a cou-

ple of days that a hundred pounds a week was a
trifle on the stage. He had soon heard of performers who worked for "nominal" salaries of
forty and fifty a week. For a manager twenty
pounds a week seemed to be a usual figure. But
in the Five Towns three pounds a week is regarded
as very goodish pay for any subordinate, and Edward Henry could not rid himself all at once of
native standards. He had therefore, with diffidence, offered three pounds a week to the aristocratic Marrier. And Mr. Marrier had not refused
it, nor ceased to smile. On three pounds a week
he haunted the best restaurants, taxicabs, and other
resorts, and his garb seemed always to be smarter
than Edward Henry's, especially in such details as
waistcoat slips.

Of course Mr. Marrier had a taxicab waiting exactly opposite the coach from which Edward Henry
descended. It was just this kind of efficient attention that was gradually endearing him to his employer.

"How goes it?" said Edward Henry curtly, as
they drove down to the Grand Babylon Hotel, now
Edward Henry's regular headquarters in London.

Said Mr. Marrier:

"I suppose you've seen another of 'em's got a
knighthood?"

"No," said Edward Henry. "Who?" He
knew that by "'em" Mr. Marrier meant the great
race of actor-managers.

"Gerald Pompey. Something to do with him being a sheriff in the City, you know. I bet you what you laike he went in for the Common Council simply in order to get even with old Pilgrim. In fact, I know he did. And now a foundation-stone-laying has dan it!"

"A foundation-stone-laying?"

"Yes. The new City Guild's building, you knaow. Royalty — Temple Bar business — sheriffs — knighthood. There you are!"

"Oh!" said Edward Henry. And then after a pause added: "Pity *we* can't have a foundation-stone-laying!"

"By the way, old Pilgrim's in the deuce and all of a haole, I heah. It's all over the Clubs." (In speaking of the Clubs, Mr. Marrier always pronounced them with a Capital letter.) "I told you he was going to sail from Tilbury on his world-tour, and have a grand embarking ceremony and seeing-off! Just laike him! Greatest advertiser the world ever saw! Well, since that P. and O. boat was lost on the Goodwins, Cora Pryde has absolutely declined to sail from Tilbury. Ab-so-lute-ly! Swears she'll join the steamer at Marseilles. And Pilgrim has got to go with her, too."

"Why?"

"Well, even Pilgrim couldn't have a grand embarking ceremony without his leading lady! He's furious, I hear."

"Why shouldn't he go with her?"

"Why not? Because he's formally announced his grand embarking ceremony! Invitations are out.

Barge from London Bridge to Tilbury, and so on!
What he wants is a good excuse for giving it up.
He'd never be able to admit that he'd had to give
it up because Cora Pryde made him! He wants
to save his face."

"Well," said Edward Henry absently, "it's a
queer world. You've got me a room at the Grand
Bab?"

"Rather!"

"Then let's go and have a look at the Regent
first," said Edward Henry.

No sooner had he expressed the wish than Mr.
Marrier's neck curved round through the window,
and with three words to the chauffeur he had de-
flected the course of the taxi.

Edward Henry had an almost boyish curiosity
about his edifice. He would go and give it a glance
at the oddest moments. And just now he had a
swift and violent desire to behold it. With all
speed the taxi shot down Shaftesbury Avenue and
swerved to the right. . . .

There it was! Yes, it really existed, the incredible edifice of his caprice and of Mr. Alloyd's con-
structive imagination! It had already reached a
height of fifteen feet; and, dozens of yards above
that, cranes dominated the sunlit air, swinging loads
of bricks in the azure; and scores of workmen
crawled about beneath these monsters. And he, Edward Henry, by a single act of volition was the author of it! He slipped from the taxi, penetrated
within the wall of hoardings, and gazed, just gazed!

A wondrous thing — human enterprise! And also a terrifying thing! . . . That building might be the tomb of his reputation. On the other hand it might be the seed of a new renown compared to which the first would be as naught! He turned his eyes away, in fear — yes, in fear!

" I say," he said, " will Sir John Pilgrim be out of bed yet, d'ye think? " He glanced at his watch. The hour was about eleven.

" He'll be at breakfast."

" I'm going to see him, then. What's his address? "

" Twenty-five Queen Anne's Gate. But do you knaow him? I do. Shall I cam with you? "

" No," said Edward Henry shortly. " You go on with my bags to the Grand Bab, and get me another taxi. I'll see you in my room at the hotel at a quarter to one. Eh? "

" Rather! " agreed Mr. Marrier, submissive.

II.

" Sole proprietor of the Regent Theatre."

These were the words which Edward Henry wrote on a visiting-card, and which procured him immediate admittance to the unique spectacle — reputed to be one of the most enthralling sights in London — of Sir John Pilgrim at breakfast.

In a very spacious front room of his flat (so celebrated for its Gobelins tapestries and its truly wonderful parquet flooring) sat Sir John Pilgrim at a large hexagonal mahogany table. At one side of the table a small square of white diaper was arranged, and on this square were an apparatus for boiling eggs, another for making toast, and a third for making coffee. Sir John, with the assistance of a young Chinaman and a fox-terrier who flitted around him, was indeed eating and drinking. The vast remainder of the table was gleamingly bare, save for newspapers and letters, opened and unopened, which Sir John tossed about. Opposite to him sat a secretary whose fluffy hair, neat white chemisette, and tender years gave her an appearance of helpless fragility in front of the powerful and ruthless celebrity. Sir John's crimson-socked left foot stuck out from the table, emerging from the left half of a lovely new pair of brown trousers, and resting on a piece of white paper. Before this white paper knelt a man in a frock-coat, who was drawing an outline on the paper round Sir John's foot.

"You *are* a bootmaker, aren't you?" Sir John was saying airily.

"Yes, Sir John."

"Excuse me!" said Sir John. "I only wanted to be sure. I fancied from the way you caressed my corn with that pencil that you might be an artist on one of the illustrated papers. My mistake!" He was bending down. Then suddenly straightening himself he called across the room: "I say, Givington, did you notice my pose then — my expression as I used the word 'caressed'? How would that do?"

And Edward Henry now observed in a corner of
the room a man standing in front of an easel and
sketching somewhat grossly thereon in charcoal.
This man said:

"If you won't bother me, Sir John, I won't bother
you."

"Ah! Givington! Ah! Givington!" murmured Sir John still more airily — at breakfast he
was either airy or nothing. "You're getting on in
the world. You aren't merely an A. R. A.— you're
making money. A year ago you'd never have had
the courage to address me in that tone. Well, I
sincerely congratulate you. . . . Here, Snip, here's
my dentist's bill — worry it, worry it! Good dog!
Worry it!"

(The dog growled now over a torn document beneath the table.)

"Miss Taft, you might see that a *communiqué*
goes out to the effect that I gave my first sitting to
Mr. Saracen Givington, A. R. A., this morning.
The activities of Mr. Saracen Givington are of interest to the world, and rightly so! You'd better
come round to the other side for the right foot, Mr.
Bootmaker. The journey is simply nothing."

And then, and not till then, did Sir John Pilgrim
turn his large and handsome middle-aged blond face
in the direction of Alderman Edward Henry
Machin.

"Pardon my curiosity," said Sir John, "but who
are you?"

"My name is Machin — Alderman Machin,"

said Edward Henry. " I sent up my card and you asked me to come in."

" Ha! " Sir John exclaimed, seizing an egg. " Will you crack an egg with me, Alderman? I can crack an egg with anybody."

" Thanks," said Edward Henry. " I'll be very glad to." And he advanced towards the table.

Sir John hesitated. The fact was that, though he dissembled his dismay with marked histrionic skill, he was unquestionably overwhelmed by astonishment. In the course of years he had airily invited hundreds of callers to crack an egg with him, — the joke was one of his favourites,— but nobody had ever ventured to accept the invitation.

" Chung," he said weakly, " lay a cover for the alderman."

Edward Henry sat down quite close to Sir John. He could discern all the details of Sir John's face and costume. The tremendous celebrity was wearing a lounge suit somewhat like his own, but instead of the coat — he had a blue dressing-jacket with crimson facings; the sleeves ended in rather long wristbands, which were unfastened, the opal cufflinks drooping each from a single hole. Perhaps for the first time in his life Edward Henry intimately understood what idiosyncratic elegance was. He could almost feel the emanating personality of Sir John Pilgrim, and he was intimidated by it; he was intimidated by its hardness, its harshness, its terrific egotism, its utterly brazen quality. Sir John's glance was the most purely arrogant that Edward

Henry had ever encountered.   It knew no reticence.
And Edward Henry thought: " When this chap
dies he'll want to die in public, with the reporters
round his bed and a private secretary taking down
messages."

" This is rather a lark," said Sir John, recovering.

" It is," said Edward Henry, who now felicitously
perceived that a lark it indeed was, and ought to be
treated as such.   " It shall be a lark! " he said to
himself.

Sir John dictated a letter to Miss Taft, and before the letter was finished the grinning Chung had
laid a place for Edward Henry, and Snip had inspected him and passed him for one of the right
sort.

" Had I said that this is rather a lark? " Sir
John enquired, the letter accomplished.

" I forget," said Edward Henry.

" Because I don't like to say the same thing twice
over if I can help it.   It *is* a lark though, isn't it? "

" Undoubtedly," said Edward Henry, decapitating
an egg.   " I only hope that I'm not interrupting
you."

" Not in the least," said Sir John.   " Breakfast
is my sole free time.   In another half-hour, I assure
you, I shall be attending to three or four things at
once."   He leant over towards Edward Henry.
" But between you and me, Alderman, quite privately, if it isn't a rude question, what did you come
for? "

" Well," said Edward Henry, " as I wrote on my

card, I'm the sole proprietor of the Regent Theatre —"

" But there is no Regent Theatre," Sir John interrupted him.

" No; not strictly. But there will be. It's in course of construction. We're up to the first floor."

" Dear me! A suburban theatre, no doubt? "

" Do you mean to say, Sir John," cried Edward Henry, " that you haven't noticed it. It's within a few yards of Piccadilly Circus."

" Really! " said Sir John. " You see my theatre is in Lower Regent Street, and I never go to Piccadilly Circus. I make a point of not going to Piccadilly Circus. Miss Taft, how long is it since I went to Piccadilly Circus? Forgive me, young woman, I was forgetting — you aren't old enough to remember. Well, never mind details. . . . And what is there remarkable about the Regent Theatre, Alderman? "

" I intend it to be a theatre of the highest class, Sir John," said Edward Henry. " Nothing but the very best will be seen on its boards."

" That's not remarkable, Alderman. We're all like that. Haven't you noticed it? "

" Then, secondly," said Edward Henry, " I am the sole proprietor. I have no financial backers, no mortgages, no partners. I have made no contracts with anybody."

" That," said Sir John, " is not unremarkable. In fact, many persons who do not happen to possess my own robust capacity for belief might not credit your statement."

"And thirdly," said Edward Henry, "every member of the audience — even in the boxes, the most expensive seats — will have a full view of the whole of the stage — or, in the alternative, at matinées, a full view of a lady's hat."

"Alderman," said Sir John gravely, "before I offer you another egg, let me warn you against carrying remarkableness too far. You may be regarded as eccentric if you go on like that. Some people, I am told, don't want a view of the stage."

"Then they had better not come to my theatre," said Edward Henry.

"All which," commented Sir John, "gives me no clue whatever to the reason why you are sitting here by my side and calmly eating my eggs and toast and drinking my coffee."

Admittedly, Edward Henry was nervous. Admittedly, he was a provincial in the presence of one of the most illustrious personages of the empire. Nevertheless he controlled his nervousness, and reflected:

"Nobody else from the Five Towns would or could have done what I am doing. Moreover, this chap is a mountebank. In the Five Towns they would kowtow to him, but they would laugh at him. They would mighty soon add *him* up. Why should I be nervous? I'm as good as he is." He finished with the thought which has inspired many a timid

man with new courage in a desperate crisis: "The
fellow can't eat me."

Then he said aloud:

"I want to ask you a question, Sir John."

"One?"

"One. Are you the head of the theatrical profession, or is Sir Gerald Pompey?"

"*Sir* Gerald Pompey?"

"*Sir* Gerald Pompey. Haven't you seen the
papers this morning?"

Sir John Pilgrim turned pale. Springing up, he
seized the topmost of an undisturbed pile of daily
papers and feverishly opened it.

"Bah!" he muttered.

He was continually thus imitating his own behaviour on the stage. The origin of his renowned
breakfasts lay in the fact that he had once played
the part of a millionaire ambassador who juggled
at breakfast with his own affairs and the affairs of
the world. The stage breakfast of a millionaire
ambassador created by a playwright on the verge of
bankruptcy had appealed to his imagination and influenced all the mornings of his life.

"They've done it just to irritate me as I'm starting off on my world's tour," he muttered, coursing
round the table. Then he stopped and gazed at
Edward Henry. "This is a political knighthood,"
said he. "It has nothing to do with the stage.
It is not like my knighthood, is it?"

"Certainly not," Edward Henry agreed. "But
you know how people will talk, Sir John. People

will be going about this very morning and saying
that Sir Gerald is at last the head of the theatrical
profession. I came here for your authoritative
opinion. I know you're unbiased."

Sir John resumed his chair.

"As for Pompey's qualifications as a head," he
murmured, "I know nothing of them. I fancy his
heart is excellent. I only saw him twice, once in
his own theatre, and once in Bond Street. I should
be inclined to say that on the stage he looks more
like a gentleman than any gentleman ought to look,
and that in the street he might be mistaken for an
actor. . . . How will that suit you?"

"It's a clue," said Edward Henry.

"Alderman," exclaimed Sir John, "I believe that
if I didn't keep a firm hand on myself I should soon
begin to like you! Have another cup of coffee.
Chung! . . . Good-bye, Bootmaker, good-bye!"

"I only want to know for certain who *is* the
head," said Edward Henry, "because I mean to in-
vite the head of the theatrical profession to lay the
corner-stone of my new theatre."

"Ah!"

"When do you start on your world's tour, Sir
John?"

"I leave Tilbury with my entire company, scenery
and effects, on the morning of Tuesday week, by the
Kandahar. I shall play first in Cairo."

"How awkward!" said Edward Henry. "I
meant to ask you to lay the stone on the very next
afternoon — Wednesday, that is!"

" Indeed ! "

" Yes, Sir John. The ceremony will be a very original affair — very original ! "

" A foundation-stone-laying ! " mused Sir John. " But if you're already up to the first floor, how can you be laying the foundation-stone on Wednesday week ? "

" I didn't say foundation-stone. I said corner-stone," Edward Henry corrected him. " An entire novelty ! That's why we can't be ready before Wednesday week."

" And you want to advertise your house by getting the head of the profession to assist? "

" That is exactly my idea."

" Well," said Sir John. " Whatever else you may lack, Mr. Alderman, you are not lacking in nerve, if you expect to succeed in *that*."

Edward Henry smiled.

" I have already heard, in a round-about way," he replied, " that Sir Gerald Pompey would not be unwilling to officiate. My only difficulty is that I'm a truthful man by nature. Whoever officiates, I shall of course have to have him labelled, in my own interests, as the head of the theatrical profession, and I don't want to say anything that isn't true."

There was a pause.

" Now, Sir John, couldn't you stay a day or two longer in London and join the ship at Marseilles instead of going on board at Tilbury? "

" But I have made all my arrangements. The

whole world knows that I am going on board at Tilbury."

Just then the door opened and a servant announced:

" Mr. Carlo Trent."

Sir John Pilgrim rushed like a locomotive to the threshold and seized both Carlo Trent's hands with such a violence of welcome that Carlo Trent's eyeglass fell out of his eye and the purple ribbon dangled to his waist.

" Come in, come in! " said Sir John. " And begin to read at once. I've been looking out of the window for you for the last quarter of an hour. Alderman, this is Mr. Carlo Trent, the well-known dramatic poet. Trent, this is one of the greatest geniuses in London. . . . Ah! You know each other? It's not surprising! No, don't stop to shake hands. Sit down here, Trent. Sit down on this chair. . . . Here, Snip, take his hat. Worry it! Worry it! Now, Trent, don't read to *me*. It might make you nervous and hurried. Read to Miss Taft and Chung, and to Mr. Givington over there. Imagine that they are the great and enlightened public. You have imagination, haven't you, being a poet? "

Sir John had accomplished the change of mood with the rapidity of a transformation-scene — in which form of art, by the way, he was a great adept.

Carlo Trent, somewhat breathless, took a manuscript from his pocket, opened it, and announced: " The Orient Pearl."

"Oh!" breathed Edward Henry.

For some thirty minutes Edward Henry listened to hexameters, the first he had ever heard. The effect of them on his moral organism was worse even than he had expected. He glanced about at the other auditors. Givington had opened a box of tubes and was spreading colours on his palette. The Chinaman's eyes were closed while his face still grinned. Snip was asleep on the parquet. Miss Taft bit the end of a pencil with her agreeable teeth. Sir John Pilgrim lay at full length on a sofa, occasionally lifting his legs. Edward Henry despaired of help in his great need. But just as his desperation was becoming too acute to be borne, Carlo Trent ejaculated the word "Curtain." It was the first word that Edward Henry had clearly understood.

"That's the first act," said Carlo Trent, wiping his face. Snip awakened.

Edward Henry rose and, in the hush, tiptoed round the sofa.

"Good-bye, Sir John," he whispered.

"You're not going?"

"I am, Sir John."

The head of his profession sat up. "How right you are!" said he. "How right you are. Trent, I knew from the first words it wouldn't do. It lacks colour. I want something more crimson, more like the brighter parts of this jacket, something —" He waved hands in the air. "The alderman agrees with me. He's going. Don't trouble to read any more, Trent. But drop in any time — any time. Chung, what o'clock is it?"

" It is nearly noon," said Edward Henry in the tone of an old friend. " Well, I'm sorry you can't oblige me, Sir John. I'm off to see Sir Gerald Pompey now."

" But who says I can't oblige you?" protested Sir John. " Who knows what sacrifices I would not make in the highest interests of the profession? Alderman, you jump to conclusions with the agility of an acrobat, but they are false conclusions! Miss Taft, the telephone! Chung, my coat! Good-bye Trent, good-bye!"

An hour later Edward Henry met Mr. Marrier at the Grand Babylon Hotel.

" Well, sir," said Mr. Marrier, " you are the greatest man that ever lived!"

" Why?"

Mr. Marrier showed him the stop-press news of a penny evening paper, which read: " Sir John Pilgrim has abandoned his ceremonious departure from Tilbury in order to lay the corner-stone of the new Regent Theatre on Wednesday week. He and Miss Cora Pryde will join the *Kandahar* at Marseilles."

" You needn't do any advertaysing," said Mr. Marrier. " Pilgrim will do all the advertaysing for you."

III.

Edward Henry and Mr. Marrier worked together admirably that afternoon on the arrangements for the corner-stone-laying. And — such was the interaction of their separate enthusiasms — it soon became apparent that all London (in the only right sense of the word "all") must and would be at the ceremony. Characteristically, Mr. Marrier happened to have a list or catalogue of all London in his pocket, and Edward Henry appreciated him more than ever. But towards four o'clock Mr. Marrier annoyed and even somewhat alarmed Edward Henry by a mysterious change of mien. His assured optimism slipped away from him. He grew uneasy, darkly preoccupied, and inefficient. At last when the clock in the room struck four, and Edward Henry failed to hear it, Mr. Marrier said:

"I'm afraid I shall have to ask you to excuse me now."

"Why?"

"I told you I had an appointment for tea at four."

"Did you? What is it?" Edward Henry demanded with an employer's instinctive assumption that souls as well as brains can be bought for such sums as three pounds a week.

"I have a lady coming to tea, here; that is, downstairs."

" In this hotel? "

" Yes."

" Who is it? " Edward Henry pursued lightly, for though he appreciated Mr. Marrier, he also despised him.   However, he found the grace to add: " May one ask? "

" It's Miss Elsie April."

" Do you mean to say, Marrier," complained Edward Henry, " that you've known Miss Elsie April all these months and never told me? . . . There aren't two, I suppose?   It's the cousin or something of Rose Euclid? "

Mr. Marrier nodded.   " The fact is," he said, " she and I are joint honorary organising secretaries for the annual conference of the Azure Society.   You know, it leads the New Thought movement in England."

" You never told me that either."

" Didn't I, sir?   I didn't think it would interest you.   Besides, both Miss April and I are comparatively new members."

" Oh! " said Edward Henry with all the canny provincial's conviction of his own superior shrewdness; and he repeated, so as to intensify this conviction and impress it on others, " Oh! "   In the undergrowth of his mind was the thought: · " How dare this man, whose brains belong to me, be the organising secretary of something that I don't know anything about and don't want to know anything about? "

" Yes," said Mr. Marrier modestly.

" I say," Edward Henry enquired warmly, with an impulsive gesture, " who is she? "

" Who is she? " repeated Mr. Marrier blankly.

" Yes. What does she do? "

" Doesn't do anything," said Mr. Marrier. " Very good amateur actress. Goes about a great deal. Her mother was on the stage. Married a wealthy wholesale corset-maker."

" Who did? Miss April? " Edward Henry had a twinge.

" No; her mother. Both parents are dead, and Miss April has an income — a considerable income."

" What do you call considerable? "

" Five or six thousand a year."

" The deuce! " murmured Edward Henry.

" May have lost a bit of it, of course," Mr. Marrier hedged. " But not much, not much! "

" Well," said Edward Henry, smiling. " What about *my* tea? Am I to have tea all by myself? "

" Will you come down and meet her? " Mr. Marrier's expression approached the wistful.

" Well," said Edward Henry, " it's an idea, isn't it? Why should I be the only person in London who doesn't know Miss Elsie April? "

It was ten minutes past four when they descended into the electric publicity of the Grand Babylon. Amid the music and the rattle of crockery and the gliding waiters and the large nodding hats that gathered more and more thickly round the tables, there was no sign of Elsie April.

"She may have been and gone away again," said Edward Henry, apprehensive.

"Oh, no! She wouldn't go away." Mr. Marrier was positive.

In the tone of a man with an income of two hundred pounds a week he ordered a table to be prepared for three.

At ten minutes to five he said:

"I hope she *hasn't* been and gone away again!"

Edward Henry began to be gloomy and resentful. The crowded and factitious gaiety of the place actually annoyed him. If Elsie April had been and gone away again, he objected to such silly feminine conduct. If she was merely late, he equally objected to such unconscionable inexactitude. He blamed Mr. Marrier. He considered that he had the right to blame Mr. Marrier because he paid him three pounds a week. And he very badly wanted his tea.

Then their four eyes, which for forty minutes had scarcely left the entrance staircase, were rewarded. She came in furs, gleaming white kid gloves, gold chains, a gold bag, and a black velvet hat.

"I'm not late, am I?" she said after the introduction.

"No," they both replied. And they both meant it. For she was like fine weather. The forty minutes of waiting were forgotten, expunged from the records of time, just as the memory of a month of rain is obliterated by one splendid sunny day.

IV.

Edward Henry enjoyed the tea, which was bad, to an extraordinary degree. He became uplifted in the presence of Miss Elsie April; whereas Mr. Marrier, strangely, drooped to still deeper depths of unaccustomed inert melancholy. Edward Henry decided that she was every bit as piquant, challenging, and delectable as he had imagined her to be on the day when he ate an artichoke at the next table to hers at Wilkins's. She coincided exactly with his remembrance of her, except that she was now slightly more plump. Her contours were effulgent — there was no other word. Beautiful she was not, for she had a turned-up nose; but what charm she radiated! Every movement and tone enchanted Edward Henry. He was enchanted not at intervals, by a chance gesture, but all the time — when she was serious, when she smiled, when she fingered her teacup, when she pushed her furs back over her shoulders, when she spoke of the weather, when she spoke of the social crisis, and when she made fun, with a certain brief absence of restraint, rather in her artichoke manner of making fun.

He thought and believed:

"This is the finest woman I ever saw!" He clearly perceived the inferiority of other women, whom nevertheless he admired and liked, such as the Countess of Chell and Lady Woldo.

It was not her brains, nor her beauty, nor her stylishness that affected him. No! It was something mysterious and dizzying that resided in every particle of her individuality.

He thought:

" I've often and often wanted to see her again. And now I'm having tea with her! " And he was happy.

" Have you got that list, Mr. Marrier? " she asked in her low and thrilling voice. So saying, she raised her eyebrows in expectation — a delicious effect, especially behind her half-raised white veil.

Mr. Marrier produced a document.

" But that's *my* list! " said Edward Henry.

" Your list? "

" I'd better tell you." Mr. Marrier essayed a rapid explanation. " Mr. Machin wanted a list of the raight sort of people to ask to the corner-stone-laying of his theatah. So I used this as a basis."

Elsie April smiled again. " Ve-ry good! " she approved.

" What *is* your list, Marrier? " asked Edward Henry.

It was Elsie who replied:

" People to be invited to the dramatic *soirée* of the Azure Society. We give six a year. No title is announced. Nobody except a committee of three knows even the name of the author of the play that is to be performed. Everything is kept a secret. Even the author doesn't know that his play has been chosen. Don't you think it's a delightful idea? . . . An offspring of the New Thought!"

He agreed that it was a delightful idea.

" Shall I be invited?" he asked.

She answered gravely: " I don't know."

" Are you going to play in it?"

She paused. . . . " Yes."

" Then you must let me come. Talking of plays —"

He stopped. He was on the edge of facetiously relating the episode of " The Orient Pearl" at Sir John Pilgrim's; but he withdrew in time. Suppose that " The Orient Pearl" was the piece to be performed by the Azure Society! It might well be. It was (in his opinion) just the sort of play that that sort of society would choose. Nevertheless he was as anxious as ever to see Elsie April act. He really thought that she could and would transfigure any play. Even his profound scorn of New Thought (a subject of which he was entirely ignorant) began to be modified — and by nothing but the enchantment of the tone in which Elsie April murmured the words, " Azure Society!"

" How soon is the performance?" he demanded.

" Wednesday week," said she.

" That's the very day of my corner-stone-laying," he said. " However, it doesn't matter. My little affair will be in the afternoon."

" But it can't be," said she solemnly. " It would interfere with us, and we should interfere with it.

Our annual conference takes place in the afternoon.
All London will be there."

Said Mr. Marrier rather shamefaced:

" That's just it, Mr. Machin.   It positively never
occurred to me that the Azure Conference is to be
on that very day.   I never thought of it until nearly
four o'clock.   And then I scarcely knew how to explain it to you.   I really don't know how it escaped
me."

Mr. Marrier's trouble was now out, and he had
declined in Edward Henry's esteem.   Mr. Marrier
was afraid of him.   Mr. Marrier's list of personages
was no longer a miracle of foresight; it was a mere
coincidence.   He doubted if Mr. Marrier was
worth even his three pounds a week.   Edward
Henry began to feel ruthless, Napoleonic.   He was
capable of brushing away the whole Azure Society
and New Thought movement into limbo.

" You must please alter your date," said Elsie
April.   And she put her right elbow on the table
and leaned her chin on it, and thus somehow established a domestic intimacy for the three amid all
the blare and notoriety of the vast tea-room.

" Oh, but I can't! " he said easily, familiarly.   It
was her occasional " artichoke " manner that had
justified him in assuming this tone.   " I can't! " he
repeated.   " I've told Sir John I can't possibly be
ready any earlier, and on the day after he'll almost
certainly be on his way to Marseilles.   Besides, I
don't *want* to alter my date.   My date is in the
papers by this time."

"You've already done quite enough harm to the movement as it is," said Elsie April stoutly but ravishingly.

"Me — harm to the movement?"

"Haven't you stopped the building of our church?"

"Oh! So you know Mr. Wrissell?"

"Very well indeed."

"Anybody else would have done the same in my place," Edward Henry defended himself. "Your cousin, Miss Euclid, would have done it, and Marrier here was in the affair with her."

"Ah!" exclaimed Elsie April. "But we didn't belong to the movement then! We didn't know. . . . Come now, Mr. Machin. Sir John Pilgrim will of course be a great show. But even if you've got him and manage to stick to him, we should beat you. You'll never get the audience you want if you don't change from Wednesday week. After all, the number of people who count in London is very small. And we've got nearly all of them. You've no idea —"

"I won't change from Wednesday week," said Edward Henry. This defiance of her put him into an extremely agitated felicity.

"Now, my dear Mr. Machin —"

He was actually aware of the charm she was exerting, and yet he discovered that he could easily withstand it.

"Now, my dear Miss April, please don't try to take advantage of your beauty!"

She sat up.   She was apparently measuring herself and him.

" Then you won't change the day, truly? "   Her
urbanity was in no wise impaired.

" I won't," he laughed lightly.   " I dare say you
aren't used to people like me, Miss April."

(She might get the better of Seven Sachs, but
not of him, Edward Henry Machin from the Five
Towns!)

" Marrier," said he suddenly, with a bluff humorous downrightness, " you know you're in a very
awkward position here, and you know you've got
to see Alloyd for me before six o'clock.   Be off
with you.   I will be responsible for Miss April."

(" I'll show these Londoners! " he said to himself.   " It's simple enough when you once get into
it.")

And he did in fact succeed in dismissing Mr.
Marrier, after the latter had talked Azure business
with Miss April for a couple of minutes.

" I must go, too," said Elsie, imperturbable, impenetrable.

" One moment," he entreated, and masterfully
signalled Marrier to depart.   After all, he was paying the fellow three pounds a week.

She watched Marrier thread his way out.   Already she had put on her gloves.

" I must go," she repeated, her rich red lips then
closed definitely.

" Have you a motor here? " Edward Henry
asked.

" No."

" Then, if I may, I'll see you home."

" You may," she said, gazing full at him. Whereby he was somewhat startled and put out of countenance.

v.

" Are we friends? " he asked roguishly.

" I hope so," she said, with no diminution of her inscrutability.

They were in a taxicab, rolling along the Embankment towards the Buckingham Palace Hotel, where she said she lived. He was happy. " Why am I happy? " he thought. " What is there in her that makes me happy? " He did not know. But he knew that he had never been in a taxicab, or anywhere else, with any woman half so elegant. Her elegance flattered him enormously. Here he was, a provincial man of business, ruffling it with the best of them! . . . And she was young in her worldly maturity. Was she twenty-seven? She could not be more. She looked straight in front of her, faintly smiling. . . . Yes, he was fully aware that he was a married man. He had a distinct vision of the angelic Nellie, of the three children, and of his mother. But it seemed to him that his own case differed in some very subtle and yet effective manner from the similar case of any other married man. And he lived, unharassed by apprehensions, in the lively joy of the moment.

" But," she said, " I hope you won't come to see me act."

" Why? "

" Because I should prefer you not to. You would not be sympathetic to me."

" Oh, yes, I should."

" I shouldn't feel it so." And then with a swift disarrangement of all the folds of her skirt she turned and faced him. " Mr. Machin, do you know why I've let you come with me? "

" Because you're a good-natured woman," he said.

She grew even graver, shaking her head.

" No! I simply wanted to tell you that you've ruined Rose, my cousin."

" Miss Euclid? Me ruined Miss Euclid? "

" Yes. You robbed her of her theatre — her one chance."

He blushed. " Excuse me," he said, " I did no such thing. I simply bought her option from her. She was absolutely free to keep the option or let it go."

" The fact remains," said Elsie April, with humid eyes, " the fact remains that she'd set her heart on having that theatre, and you failed her at the last instant. And she has nothing, and you've got the theatre entirely in your own hands. I'm not so silly as to suppose that you can't defend yourself legally. But let me tell you that Rose went to the United States heart-broken, and she's playing to empty houses there — empty houses! Whereas she might have been here in London, interested in her theatre, and preparing for a successful season."

"I'd no idea of this," breathed Edward Henry. He was dashed. "I'm awfully sorry!"

"Yes, no doubt. But there it is!"

Silence fell. He knew not what to say. He felt himself in one way innocent, but he felt himself in another way blackly guilty. His remorse for the telephone-trick which he had practised on Rose Euclid burst forth again after a long period of quiescence simulating death, and actually troubled him. . . . No, he was not guilty! He insisted in his heart that he was not guilty! And yet — and yet —

No taxicab ever travelled so quickly as that taxicab. Before he could gather together his forces it had arrived beneath the awning of the Buckingham Palace Hotel.

His last words to her were:

"Now, I sha'nt change the day of my stone-laying. But don't worry about your conference. You know it'll be perfectly all right." He spoke archly, with a brave attempt at cajolery; but in the recesses of his soul he was not sure that she had not defeated him in this their first encounter. However, Seven Sachs might talk as he chose — she was not such a persuasive creature as all that! She had scarcely even tried to be persuasive.

At about a quarter-past six, when he saw his underling again, he said to Mr. Marrier:

"Marrier, I've got a great idea. We'll have that

corner-stone-laying at night. After the theatres.
Say half-past eleven. Torchlight! Fireworks from
the cranes! It'll tickle old Pilgrim to death. I
shall have a marquee with match-boarding sides fixed
up inside, and heat it with a few of those smoke-
less stoves. We can easily lay on electricity. It
will be absolutely the most sensational stone-laying
that ever was. It'll be in all the papers all over
the blessed world. Think of it! Torches! Fireworks from the cranes! . . . But I won't change
the day — neither for Miss April nor anybody else."

Mr. Marrier dissolved in laudations.

"Well," Edward Henry agreed with false diffidence, " it'll knock spots off some of 'em in this
town!"

He felt that he had snatched victory out of de-
feat. But the next moment he was capable of feeling that Elsie April had defeated him even in his
victory. Anyhow, she was a most disconcerting and
fancy-monopolising creature.

There was one source of unsullied gratification:
he had shaved off his beard.

VI.

"Come up here, Sir John," Edward Henry
called. " You'll see better, and you'll be out of the
crowd. And I'll show you something."

He stood, in a fur coat, at the top of a short
flight of rough-surfaced steps between two un-
plastered walls — a staircase which ultimately was
to form part of an emergency exit from the dress-

circle of the Regent Theatre. Sir John Pilgrim, also in a fur coat, stood near the bottom of the steps, with a glare of a Wells light full on him and throwing his shadow almost up to Edward Henry's feet. Around, Edward Henry could descry the vast mysterious forms of the building's skeleton — black in places, but in other places lit up by bright rays from the gaiety below, and showing glimpses of that gaiety in the occasional revelation of a woman's cloak through slits in the construction. High over-head, two gigantic cranes interlaced their arms; and even higher than the cranes, shone the stars of the clear spring night.

The hour was nearly half-past twelve. The cere-mony was concluded — and successfully concluded. All London had indeed been present. Half the aristocracy of England, and far more than half the aristocracy of the London stage! The entire preci-osity of the metropolis! Journalists with influence enough to plunge the whole of Europe into war! In one short hour Edward Henry's right hand (peeping out from the superb fur coat which he had had the wit to buy) had made the acquaintance of scores upon scores of the most celebrated right hands in Britain. He had the sensation that in fu-ture, whenever he walked about the best streets of the West End, he would be continually compelled to stop and chat with august and renowned acquaint-ances, and that he would always be taking off his hat to fine ladies who flashed by nodding from powerful motor-cars. Indeed, Edward Henry was surprised at the number of famous people who seemed to have nothing to do but attend advertising rituals at midnight or thereabouts. Sir John Pilgrim had, as Marrier predicted, attended to the advertisements. But Edward Henry had helped. And on the day itself the evening newspapers had taken the bit between their teeth and run off with the affair at a great pace. The affair was on all the contents-bills hours before it actually happened. Edward Henry had been interviewed several times, and had rather enjoyed that. Gradually he had perceived that his novel idea for a corner-stone-laying had caught the facile imagination of the London populace. For that night at least he was famous — as famous as anybody!

Sir John had made a wondrous picturesque figure of himself as, in a raised corner of the crowded and beflagged marquee, he had flourished a trowel and talked about the great and enlightened public, and about the highest function of the drama, and about the duty of the artist to elevate, and about the solemn responsibility of theatrical managers, and about the absence of petty jealousies in the world of the stage. Everybody had vociferously applauded, while reporters turned rapidly the pages of their note-books. "Ass!" Edward Henry had said to himself with much force and sincerity,— meaning Sir John,— but he too had vociferously applauded; for he was from the Five Towns, and in the Five Towns people are like that! Then Sir John had declared the corner-stone well and truly laid (it was

on the corner which the electric sign of the future
was destined to occupy), and, after being thanked,
had wandered off shaking hands here and there absently, to arrive at length in the office of the clerk
of the works, where Edward Henry had arranged
suitably to refresh the stone-layer and a few choice
friends of both sexes.

He had hoped that Elsie April would somehow
reach that little office. But Elsie April was absent,
indisposed. Her absence made the one blemish on
the affair's perfection. Elsie April, it appeared,
had been struck down by a cold which had entirely
deprived her of her voice, so that the performance
of the Azuré Society's Dramatic Club, so eagerly
anticipated by all London, had had to be postponed.
Edward Henry bore the misfortune of the Azure
Society with stoicism, but he had been extremely
disappointed by the invisibility of Elsie April at his
stone-laying. His eyes had wanted her.

Sir John, awaking apparently out of a dream
when Edward Henry had summoned him twice,
climbed the uneven staircase and joined his host and
youngest rival on the insecure planks and gangways
that covered the first floor of the Regent Theatre.

" Come higher," said Edward Henry, mounting
upward to the beginnings of the second story, above
which hung suspended from the larger crane the
great cage that was employed to carry brick and
stone from the ground.

The two fur coats almost mingled.

"Well, young man," said Sir John Pilgrim, "your troubles will soon be beginning."

Now Edward Henry hated to be addressed as "young man," especially in the patronising tone which Sir John used. Moreover, he had a suspicion that in Sir John's mind was the illusion that Sir John alone was responsible for the creation of the Regent Theatre — that without Sir John's aid as a stone-layer it could never have existed.

"You mean my troubles as a manager?" said Edward Henry grimly.

"In twelve months from now, before I come back from my world's tour, you'll be ready to get rid of this thing on any terms. You will be wishing that you had imitated my example and kept out of Piccadilly Circus. Piccadilly Circus is sinister, my Alderman — sinister."

"Come up into the cage, Sir John," said Edward Henry. "You'll get a still better view. Rather fine, isn't it, even from here?"

He climbed up into the cage and helped Sir John to climb.

And, standing there in the immediate silence, Sir John murmured with emotion:

"We are alone with London!"

Edward Henry thought:

"Cuckoo!"

They heard footsteps resounding on loose planks in a distant corner.

"Who's there?" Edward Henry called.

"Only me!" replied a voice. "Nobody takes any notice of me!"

"Who is it?" muttered Sir John.

"Alloyd, the architect," Edward Henry answered, and then calling loud: "Come up here, Alloyd."

The muffled and coated figure approached, hesitated, and then joined the other two in the cage.

"Let me introduce Mr. Alloyd, the architect — Sir John Pilgrim," said Edward Henry.

"Ah!" said Sir John, bending towards Alloyd. "Are you the genius who draws those amusing little lines and scrawls on transparent paper, Mr. Alloyd? Tell me, are they really necessary for a building, or do you only do them for your own fun? Quite between ourselves, you know! I've often wondered."

Said Mr. Alloyd with a pale smile:

"Of course everyone looks on the architect as a joke!" The pause was somewhat difficult.

"You promised us rockets, Mr. Machin," said Sir John. "My mind yearns for rockets."

"Right you are!" Edward Henry complied. Close by, but somewhat above them, was the crane-engine, manned by an engineer whom Edward Henry was paying for overtime. A signal was given, and the cage containing the proprietor and the architect of the theatre and Sir John Pilgrim bounded most startlingly up into the air. Simultaneously it began to revolve rapidly on its cable, as such cages will, whether filled with bricks or with celebrities.

"Oh!" ejaculated Sir John, terror-struck, clinging hard to the side of the cage.

"Oh!" ejaculated Mr. Alloyd, also clinging hard.

"I want you to see London," said Edward Henry, who had been through the experience before.

The wind blew cold above the chimneys.

The cage came to a standstill exactly at the peak of the other crane. London lay beneath the trio. The curves of Regent Street and of Shaftesbury Avenue, the right lines of Piccadilly, Lower Regent Street, and Coventry Street, were displayed at their feet as on an illuminated map, over which crawled mannikins and toy autobuses. At their feet a long procession of automobiles were sliding off, one after another, with the guests of the evening. The metropolis stretched away, lifting to the north, and sinking to the south into jewelled river on whose curved bank rose messages of light concerning whisky, tea, and beer. The peaceful nocturnal roar of the city, dwindling every moment now, reached them like an emanation from another world.

"You asked for a rocket, Sir John," said Edward Henry. "You shall have it."

He had taken a box of fuses from his pocket. He struck one, and his companions in the swaying cage now saw that a tremendous rocket was hung to the peak of the other crane. He lighted the fuse. . . . An instant of deathly suspense! . . . And then with a terrific and a shattering bang and splutter the rocket shot towards the kingdom of heaven, and there burst into a vast dome of red blossoms which, irradiating a square mile of roofs, descended slowly and softly on the West End like a benediction.

"You always want crimson, don't you, Sir John?" said Edward Henry, and the easy cheeriness of his voice gradually tranquillised the alarm natural to two very earthly men who for the first time found themselves suspended insecurely over a gulf.

"I have seen nothing so impressive since the Russian ballet," murmured Mr. Alloyd, recovering.

"You ought to go to Siberia, Alloyd," said Edward Henry.

Sir John Pilgrim, pretending now to be extremely brave, suddenly turned on Edward Henry and in a convulsive grasp seized his hand.

"My friend," he said hoarsely, "a thought has just occurred to me: you and I are the two most remarkable men in London!" He glanced up as the cage trembled. "How thin that steel rope seems!"

The cage slowly descended, with many twists.

Edward Henry said not a word. He was too deeply moved by his own triumph to be able to speak.

"Who else but me," he reflected, exultant, "could have managed this affair as I've managed it? Did anyone else ever take Sir John Pilgrim up into the sky like a load of bricks, and frighten his life out of him?"

As the cage approached the platforms of the first story he saw two people waiting there; one he recognised as the faithful, harmless Marrier; the other was a woman.

"Someone here wants you urgently, Mr. Machin!" cried Marrier.

"By Jove," exclaimed Alloyd under his breath, "what a beautiful figure! No girl as attractive as that ever wanted *me* urgently! Some folks do have luck!"

The woman had moved a little away when the cage landed. Edward Henry followed her along the planking.

It was Elsie April.

"I thought you were ill in bed," he breathed, astounded.

Her answering voice reached him, scarcely audible:

"I'm only hoarse. My cousin Rose has arrived to-night in secret at Tilbury by the *Minnetonka*."

"The *Minnetonka!*" he muttered. Staggering coincidence! Mystic heralding of misfortune!

"I was sent for," the pale ghost of a delicate voice continued. "She's broken, ruined; no courage left. Awful fiasco in Chicago! She's hiding now at a little hotel in Soho. She absolutely declined to come to my hotel. I've done what I could for the moment. As I was driving by here just now I saw the rocket, and I thought of you. I thought you ought to know it. I thought it was my duty to tell you."

She held her muff to her mouth. She seemed to be trembling.

A heavy hand was laid on his shoulder.

"Excuse me, sir," said a strong, rough voice. "Are you the gent that fired off the rocket? It's against the law to do that kind o' thing here, and you ought to know it. I shall have to trouble you —"

It was a policeman of the C division.

Sir John was disappearing, with his stealthy and conspiratorial air, down the staircase.

CHAPTER VIII

DEALING WITH ELSIE

I.

THE headquarters of the Azure Society were situate in Marloes Road, for no other reason than that it happened so. Though certain famous people inhabit Marloes Road, no street could well be less fashionable than this thoroughfare, which is very arid and very long, and a very long way off the centre of the universe.

" The Azure Society, you know! " Edward Henry added when he had given the exact address to the chauffeur of the taxi.

The chauffeur, however, did not know, and did not seem to be ashamed of his ignorance. His attitude indicated that he despised Marloes Road, and was not particularly anxious for his vehicle to be seen therein, especially on a wet night, but that nevertheless he would endeavour to reach it. When he did reach it, and observed the large concourse of shining automobiles that struggled together in the rain in front of the illuminated number named by Edward Henry, the chauffeur admitted to himself that for once he had been mistaken, and his manner of receiving money from Edward Henry was generously respectful.

Originally the headquarters of the Azure Society had been a seminary and schoolmistress' house. The thoroughness with which the buildings had been transformed showed that money was not among the things which the society had to search for. It had rich resources, and it had also high social standing; and the deferential commissionaires at the doors and the fluffy-aproned, appealing girls who gave away programmes in the foyer were a proof that the society, while doubtless anxious about such subjects as the persistence of individuality after death, had no desire to reconstitute the community on a democratic basis. It was above such transient trifles of reform, and its high endeavours were confined to questions of immortality, of the infinite, of sex, and of art: which questions it discussed in fine raiment and with all the punctilio of courtly politeness.

Edward Henry was late, in common with some two hundred other people of whom the majority were elegant women wearing Paris or almost Paris gowns with a difference. As on the current of the variegated throng he drifted through corridors into the bijou theatre of the society, he could not help feeling proud of his own presence there; and yet at the same time he was scorning, in his Five Towns way, the preciosity and the simperings of these his fellow creatures. Seated in the auditorium, at the end of a row, he was aware of an even keener satisfaction as people bowed and smiled at him; for the theatre was so tiny and the reunion so choice that it was obviously an honour and a distinction to have been invited to such an exclusive affair. To the evening first fixed for the dramatic *soirée* of the Azure Society he had received no invitation. But shortly after the postponement due to Elsie April's indisposition an envelope addressed by Marrier himself, and containing the sacred card, had arrived for him in Bursley. His instinct had been to ignore it, and for two days he had ignored it, and then he noticed in one corner the initials " E. A." Strange that it did not occur to him immediately that E. A. stood, or might stand, for Elsie April!

Reflection brings wisdom and knowledge. In the end he was absolutely convinced that E. A. stood for Elsie April; and at the last moment, deciding that it would be the act of a fool and a coward to decline what was practically a personal request from a young and enchanting woman, he had come to London — short of sleep, it is true, owing to local convivialities, but he had come. And, curiously, he had not communicated with Marrier. Marrier had been extremely taken up with the dramatic *soirée* of the Azure Society, which Edward Henry justifiably but quite privately resented. Was he not paying three pounds a week to Marrier?

And now, there he sat, known, watched, a notoriety, the card who had raised Pilgrim to the skies, probably the only theatrical proprietor in the crowded and silent audience; and he was expecting anxiously to see Elsie April again — across the footlights! He had not seen her since the night of the stone-laying, over a week earlier. He had not sought to see her. He had listened then to the delicate tones of her weak, whispering, thrilling voice, and had expressed regret for Rose Euclid's plight. But he had done no more. What could he have done? Clearly he could not have offered money to relieve the plight of Rose Euclid, who was the cousin of a girl as wealthy and as sympathetic as Elsie April. To do so would have been to insult Elsie. Yet he felt guilty none the less. An odd situation! The delicate tones of Elsie's weak, whispering, thrilling voice on the scaffolding haunted his memory, and came back with strange clearness as he sat waiting for the curtain to ascend.

There was an outburst of sedate applause, and a turning of heads to the right. Edward Henry looked in that direction. Rose Euclid herself was bowing from one of the two boxes on the first tier. Instantly she had been recognised and acknowledged, and the clapping had in nowise disturbed her. Evidently she accepted it as a matter of course. How famous, after all, she must be, if such an audience would pay her such a meed! She was pale, and dressed glitteringly in white. She seemed younger, more graceful, much more handsome, more in accordance with her renown. She was at home and at ease up there in the brightness of publicity. The imposing legend of her long career had survived the eclipse in the United States. Who could have guessed that some ten days before she had landed heart-broken and ruined at Tilbury from the *Minnetonka?*

Edward Henry was impressed.

" She's none so dusty ! " he said to himself in the incomprehensible slang of the Five Towns. The phrase was a high compliment to Rose Euclid, aged fifty and looking anything you like over thirty. It measured the extent to which he was impressed.

Yes, he felt guilty. He had to drop his eyes, lest hers should catch them. He examined guiltily the programme, which announced " The New Don Juan," a play " in three acts and in verse "— author unnamed. The curtain went up.

II.

And with the rising of the curtain began Edward Henry's torture and bewilderment. The scene disclosed a cloth upon which was painted, to the right, a vast writhing purple cuttlefish whose finer tentacles were lost above the proscenium-arch, and to the left an enormous crimson oblong patch with a hole in it. He referred to the programme, which said: " Act. I. A castle in the forest," and also " Scenery and costumes designed by Saracen Givington, A.R.A." The cuttlefish, then, was the purple forest, or perhaps one tree in the forest, and the oblong patch was the crimson castle. The stage remained empty, and Edward Henry had time to perceive that the footlights were unlit, and that rays came only from the flies and from the wings.

He glanced round. Nobody had blenched. Quite confused, he referred again to the programme and deciphered in the increasing gloom, " Lighting by Cosmo Clark," in very large letters.

Two yellow-clad figures of no particular sex glided into view, and at the first words which they uttered Edward Henry's heart seemed in apprehension to cease to beat. A fear seized him. A few more words, and the fear became a positive assurance and realisation of evil. " The New Don Juan " was simply a pseudonym for Carlo Trent's " Orient Pearl "! . . . He had always known that it would be. Ever since deciding to accept the invitation he had lived under just that menace. " The Orient Pearl " seemed to be pursuing him like a sinister destiny.

Weakly he consulted yet again the programme. Only one character bore a name familiar to the Don Juan story; to wit, " Haidee "; and opposite that name was the name of Elsie April. He waited for her,— he had no other interest in the evening,— and he waited in resignation. A young female troubadour (styled in the programme " the messenger ") emerged from the unseen depths of the forest in the wings and ejaculated to the hero and his friend: " The woman appears." But it was not Elsie that appeared. Six times that troubadour messenger emerged and ejaculated, " The woman appears," and each time Edward Henry was disappointed. But at the seventh heralding — the heralding of the seventh and highest heroine of this drama in hexameters — Elsie did at length appear.

And Edward Henry became happy. He under-

stood little more of the play than at the historic
breakfast-party of Sir John Pilgrim; he was well confirmed in his belief that the play was exactly as pre-
posterous as a play in verse must necessarily be; his
manly contempt for verse was more firmly established than ever — but Elsie April made an exquisite
figure between the castle and the forest; her voice
did really set up physical vibrations in his spine.
He was deliciously convinced that if she remained
on the stage from everlasting to everlasting, just so
long could he gaze thereat without surfeit and without other desire. The mischief was that she did not
remain on the stage. With despair he saw her
depart; and the close of the act was ashes in his
mouth.

The applause was tremendous. It was not as tremendous as that which had greeted the plate-smash-
ing comedy at the Hanbridge Empire, but it was
far more than sufficiently enthusiastic to startle and
shock Edward Henry. In fact, his cold indifference
was so conspicuous amid that fever, that in order
to save his face he had to clap and to smile.

And the dreadful thought crossed his mind, tra-
versing it like the shudder of a distant earthquake
that presages complete destruction:

"Are the ideas of the Five Towns all wrong?
Am I a provincial after all?"

For hitherto, though he had often admitted to
himself that he was a provincial, he had never done
so with sincerity; but always in a manner of playful
and rather condescending bandinage.

III.

" Did you ever see such scenery and costumes? "
some one addressed him suddenly when the applause
had died down.   It was Mr. Alloyd, who had advanced up the aisle from the back row of the stalls.

" No, I never did! " Edward Henry agreed.

" It's wonderful how Givington has managed to
get away from the childish realism of the modern
theatre," said Mr. Alloyd, " without being ridiculous."

" You think so! " said Edward Henry judicially.
" The question is, Has he? "

" Do you mean it's too realistic for you? " cried
Mr. Alloyd.   " Well, you *are* advanced!   I didn't
know you were as anti-representational as all that! "

" Neither did I! " said Edward Henry.   " What
do you think of the play? "

" Well," answered Mr. Alloyd low and cautiously, with a somewhat shamed grin, " between you
and me, I think the play's bosh."

" Come, come! " Edward Henry murmured as if
in protest.

The word " bosh " was almost the first word of
the discussion which he had comprehended, and the
honest familiar sound of it did him good.   Nevertheless, keeping his presence of mind, he had for-
borne to welcome it openly.   He wondered what on
earth " anti-representational " could mean.   Similar
conversations were proceeding around him, and each
could be very closely heard, for the reason that, the

audience being frankly intellectual and anxious to exchange ideas, the management had wisely avoided the expense and noise of an orchestra. The entr'acte was like a *conversazione* of all the cultures.

" I wish you'd give us some scenery and costumes like this in *your* theatre," said Alloyd as he strolled away.

The remark stabbed him like a needle; the pain was gone in an instant, but it left a vague fear behind it, as of the menace of a mortal injury. It is a fact that Edward Henry blushed and grew gloomy, and he scarcely knew why. He looked about him timidly, half defiantly. A magnificently arrayed woman in the row in front, somewhat to the right, leaned back and towards him, and behind her fan said:

" You're the only manager here, Mr. Machin! How alive and alert you are! " Her voice seemed to be charged with a hidden meaning.

" D'you think so? " said Edward Henry. He had no idea who she might be. He had probably shaken hands with her at his stone-laying, but if so he had forgotten her face. He was fast becoming one of the oligarchical few who are recognised by far more people than they recognise.

" A beautiful play! " said the woman. " Not merely poetic, but intellectual. And an extraordinarily acute criticism of modern conditions! "

He nodded. " What do you think of the scenery? " he asked.

" Well, of course candidly," said the woman, " I think it's silly. I dare say I'm old-fashioned."

" I dare say," murmured Edward Henry.

" They told me you were very ironic," said she, flushing but meek.

" They! " Who? Who in the world of London had been labelling him as ironic? He was rather proud.

" I hope if you *do* do this kind of play,— and we're all looking to you, Mr. Machin," said the lady making a new start,—" I hope you won't go in for these costumes and scenery. That would never do ! "

Again the stab of the needle!

" It wouldn't," he said.

" I'm delighted you think so," said she.

An orange telegram came travelling from hand to hand along that row of stalls, and ultimately, after skipping a few persons, reached the magnificently arrayed woman, who read it and then passed it to Edward Henry.

" Splendid! " she exclaimed. " Splendid! "

Edward Henry read: " Released. Isabel."

" What does it mean? "

" It's from Isabel Joy — at Marseilles."

" Really! "

Edward Henry's ignorance of affairs round about the centre of the universe was occasionally distressing — to himself in particular. And just now he gravely blamed Mr. Marrier, who had neglected to post him about Isabel Joy. But how could Mar-

rier honestly earn his three pounds a week if he was
occupied night and day with the organising and management of these precious dramatic *soirées?* Edward Henry decided that he must give Mr. Marrier
a piece of his mind at the first opportunity.

" Don't you know ? " questioned the dame.

" How should I ? " he parried. " I'm only a
provincial."

" But surely," pursued the dame, " you knew we'd
sent her round the world. She started on the *Kandahar,* the ship that you stopped Sir John Pilgrim
from taking. She almost atoned for his absence at
Tilbury. Twenty-five reporters, anyway ! "

Edward Henry sharply slapped his thigh, which
in the Five Towns signifies, " I shall forget my own
name next."

Of course ! Isabel Joy was the advertising emissary of the Militant Suffragette Society, sent forth
to hold a public meeting and make a speech in the
principal ports of the world. She had guaranteed
to circuit the globe and to be back in London within
a hundred days, to speak in at least five languages,
and to get herself arrested at least three times en
route. Of course ! Isabel Joy had possessed a
very fair share of the newspapers on the day before
the stone-laying, but Edward Henry had naturally
had too many preoccupations to follow her exploits.
After all, his momentary forgetfulness was rather
excusable.

" She's made a superb beginning ! " said the resplendent dame, taking the telegram from Edward

Henry and inducting it into another row. " And before three months are out she'll be the talk of the entire earth. You'll see!"

" Is everybody a suffragette here?" asked Edward Henry simply, as his eyes witnessed the satisfaction spread by the voyaging telegram.

" Practically," said the dame. " These things always go hand in hand," she added in a deep tone.

" What things?" the provincial demanded.

But just then the curtain rose on the second act.

IV.

" Won't you cam up to Miss April's dressing-room?" said Mr. Marrier, who in the midst of the fulminating applause after the second act seemed to be inexplicably standing over him, having appeared in an instant out of nowhere like a genie.

The fact was that Edward Henry had been gently and innocently dozing. It was in part the deep obscurity of the auditorium, in part his own physical fatigue, and in part the secret nature of poetry that had been responsible for this restful slumber. He had remained awake without difficulty during the first portion of the act, in which Elsie April — the orient pearl — had had a long scene of emotion and tears, played, as Edward Henry thought, magnificently in spite of its inherent ridiculousness; but later, when gentle *Haidee* had vanished away and the fateful troubadour messenger had begun to resume her announcements of " The woman appears," Edward Henry's soul had miserably yielded to his

body and to the temptation of darkness. The upturned lights and the ringing hosannahs had roused
him to a full sense of sin, but he had not quite recovered all his faculties when Marrier startled him.

"Yes, yes! Of course! I was coming," he answered a little petulantly. But no petulance could
impair the beaming optimism on Mr. Marrier's features. To judge by those features, Mr. Marrier,
in addition to having organised and managed the
soirée, might also have written the piece and played
every part in it, and founded the Azure Society and
built its private theatre. The hour was Mr. Marrier's.

Elsie April's dressing-room was small and very
thickly populated, and the threshold of it was
barred by eager persons who were half in and half
out of the room. Through these Mr. Marrier's
authority forced a way. The first man Edward
Henry recognised in the tumult of bodies was Mr.
Rollo Wrissell, whom he had not seen since their
meeting at Slosson's.

"Mr. Wrissell," said the glowing Marrier, "let
me introduce Mr. Alderman Machin, of the Regent
Theatah."

"Clumsy fool!" thought Edward Henry, and
stood as if entranced.

But Mr. Wrissell held out a hand with the perfection of urbane *insouciance*.

"How d'you do, Mr. Machin?" said he. "I
hope you'll forgive me for not having followed your
advice."

This was a lesson to Edward Henry. He learnt that you should never show a wound, and if possible never feel one. He admitted that in such details of social conduct London might be in advance of the Five Towns, despite the Five Towns' admirable downrightness.

Lady Woldo was also in the dressing-room, glorious in black. Her beauty was positively disconcerting, and the more so on this occasion as she was bending over the faded Rose Euclid, who sat in a corner surrounded by a court. This court, comprising comparatively uncelebrated young women and men, listened with respect to the conversation of the peeress (who called Rose "my dear"), the great star-actress, and the now somewhat notorious Five Towns character, Edward Henry Machin.

"Miss April is splendid, isn't she?" said Edward Henry to Lady Woldo.

"Oh! My word, yes!" replied Lady Woldo nicely, warmly, yet with a certain perfunctoriness. Edward Henry was astonished that everybody was not passionately enthusiastic about the charm of Elsie's performance. Then Lady Woldo added: "But what a part for Miss Euclid! What a part for her!"

And there were murmurs of approbation.

Rose Euclid gazed at Edward Henry palely and weakly. He considered her much less effective here than in her box. But her febrile gaze was effective enough to produce in him the needle-stab again, the feeling of gloom, of pessimism, of being gradually overtaken by an unseen and mysterious avenger.

"Yes, indeed!" said he.

He thought to himself: "Now's the time for me to behave like Edward Henry Machin, and teach these people a thing or two!" But he could not.

A pretty young girl summoned all her forces to address the great proprietor of the Regent, to whom, however, she had not been introduced, and with a charming nervous earnest lisp said:

"But don't you think it's a great play, Mr. Machin?"

"Of course!" he replied, inwardly employing the most fearful and shocking anathemas.

"We were sure *you* would!"

The young people glanced at each other with the satisfaction of proved prophets.

"D'you know that not another manager has taken the trouble to come here!" said a second earnest young woman.

Edward Henry's self-consciousness was now acute. He would have paid a ransom to be alone on a desert island in the Indian seas. He looked downwards, and noticed that all these bright eager persons, women and men, were wearing blue stockings or socks."

"Miss April is free now," said Marrier in his ear.

The next instant he was talking alone to Elsie in another corner, while the rest of the room respectfully observed.

"So you deigned to come!" said Elsie April. "You did get my card!"

A little paint did her no harm, and the accentuation of her eyebrows and lips and the calculated disorder of her hair were not more than her powerful effulgent physique could stand. In a costume of green and silver she was magnificent, overwhelmingly magnificent.

Her varying voice and her glance, at once sincere, timid, and bold, produced the most singular sensations behind Edward Henry's soft-frilled shirt-front. And he thought that he had never been through any experience so disturbing and so fine as just standing in front of her.

"I ought to be saying nice things to her," he reflected; but, no doubt because he had been born in the Five Towns, he could not formulate in his mind a single nice thing.

"Well, what do you think of it?" she asked, looking full at him, and the glance too had a strange significance. It was as if she had said: "Are you a man, or aren't you?"

"I think you're splendid," he exclaimed.

"Now please!" she protested. "Don't begin in that strain. I know I'm very good for an amateur —"

"But really! I'm not joking!"

She shook her head.

"What do you think of my part for Rose? Wouldn't she be tremendous in it? Wouldn't she be tremendous? What a chance!"

He was acutely uncomfortable, but even his discomfort was somehow a joy.

" Yes," he admitted.   " Yes."

" Oh!   Here's Carlo Trent," said she.

He heard Trent's triumphant voice carrying the end of a conversation into the room: " If he hadn't been going away," Carlo Trent was saying, " Pilgrim would have taken it.   Pilgrim —"

The poet's eyes met Edward Henry's, and the sentence was never finished.

" How d'ye do, Machin? " murmured the poet.

Then a bell began to ring and would not stop.

" You're staying for the reception afterwards? " said Elsie April as the room emptied.

" Is there one? "

" Of course."

It seemed to Edward Henry that they exchanged silent messages.

v.

Some time after the last hexameter had rolled forth, and the curtain had finally fallen on the immense and rapturous success of Carlo Trent's play in three acts and in verse, Edward Henry, walking about the crowded stage where the reception was being held, encountered Elsie April, who was still in her gorgeous dress of green and silver.   She was chatting with Marrier, who instantly left her, thus displaying a discretion such as an employer would naturally expect from a factotum to whom he was paying three pounds a week.

Edward Henry's heart began to beat in a manner which troubled him and made him wonder what could be happening at the back of the soft-frilled shirt-front that he had obtained in imitation of Mr. Seven Sachs.

"Not much elbow-room here!" he said lightly. He was very anxious to be equal to the occasion.

She gazed at him under her emphasized eyebrows. He noticed that there were little touches of red on her delightful nostrils.

"No," she answered with direct simplicity. "Suppose we try somewhere else."

She turned her back on all the amiable and intellectual babble, descended three steps on the prompt side, and opened a door. The swish of her brocaded spreading skirt was loud and sensuous. He followed her into an obscure chamber in which several figures were moving to and fro and talking.

"What's this place?" he asked. Involuntarily his voice was diminished to a whisper.

"It's one of the discussion-rooms," said she. "It used to be a classroom, I expect, before the society took the buildings over. You see the theatre was the general schoolroom."

They sat down inobtrusively in an embrasure. None among the mysterious moving figures seemed to remark them.

"But why are they talking in the dark?" Edward Henry asked behind his hand.

"To begin with, it isn't quite dark," she said. "There's the light of the street-lamp through the

window. But it has been found that serious dis-
cussions can be carried on much better without too
much light. . . . I'm not joking." (It was as if
in the gloom her ears had caught his faint sardonic
smile.)

Said the voice of one of the figures:

" Can you tell me what is the origin of the decay
of realism? Can you tell me that? "

Suddenly, in the ensuing silence, there was a click
and a tiny electric lamp shot its beam. The hand
which held the lamp was the hand of Carlo Trent.
He raised it and flashed the trembling ray in the in-
quirer's face. Edward Henry recalled Carlo's objection to excessive electricity in the private drawing-room at Wilkins's.

" Why do you ask such a question? " Carlo Trent
challenged the enquirer, brandishing the lamp. " I
ask you why do you ask it? "

The other also drew forth a lamp and, as it were,
cocked it and let it off at the features of Carlo
Trent. And thus the two stood, statuesque and
lit, surrounded by shadowy witnesses of the discussion.

The door creaked and yet another figure, sil-
houetted for an instant against the illumination of
the stage, descended into the discussion-chamber.

Carlo Trent tripped towards the newcomer, bent
with his lamp, lifted delicately the hem of the newcomer's trousers, and gazed at the colour of his sock,
which was blue.

" All right! " said he.

" The champagne and sandwiches are served," said the newcomer.

" You've not answered me, sir," Carlo Trent faced once more his opponent in the discussion. " You've not answered me."

Whereupon, the lamps being extinguished, they all filed forth, the door swung to of its own accord, shutting out the sound of babble from the stage, and Edward Henry and Elsie April were left silent and solitary to the sole ray of the street-lamp.

All the Five Towns shrewdness in Edward Henry's character, all the husband in him, all the father in him, all the son in him, leapt to his lips and tried to say to Elsie, " Shall *we* go and inspect the champagne and sandwiches too? " and failed to say these incantatory words of salvation!

And the romantic adventurous fool in him rejoiced at their failure. For he was adventurously happy in his propinquity to that simple and sincere creature. He was so happy, and his heart was so active, that he even made no caustic characteristic comment on the singular behaviour of the beings who had just abandoned them to their loneliness. He was also proud because he was sitting alone nearly in the dark with a piquant and wealthy, albeit amateur, actress who had just participated in a triumph at which the spiritual aristocracy of London had assisted.

VI.

Two thoughts ran through his head, shooting in and out and to and fro among his complex sensations of pleasure. The first was that he had never been in such a fix before, despite his enterprising habits. And the second was that neither Elsie April nor anybody else connected with his affairs in London had ever asked him whether he was married, nor assumed by any detail of behaviour towards him that there existed the possibility of his being married. Of course he might, had he chosen, have informed a few of them that a wife and children possessed him, but then, really, would not that have been equivalent to attaching a label to himself " Married " ?— a procedure which had to him the stamp of provinciality.

Elsie April said nothing. And as she said nothing he was obliged to say something, if only to prove to both of them that he was not a mere tongue-tied provincial. He said:

" You know I feel awfully out of it here in this society of yours! "

" Out of it? " she exclaimed, and her voice thrilled as she resented his self-depreciation.

" It's over my head — right over it! "

" Now, Mr. Machin," she said, dropping somewhat that rich, low voice, " I quite understand that there are some things about the society you don't like, trifles that you're inclined to laugh at. *I* know that. Many of us know it. But it can't be helped in an organisation like ours. It's even essential. Don't be too hard on us. Don't be sarcastic."

" But I'm not sarcastic! " he protested.

" Honest?" She turned to him quickly. He could descry her face in the gloom, and the forward bend of her shoulders, and the backward sweep of her arms resting on the seat, and the straight droop of her Egyptian shawl from her inclined body.

" Honest!" he solemnly insisted.

The exchange of this single word was so intimate that it shifted their conversation to a different level — a level at which each seemed to be assuring the other that intercourse between them could never be aught but utterly sincere thenceforward, and that indeed in future they would constitute a little society of their own, ideal in its organisation.

" Then you're too modest," she said decidedly. " There was no one here to-night who's more respected than you are. No one! Immediately I first spoke to you — I daresay you don't remember that afternoon at the Grand Babylon Hotel — I knew you weren't like the rest. And don't I know them? Don't I know them?"

" But how did you know I'm not like the rest?" asked Edward Henry. The line which she was taking had very much surprised him, and charmed him. The compliment, so serious and urgent in tone, was intensely agreeable, and it made an entirely new experience in his career. He thought: " Oh! There's no mistake about it. These London women are marvellous! They're just as straight and in earnest as the best of our little lot down there. But they've got something else. There's no comparison!" The unique word to describe the indescribable floated into his head: "Scrumptuous!" What could not life be with such semi-divine creatures? He dreamt of art drawing-rooms softly shaded at midnight. And his attitude towards even poetry was modified.

"I knew you weren't like the rest," said she, "by your look; by the way you say everything you *do* say. We all know it. And I'm sure you're far more than clever enough to be perfectly aware that we all know it. Just see how everyone looked at you to-night!"

Yes, he had in fact been aware of the glances.

"I think I ought to tell you," she went on, "that I was rather unfair to you that day in talking about my cousin — in the taxi. You were quite right to refuse to go into partnership with her. She thinks so too. We've talked it over, and we're quite agreed. Of course it did seem hard — at the time, and her bad luck in America seemed to make it worse. But you were quite right. You can work much better alone. You must have felt that instinctively — far quicker than we felt it."

"Well," he murmured, confused, "I don't know —"

Could this be she who had too openly smiled at his skirmish with an artichoke?

"Oh, Mr. Machin," she burst out, "you've got an unprecedented opportunity, and, thank Heaven, you're the man to use it! We're all expecting so much from you, and we know we sha'n't be disappointed."

" D'ye mean the theatre?" he asked, alarmed as it were amid rising waters.

" The theatre," said she gravely. " You're the one man that can save London. No one *in* London can do it! . . . *You* have the happiness of knowing what your mission is, and of knowing too that you are equal to it. What good fortune! I wish I could say as much for myself. I want to do something! I try! But what can I do? Nothing — really! You've no idea of the awful loneliness that comes from a feeling of inability."

" Loneliness!" he repeated. " But surely —" He stopped.

" Loneliness," she insisted. Her little chin was now in her little hand, and her dim face upturned.

And suddenly a sensation of absolute and marvellous terror seized Edward Henry. He was more afraid than he had ever been — and yet once or twice in his life he had felt fear. His sense of true perspective — one of his most precious qualities — returned. He thought: " I've got to get out of this." Well, the door was not locked. It was only necessary to turn the handle, and security lay on the other side of the door! He had but to rise and walk. And he could not. He might just as well have been manacled in a prison-cell. He was under an enchantment.

" A man," murmured Elsie, " a man can never realise the loneliness —" She ceased.

He stirred uneasily.

" About this play," he found himself saying.

And yet why should he mention the play in his fright? He pretended to himself not to know why.   But he knew why.   His instinct had seen in the topic of the play the sole avenue of salvation.

" A wonderful thing, isn't it? "

" Oh, yes," he said; and then, most astonishingly to himself, added: " I've decided to do it."

" We knew you would," she said calmly.   " At any rate I did. . . . You'll open with it of course."

" Yes," he answered desperately, and proceeded, with the most extraordinary bravery: " If you'll act in it."

Immediately on hearing these last words issue from his mouth he knew that a fool had uttered them, and that the bravery was mere rashness; for Elsie's responding gesture reinspired him afresh with the exquisite terror which he had already begun to conjure away.

" You think Miss Euclid ought to have the part," he added quickly, before she could speak.

" Oh, I do! " cried Elsie positively and eagerly. " Rose will do simply wonders with that part.   You see she can speak verse.   I can't.   I'm nobody.   I only took it because —"

" Aren't you anybody? " he contradicted. " Aren't you anybody?   I can just tell you —"

There he was again, bringing back the delicious terror!   An astounding situation!

But the door creaked.   The babble from the stage invaded the room.   And in a second the enchantment was lifted from him.   Several people entered. He sighed, saying within himself to the disturbers:

"I'd have given you a hundred-pound piece if you'd been five minutes sooner."

And yet simultaneously he regretted their arrival. And, more curious still, though he well remembered the warning words of Mr. Seven Sachs concerning Elsie April, he did not consider that they were justified. She had not been a bit persuasive . . . only . . .

VII.

He sat down to the pianisto with a strange and agreeable sense of security. It is true that, owing to the time of year, the drawing-room had been, in the figurative phrase, turned upside down by the process of spring-cleaning, which his unexpected arrival had surprised in fullest activity. But he did not mind that. He abode content among rolled carpets, a swathed chandelier, piled chairs, and walls full of pale rectangular spaces where pictures had been. Early that morning, after a brief night spent partly in bed and partly in erect contemplation of his immediate past and his immediate future, he had hurried back to his pianisto and his home — to the beings and things that he knew and that knew him.

In the train he had had the pleasure of reading in sundry newspapers that "The Orient Pearl," by Carlo Trent (who was mentioned in terms of startling respect and admiration), had been performed on the previous evening at the dramatic *soirée* of the

Azure Society, with all the usual accompaniments of secrecy and exclusiveness, in its private theatre in Kensington, and had been accepted on the spot by Mr. E. H. Machin ("that most enterprising and enlightened recruit to the ranks of theatrical managers") for production at the new Regent Theatre. And further, that Mr. Machin intended to open with it. And still further, that his selection of such a play, which combined in the highest degree the poetry of Mr. W. B. Yeats with the critical intellectuality of Mr. Bernard Shaw, was of excellent augury for London's dramatic future, and that the "upward movement" must on no account be thought to have failed because of the failure of certain recent ill-judged attempts, by persons who did not understand their business, to force it in particular directions. And still further, that he, Edward Henry, had engaged for the principal part Miss Rose Euclid, perhaps the greatest emotional actress the English-speaking peoples had ever had, but who unfortunately had not been sufficiently seen of late on the London stage, and that this would be her first appearance after her recent artistic successes in the United States. And lastly, that Mr. Marrier (whose name would be remembered in connection with . . . etc., etc.) was Mr. E. H. Machin's acting manager and technical adviser. Edward Henry could trace the hand of Marrier in all the paragraphs. Marrier had lost no time.

Mrs. Machin, senior, came into the drawing-room just as he was adjusting the "Tannhäuser" overture to the mechanicien. The piece was one of his major favourites.

" This is no place for you, my lad," said Mrs. Machin grimly, glancing round the room. " But I came to tell ye as th' mutton's been cooling at least five minutes. You gave out as you were hungry."

" Keep your hair on, Mother," said he, springing up.

Barely twelve hours earlier he had been mincing among the elect and the select and the intellectual and the poetic and the aristocratic; among the lah-di-dah and Kensingtonian accents; among rouged lips and blue hose and fixed simperings; in the centre of the universe. And he had conducted himself with considerable skill accordingly. Nobody, on the previous night, could have guessed from the cut of his fancy waistcoat, or the judiciousness of his responses to remarks about verse, that his wife often wore a white apron, or that his mother was — the woman she was! He had not unskillfully caught many of the tricks of that metropolitan environment. But now they all fell away from him, and he was just Edward Henry — nay, he was almost the old Denry again.

" Who chose this mutton? " he asked as he bent over the juicy and rich joint and cut therefrom exquisite thick slices with a carving-knife like a razor.

" *I* did, if ye want to know," said his mother. " Anything amiss with it? " She challenged.

" No. It's fine."

" Yes," said she, " I'm wondering whether you get

aught as good as that in these grand hotels, as you call 'em."

"We don't," said Edward Henry. First, it was true, and secondly he was anxious to be propitiatory, for he had a plan to further.

He looked at his wife. She was not talkative, but she had received him in the hall with every detail of affection, if a little absent-mindedly, owing to the state of the house. She had not been caustic, like his mother, about this male incursion into spring-cleaning. She had not informed the surrounding air that she failed to understand why them as were in London couldn't stop in London for a bit, as his mother had. Moreover, though the spring-cleaning fully entitled her to wear a white apron at meals, she was not wearing a white apron, which was a sign to him that she still loved him enough to want to please him. On the whole, he was fairly optimistic about his plan of salvation. Nevertheless, it was not until nearly the end of the meal, when one of his mother's ample pies was being consumed, that he began to try to broach it.

"Nell," he said, "I suppose you wouldn't care to come to London with me?"

"Oh!" she answered smiling, a smile of a peculiar quality. It was astonishing how that simple woman could put just one-tenth of one per cent. of irony into a good-natured smile. "What's the meaning of this?" Then she flushed. The flush touched Edward Henry in an extraordinary manner.

("To think," he reflected, incredulously, "that

only last night I was talking in the dark to Elsie April — and here I am now!" And he remembered the glory of Elsie's frock, and her thrilling voice in the gloom, and that pose of hers as she leaned dimly forward.)

"Well," he said aloud, as naturally as he could. "That theatre's beginning to get up on its hind legs now, and I should like you to see it."

A difficult pass for him, as regards his mother! This was the first time he had ever overtly spoken of the theatre in his mother's presence. In the best bedroom he had talked of it, but even there with a certain self-consciousness and false casualness. Now his mother stared straight in front of her with an expression of which she alone among human beings had the monopoly.

"I should like to," said Nellie generously.

"Well," said he, "I've got to go back to town to-morrow. Wilt come with me, lass?"

"Don't be silly, Edward Henry," said she. "How can I leave Mother in the middle of all this spring-cleaning?"

"You needn't leave Mother. We'll take her too," said Edward Henry lightly.

"You won't!" observed Mrs. Machin.

"I *have* to go to-morrow, Nell," said Edward Henry. "And I was thinking you might as well come with me. It will be a change for you."

(He said to himself: "And not only have I to go to-morrow, but you absolutely must come with me, my girl. That's the one thing to do.")

" It would be a change for me," Nellie agreed. She was beyond doubt flattered and calmly pleased. " But I can't possibly come to-morrow. You can see that for yourself, dear."

" No, I can't! " he cried impatiently. " What does it matter? Mother'll be here. The kids'll be all right. After all, spring cleaning isn't the day of judgment."

" Edward Henry," said his mother, cutting in between them like a thin blade, " I wish you wouldn't be blasphemous. London's London, and Bursley's Bursley." She had finished.

" It's quite out of the question for me to come to-morrow, dear. I must have notice. I really must."

And Edward Henry saw with alarm that Nellie had made up her mind, and that the flattered calm pleasure in his suggestion had faded from her face.

" Oh, dash these domesticated women! " he thought, and shortly afterwards departed, brooding, to the offices of the Thrift Club.

VIII.

He timed his return with exactitude, and, going straight up-stairs to the chamber known indifferently as " Maisie's room " or " nurse's room," sure enough he found the three children there alone! They were fed, washed, night-gowned, and even dressing-gowned; and this was the hour when, while Nurse repaired the consequences of their revolutionary conduct in the bathroom and other places, they were left to themselves.   Robert lay on the hearth-rug, the insteps of his soft, pink feet rubbing idly against the pile of the rug, his elbows digging into the pile, his chin on his fists, and a book perpendicularly beneath his eyes.   Ralph, careless adventurer rather than student, had climbed to the glittering brass rail of Maisie's new bedstead, and was thereon imitating a recently seen circus performance.   Maisie, in the bed according to regulation, and lying on the flat of her back, was singing nonchalantly to the ceiling. Carlo, unaware that at that moment he might have been a buried corpse but for the benignancy of Providence in his behalf, was feeling sympathetic towards himself because he was slightly bored.

"Hello, kids!"   Edward Henry greeted them. As he had seen them before midday dinner, the more formal ceremonies of salutation after absence, so hateful to the Five Towns temperament, were happily over and done with.

Robert turned his head slightly, inspected his father with a judicial detachment that hardly escaped the inimical, and then resumed his book.

("No one would think," said Edward Henry to himself, "that the person who has just entered this room is the most enterprising and enlightened of West End theatrical managers.")

"'Ello, Father!" shrilled Ralph.   "Come and help me to stand on this wire rope."

"It isn't a wire rope," said Robert from the hearth-rug, without stirring.   "It's a brass rail."

"Yes, it is a wire rope, because I can make it

bend," Ralph retorted, bumping down on the thing. "Anyhow, it's going to be a wire rope."

Maisie simply stuck several fingers into her mouth, shifted to one side, and smiled at her father in a style of heavenly and mischievous flirtatiousness.

"Well, Robert, what are you reading?" Edward Henry inquired in his best fatherly manner, half authoritative and half humorous, while he formed part of the staff of Ralph's circus.

"I'm not reading, I'm learning my spellings," replied Robert.

Edward Henry, knowing that the discipline of filial politeness must be maintained, said: "'Learning my spellings'— what?"

"Learning my spellings, Father," Robert consented to say, but with a savage air of giving way to the unreasonable demands of affected fools. Why indeed should it be necessary in conversation always to end one's sentence with the name or title of the person addressed?

"Well, would you like to go to London with me?"

"When?" the boy demanded cautiously. He still did not move, but his ears seemed to prick up.

"To-morrow?"

"No thanks . . . Father." His ears ceased their activity.

"No? Why not?"

"Because there's a spellings examination on Friday, and I'm going to be top boy."

It was a fact that the infant (whose programmes were always somehow arranged in advance, and were in his mind absolutely unalterable) could spell the most obstreperous words. Quite conceivably he could spell better than his father, who still showed an occasional tendency to write "separate" with three e's and only one a.

"London's a fine place," said Edward Henry.

"I know," said Robert negligently.

"What's the population of London?"

"I don't know," said Robert with curtness, though he added after a pause: "But I can spell population — p-o-p-u-l-a-t-i-o-n."

"*I'll* come to London, Father, if you'll have me," said Ralph, grinning good-naturedly.

"Will you!" said his father.

"Fahver," asked Maisie, wriggling, "have you brought me a doll?"

"I'm afraid I haven't."

"Mother said p'r'aps you would."

It was true, there had been talk of a doll; he had forgotten it.

"I tell you what I'll do," said Edward Henry, "I'll take you to London, and you can choose a doll in London. You never saw such dolls as there are in London — talking dolls that shut and open their eyes and say Papa and Mamma, and all their clothes take off and on."

"Do they say ' Father?'" growled Robert.

"No, they don't," said Edward Henry.

"Why don't they?" growled Robert.

"When will you take me?" Maisie almost squealed.

" To-morrow."

" Certain sure, Father? "

" Yes."

" You promise, Father? "

" Of course I promise."

Robert at length stood up to judge for himself
this strange and agitating caprice of his father's for
taking Maisie to London. He saw that, despite
spellings, it would never do to let Maisie alone go.
He was about to put his father through a cross-ex-
amination, but Edward Henry dropped Ralph, who
had been climbing up him as up a telegraph-pole, on
to the bed and went over to the window, nervously,
and tapped thereon.

Carlo followed him, wagging an untidy tail.

" Hello, Trent! " murmured Edward Henry,
stooping and patting the dog.

Ralph exploded into loud laughter.

" Father's called Carlo ' Trent,' he roared.
" Father, have you forgotten his name's Carlo? "
It was one of the greatest jokes that Ralph had
heard for a long time.

Then Nellie hurried into the room, and Edward
Henry, with a " Mustn't be late for tea," as hurriedly left it.

Three minutes later, while he was bent over the
lavatory basin, someone burst into the bathroom.
He lifted a soapy face.

It was Nellie, with disturbed features.

" What's this about your positively promising to
take Maisie to London to-morrow to choose a doll? "

" I'll take 'em all," he replied with absurd levity.
" And you too ! "

" But really ——" she pouted, indicating that he
must not carry the ridiculous too far.

" Look here, d——n it," he said impulsively, " I
want you to come. And I want you to come to-
morrow. I knew it was the confounded infants you
wouldn't leave. You don't mean to tell me you can't
arrange it —— a woman like you ! "

She hesitated.

" And what am I to do with three children in a
London hotel ? "

" Take Nurse, naturally."

" Take Nurse ? " she cried.

He imitated her with a grotesque exaggeration,
yelling loudly, " Take Nurse ? " Then he planted
a soap-sud on her fresh cheek.

She wiped it off carefully and smacked his arm.
The next moment she was gone, having left the door
open.

" He *wants* me to go to London to-morrow," he
could hear her saying to his mother on the landing.

" Confound it ! " he thought. " Didn't she know
that at dinner-time ? "

" Bless us ! " His mother's voice.

" And take the children —— and Nurse ! " his wife
continued in a tone to convey the fact that she was
just as much disturbed as her mother-in-law could
possibly be by the eccentricities of the male.

" He's his father all over, that lad is ! " said his
mother strangely.

And Edward Henry was impressed by these words, for not once in seven years did his mother mention his father.

Tea was an exciting meal.

"You'd better come too, Mother," said Edward Henry audaciously. "We'll shut the house up."

"I come to no London," said she.

"Well, then, you can use the motor as much as you like while we're away."

"I go about gallivanting in no motor," said his mother. "It'll take me all my time to get this house straight against you come back."

"I haven't a *thing* to go in!" said Nellie with a martyr's sigh.

After all (he reflected), though domesticated, she was a woman.

He went to bed early. It seemed to him that his wife, his mother, and the nurse were active and whispering up and down the house till the very middle of the night. He arose not late, but they were all three afoot before him, active and whispering.

IX.

He found out on the morning after the highly complex transaction of getting his family from Bursley to London that London held more problems for him than ever. He was now not merely the proprietor of a theatre approaching completion, but really a theatrical manager with a play to produce, artistes to engage, and the public to attract. He had made two appointments for that morning at the

Majestic (he was not at the Grand Babylon, because his wife had once stayed with him at the Majestic, and he did not want to add to his anxieties the business of accustoming her to a new and costlier luxury) : one appointment at nine with Marrier, and the other at ten with Nellie, family, and Nurse. He had expected to get rid of Marrier before ten.

Among the exciting mail which Marrier had collected for him from the Grand Babylon and elsewhere was the following letter:

Buckingham Palace Hotel.

DEAR FRIEND: We are all so proud of you. I should like some time to finish our interrupted conversation. Will you come and have lunch with me one day here at 1.30? You needn't write. I know how busy you are. Just telephone you are coming. But don't telephone between 12 and 1, because at that time I *always* take my constitutional in St. James's Park.

Yours sincerely,

E. A.

"Well," he thought. "That's a bit thick, that is! She's stuck me up with a dramatist I don't believe in, and a play I don't believe in, and an actress I don't believe in, and now she —"

Nevertheless, to a certain extent he was bluffing himself; for, as he pretended to put Elsie April back into her place, he had disturbing and delightful visions of her. A clever creature! Uncannily clever! Wealthy! Under thirty! Broad-minded! No provincial prejudices! . . . Her voice, that always affected his spine! Her delicious flattery! . . . She was no mean actress either! And the multifariousness of her seductive charm! In fact, she was a regular woman of the world, such as you would read about — if you did read! . . . He was sitting with her again in the obscurity of the discussion-room at the Azure Society's establishment. His heart was beating again.

Pooh! . . .

A single wrench, and he ripped up the letter and cast it into one of the red-lined waste-paper baskets with which the immense and rather shabby writing-room of the Majestic was dotted.

Before he had finished dealing with Mr. Marrier's queries and suggestions — some ten thousand in all — the clock struck, and Nellie tripped into the room. She was in black silk, with hints here and there of gold chains. As she had explained, she had nothing to wear, and was therefore obliged to fall back on the final resource of every woman in her state. For in this connection " nothing to wear " signified " nothing except my black silk "— at any rate, in the Five Towns.

" Mr. Marrier — my wife. Nellie, this is Mr. Marrier."

Mr. Marrier was profuse: no other word would describe his demeanour. Nellie had the timidity of a young girl. Indeed, she looked quite youthful, despite the aging influences of black silk.

" So that's your Mr. Marrier! I understood from you he was a clerk! " said Nellie tartly, suddenly retransformed into the shrewd matron as soon as Mr. Marrier had profusely gone. She had conceived Marrier as a sort of Penkethman. Edward Henry had hoped to avoid this interview.

He shrugged his shoulders in answer to his wife's remark.

" Well," he said, " where are the kids? "

" Waiting in the lounge with Nurse, as you said to be." Her mien delicately informed him that while in London his caprices would be her law, which she would obey without seeking to comprehend.

" Well," he went on, " I expect they'd like the parks as well as anything. Suppose we take 'em and show 'em one of the parks? Shall we? Besides, they must have fresh air."

" All right," Nellie agreed. " But how far will it be? "

" Oh," said Edward Henry, " we'll crowd into a taxi ! "

They crowded into a taxi, and the children found their father in high spirits. Maisie mentioned the doll. In a minute the taxi had stopped in front of a toy-shop surpassing dreams, and they invaded the toy-shop like an army. When they emerged, after a considerable interval, Nurse was carrying an enormous doll, and Nellie was carrying Maisie, and Ralph was lovingly stroking the doll's real shoes. Robert kept a profound silence — a silence which had begun in the train.

" You haven't got much to say, Robert," his father remarked when the taxi set off again.

" I know," said Robert gruffly. Among other things, he resented his best clothes on a week-day.

" What do you think of London? "

" I don't know," said Robert.

His eyes never left the window of the taxi.

Then they visited the theatre — a very fatiguing enterprise, and also, for Edward Henry, a very nervous one.   He was as awkward in displaying that inchoate theatre as a newly-made father with his firstborn.   Pride and shame fought for dominion over him.   Nellie was full of laudations.   Ralph enjoyed the ladders.

" I say," said Nellie, apprehensive for Maisie, on the pavement, " this child's exhausted already.   How big's this park of yours?   Because neither Nurse nor I can carry her very far."

" We'll buy a pram," said Edward Henry.   He was staring at a newspaper placard which said: " Isabel Joy on the war-path again.   Will she win? "

" But —"

" Oh, yes, we'll buy a pram!   Driver —"

" A pram isn't enough.   You'll want coverings for her, in this wind."

" Well, we'll buy the necessary number of eiderdowns and blankets, then," said Edward Henry. " Driver —"

A tremendous business!   For, in addition to making the purchases, he had to feed his flock in an A-B-C shop, where among the unoccupied waitresses Maisie and her talkative winking doll enjoyed a triumph.   Still, there was plenty of time.

At a quarter-past twelve he was displaying the varied landscape beauties of the park to his family. Ralph insisted on going to the bridge over the lake, and Robert silently backed him.   And therefore the

entire party went. But Maisie was afraid of the
water, and cried. Now, the worst thing about
Maisie was that when once she had begun to cry it
was very difficult to stop her. Even the most remarkable dolls were powerless to appease her dis-
tress.

" Give me the confounded pram, Nurse," said
Edward Henry, " I'll cure her."

But he did not cure her. However, he had to
stick grimly to the perambulator. Nellie tripped
primly in black silk on one side of it. Nurse had the
wayward Ralph by the hand. And Robert, taciturn,
stalked alone, adding up London and making a very,
small total of it.

Suddenly Edward Henry halted the perambulator
and, stepping away from it, raised his hat. An excessively elegant young woman leading a Pekinese by
a silver chain stopped as if smitten by a magic dart
and held spellbound.

" How do you do, Miss April? " said Edward
Henry loudly. " I was hoping to meet you. This
is my wife. Nellie, this is Miss April." Nellie
bowed stiffly in her black silk. Naught of the fresh
maiden about her now! And it has to be said that
Elsie April, in all her young and radiant splendour
and woman-of-the-worldliness, was equally stiff.
" And there are my two boys. And this is my little
girl in the pram."

Maisie screamed, and pushed an expensive doll
out of the perambulator. Edward Henry saved it
by its boot as it fell.

" And this is her doll.   And this is Nurse," he finished.   " Fine breezy morning, isn't it ? "

In due course the processions moved on.

" Well, that's done ! " Edward Henry muttered
to himself, and sighed.

CHAPTER IX

THE FIRST NIGHT

I.

IT was upon an evening in June — and a fine evening, full of the exquisite melancholy of summer in a city — that Edward Henry stood before a window, drumming thereon as he had once, a less experienced man with hair slightly less gray, drummed on the table of the mighty and arrogant Slosson. The window was the window of the managerial room of the Regent Theatre. And he could scarcely believe it, he could scarcely believe that he was not in a dream, for the room was papered, carpeted and otherwise furnished. Only its electric light fittings were somewhat hasty and provisional, and the white ceiling showed a hole and a bunch of wires, like the nerves of a hollow tooth, whence one of Edward Henry's favourite chandeliers would ultimately depend.

The whole of the theatre was at least as far advanced toward completion as that room. A great deal of it was more advanced; for instance the auditorium, foyer, and bars, which were utterly finished, so far as anything ever is finished in a changing world. Wonders, marvels, and miracles had been accomplished. Mr. Alloyd, in the stress of the job, had even ceased to bring the Russian ballet into his conversations. Mr. Alloyd, despite a growing tendency to prove to Edward Henry by authentic anecdote about midnight his general proposition that women as a sex treated him with shameful unfairness, had gained the high esteem of Edward Henry as an architect. He had fulfilled his word about those properties of the auditorium which had to do with hearing and seeing — in-so-much that the auditorium was indeed unique in London. And he had taken care that the clerk of the Works took care that the builder did not give up heart in the race with time.

Moreover he had maintained the peace with the terrible London County Council, all of whose inspecting departments seemed to have secretly decided that the Regent Theatre should be opened, not in June as Edward Henry had decided but at some vague future date toward the middle of the century. Months earlier Edward Henry had ordained and announced that the Regent Theatre should be inaugurated on a given date in June, at the full height of splendour of the London season, and he had astounded the theatrical world by adhering through thick and thin to that date, and had thereby intensified his reputation as an eccentric; for the oldest inhabitant of that world could not recall a case in which the opening of a new theatre had not been promised for at least three widely different dates.

Edward Henry had now arrived at the eve of the

date, and if he had arrived there in comparative
safety, with a reasonable prospect of avoiding complete shame and disaster, he felt and he admitted
that the credit was due as much to Mr. Alloyd as to
himself. Which only confirmed an early impression
of his that architects were queer people — rather
like artists and poets in some ways, but with a basis
of bricks and mortar to them.

His own share in the enterprise of the Regent had
in theory been confined to engaging the right people
for the right tasks and situations; and to signing
checks. He had depended chiefly upon Mr. Marrier, who, growing more radiant every day, had
gradually developed into a sort of chubby Napoleon,
taking an immense delight in detail and in choosing
minor hands at round-sum salaries on the spur of
the moment. Mr. Marrier refused no call upon his
energy. He was helping Carlo Trent in the production and stage-management of the play. He
dried the tears of girlish neophytes at rehearsals.
He helped to number the stalls. He showed a passionate interest in the tessellated pavement of the entrance. He taught the managerial typewriting girl
how to make afternoon tea. He went to Hitchin to
find a mediæval chair required for the third act,
and found it. In a word he was fully equal to the
post of acting manager. He managed! He managed everything and everybody except Edward
Henry, and except the press-agent, a functionary
whose conviction of his own indispensability and importance was so sincere that even Marrier shared

it and left him alone in his Bismarckian operations. The press-agent, who sang in musical comedy chorus at night, knew that if the Regent Theatre succeeded, it would be his doing and his alone.

And yet Edward Henry, though he had delegated everything, had yet found a vast amount of work to do; and was thereby exhausted. That was why he was drumming on the pane. That was why he was conscious of a foolish desire to shove his fist through the pane. During the afternoon he had had two scenes with two representatives of the Libraries (so called because they deal in theatre-tickets and not in books) who had declined to take up any of his tickets in advance. He had commenced an action against a firm of bill posters. He had settled an incipient strike in the " limes " department, originated by Mr. Cosmo Clark's views about lighting. He had dictated answers to seventy-nine letters of complaint from unknown people concerning the supply of free seats for the first night. He had responded in the negative to a request from a newspaper critic who, on the score that he was deaf, wanted a copy of the play. He had replied finally to an official of the County Council about the smoke trap over the stage. He had replied finally to another official of the County Council about the electric sign. He had attended to a new curiosity on the part of another official of the County Council about the iron curtain. And he had been almost rude to still another official of the County Council about the wiring of the electric light in the dressing-rooms. He had been unmistakably and pleasurably rude in writing to Slossons about their criticisms of the lock on the door of Lord Woldo's private entrance to the theatre. Also he had arranged with the representative of the Chief Commissioner of Police concerning the carriage regulations for " setting-down and taking-up."

And he had indeed had more than enough. His nerves, though he did not know it, and would have scorned the imputation, were slowly giving way. Hence, really, the danger to the pane! Through the pane, in the dying light he could see a cross-section of Shaftesbury Avenue, and an aged newspaper lad leaning against a lamp-post and displaying a poster which spoke of Isabel Joy. Isabel Joy yet again! That little fact of itself contributed to his exasperation. He thought, considering the importance of the Regent Theatre and the salary he was paying to his press-agent, that the newspapers ought to occupy their pages solely with the metropolitan affairs of Edward Henry Machin. But the wretched Isabel had, as it were, got London by the throat. She had reached Chicago from the West, on her triumphant way home, and had there contrived to be arrested, according to boast, but she was experiencing much more difficulty in emerging from the Chicago prison than in entering it. And the question was now becoming acute whether the emissary of the militant Suffragettes would arrive back in London within the specified period of a hundred days. Naturally, London was holding its breath. London will keep calm during moderate crises — such as a

national strike or the agony of the House of Lords
— but when the supreme excitation is achieved London
knows how to let itself go.

" If you please, Mr. Machin —"

He turned. It was his typewriter, Miss Lindop,
a young girl of some thirty-five years, holding a
tea-tray.

" But I've had my tea once! " he snapped.

" But you've not had your dinner, sir, and it's
half-past eight! " she pleaded.

He had known this girl for less than a month and
he paid her fewer shillings a week than the years
of her age, and yet somehow she had assumed a
worshipping charge of him, based on the idea that
he was incapable of taking care of himself. To
look at her appealing eyes one might have thought
that she would have died to insure his welfare.

" And they want to see you about the linoleum
for the gallery stairs," she added timidly. " The
County Council man says it must be taken up."

The linoleum for the gallery stairs! Something
snapped in him. He almost walked right through
the young woman and the tea-tray.

" I'll linoleum them! " he bitterly exclaimed, and
disappeared.

II.

Having duly " linoleumed them," or rather having
very annoyingly quite failed to " linoleum them,"
Edward Henry continued his way up the right-
hand gallery staircase and reached the auditorium,

where to his astonishment a good deal of electricity, at one penny three farthings a unit, was blazing. Every seat in the narrow and high-pitched gallery, where at the sides the knees of one spectator would be on a level with the picture-hat of the spectator in the row beneath, had a perfect and entire view of the proscenium opening. And Edward Henry now proved this unprecedented fact by climbing to the topmost corner seat and therefrom surveying the scene of which he was monarch. The boxes were swathed in their new white dust sheets; and likewise the higgledy-piggledy stalls, not as yet screwed down to the floor, save three or four stalls in the middle of the front row, from which the sheet had been removed. On one of these seats, far off though it was, he could descry a paper bag,—probably containing sandwiches,— and on another a pair of gloves and a walking-stick. Several alert ladies with sketchbooks walked uneasily about in the aisles. The orchestra was hidden in the well provided for it, and apparently murmuring in its sleep. The magnificent drop-curtain, designed by Saracen Givington, A. R. A., concealed the stage.

Suddenly Mr. Marrier and Carlo Trent appeared through the iron door that gave communication — to initiates — between the wings and the auditorium; they sat down in the stalls. And the curtain rose with a violent swish, and disclosed the first " set " of " The Orient Pearl."

" What about that amber, Cosmo? " Mr. Marrier cried thickly, after a pause, his mouth occupied with sandwich.

" There you are! " came the reply.

" Right! " said Mr. Marrier.   " Strike! "

" Don't strike! " contradicted Carlo Trent.

" Strike, I tell you!   We must get on with the second act."   The voices resounded queerly in the empty theatre.

The stage was invaded by scene shifters before the curtain could descend again.

Edward Henry heard a tripipng step behind him. It was the faithful typewriting girl.

" I say," he said.   " Do you mind telling me what's going on here?   It's true that in the rush of more important business I'd almost forgotten that a theatre is a place where they perform plays."

" It's the dress-rehearsal, Mr. Machin," said the woman, startled and apologetic.

" But the dress-rehearsal was fixed for three o'clock," said he.   " It must have been finished three hours ago."

" I think they've only just done the first act," the woman breathed.   " I know they didn't begin till seven.   Oh!   Mr. Machin, of course it's no affair of mine, but I've worked in a good many theatres, and I do think it's such a mistake to have the dress-rehearsal quite private.   If you get a hundred or so people in the stalls, then it's an audience, and there's much less delay and everything goes much better.   But when it's private a dress-rehearsal is just like any other rehearsal."

"Only more so, perhaps," said Edward Henry, smiling.

He saw that he had made her happy; but he saw also that he had given her empire over him.

"I've got your tea here," she said, rather like a hospital nurse now. "Won't you drink it?"

"I'll drink it if it's not stewed," he muttered.

"Oh!" she protested. "Of course it isn't! I poured it off the leaves into another teapot before I brought it up."

She went behind the barrier, and reappeared balancing a cup of tea with a slice of sultana cake edged on the saucer. And as she handed it to him — the sustenance of rehearsals — she gazed at him and he could almost hear her eyes saying: "You poor thing!"

There was nothing that he hated so much as to be pitied.

"You go home!" he commanded.

"Oh, but —"

"You go home! See?" He paused, threatening. "If you don't clear out on the tick, I'll chuck this cup and saucer down into the stalls."

Horrified, she vanished.

He sighed his relief.

After some time, the leader of the orchestra climbed into his chair, and the orchestra began to play, and the curtain went up again, on the second act of the masterpiece in hexameters. The new scenery, which Edward Henry had with extraordi-

nary courage insisted on Saracen Givington substituting for the original incomprehensibilities displayed
at the Azure Society's performance, rather pleased
him. Its colouring was agreeable, and it did resemble something definite. You could, though perhaps not easily, tell what it was meant to represent.
The play proceeded, and the general effect was sur-
prisingly pleasant to Edward Henry. And then
Rose Euclid as Haidee came on for the great scene
of the act. From the distance of the gallery she
looked quite passably youthful, and beyond question
she had a dominating presence in her resplendent
costume. She was incomparably and amazingly better than she had been at the few previous rehearsals
which Edward Henry had been unfortunate enough
to witness. She even reminded him of his earliest
entrancing vision of her.

"Some people may *like* this!" he admitted, with
a gleam of optimism. Hitherto, for weeks past, he
had gone forward with his preparations in the most
frigid and convinced pessimism. It seemed to him
that he had become involved in a vast piece of ma-
chinery, and that nothing short of blowing the
theatre up with dynamite would bring the cranks and
pistons to a stop. And yet it seemed to him also
that everything was unreal, that the contracts he
signed were unreal, and the proofs he passed, and
the posters he saw on the walls of London, and the
advertisements in the newspapers. Only the checks
he drew had the air of being real. And now, in a
magic flash, after a few moments gazing at the

stage, he saw all differently. He scented triumph from afar off, as one sniffs the tang of the sea. On the morrow he had to meet Nellie at Euston, and he had shrunk from meeting her, with her terrible remorseless, provincial, untheatrical common sense; but now, in another magic flash, he envisaged the meeting with a cock-a-doodle-doo of hope. Strange! He admitted it was strange.

And then he failed to hear several words spoken by Rose Euclid. And then a few more. As the emotion of the scene grew, the proportion of her words audible in the gallery diminished. Until she became, for him, totally inarticulate, raving away there and struggling in a cocoon of hexameters.

Despair seized him. His nervous system, every separate nerve of it, was on the rack once more.

He stood up in a sort of paroxysm and called loudly across the vast intervening space:

"Speak more distinctly, please."

A fearful silence fell upon the whole theatre. The rehearsal stopped. The building itself seemed to be staggered. Somebody had actually demanded that words should be uttered articulately!

Mr. Marrier turned toward the intruder, as one determined to put an end to such singularities.

"Who's up theyah?"

"I am," said Edward Henry. "And I want it to be clearly understood in my theatre that the first thing an actor has to do is to make himself heard. I daresay I'm devilish odd, but that's how I look at it."

"Whom do you mean, Mr. Machin?" asked Marrier in a different tone.

"I mean Miss Euclid of course. Here I've spent Heaven knows how much on the acoustics of this theatre, and I can't make out a word she says. I can hear all the others. And this is the dress-rehearsal!"

"You must remember you're in the gallery," said Mr. Marrier firmly.

"And what if I am! I'm not giving gallery seats away to-morrow night. It's true I'm giving half the stalls away, but the gallery will be paid for."

Another silence.

Said Rose Euclid sharply, and Edward Henry caught every word with the most perfect distinctness:

"I'm sick and tired of people saying they can't make out what I say! They actually write me letters about it! Why *should* people make out what I say?"

She quitted the stage.

Another silence. . . .

"Ring down the curtain," said Mr. Marrier in a thrilled voice.

III.

Shortly afterward Mr. Marrier came into the managerial office, lit up now, where Edward Henry was dictating to his typewriter and hospital nurse, who, having been caught in hat and jacket on the threshold, had been brought back and was tapping his words direct on to the machine.

It was a remarkable fact that the sole proprietor of the Regent Theatre was now in high spirits and good-humour.

"Well, Marrier, my boy," he saluted the acting manager, "how are you getting on with that rehearsal?"

"Well, sir," said Mr. Marrier, "I'm not getting on with it. Miss Euclid refuses absolutely to proceed. She's in her dressing-room."

"But why?" enquired Edward Henry with bland surprise. "Doesn't she *want* to be heard by her gallery-boys?"

Mr. Marrier showed a feeble smile.

"She hasn't been spoken to like that for thirty years," said he.

"But don't you agree with me?" asked Edward Henry.

"Yes," said Marrier, "I *agree* with you—"

"And doesn't your friend Carlo want his precious hexameters to be heard?"

"We baoth agree with you," said Marrier. "The fact is, we've done all we could, but it's no use. She's splendid; only—" He paused.

"Only you can't make out ten per cent. of what she says," Edward Henry finished for him. "Well, I've got no use for that in my theatre." He found a singular pleasure in emphasising the phrase, "my theatre."

"That's all very well," said Marrier. "But what are you going to *do* about it? I've tried everything.

You've come in and burst up the entire show, if
you'll forgive my saying saoh! "

" Do? " exclaimed Edward Henry. " It's perfectly simple. All you have to do is to act. God
bless my soul, aren't you getting fifteen pounds
a week, and aren't you my acting manager?
Act, then! You've done enough hinting. You've
proved that hints are no good. You'd have known
that from your birth up, Marrier, if you'd been
born in the Five Towns. Act, my boy."

" But haow? If she won't go on, she won't."

" Is her understudy in the theatre? "

" Yes. It's Miss Cunningham, you knaow."

" What salary does she get? "

" Ten pounds a week."

" What for? "

" Well — partly to understudy, I suppose."

" Let her earn it, then. Go on with the rehearsal. And let her play the part to-morrow night.
She'll be delighted, you bet."

" But — "

" Miss Lindop," Edward Henry interrupted,
" will you please read to Mr. Marrier what I've
dictated? " He turned to Marrier. " It's an interview with myself for one of to-morrow's papers."

Miss Lindop, with tears in her voice if not in
her eyes, obeyed the order and, drawing the paper
from the machine, read its contents aloud.

Mr. Marrier started back — not in the figurative
but in the literal sense — as he listened.

" But you'll never send that out! " he exclaimed.

" Why not? "

" No paper will print it! "

" My dear Marrier," said Edward Henry. " Don't be a simpleton. You know as well as I do that half-a-dozen papers will be delighted to print it. And all the rest will copy the one that does print it. It'll be the talk of London to-morrow, and Isabel Joy will be absolutely snuffed out."

" Well," said Mr. Marrier. " I never heard of such a thing! "

" Pity you didn't, then! "

Mr. Marrier moved away.

" I say," he murmured at the door. " Don't you think you ought to read that to Rose first? "

" I'll read it to Rose like a bird," said Edward Henry.

Within two minutes — it was impossible to get from his room to the dressing-rooms in less — he was knocking at Rose Euclid's door. " Who's there? " said a voice. He entered and then replied, " I am."

Rose Euclid was smoking a cigarette and scratching the arm of an easy-chair behind her. Her maid stood near by with a whisky-and-soda.

" Sorry you can't go on with the rehearsal, Miss Euclid," said Edward Henry very quickly. " However, we must do the best we can. But Mr. Marrier thought you'd like to hear this. It's part of an interview with me that's going to appear to-morrow in the press."

Without pausing, he went on to read: "'I found Mr. Alderman Machin, the hero of the Five Towns and the proprietor and initiator of London's newest and most up-to-date and most intellectual theatre, surrounded by a complicated apparatus of telephones and typewriters in his managerial room at the Regent. He received me very courteously. "Yes," he said in response to my question, " The rumour is quite true. The principal part in ' The Orient Pearl' will be played on the first night by Miss Euclid's understudy, Miss Olga Cunningham, a young woman of very remarkable talent. No; Miss Euclid is not ill or even indisposed. But she and I have had a grave difference of opinion. The point between us was whether Miss Euclid's speeches ought to be clearly audible in the auditorium. I considered they ought. I may be wrong. I may be provincial. But that was and is my view. At the dress-rehearsal, seated in the gallery, I could not hear her lines. I objected. She refused to consider the subject or to proceed with the rehearsal. *Hinc illæ lachrymæ!*" . . . "Not at all," said Mr. Machin in reply to a question, " I have the highest admiration for Miss Euclid's genius. I should not presume to dictate to her as to her art. She has had a very long experience of the stage, very long, and doubtless knows better than I do. Only, the Regent happens to be my theatre, and I'm responsible for it. Every member of the audience will have a complete uninterrupted view of the stage, and I intend that every member of the audience, shall hear every word that is uttered on the stage. I'm odd, I know. But then I've a reputation for oddness to keep up. And by the way I'm sure that Miss Cunningham will make a great reputation for herself." ' "

" Not while I'm here, she won't! " exclaimed Rose Euclid standing up, and enunciating her words with marvellous clearness.

Edward Henry glanced at her, and then continued to read: " Suggestions for headlines. ' Piquant quarrel between manager and star actress.' ' Unparalleled situation.' ' Trouble at the Regent Theatre.' "

" Mr. Machin," said Rose Euclid, " you are not a gentleman."

" You'd hardly think so, would you? " mused Edward Henry, as if mildly interested in this new discovery of Miss Euclid's.

" Maria," said the star to her maid, " go and tell Mr. Marrier I'm coming."

" And I'll go back to the gallery," said Edward Henry. " It's the place for people like me, isn't it? I daresay I'll tear up this paper later, Miss Euclid — we'll see."

IV.

On the next night a male figure in evening dress and a pale overcoat might have been seen standing at the corner of Piccadilly Circus and Lower Regent Street, staring at an electric sign in the shape

of a shield which said in its glittering, throbbing
speech of incandescence:

THE REGENT
ROSE EUCLID
IN
THE ORIENT PEARL

The figure crossed the Circus, and stared at the
sign from a new point of view.   Then it passed along
Coventry Street, and stared at the sign from yet
another point of view.   Then it reached Shaftesbury Avenue, and stared again.   Then it returned
to its original station.   It was the figure of Edward
Henry Machin, savouring the glorious electric sign
of which he had dreamed.   He lit a cigarette, and
thought of Seven Sachs gazing at the name of Seven
Sachs in fire on the façade of a Broadway theatre
in New York.   Was not this London phenomenon
at least as fine?   He considered it was.   The Regent Theatre existed — there it stood!   (What a
name for a theatre!)   Its windows were all illuminated.   Its entrance-lamps bathed the pavement in
light, and in this radiance stood the commissionaires
in their military pride and their new uniforms.   A
line of waiting automobiles began a couple of yards
to the north of the main doors and continued round
all sorts of dark corners and up all manner of back
streets toward Golden Square itself.   Marrier had
had the automobiles counted and had told him the
number —, but such was Edward Henry's condition
that he had forgotten.   A row of boards reared on

the pavement against the walls of the façade said:
" Stalls Full," " Private Boxes Full," " Dress Circle
Full," " Upper Circle Full," " Pit Full," " Gallery
Full." And attached to the ironwork of the glazed
entrance canopy was a long board which gave the
same information in terser form: " House Full."
The Regent had indeed been obliged to refuse quite
a lot of money on its opening night.

After all, the inauguration of a new theatre was
something, even in London! Important personages
had actually begged the privilege of buying seats
at normal prices, and had been refused. Unim-
portant personages, such as those who boast in the
universe that they had never missed a first night in
the West End for twenty, thirty, or even fifty years,
had tried to buy seats at abnormal prices, and had
failed; which was in itself a tragedy. Edward
Henry at the final moment had yielded his wife's
stall to the instances of a Minister of the Crown,
and at Lady Woldo's urgent request had put her into
Lady Woldo's private landowner's box, where also
was Miss Elsie April who " had already had
the pleasure of meeting Mrs. Machin." Edward
Henry's first night was an event of magnitude. And
he alone was responsible for it. His volition alone
had brought into being that grand edifice whose
light yellow walls now gleamed in nocturnal mystery
under the shimmer of countless electric bulbs.

" There goes pretty nigh forty thousand pounds
of my money! " he reflected, excitedly.

And he reflected:

" After all, I'm somebody."

Then he glanced down Lower Regent Street and saw Sir John Pilgrim's much larger theatre, now sublet to a tenant who also was lavish with displays of radiance. And he reflected that on first nights Sir John Pilgrim, in addition to doing all that he himself had done, would hold the great rôle on the stage throughout the evening. And he admired the astounding, dazzling energy of such a being, and admitted ungrudgingly:

" He's somebody too! I wonder what part of the world he's illuminating just now! "

Edward Henry did not deny to his soul that he was extremely nervous. He would not and could not face even the bare possibility that the first play presented at the new theatre might be a failure. He had meant to witness the production incognito among the crowd in the pit or in the gallery. But, after visiting the pit a few moments before the curtain went up, he had been appalled by the hardhearted levity of the pit's remarks on things in general. The pit did not seem to be in any way chastened or softened by the fact that a fortune, that reputations, that careers were at stake. He had fled from the packed pit. (As for the gallery, he decided that he had already had enough of the gallery.)

He had wandered about corridors and to and fro in his own room and in the wings, and even in the basement, as nervous as a lost cat or an author, and as self-conscious as a criminal who knows him-

self to be on the edge of discovery. It was a fact
that he could not look people in the eyes. The reception of the first act had been fairly amiable, and
he had suffered horribly as he listened for the applause. Catching sight of Carlo Trent in the distance of a passage, he had positively run away from
Carlo Trent. The first entr'acte had seemed to last
for about three months. Its nightmarish length had
driven him almost to lunacy. The " feel " of the
second act, so far as it mystically communicated itself to him in his place of concealment, had been
better. At the end of the second fall of the curtain the applause had been enthusiastic. Yes, enthusiastic!

Curiously, it was the revulsion caused by this new
birth of hope that, while the third act was being
played, had driven him out of the theatre. His
wild hope needed ozone. His breast had to ex-
pand in the boundless prairie of Piccadilly Circus.
His legs had to walk. His arms had to swing.

Now he crossed the Circus again to his own pavement and gazed like a stranger at his own posters.
On several of them, encircled in a scarlet ring, was
the sole name of Rose Euclid — impressive! (And
smaller, but above it, the legend " E. H. Machin.
Sole proprietor.") He asked himself impartially,
as his eyes uneasily left the poster and slipped round
the Circus, deserted save by a few sinister and idle
figures at that hour, " Should I have sent that interview to the papers, or shouldn't I? . . . I wonder.
I expect some folks would say on the whole I've

been rather hard on Rose since I first met her! . . .
Anyhow, she's speaking up all right to-night!" He
laughed shortly.

A newsboy floated up from the Circus bearing
a poster with the name of Isabel Joy on it in large
letters.

He thought:

"Be blowed to Isabel Joy!"

He did not care a fig for Isabel Joy's competition
now.

And then a small door opened in the wall close
by, and an elegant, cloaked woman came out on to
the pavement. The door was the private door leading to the private box of Lord Woldo, owner of
the ground upon which the Regent Theatre was
built. The woman he recognised with confusion
as Elsie April, whom he had not seen alone since the
Azure Society's night.

"What are you doing out here, Mr. Machin?"
she greeted him with pleasant composure.

"I'm thinking," said he.

"It's going splendidly," she remarked. "Really!
I'm just running round to the stage door to meet
dear Rose as she comes off. What a delightful woman your wife is! So pretty, and so sen-
sible!"

She disappeared round the corner before he could
compose a suitable husband's reply to this lauda-
tion of a wife.

Then the commissionaires at the entrance seemed
to start into life. And then suddenly several pre-

occupied men strode rapidly out of the theatre, but-
toning their coats, and vanished, phantom-like.
Critics, on their way to destruction!

The performance must be finishing. Hastily he
followed in the direction taken by Elsie April.

He was in the wings, on the prompt side. Close
by stood the prompter, an untidy youth with im-
perfections of teeth, clutching hard at the red-scored
manuscript of " The Orient Pearl." Sundry players, of varying stellar degrees, were posed around
in the opulent costumes designed by Saracen Givington, A. R. A. Miss Lindop was in the back-
ground, ecstatically happy, her cheeks a race-course
of tears. Afar off, in the centre of the stage, alone,
stood Rose Euclid, gorgeous in green and silver,
bowing and bowing and bowing — bowing before
the storm of approval and acclamation that swept
from the auditorium across the footlights.

With a sound like that of tearing silk, or of a gigantic contralto mosquito, the curtain swished down,
and swished up, and swished down again. Bouquets
flew on to the stage from the auditorium (a custom
newly imported from the United States by Miss Euclid, and encouraged by her, though contrary to the
lofty canons of London taste). The actress already
held one huge trophy, shaped as a crown, to her
breast. She hesitated, and then ran to the wings,
and caught Edward Henry by the wrist impulsively,
madly. They shook hands in an ecstasy. It was
as though they recognised in one another a funda-
mental and glorious worth; it was as though no

words could ever express the depth of appreciation, affection and admiration which each intensely felt for the other; it was as though this moment were the final consecration of twin lives whose long, loyal comradeship had never been clouded by the faintest breath of mutual suspicion. Rose Euclid was still the unparalleled star, the image of grace and beauty and dominance upon the stage. And yet quite clearly Edward Henry saw close to his the wrinkled, damaged, daubed face and thin neck of an old woman; and it made no difference.

"Rose!" cried a strained voice, and Rose Euclid wrenched herself from him and tumbled with half a sob into the clasping arms of Elsie April.

"You've saved the intellectual theatah for London, my boy! That's what you've done!" Marrier was now gripping his hand. And Edward Henry was convinced that he had.

The strident vigour of the applause showed no diminution. And through the thick heavy rain of it could be heard the monotonous insistent detonations of one syllable:

"'Thor! 'Thor! 'Thor! 'Thor! 'Thor!"

And then another syllable was added:

"Speech! Speech! Speech! Speech!"

Mechanically Edward Henry lit a cigarette. He had no consciousness of doing so.

"Where is Trent?" people were asking.

Carlo Trent appeared up a staircase at the back of the stage.

"You've got to go on," said Marrier. "Now,

pull yourself togethah. The Great Beast is calling for you. Say a few wahds."

Carlo Trent in his turn seized the hand of Edward Henry, and it was for all the world as though he were seizing the hand of an intellectual and poetic equal, and wrung it.

" Come now! " Mr. Marrier, beaming, admonished him, and then pushed.

" What must I say? " stammered Carlo.

" Whatever comes into your head."

" All right! I'll say something."

A man in a dirty white apron, drew back the heavy mass of the curtain about eighteen inches, and, Carlo Trent stepping forward, the glare of the footlights suddenly lit his white face. The applause, now multiplied fivefold and become deafening, seemed to beat him back against the curtain. His lips worked. He did not bow.

" Cam back, you fool! " whispered Marrier.

And Carlo Trent stepped back into safe shelter.

" Why didn't you say something? "

" I c-couldn't," murmured the greatest dramatic poet in the world; and began to cry.

" Speech! Speech! Speech! Speech! "

" Here! " said Edward Henry gruffly. " Get out of my way! I'll settle 'em. Get out of my way! " And he riddled Carlo Trent with a fusillade of savagely scornful glances.

The man in the apron obediently drew back the curtain again, and the next second Edward Henry was facing an auditorium crowded with his patrons.

Everybody was standing up, chiefly in the aisles and crowded at the entrances, and quite half the people were waving, and quite a quarter of them were shouting. He bowed several times. An age elapsed. His ears were stunned. But it seemed to him that his brain was working with marvellous perfection. He perceived that he had been utterly wrong about " The Orient Pearl." And that all his advisers had been splendidly right. He had failed to catch its charm and to feel its power. But this audience — this magnificent representative audience drawn from London in the brilliant height of the season — had not failed.

It occurred to him to raise his hand. And as he raised his hand it occurred to him that his hand held a lighted cigarette. A magic hush fell upon the magnificent audience, which owned all that endless line of automobiles outside. Edward Henry, in the hush, took a pull at his cigarette.

"Ladies and gentlemen," he said, pitching his voice well, for municipal politics had made him a practised public speaker, " I congratulate you. This evening you — have succeeded! "

There was a roar, confused, mirthful, humorously protesting. He distinctly heard a man in the front row of the stalls say: " Well, for sheer nerve —! " And then go off into a peal of laughter.

He smiled and retired.

Marrier took charge of him.

" You merit the entire confectioner's shop! " exclaimed Marrier, aghast, admiring, triumphant.

Now Edward Henry had had no intention of meriting cake. He had merely followed in speech the secret train of his thought. But he saw that he had treated a West End audience as a West End audience had never before been treated, and that his audacity had conquered. Hence he determined not to refuse the cake.

" Didn't I tell you I'd settle 'em? " said he.

The band played " God Save the King."

VI.

One hour later, in the double-bedded chamber at the Majestic, as his wife lay in bed and he was methodically folding up a creased white tie and inspecting his chin in the mirror, he felt that he was touching again, after an immeasurable interval, the rock-bottom of reality. Nellie, even when he could see only her face, and that in a mirror, was the most real phenomenon in his existence, and she possessed the strange faculty of dispelling all unreality round about her.

" Well," he said. " How did you get on in the box? "

" Oh! " she replied, " I got on very well with the Woldo woman. She's one of our sort. But I'm not so set up with your Elsie April."

" Dash this collar! "

Nellie continued:

" And I can tell you another thing. I don't envy Mr. Rollo Wrissel."

" What's Wrissel got to do with it? "

" She means to marry him."

" Elsie April means to marry Wrissel? "

" He was in and out of the box all night. It was as plain as a pikestaff."

" What's amiss with my Elsie April? " Edward Henry demanded.

" She's a thought too *pleasant* for my taste," answered Nellie.

Astonishing, how pleasantness is regarded with suspicion in the Five Towns, even by women who can at a pinch be angels!

VII.

Often during the brief night he gazed sleepily at the vague next bed and mused upon the extraordinariness of women's consciences. His wife slept like an innocent. She always did. It was as though she gently expired every evening and returned gloriously to life every morning. The sunshiny hours between three and seven were very long to him, but it was indisputable that he did not hear the clock strike six, which was, at any rate, proof of a little sleep to the good. At five minutes past seven he thought he heard a faint rustling noise in the corridor, and he arose and tiptoed to the door and opened it. Yes, the Majestic had its good qualities! He had ordered that all the London morning daily papers should be laid at his door as early as possible, and there the pile was, somewhat damp, and as fresh as fruit, with a slight odour of ink. He took it in.

His heart was beating as he climbed back into bed with it and arranged pillows so that he could sit up, and unfolded the first paper. Nellie had not stirred.

Once again he was disappointed in the prominence given by the powerful London press to his London enterprise. In the first newspaper, a very important one, he positively could not find any criticism of the Regent's first night. There was nearly a page of the offensive Isabel Joy, who was now appealing, through the newspapers, to the President of the United States. Isabel had been christened the World-Circler, and the special correspondents of the entire earth were gathered about her carpeted cell. Hope still remained that she would reach London within the hundred days. An unknown adherent of the cause for which she suffered had promised to give ten thousand pounds to that cause if she did so. Furthermore, she was receiving over sixty proposals of marriage a day. And so on and so on! Most of this he gathered in an instant from the headlines alone. Nauseating!

Another annoying item in the paper was a column and a half given to the foundation-stone laying of the First New Thought Church, in Dean Street, Soho — about a couple of hundred yards from its original site. He hated the First New Thought Church as one always hates that to which one has done an injury.

Then he found what he was searching for: " Regent Theatre. Production of poetical drama at London's latest playhouse." After all, it was well situated in the paper, on quite an important page, and there was over a column of it. But in his nervous excitation his eyes had missed it. His eyes now read it. Over half of it was given to a discussion of the Don Juan legend and the significance of the Byronic character of Haidee — obviously written before the performance. A description of the plot occupied most of the rest, and a reference to the acting ended it. "Miss Rose Euclid in the trying and occasionally beautiful part of Haidee was all that her admirers could have wished " . . . "Miss Cunningham distinguished herself by her diction and bearing in the small part of the Messenger." The final words were: "The reception was quite favourable."

"Quite favourable," indeed! Edward Henry had a chill. Good heavens, was not the reception ecstatically, madly, foolishly enthusiastic? "Why!" he exclaimed within, "I never saw such a reception!" It was true; but then he had never seen any other first night. He was shocked, as well as chilled. And for this reason: For weeks past all the newspapers, in their dramatic gossip, had contained highly sympathetic references to his enterprise. According to the paragraphs, he was a wondrous man, and the theatre was a wondrous house, the best of all possible theatres, and Carlo Trent was a great writer, and Rose Euclid exactly as marvellous as she had been a quarter of a century before, and the prospects of the intellectual-

poetic drama in London so favourable as to amount
to a certainty of success.

In those columns of dramatic gossip there was no
flaw in the theatrical world. In those columns of
dramatic gossip no piece ever failed, though sometimes a piece was withdrawn, regretfully and against
the wishes of the public, to make room for another
piece. In those columns of dramatic gossip theatrical managers, actors, and especially actresses, and
even authors, were benefactors of society, and therefore they were treated with the deference, the gentle-
ness, the heartfelt sympathy which benefactors of
society merit and ought to receive.

The tone of the criticism of the first night was
different — it was subtly, not crudely, different.
But different it was.

The next newspaper said the play was bad and
the audience indulgent. It was very severe on Carlo
Trent, and very kind to the players, whom it regarded as good men and women in adversity — with
particular laudations for Miss Rose Euclid and the
Messenger. The next newspaper said the play was a
masterpiece, and would be so hailed in any country but
England. England, however —! Unfortunately
this was a newspaper whose political opinions Edward Henry despised. The next newspaper praised
everything and everybody, and called the reception
tumultuously enthusiastic. And Edward Henry felt
as though somebody, mistaking his face for a slice
of toast, had spread butter all over it. Even the
paper's parting assurance that the future of the

higher drama in London was now safe beyond question did not remove this delusion of butter.

The two following newspapers were more sketchy or descriptive, and referred at some length to Edward Henry's own speech, with a kind of sub-hint that Edward Henry had better mind what he was about. Three illustrated papers had photographs of scenes and figures, but nothing important in the matter of criticism. The rest were " neither one thing nor the other," as they say in the Five Towns. On the whole, an inscrutable press, a disconcerting, a startling, an appetite-destroying, but not a hopeless press. The general impression which he gathered from his perusals was that the author was a pretentious dullard, an absolute criminal, a genius; that the actors and actresses were all splendid and worked hard, though conceivably one or two of them had been set impossible tasks — to wit, tasks unsuited to their personalities; that he himself was a Napoleon, a temerarious individual, an incomprehensible fellow; and that the future of the intellectual-poetic drama in London was not a topic of burning actuality. . . . He remembered sadly the superlative-laden descriptions, in those same newspapers, of the theatre itself, a week or two back, the unique theatre in which the occupant of every seat had a complete and uninterrupted view of the whole of the proscenium opening. Surely that fact alone ought to have ensured proper treatment for him!

Then Nellie woke up, and saw the scattered newspapers.

"Well," she asked; "what do they say?"

"Oh!" he replied lightly, with a laugh. "Just about what you'd expect. Of course you know what a first-night audience always is. Too generous. And ours was, particularly. Miss April saw to that. She had the Azure Society behind her, and she was determined to help Rose Euclid. However, I should say it was all right — I should say it was quite all right. I told you it was a gamble, you know."

When Nellie, dressing, said that she considered she ought to go back home that day, he offered no objection. Indeed he rather wanted her to go. Not that he had a desire to spend the whole of his time at the theatre, unhampered by provincial women in London. On the contrary, he was aware of a most definite desire not to go to the theatre. He lay in bed and watched with careless curiosity the rapid processes of Nellie's toilette. He had his breakfast on the dressing-table (for he was not at Wilkins's, neither at the Grand Babylon). Then he helped her to pack, and finally he accompanied her to Euston, where she kissed him with affectionate common sense and caught the twelve five. He was relieved that nobody from the Five Towns happened to be going down by that train.

As he turned away from the moving carriage, the evening papers had just arrived at the bookstalls. He bought the four chief organs — one green, one yellowish, one white, one pink — and scanned them

self-consciously on the platform.   The white organ
had a good heading: "Re-birth of the intellectual
drama in London.   What a provincial has done.
Opinions of the leading men."   Two columns altogether!   There was, however, little in the two columns.   The leading men had practised a sagacious
caution.   They, like the press as a whole, were obviously waiting to see which way the great elephan-
tine public would jump.   When the enormous animal had jumped, they would all exclaim: "What
did I tell you?"   The other critiques were colour-
less.   At the end of the green critique occurred the
following sentence: "It is only fair to state, nevertheless, that the play was favourably received by
an apparently enthusiastic audience."

"Nevertheless!" . . . "Apparently!"

Edward Henry turned the page to the theatrical
advertisements.

Unreal!   Fantastic!   Was   this   he,   Edward
Henry?   Could it be still his mother's son?

Still —"matinées every Wednesday and Saturday." "*Every* Wednesday and Saturday." That word implied and necessitated a long run, anyhow a run extending over months. That word comforted him. Though he knew as well as you do that Mr. Marrier had composed the advertisement, and that he himself was paying for it, it comforted him. He was just like a child.

VIII.

" I say, Cunningham's made a hit! " Mr. Marrier almost shouted at him as he entered the managerial room at the Regent.

" Cunningham? Who's Cunningham? "

Then he remembered. She was the girl who played the Messenger. She had only three words to say, and to say them over and over again; and she had made a hit!

" Seen the notices? " asked Marrier.

" Yes, — What of them? "

" Oh! Well! " Marrier drawled. " What would you expect? "

" That's just what *I* said! " observed Edward Henry.

" You did, did you? " Mr. Marrier exclaimed, as if extremely interested by this corroboration of his views.

Carlo Trent strolled in; he remarked that he happened to be just passing. But the discussion of the situation was not carried very far.

That evening the house was nearly full, except the

pit and the gallery, which were nearly empty. Applause was perfunctory.

"How much?" Edward Henry enquired of the box-office manager when figures were added together.

"Thirty-one pounds two shillings."

"Hem!"

"Of course," said Mr. Marrier. "In the height of the London season, with so many counter-attractions —! Besides, they've got to get used to the idea of it."

Edward Henry did not turn pale. Still, he was aware that it cost him a trifle over sixty pounds "to ring the curtain up" at every performance, and this sum took no account of expenses of production nor of author's fees. The sum would have been higher, but he was calculating as rent of the theatre only the ground-rent plus six per cent. on the total price of the building.

What disgusted him was the duplicity of the first-night audience, and he said to himself violently: "I was right all the time, and I knew I was right! Idiots! Chumps! Of course I was right!"

On the third night the house held twenty-seven pounds and sixpence.

"Naturally," said Mr. Marrier. "In this hot weathah —! I never knew such a hot June! It's the open-air places that are doing us in the eye. In fact I heard to-day that the White City is packed. They simply can't bank their money quick enough."

It was on that day that Edward Henry paid salaries. It appeared to him that he was providing half London with a livelihood: acting managers, stage managers, assistant ditto, property men, stage hands, electricians, prompters, call boys, box-office staff, general staff, dressers, commissionaires, programme girls, cleaners, actors, actresses, understudies, to say nothing of Rose Euclid at a purely nominal salary of one hundred pounds a week. The tenants of the bars were grumbling, but happily he was getting money from them.

The following day was Saturday. It rained — a succession of thunderstorms. The morning and the evening performances produced together sixty-eight pounds.

"Well," said Mr. Marrier. "In this kind of weathah you can't expect people to come out, can you? Besides, this cursed week-ending habit —"

Which conclusions did not materially modify the harsh fact that Edward Henry was losing over thirty pounds a day — or at the rate of over ten thousand pounds a year.

He spent Sunday between his hotel and his club, chiefly in reiterating to himself that Monday began a new week and that something would have to occur on Monday.

Something did occur.

Carlo Trent lounged into the office early. The man was forever being drawn to the theatre as by an invisible but powerful elastic cord. The papers had a worse attack than ever of Isabel Joy, for she had been convicted of transgression in a Chicago court of law, but a tremendous lawyer from St. Louis had loomed over Chicago and, having examined the documents in the case, was hopeful of getting the conviction quashed. He had discovered that in one and the same document " Isabel " had been spelt " Isobel," and, worse, Illinois had been deprived by a careless clerk of one of its " l's." He was sure that by proving these grave irregularities in American justice he could win on appeal.

Edward Henry glanced up suddenly from the newspaper. He had been inspired.

" I say, Trent," he remarked, without any warning or preparation, " you're not looking at all well. I want a change myself. I've a good mind to take you for a sea voyage."

" Oh ! " grumbled Trent. " I can't afford sea voyages."

" *I* can ! " said Edward Henry. " And I shouldn't dream of letting it cost you a penny. I'm not a philanthropist. But I know as well as anybody that it will pay us theatrical managers to keep you in health."

" You're not going to take the play off ? " Trent demanded suspiciously.

" Certainly not ! " said Edward Henry.

" What sort of a sea voyage ? "

" Well — what price the Atlantic ? Been to New York ? . . . Neither have I ! Let's go. Just for the trip. It'll do us good."

" You don't mean it ! " murmured the greatest dramatic poet, who had never voyaged farther than the Isle of Wight. His eyeglass swung to and fro.

Edward Henry feigned to resent this remark.

"Of course I mean it. Do you take me for a blooming gas-bag?" He rose. "Marrier!" Then more loudly: "Marrier!" Mr. Marrier entered. "Do you know anything about the sailings to New York?"

"Rather!" said Mr. Marrier, beaming. After all he was a most precious aid.

"We may be able to arrange for a production in New York," said Edward Henry to Carlo, mysteriously.

Mr. Marrier gazed at one and then at the other, puzzled.

CHAPTER X

ISABEL

I.

THROUGHOUT the voyage of the *Lithuania* from Liverpool to New York, Edward Henry, in common with some two thousand other people on board, had the sensation of being hurried. He who in a cab rides late to an important appointment arrives with muscles fatigued by mentally aiding the horse to move the vehicle along. Thus were Edward Henry's muscles fatigued, and the muscles of many others; but just as much more so as the *Lithuania* was bigger than a cab.

For the *Lithuania,* having been seriously delayed in Liverpool by men who were most ridiculously striking for the fantastic remuneration of one pound a week, was engaged on the business of making new records. And every passenger was personally determined that she should therein succeed. And, despite very bad June weather toward the end, she did sail past the Battery on a grand Monday morning with a new record to her credit.

So far, Edward Henry's plan was not miscarrying. But he had a very great deal to do and very little time in which to do it, and whereas the muscles of

339

the other passengers were relaxed as the ship drew
to her berth Edward Henry's muscles were only
more tensely tightened.   He had expected to see
Mr. Seven Sachs on the quay, for in response to
his telegram from Queenstown, the illustrious actor-
author had sent him an agreeable wireless message
in full Atlantic; the which had inspired Edward
Henry to obtain news by Marconi both from London
and New York, at much expense; from the east he
had had daily information of the dwindling receipts
at the Regent Theatre, and from the west daily information concerning Isabel Joy.   He had not, however, expected Mr. Seven Sachs to walk into the
Lithuania's music-saloon an hour before the ship
touched the quay.   Nevertheless this was what Mr.
Seven Sachs did, by the exercise of those mysterious
powers wielded by the influential in democratic com-
munities.

"And what are you doing here?" Mr. Seven
Sachs greeted Edward Henry with geniality.

Edward Henry lowered his voice.

"I'm throwing good money after bad," said he.

The friendly grip of Mr. Seven Sach's hand did
him good, reassured him, and gave him courage.
He was utterly tired of the voyage, and also of the
poetical society of Carlo Trent, whose passage had
cost him thirty pounds, considerable boredom, and
some sick-nursing during the final days and nights.
A dramatic poet with an appetite was a full dose for
Edward Henry; but a dramatic poet who lay on
his back and moaned for naught but soda water and

dry land amounted to more than Edward Henry could conveniently swallow.

He directed Mr. Sachs's attention to the anguished and debile organism which had once been Carlo Trent, and Mr. Sachs was so sympathetic that Carlo Trent began to adore him, and Edward Henry to be somewhat disturbed in his previous estimate of Mr. Sachs's common sense. But at a favourable moment Mr. Sachs breathed humorously into Edward Henry's ear the question:

" What have you brought *him* out for? "

" I've brought him out to lose him."

As they pushed through the bustle of the enormous ship, and descended from the dizzy eminence of her boat deck by lifts and ladders down to the level of the windy, sun-steeped rock of New York, Edward Henry said:

" Now I want you to understand, Mr. Sachs, that I haven't a minute to spare. I've just looked in for lunch."

" Going on to Chicago? "

" She isn't in Chicago, is she? " demanded Edward Henry, aghast. " I thought she'd reached New York! "

" Who? "

" Isabel Joy."

" Oh! Isabel's in New York, sure enough. She's right here. They say she'll have to catch the *Lithuania* if she's going to get away with it."

" Get away with what? "

" Well — the goods."

The precious words reminded Edward Henry of an evening at Wilkins's, and raised his spirits even higher. It was a word he loved.

"And I've got to catch the *Lithuania,* too!" said he. "But Trent doesn't know! . . . And, let me tell you, she's going to do the quickest turn round that any ship ever did. The purser assured me she'll leave at noon to-morrow unless the world comes to an end in the meantime. Now what about a hotel?"

"You'll stay with me — naturally."

"But —" Edward Henry protested.

"Oh, yes, you will. I shall be delighted."

"But I must look after Trent."

"He'll stay with me too — naturally. I live at the Stuyvesant Hotel, you know, on Fifth. I've a pretty good private suite there. I shall arrange a little supper for to-night. My automobile is here."

"Is it possible that I once saved your life and have forgotten all about it?" Edward Henry exclaimed. "Or do you treat everybody like this?"

"We like to look after our friends," said Mr. Sachs simply.

In the terrific confusion of the quay, where groups of passengers were mounted like watch dogs over hillocks of baggage, Mr. Sachs stood continually between the travellers and the administrative rigours and official incredulity of a proud republic. And in the minimum of time the fine trunk of Edward Henry and the modest packages of the poet were on the roof of Mr. Sachs's vast car, the three men were inside, and the car was leaping, somewhat in the manner of a motor boat at full speed, over the cobbles of a wide, mediæval street.

" Quick! " thought Edward Henry. " I haven't a minute to lose! "

His prayer reached the chauffeur. Conversation was difficult; Carlo Trent groaned. Presently they rolled less perilously upon asphalt, though the equipage still lurched. Edward Henry was forever bending his head toward the window aperture in order to glimpse the roofs of the buildings, and never seeing the roofs.

" Now we're on Fifth," said Mr. Sachs, after a fearful lurch, with pride.

Vistas of flags, high cornices, crowded pavements, marble, jewelry behind glass — the whole seen through a roaring phantasmagoria of competing and menacing vehicles!

And Edward Henry thought:

" This is my sort of place! "

The jolting recommenced. Carlo Trent rebounded, limply groaning, between cushions and upholstery. Edward Henry tried to pretend that he was not frightened. Then there was a shock as of the concussion of two equally unyielding natures. A pane of glass in Mr. Seven Sachs's limousine flew to fragments and the car stopped.

" I expect that's a spring gone! " observed Mr. Sachs with tranquillity. " Will happen, you know, sometimes! "

Everybody got out. Mr. Sachs's presumption

was correct. One of the back wheels had failed to
leap over a hole in Fifth Avenue some eighteen
inches deep and two feet long.

" What is that hole? " asked Edward Henry.

" Well," said Mr. Sachs. " It's just a hole.
We'd better transfer to a taxi." He gave calm orders to his chauffeur.

Four empty taxis passed down the sunny magnifi-
cence of Fifth Avenue and ignored Mr. Sachs's
urgent waving. The fifth stopped. The baggage
was strapped and tied to it: which process occupied
much time. Edward Henry, fuming against delay,
gazed around. A nonchalant policeman on a superb
horse occupied the middle of the road. Tram cars
passed constantly across the street in front of his
caracoling horse, dividing a route for themselves in
the wild ocean of traffic as Moses cut into the Red
Sea. At intervals a knot of persons, intimidated and
yet daring, would essay the voyage from one pavement to the opposite pavement; there was no half-
way refuge for these adventurers, as in decrepit
London; some apparently arrived; others seemed to
disappear forever in the feverish welter of confused
motion and were never heard of again. The policeman, easily accommodating himself to the caracolings
of his mount, gazed absently at Edward Henry, and
Edward Henry gazed first at the policeman, and
then at the high decorated grandeur of the buildings,
and then at the Assyrian taxi into which Mr. Sachs
was now ingeniously inserting Carlo Trent. He
thought:

"No mistake — this street is alive. But what cemeteries they must have!"

He followed Carlo, with minute precautions, into the interior of the taxi. And then came the supremely delicate operation — that of introducing a third person into the same vehicle. It was accomplished; three chins and six knees fraternized in close intimacy; but the door would not shut. Wheezing, snorting, shaking, complaining, the taxi drew slowly away from Mr. Sachs's luxurious automobile and left it forlorn to its chauffeur. Mr. Sachs imperturbably smiled. ("I have two other automobiles," said Mr. Sachs.) In some sixty seconds the taxi stopped in front of the tremendous glass awning of the Stuyvesant. The baggage was unstrapped; the passengers were extracted one by one from the cell, and Edward Henry saw Mr. Sachs give two separate dollar bills to the driver.

"By Jove!" he murmured.

"I beg your pardon," said Mr. Sachs politely.

"Nothing!" said Edward Henry.

They walked into the hotel, and passed through a long succession of corridors and vast public rooms surging with well-dressed men and women.

"What's all this crowd for?" asked Edward Henry.

"What crowd?" asked Mr. Sachs, surprised.

Edward Henry saw that he had blundered.

"I prefer the upper floors," remarked Mr. Sachs as they were being flung upward in a gilded elevator, and passing rapidly all numbers from 1 to 14.

The elevator made an end of Carlo Trent's manhood. He collapsed. Mr. Sachs regarded him, and then said:

" I think I'll get an extra room for Mr. Trent. He ought to go to bed."

Edward Henry enthusiastically concurred.

" And stay there! " said Edward Henry.

Pale Carlo Trent permitted himself to be put to bed. But, therein, he proved fractious. He was anxious about his linen. Mr. Sachs telephoned from the bedside, and a laundry maid came. He was anxious about his best lounge suit. Mr. Sachs telephoned, and a valet came. Then he wanted a siphon of soda water, and Mr. Sachs telephoned, and a waiter came. Then it was a newspaper he required. Mr. Sachs telephoned and a page came. All these functionaries, together with two reporters, peopled Mr. Trent's bedroom more or less simultaneously. It was Edward Henry's bright notion to add to them a doctor — a doctor whom Mr. Sachs knew, a doctor who would perceive at once that bed was the only proper place for Carlo Trent.

" Now," said Edward Henry, when he and Mr. Sachs were participating in a private lunch amid the splendours and the grim silent service of the latter's suite at the Stuyvesant, " I have fully grasped the fact that I am in New York. It is one o'clock and after, and as soon as ever this meal is over, I have just *got* to find Isabel Joy. You must understand that on this trip New York for me is merely a town where Isabel Joy happens to be."

"Well," replied Mr. Sachs. "I reckon I can put you on to that. *She's going to be photographed at two o'clock by Rentoul Smiles.* I happen to know because Rent's a particular friend of mine."

"A photographer, you say?"

Mr. Sachs controlled himself. "Do you mean to say you've not heard of Rentoul Smiles? . . . Well, he's called 'Man's photographer.' He has never photographed a woman! Won't! At least, wouldn't! But he's going to photograph Isabel! So you may guess that he considers Isabel *some* woman, eh?"

"And how will that help me?" inquired Edward Henry.

"Why! I'll take you up to Rent's," Mr. Sachs comforted him. "It's close by — corner of Thirty-ninth and Fifth."

"Tell me," Edward Henry demanded, with immense relief. "She hasn't got herself arrested yet, has she?"

"No. And she won't."

"Why not?"

"The police have been put wise," said Mr. Sachs.

"Put wise?"

"Yes. *Put wise!*"

"I see," said Edward Henry.

But he did not see. He only half saw.

"As a matter of fact," said Mr. Sachs, "Isabel can't get away with the goods unless she fixes the police to lock her up for a few hours. And she'll

not succeed in that.   Her hundred days are up in
London next Sunday.   So there'll be no time for her
to be arrested and bailed out either at Liverpool or
Fishguard.   And that's her only chance.   I've seen
Isabel, and if you ask me my opinion she's down
and out."

"Never mind!" said Edward Henry with glee.

"I guess what you are after her for," said Mr.
Seven Sachs, with an air of deep knowledge.

"The deuce you do!"

"Yes, sir!   And let me tell you that dozens of
'em have been after her already.   But she wouldn't!
Nothing would tempt her."

"Never mind!" Edward Henry smiled.

II.

When Edward Henry stood by the side of Mr.
Sachs in a doorway half shielded by a portière, and
gazed unseen into the great studio of Mr. Rentoul
Smiles, he comprehended that he was indeed under
powerful protection in New York.   At the entrance
on Fifth Avenue he and Sachs had passed through
a small crowd of assorted men, chiefly young, whom
Sachs had greeted in the mass with the smiling
words, "Well, boys!"   Other men were within.
Still another went up with them in the elevator, but
no further.   They were reporters of the entire
world's press, to each of whom Isabel Joy had been
specially "assigned."   They were waiting; they
would wait.   Mr. Rentoul Smiles, having been
warned by telephone of the visit of his beloved

friend Seven Sachs and his English protégé had
been received at Smile's outer door by a clerk who
knew exactly what to do with them, and did it.

" Is she here ? " Mr. Sachs had murmured.

" Yep," the clerk had negligently replied.

And now Edward Henry beheld the objective of
his pilgrimage, her whose personality, portrait, and
adventures had been filling the newspapers of two
hemispheres for three weeks. She was not realis-
tically like her portraits. She was a little, thin,
pale, obviously nervous woman, of any age from
thirty-five to fifty, with fair untidy hair, and pale
grey-blue eyes that showed the dreamer, the idealist,
and the harsh fanatic. She looked as though a moderate breeze would have overthrown her, but she
also looked, to the enlightened observer, as though
she would recoil before no cruelty and no suffering
in pursuit of her vision. The blind dreaming force
behind her apparent frailty would strike terror into
the heart of any man intelligent enough to understand it. Edward Henry had an inward shudder.
" Great Scott! " he reflected. " I shouldn't like
to be ill and have Isabel for a nurse ! "

And his mind at once flew to Nellie, and then to
Elsie April. " And so she's going to marry Wrissell ! " he reflected, and could scarcely believe it.

Then he violently wrenched his mind back to the
immediate objective. He wondered why Isabel
Joy should wear a bowler hat and mustard-coloured
jacket that resembled a sporting man's overcoat; and
why these garments suited her. With a whip in

her hand she could have sat for a jockey. And yet she was a woman, and very feminine, and probably old enough to be Elsie April's mother! A disconcerting world, he thought.

The "man's photographer," as he was described in copper on Fifth Avenue and in gold on his own doors, was a big, loosely-articulated male, who loured over the trifle Isabel like a cloud over a sheep in a great field. Edward Henry could only see his broad bending back as he posed in athletic attitudes behind the camera.

Suddenly Rentoul Smiles dashed to a switch, and Isabel's wistful face was transformed into that of a drowned corpse, into a dreadful harmony of greens and purples.

"Now," said Rentoul Smiles, in a deep voice that was like a rich unguent. "We'll try again. We'll just play around that spot. Look into my eyes. Not *at* my eyes, my dear woman, *into* them! Just a little more challenge — a little more! That's it. Don't wink, for the land's sake! Now!"

He seized a bulb at the end of a tube and slowly squeezed — squeezed it tragically and remorselessly, twisting himself as if suffering in sympathy with the bulb, and then in a wide sweeping gesture he flung the bulb on to the top of the camera, and ejaculated:

"Ha!"

Edward Henry thought:

"I would give ten pounds to see Rentoul Smiles photograph Sir John Pilgrim." But the next instant the forgotten sensation of hurry was upon him once more. Quick, quick, Rentoul Smiles! Edward Henry's scorching desire was to get done and leave New York.

"Now, Miss Isabel," Mr. Smiles proceeded, exasperatingly deliberate, " d'you know, I feel kind of guilty? I have got a little farm out in Westchester County and I'm making a little English pathway up the garden with a gate at the end. I woke up this morning and began to think about the quaint English form of that gate, and just how I would have it." He raised a finger. " But I ought to have been thinking about you. I ought to have been saying to myself, ' To-day I have to photograph Isabel Joy,' and trying to understand in meditation the secrets of your personality. I'm sorry! Now, don't talk. Keep like that. Move your head round. Go on! Go on! Move it! Don't be afraid. This place belongs to you. It's yours. Whatever you do, we've got people here who'll straighten up after you. . . . D'you know why I've made money? I've made money so that I can take *you* this afternoon, and tell a two-hundred-dollar client to go to the deuce. That's why I've made money. Put your back against the chair, like an Englishwoman. That's it. No, don't *talk,* I tell you. Now look joyful, hang it! Look joyful. . . . No, no! Joy isn't a contortion. It's something right deep down. There, there! "

The lubricant voice rolled on while Rentoul Smiles manipulated the camera. He clasped the bulb again, and again threw it dramatically away.

" I'm through!" he said. " Don't expect anything very grand, Miss Isabel. What I've been trying to do this afternoon is my interpretation of you as I've studied your personality in your speeches. If I believed wholly in your cause, or if I wholly disbelieved in it, my work would not have been good. Any value that it has will be due to the sympathetic impartiality of my spiritual attitude. Although "— he menaced her with the licenced familiarity of a philosopher —" Although, lady, I must say that I felt you were working against me all the time. . . . This way!"

(Edward Henry, recalling the comparative simplicity of the London photographer at Wilkins's, thought: " How profoundly they understand photography in America!")

Isabel Joy rose and glanced at the watch in her bracelet; then followed the direction of the male hand, and vanished.

Rentoul Smiles turned instantly to the other doorway.

" How do, Rent?" said Seven Sachs, coming forward.

" How do, Seven?" Mr. Rentoul Smiles winked.

" This is my good friend, Alderman Machin, the theatre-manager from London."

" Glad to meet you, sir."

" She's not gone, has she?" asked Sachs hurriedly.

" No, my housekeeper wanted to talk to her. Come along."

And in the waiting room, full of permanent examples of the results of Mr. Rentoul Smiles's spiritual attitude toward his fellow men, Edward Henry was presented to Isabel Joy. The next instant the two men and the housekeeper had unobtrusively retired, and he was alone with his objective. In truth Seven Sachs was a notable organiser.

III.

She was sitting down in a cosy-corner, her feet on a footstool, and she seemed a negligible physical quantity as he stood in front of her. This was she who had worsted the entire judicial and police system of Chicago, who spoke pentecostal tongues, who had circled the globe, and held enthralled — so journalists computed — more than a quarter of a million of the inhabitants of Marseilles, Athens, Port Said, Candy, Calcutta, Bangkok, Hong Kong, Tokio, Hawaii, San Francisco, Salt Lake City, Denver, Chicago, and lastly New York! This was she!

" I understand we're going home on the same ship! " he was saying.

She looked up at him, almost appealingly.

" You won't see anything of me, though," she said.

" Why not? "

" Tell me," said she, not answering his question. " What do they say of me, really, in England? I don't mean the newspapers. For instance, well,— the Azure Society. Do you know of it? "

He nodded.

" Tell me," she repeated.

He related the episode of the telegram at the private first performance of " The Orient Pearl."

She burst out, in a torrent of irrelevant protest:

" The New York police have not treated me right. It would have cost them nothing to arrest me and let me go. But they wouldn't. Every man in the force — you hear me, every man — has had strict orders to leave me unmolested. It seems they resent my dealings with the police in Chicago, where I brought about the dismissal of four officers, so they say. And so I'm to be boycotted in this manner! Is that argument, Mr. Machin? Tell me. You're a man, but honestly, is it argument? Why, it's just as mean and despicable as brute force."

" I agree with you," said Edward Henry softly.

" Do you really think it will harm the militant cause? Do they *really* think so? No, it will only harm me. I made a mistake in tactics. I trusted — fool! — to the chivalry of the United States. I might have been arrested in a dozen cities, but I, on purpose, reserved my last two arrests for Chicago and New York, for the sake of the superior advertisement, you see! I never dreamt! — Now it's too late. I am defeated! I shall just arrive in London on the hundredth day. I shall have made speeches at all the meetings. But I shall be short of one arrest. And the ten thousand pounds will be lost to the cause. The militants here — such as they are — are as disgusted as I am. But they scorn me. And are they not right? Are they not right? There should be no quarter for the vanquished."

"Miss Joy," said Edward Henry, "I've come over from England specially to see you. I want to make up the loss of that ten thousand pounds as far as I can. I'll explain at once. I'm running a poetical play of the highest merit, called 'The Orient Pearl,' at my new theatre in Piccadilly Circus. If you will undertake a small part in it, a part of three words only, I'll pay you a record salary — sixty-six pounds thirteen and fourpence a word, two hundred pounds a week!"

Isabel Joy jumped up.

"Are you another of them, then?" she muttered. "I did think from the look of you that you would know a gentlewoman when you met one! Did you imagine for the thousandth part of one second that I would stoop —"

"Stoop!" exclaimed Edward Henry. "My theatre is not a music-hall —"

"You want to make it into one!" she stopped him.

"Good-day to you," she said. "I must face those journalists again, I suppose. Well, even they — ! I came alone in order to avoid them. But it was hopeless. Besides, is it my duty to avoid them — after all?"

It was while passing through the door that she uttered the last words.

" Where is she? " Seven Sachs enquired, entering.

" Fled! " said Edward Henry.

" Everything all right? "

" Quite! "

Mr. Rentoul Smiles came in.

" Mr. Smiles," said Edward Henry, " did you ever photograph Sir John Pilgrim? "

" I did, on his last visit to New York. Here you are! "

He pointed to his rendering of Sir John.

" What did you think of him? "

" A great actor, but a mountebank, sir."

During the remainder of the afternoon Edward Henry saw the whole of New York, with bits of the Bronx and Yonkers in the distance, from Seven Sach's second automobile. In his third automobile he went to the theatre and saw Seven Sachs act to a house of over two thousand dollars. And lastly he attended a supper and made a speech. But he insisted upon passing the remainder of the night on the *Lithuania*. In the morning Isabel Joy came aboard early and irrevocably disappeared into her berth. And from that moment Edward Henry spent the whole secret force of his individuality in fervently desiring the *Lithuania* to start. At two o'clock, two hours late, she did start. Edward Henry's farewells to the admirable and hospitable Mr. Sachs were somewhat absent-minded, for already his heart was in London. But he had sufficient presence of mind to make certain final arrangements.

" Keep him at least a week," said Edward Henry to Seven Sachs, " and I shall be your debtor for ever and ever."

He meant Carlo Trent, still bedridden.

As from the receding ship he gazed in abstraction at the gigantic, inconvenient word — common to three languages — which is the first thing seen by the arriving, and the last thing seen by the departing, visitor, he meditated:

" The dearness of living in the United States has certainly been exaggerated."

For his total expenses, beyond the confines of the quay, amounted to one cent, disbursed to buy an evening paper which had contained a brief interview with himself concerning the future of the intellectual drama in England. He had told the pressman that " The Orient Pearl " would run a hundred nights. Save for putting " The Orient Girl " instead of " The Orient Pearl," and two hundred nights instead of one hundred nights, this interview was tolerably accurate.

IV.

Two entire interminable days of the voyage elapsed before Edward Henry was clever enough to encounter Isabel Joy — the most famous and the least visible person on the ship. He remembered that she had said: " You won't see anything of me."

It was easy to ascertain the number of her state-room — a double-berth which she shared with no-body. But it was less easy to find out whether she ever left it, and if so, at what time of day. He could not mount guard in the long corridor; and the stewardesses on the *Lithuania* were mature, experi-enced and uncommunicative women, their sole weak-ness being an occasional tendency to imagine that they, and not the captain, were in supreme charge of the steamer. However, Edward Henry did at last achieve his desire. And on the third morning, at a little before six o'clock, he met a muffled Isabel Joy on the D deck. The D deck was wet, having just been swabbed; and a boat, chosen for that dawn's boat drill, ascended past them on its way from the sea level to the busy boat deck above; on the other side of an iron barrier, large crowds of early-rising third-class passengers were standing and talking, and staring at the oblong slit of sea which was the only prospect offered by the D deck; it was the first time that Edward Henry aboard had ever set eyes on a steerage passenger; with all the con-ceit natural to the occupant of a costly stateroom, he had unconsciously assumed that he and his like had sole possession of the ship.

Isabel responded to his greeting in a very natural way. The sharp freshness of the summer morning at sea had its tonic effect on both of them; and as for Edward Henry, he lunged and plunged at once into the subject which alone preoccupied and exas-perated him. She did not seem to resent it.

" You'd have the satisfaction of helping on a
thing that all your friends say ought to be helped,"
he argued. " Nobody but you can do it. Without
you, there'll be a frost. You would make a lot of
money, which you could spend in helping on things
of your own. And surely it isn't the publicity that
you're afraid of! "

" No," she agreed. " I'm not afraid of publicity." Her pale grey-blue eyes shone as they regarded the secret dream that for her hung always
unseen in the air. And she had a strange, wistful,
fragile, feminine mien in her mannish costume.

" Well then —"

" But can't you see it's humiliating? " cried she,
as if interested in the argument.

" It's not humiliating to do something that you
can do well — I know you can do it well — and get
a large salary for it, and make the success of a big
enterprise by it. If you knew the play —"

" I do know the play," she said. " We'd lots
of us read it in manuscript long ago."

Edward Henry was somewhat dashed by this information.

" Well, what do you think of it? "

" I think it's just splendid! " said she with enthusiasm.

" And will it be any worse a play because you act
a small part in it? "

" No," she said shortly.

" I expect you think it's a play that people ought
to go and see, don't you? "

" I do, Mr. Socrates," she admitted.

He wondered what she could mean, but continued :
" What does it matter what it is that brings the audience into the theatre, so long as they get there and have to listen? "

She sighed.

" It's no use discussing with you," she murmured. " You're too simple for this world. I daresay you're honest enough — in fact I think you are — but there are so many things that you don't understand. You're evidently incapable of understanding them."

" Thanks! " he replied, and paused to recover his self-possession. " But let's get right down to business now. If you'll appear in this play, I'll not merely give you two hundred pounds a week, but I'll explain to you how to get arrested and still arrive in triumph in London before midnight on Sunday."

She recoiled a step, and raised her eyes.

" How? " she demanded, as with a pistol.

" Ah! " he said. " That's just it. How? Will you promise? "

" I've thought of everything," she said musingly. " If the last day was any day but Sunday I could get arrested on landing and get bailed out, and still be in London before night. But on Sunday — no! So you needn't talk like that."

" Still," he said, " it can be done."

" How," she demanded again.

" Will you sign a contract with me, if I tell you?

. . . Think of what your reception in London will be if you win after all! Just think!"

Those pale eyes ·gleamed, for Isabel Joy had tasted the noisy flattery of sympathetic and of adverse crowds, and her being hungered for it again; the desire of it had become part of her nature.

She walked away, her hands in the pockets of her ulster, and returned.

"What is your scheme?"

"You'll sign?"

"Yes, if it works."

"I can trust you?"

The little woman of forty or so blazed up. "You can refrain from insulting me by doubting my word," said she.

"Sorry! Sorry!" he apologised.

V.

That same evening, in the colossal many-tabled dining-saloon of the *Lithuania* Edward Henry sat as usual to the left of the purser's empty chair at the purser's table, where were about a dozen other men. A page brought him a marconigram. He opened it, and read the single word "Nineteen." It was the amount of the previous evening's receipts at the Regent, in pounds. He was now losing something like forty pounds a night — without counting the expenses of the present excursion. The band began to play as the soup was served, and the ship rolled politely, gently, but nevertheless unmistakably, accomplishing one complete roll to about sixteen

bars of the music. Then the entire saloon was
suddenly excited. Isabel Joy had entered. She
was in the gallery, near the orchestra, at a small
table alone. Everybody became aware of the fact
in an instant, and scores of necks on the lower floor
were twisted to glimpse the celebrity on the upper.
It was remarked that she wore a magnificent evening
dress.

One subject of conversation now occupied all the
tables. And it was fully occupying the purser's table
when the purser, generally a little late, owing to the
arduousness of his situation on the ship, entered and
sat down. Now the purser was a Northerner, from
Durham, a delightful companion in his lighter
moods, but dour, and with a high conception of authority and of the intelligence of dogs. He would
relate that when he and his wife wanted to keep a
secret from their Yorkshire terrier they had to spell
the crucial words in talk, for the dog understood
their every sentence.

The purser's views about the cause represented by
Isabel Joy were absolutely clear. None could mistake them, and the few clauses which he curtly added
to the discussion rather damped the discussion, and
there was a pause.

"What should you do, Mr. Purser," said Edward Henry, "if she began to play any of her tricks
here?"

"If she began to play any of her tricks on this
ship," answered the purser, putting his hands on his
stout knees, "we should know what to do."

" Of course you can arrest? "

" Most decidedly. I could tell you things —"
The purser stopped, for experience had taught him
to be very discreet with passengers until he had
voyaged with them at least ten times. He concluded: " The captain is the representative of English law on an English ship."

And then, in the silence created by the resting
orchestra, all in the saloon could hear a clear, pier-
cing woman's voice, oratorical at first and then quick-
ening:

" Ladies and gentlemen: I wish to talk to you to-
night on the subject of the injustice of men to
women." Isabel Joy was on her feet and leaning
over the gallery rail. As she proceeded, a startled
hush changed to uproar. And in the uproar could
be caught now and then a detached phrase, such
as " For example, this man-governed ship."

Possibly it was just this phrase that roused the
Northerner in the purser. He rose, and looked toward the captain's table. But the captain was not
dining in the saloon that evening. Then he strode
to the centre of the saloon, beneath the renowned
dome which has been so often photographed for the
illustrated papers, and sought to destroy Isabel
Joy with a single marine glance. Having failed,
he called out loudly:

" Be quiet, madam. Resume your seat."

Isabel Joy stopped for a second, gave him a glance
far more homicidal than his own, and resumed her
discourse.

"Steward," cried the purser, "take that woman out of the saloon."

The whole complement of first-class passengers was now standing up, and many of them saw a plate descend from on high, and grace the purser's shoulder. With the celerity of a sprinter the man of authority from Durham disappeared from the ground floor and was immediately seen in the gallery. Accounts differed, afterward, as to the exact order of events; but it is certain that the leader of the band lost his fiddle, which was broken by the lusty Isabel on the Purser's head. It was known later that Isabel, though not exactly in irons, was under arrest in her stateroom.

"She really ought to have thought of that for herself, if she's as smart as she thinks she is," said Edward Henry privately.

VI.

Though he was on the way to high success, his anxieties and solicitudes seemed to increase every hour. Immediately after Isabel Joy's arrest he became more than ever a crony of the Marconi operator, and began to despatch vivid and urgent telegrams to London, without counting the cost. On the next day he began to receive replies. (It was the most interesting voyage that the Marconi operator had had since the sinking of the *Catherine of Siena,* in which episode his promptness through the air had certainly saved two hundred lives.) Edward Henry could scarcely sleep, so intense was his

longing for Sunday night — his desire to be safe in
London with Isabel Joy! Nay, he could not
properly eat! And then the doubt entered his mind
whether, after all, he would get to London on Sunday night. For the *Lithuania* was lagging. She
might have been doing it on purpose to ruin him.
Every day, in the auction-pool on the ship's run, it
was the holder of the low field that pocketed the
money of his fellow men. The *Lithuania* actually
descended below five hundred and forty knots
in the twenty-four hours. And no authoritative explanation of this behaviour was ever given. Upon
leaving New York there had been talk of reaching
Fishguard on Saturday evening. But now the prophesied moment of arrival had been put forward to
noon on Sunday. Edward Henry's sole consolation
was that each day on the eastward trip consisted of
only twenty-three hours.

Further, he was by no means free from apprehension about the personal liberty of Isabel Joy.
Isabel had exceeded the programme arranged between
them. It had been no part of his scheme that she
should cast plates, nor even break violins on the
shining crown of an august purser. The purser
was angry, and he had the captain, a milder man,
behind him. When Isabel Joy threatened a hunger-
strike if she was not immediately released, the purser signified that she might proceed with her hunger-
strike; he well knew that it would be impossible for
her to expire of inanition before the arrival at Fishguard,

The case was serious, because Isabel Joy had
created a precedent. Policemen and cabinet minis-
ters had for many months been regarded as the law-
ful prey of militants, but Isabel Joy was the first of
the militants to damage property and heads which
belonged to persons of neither of these classes. And
the authorities of the ship were assuredly inclined to
hand Isabel Joy over to the police at Fishguard.
What saved the situation for Edward Henry was the
factor which saved most situations, namely, public
opinion. When the saloon clearly realised that
Isabel Joy had done what she had done with the
pure and innocent aim of winning a wager, all that
was Anglo-Saxon in the saloon ranged itself on the
side of true sport, and the matter was lifted above
mere politics. A subscription was inaugurated to buy
a new fiddle, and to pay for shattered crockery. And
the amount collected would have purchased, after
settling for the crockery, a couple of dozen new fid-
dles. The unneeded balance was given to seamen's
orphanages. The purser was approached. The
captain was implored. Influence was brought to
bear. In short — the wheels that are within
wheels went duly round. And Miss Isabel Joy,
after apologies and promises, was unconditionally released.

But she had been arrested.

And then, early on Sunday morning, the ship met
a storm that had a sad influence on divine service, a
storm of the eminence that scares even the brass-
buttoned occupants of liners' bridges. The rumour

went round the ship that the captain would not call
at Fishguard in such weather.

Edward Henry was ready to yield up his spirit
in this fearful crisis, which endured two hours. The
captain did call at Fishguard, in pouring rain, and
men came aboard selling Sunday newspapers that
were full of Isabel's arrest on the steamer, and of
the nearing triumph of her arrival in London before midnight. And newspaper correspondents also
came aboard, and all the way on the tender, and in
the sheds, and in the train, Edward Henry and
Isabel Joy were subjected to the journalistic experi-
ments of hardy interviewers. The train arrived at
Paddington at 9 P. M. Isabel had won by three
hours. The station was a surging throng of open-
mouthed people. Edward Henry would not lose
sight of his priceless charge, but he sent Marrier to
despatch a telegram to Nellie, whose wifely interest
in his movements he had till then either forgotten or
ignored.

And even now his mind was not free. He saw in
front of him still twenty-four hours of anguish.

VII.

The next night, just before the curtain went up,
he stood on the stage of the Regent Theatre, and it
is a fact that he was trembling — not with fear but
with simple excitement.

Through what a day he had passed! There had
been the rehearsal in the morning; it had gone off
very well, save that Rose Euclid had behaved im-

possibly, and that the Cunningham girl, the hit of
the piece but ousted from her part, had filled the
place with just lamentations and recriminations.

And then had followed the appalling scene with
Rose Euclid. Rose, leaving the theatre for lunch,
had beheld the workmen removing her name from
the electric sign and substituting that of Isabel Joy.
She was a woman and an artist, and it would have
been the same had she been a man and an artist. She
would not submit to this inconceivable affront. She
had resigned her rôle. She had ripped her contract
to bits and flung the bits to the breeze. Upon the
whole Edward Henry had been glad. He had sent
for Miss Cunningham, who was Rose's understudy,
had given her instructions, called another rehearsal
for the afternoon and effected a saving of nearly
half Isabel Joy's fantastic salary. Then he entered
into financial negotiations with four evening papers
and managed to buy, at a price, their contents-bills
for the day. So that all the West End was filled
with men and boys wearing like aprons posters which
bore the words: "Isabel Joy to appear at the Regent to-night." A great and original stroke!

And now he gazed through the peep-hole of the
curtain upon a crammed and half-delirious auditorium. The assistant stage manager ordered him
off. The curtain went up on the drama in hexameters. He waited in the wings, and spoke soothingly
to Isabel Joy who, looking juvenile in the airy costume
of the Messenger, stood flutteringly agog for
her cue. . . . He heard the thunderous crashing

roar that met her entrance. He did not hear her line.

He walked forth to the glazed balcony at the front of the house, where in the entr'actes dandies smoked cigarettes baptised with girlish names. He could see Piccadilly Circus, and he saw Piccadilly Circus thronged with a multitude of loafers, who were happy in the mere spectacle of Isabel Joy's name glowing on an electric sign. He went back at last to the managerial room. Marrier was there, hero-worshipping.

" Got the figures yet? " he asked.

Marrier beamed.

" Two hundred and sixty pounds. As long as it keeps up it means a profit of getting on for two hundred a naight! "

" But, dash it, man,— the house only holds two hundred and thirty! "

" But my good sir," said Marrier, " they're paying ten shillings a-piece to stand up in the dress-circle."

Edward Henry dropped into a chair at the desk. A telegram was lying there, addressed to himself.

" What's this? " he demanded.

" Just cam."

He opened it, and read: " I absolutely forbid this monstrous outrage on a work of art. Trent."

" Bit late in the day, isn't he? " said Edward Henry, showing the telegram to Marrier.

" Besides," Marrier observed, " he'll come round when he knows what his royalties are."

" Well," said Edward Henry, " I'm going to bed."
And he gave a devastating yawn.

VIII.

One afternoon Edward Henry sat in the king of
all the easy chairs in the drawing-room of his house
in Trafalgar Road, Bursley. Although the month
was September, and the weather warm even for September, a swansdown quilt lay spread upon his knees.
His face was pale, his hands were paler; but his eye
was clear and his visage enlightened. His beard
had grown to nearly its original dimensions. On
a chair by his side were a number of letters to
which he had just dictated answers. At a neighbouring table a young clerk was using a typewriter.
Stretched at full length on the sofa was Robert
Machin, engaged in the perusal of the second edi-
tion of that day's *Signal*. Of late Robert, having exhausted nearly all available books, had been
cultivating during his holidays an interest in jour-
nalism, and he would give great accounts, in the
nursery, of events happening in each day's instal-
ment of the *Signal's* sensational serial. His heels
kicked idly one against the other.

A powerful voice resounded in the lobby, and
Doctor Stirling entered the room with Nellie.

" Well, Doc! " Edward Henry greeted him.

" So you're in full blast again! " observed the
doctor, using a metaphor invented by the population
of a district where the roar of furnaces wakens the
night.

" No ! " Edward Henry protested, as an invalid
always will. " I'm only just keeping an eye on one
or two pressing things."

" Of course he's in full blast ! " said Nellie with
calm conviction.

" What's this I hear about ye ganging away to the
seaside, Saturday ? " asked the doctor.

" Well, can't I ? " said Edward Henry.

" Ye can," said the doctor. " Let's have a look
at ye, man."

" What was it you said I've had ? " Edward
Henry questioned.

" Colitis."

" Yes, that's the word. I thought I couldn't have
got it wrong. Well, you should have seen my
mother's face when I told her what you called it.
She said, ' He may call it that if he's a mind to, but
we had another name for it in my time.' You
should have heard her sniff ! . . . Look here, Doc,
do you know you've had me down now for pretty
near three months ? "

" Nay," said Stirling. " It's yer own obstinacy
that's had ye down, man. If ye'd listened to yer
London doctor at first, mayhap ye wouldn't have had
to travel from Euston in an invalid's carriage. If
ye hadn't had the misfortune to be born an obstinate
simpleton ye'd ha' been up and about six weeks back.
But there's no doing anything with you geniuses.
It's all nerves with you and your like."

" Nerves ! " exclaimed Edward Henry, pretending
to scorn. But he was delighted at the diagnosis.

" Nerves," repeated the doctor firmly. " Ye go gadding off to America. Ye get yeself mixed up in theatres. . . . How's the theatre? I see yer famous play's coming to end next week."

" And what if it is?" said Edward Henry, jealous for reputations, including his own. " It will have run for a hundred and one nights. And right through August, too! No modern poetry play ever did run as long in London, and no other ever will. I've given the intellectual theatre the biggest ad. it ever had. And I've made money on it. I should have made more if I'd ended the run a fortnight ago, but I was determined to pass the hundredth night. And I shall do! "

" And what are ye for giving next? "

" I'm not for giving anything next, Doc. I've let the Regent for five years at seven thousand five hundred pounds a year to a musical comedy syndicate, since you're so curious. And when I've paid the ground rent and taxes and repairs and something toward a sinking-fund, and six per cent. on my capital I shall have not far off two thousand pounds a year clear annual profit. You may say what you like, but that's what I call business! "

It was a remarkable fact that, while giving unde-manded information to Doctor Stirling, Edward Henry was in reality defending himself against the accusations of his wife — accusations which, by the way, she had never uttered, but which he thought he read sometimes in her face. He might of course have told his wife these agreeable details directly, and in private. But he was a husband, and, like many husbands, apt to be indirect.

Nellie said not a word.

" Then you're giving up London? " The doctor rose to depart.

" I am," said Edward Henry, almost blushing.

" Why? "

" Well," the genius answered. " Those theatrical things are altogether too exciting and risky! And they're such queer people — Great Scott! I've come out on the right side, as it happens, but — well, I'm not as young as I was. I've done with London. The Five Towns are good enough for me."

Nellie, unable to restrain a note of triumph, indiscreetly remarked with just the air of superior sagacity that in a wife drives husbands to fury and to foolishness:

" I should think so, indeed! "

Edward Henry leaped from his chair, and the swansdown quilt swathed his slippered feet.

" Nell," he exploded, clenching his hand. " If you say that once more in that tone — once more, mind! — I'll go and take a flat in London to-morrow! "

The doctor crackled with laughter. Nellie smiled. Even Robert, who had completely ignored the doctor's entrance, glanced round with creased brows.

" Sit down, dearest," Nellie quietly enjoined the invalid.

But he would not sit down, and, to show his independence, he helped his wife to escort Stirling into the lobby.

Robert, now alone with the ignored young clerk tapping at the table, turned toward him, and in his deliberate, judicial, disdainful, childish voice said to him:

" Isn't Father a funny man? "

THE END